YOU DON'T HAVE A SHOT

ALSO BY RACQUEL MARIE

Ophelia After All

RACQUEL MARIE

FEIWEL AND FRIENDS
NEW YORK

A Feiwel and Friends Book
An imprint of Macmillan Publishing Group, LLC
120 Broadway, New York, NY 10271 • fiercereads.com

Our books may be purchased in bulk for promotional, educational, or business use. Please contact your local bookseller or the Macmillan Corporate and Premium Sales Department at (800) 221-7945 ext. 5442 or by email at MacmillanSpecialMarkets@macmillan.com.

Library of Congress Cataloging-in-Publication Data is available.

First edition, 2023
Book design by Aurora Parlegreco
Feiwel and Friends logo designed by Filomena Tuosto
Printed in the United States of America.

ISBN 978-1-250-83629-8 (hardcover)
1 3 5 7 9 10 8 6 4 2

For Dad,

It goes beyond words, but let's start with these ones:

I love you. Thank you for everything.

And for soccer,

Thanks for introducing my parents.

I promise I never stopped loving you.

ONE

COACH IS GOING TO KILL US.

Like actually our-asses-are-grass, possibly-bench-us-for-all-of-senior-year Kill Us. In my defense, I only went to the beach with the rest of the team last night to keep them out of trouble and make sure they at least marginally practiced. But given that I brought the Aguardiente just to spite Dad, lit the bonfire that poured smoke into their lungs since I didn't want them to freeze, then proceeded to lead the girls in intense, tipsy drills well into the evening, redistributing the blame doesn't bode well for me. Besides, we're not that late.

I check the time on my phone. *Shit.*

Still scrubbing my teeth and tongue clean of any lingering booze, I shout around my toothbrush that Ovie and Dina need to haul ass or I'm leaving them behind and telling Coach to let the benchwarmers take a crack at their positions. They're two of our best players and Ovie is Coach's daughter, so it's an empty threat. But when you're captain, it's inevitable that you make it every once in a while, even to your best friends.

"Checking that your breath is fresh for when you see your *girlfriend*?" Dina's head pops into the doorway, her short, dark curls already pulled into a high ponytail and fly-aways pushed back with navy-blue prewrap that matches our jerseys.

I spit into the sink. "Some of us just care about basic hygiene." I toss her my deodorant.

"Stench is a secret weapon, my friend," she replies, winking. Thankfully, she still uncaps the deodorant and applies it liberally. None of us had time to shower and, even wearing our clean uniforms that we doused in an ancient bottle of vanilla body spray we found in Ovie's bag, we reek.

"Don't get Vale all flustered before the game!" Ovie shouts as she runs past the bathroom, slides in hand. Her voice echoes down the hall. "Dammit, where are my cleats?"

"Go help your actual girlfriend before we end up later than we already are," I tell Dina. She rolls her eyes but leaves. If Ovie's cheer moments later is any indication, Dina found her cleats.

I splash my face with water and kick Dina's bathroom door shut before I do what I always do before a big game. I give myself seven seconds to panic. Seven seconds to worry that this'll be it—our winning streak over, my best shot at a college scholarship out the door, another victory for Leticia and failure in Dad's eyes.

1. The Hillcrest Tigers have a top-tier coach who was flown in from Brazil to train them. I love Coach, but

her credentials don't compare, and their season's undefeated streak rivals our own.

2. The Venn diagram of players who got wasted last night and players who sprinted up and down the sand for hours per my equally wasted commands, ankles and knees wobbling about, would be a nearly perfect circle. If anyone got more than four hours of sleep and didn't wake up sore, it would be a miracle.
3. Even when we're playing at our best, Hillcrest is a better team. I can admit that to myself in the privacy of my head, even if I'd deny it out loud. We're playing at a disadvantage after last night.
4. If we lose like this—hungover, sleep-deprived, bodies aching from my drunken, self-sabotaging antics—they don't get anything, not really. *She* doesn't get anything.
5. But if we lose, I'm toast.
6. Leticia Ortiz. Pain in my ass since I was eleven years old. Hillcrest team captain and the biggest obstacle standing between me and my goals. Literally.
7. Dad. Dad will be watching.

I take a deep breath and tug at my Ravens jersey so the large, white number seven across my back isn't so wrinkled. The panic still brims beneath the surface, but I'll keep it at bay. Because I have to.

I throw the door open, hike my bag onto my shoulder, and

grab my car keys. "Vámonos, bitches!" *Don't let them see the fear, don't let them see the panic.* "Let's get this shit over with."

My friends race out the door behind me, bags and cleats banging against their bodies. I only make it into the minivan—which Jorge and I inherited when Mami passed—a minute before the girls, but I lay on the horn for the dramatics.

As payback, they stop to play rock-paper-scissors over who gets shotgun. Dina wins and kisses Ovie quickly before sliding into the seat. Ovie, pouting, hops in the back and scoots to the middle.

"I call aux," Dina says, while I turn off her street and try to keep from speeding all the way to school. Hyperpop bursts out of the speakers, the volume still at full blast from when Ovie drove us home last night as our designated driver. She lost that game of rock-paper-scissors too.

"Shit, my mom is calling!" Ovie shouts over the music. "What do I do?"

"Answer, so she doesn't think you died in a ditch," I reply, picking up speed ever so slightly. The green light gods have been blessing us thus far, but I'm scared to push our luck. The absolute last thing we need is to get pulled over.

Dina turns down the music as Ovie lifts her phone to her ear. "Hey, Mom! How are you feeling today?" Dina and I both groan. "No—no, yeah . . . no, we—Mom, we're on our way. No—no, yes, yes, ma'am. Yes, ma'am. Okay, love you. Bye."

"On a scale from an extra lap around the field to three rounds of deadlies, how screwed are we?" I ask. We started calling "suicides"—sprinting to and from increasingly farther points on the field—"deadlies" back when we all met in fifth-grade PE.

"Based on her tone, I'd say closer to being benched for opening lineup," Ovie says, wincing.

I hit the steering wheel and fight the urge to stomp on the gas. "Fuck."

"Bright news is Hillcrest is also running late because of traffic, so we're slightly less screwed than we would be otherwise."

"Thank you, Hell-crest," Dina says.

I think of Leticia, smug in her team's bougie private school bus and garish red jersey. Meanwhile we smell like ass in our bland navy blue uniforms, and half the vents in this ancient car are broken from my little brother jamming Play-Doh in them.

I shake Leticia out of my head. My mind starts to shrink down to the precision it reaches during a game. Nothing to focus on but me and the ball. Every thought fading into instincts that have been drilled into me from the time I could walk.

My friends must notice my mental shift because Dina whips out her earbuds and plugs them in to her phone, privately blasting her music. I see Ovie twist herself into whatever stretches she can manage in the back seat. We may be fuckups right now, late and smelly and in trouble, but we're transitioning into who we are on the field: a force to be reckoned with.

COACH DOESN'T SAY ANYTHING TO US when we arrive. She's waiting at the edge of the parking lot, her dark brown skin and tightly coiled black hair glistening in the sun. All she does is nod toward our locker rooms. Ovie stops to kiss her on the cheek, though, and I notice her posture soften.

I squint up at the bleachers. Jorge's hunched in the upper corner, scowling at something in his notebook, far from any of the other sophomores who've got siblings or girlfriends on the team. Matteo sits beside him, mindlessly running his toy cars over the ridges in the benches.

Dad stands separately, front and center, watching me show up late for the biggest game of the season. He always camps out as close as he can get to the sidelines. As close as he can get to me. I look away and catch up to my friends.

The locker room is in full-blown pregame chaos. Our team playlist echoes in the humble concrete room, the girls dancing and singing along as they tie up their hair and laces.

I nod to a few of them on the way to my locker. Others I

ignore, like irrelevant Sarah, who jokes that Coach was ready to send out a search party for us. I overheard her tell one of the other benchwarmers last night that the only reason Coach let me play dictator over the team this year is because Ovie's my best friend. But Sarah's graduating in a few weeks with nothing to show but a handful of Division III offers accompanied by mediocre scholarships, so I brush aside her judgment. I can only handle so much when whatever peace I was finding in the car has already been disturbed by Dad's and Coach's dual disappointment. I kick off my black Chucks and start yanking on my game socks when I notice the volume of chatter has dropped suspiciously low.

"Sorry to interrupt the party. We're just looking for a bathroom," a disgustingly familiar voice says, carrying from a few rows away. "Half the toilets in the guest locker room are clogged."

On socked feet, I jog toward our visitors. Leticia is flanked by two teammates in the open doorway, the light behind her providing a false halo against her close-cropped black curls. Her eyes find mine, and whatever semblance of civility she was willing to extend to the rest of my team melts away.

"Oh hey, Princesa." Her face breaks into a sharp smile. "Might as well offer my condolences over the death of your undefeated streak while I'm here."

The nickname comes with the territory of having "Castillo" in my last name, Castillo-Green. One part Mami's Colombian heritage, one part Dad's Irish American. I ignore it, as I've opted to do since she came up with it years ago.

"That's a little optimistic, don't you think? I mean, I've seen you play, so I know that your team doesn't like to plan ahead, but you may want to give this one a bit more time."

Her devilish smirk creeps wider. "We like to be proactive. Your midfielders"—she pauses to give me a once-over—"could learn a thing or two."

"Public bathrooms are by the snack bar on the field," I say through a tight mouth. "You'll find it right beside the measly guest crowd that came to watch you lose."

"Wow. Home team advantage is a lot to brag about," she says. "Though I guess beggars can't be choosers when you're scraping the bottom of the barrel for things to be proud of." She winks. "See you on the field."

I exhale as the door shuts behind her, unaware I was even holding my breath.

I had the misfortune of meeting Leticia when we ended up on the same Under-12 team at a sleepaway soccer camp. At first, I was excited by the prospect of playing with another Latina from SoCal, especially since Ovie and Dina, who'd already been going to the camp for years, weren't on my team. I thought I could make a friendship that lasted beyond the summer, taking it home with me alongside the memories and bruises.

But the more I tried to be Leticia's friend—inviting her to eat Popsicles with me after games or offering her a pair of neon-yellow laces my mom bought for me at the dollar store—the more she seemed determined to ignore me. The only times she acknowledged my existence were to yell at me for being a shitty defender who was always too eager to leave my post and play offense. I went up to her after we lost our final game and tried to correct the way she was checking her pulse, but before I could even apologize for whatever I'd done to earn her disdain, she stormed off. I figured she blamed me for the loss, and that ended any and all attempts at befriending her. The next summer, we were immediately at each other's throats. And thus the rivalry was born.

By the summer after that, Matteo was born and Mami was dead and summer camp was the least of my concerns. Dina and Ovie were over it anyway, and since Leticia graduated to playing club during the summer and high school during the spring, I doubt she ever went back either.

"Val-ayeeee?" Dina stretches out the end of my nickname.

I shake free of my memories. "Huh?"

"She's gone. You can stop drooling."

"Go put your shin guards on." I shove past her as she laughs. Not wanting to push my luck with Coach any more than I already have today, I finish gearing up. The locker room is mostly empty now, but I don't have another seven seconds to spare to panic again. I give my reflection in my dingy locker mirror a quick glance, and then sprint out into the sunlight.

We're not losing. But we're definitely not winning.

Despite her annoyance, Coach still starts me, Dina, and Ovie. She couldn't afford to bench us even if she wanted to. We're a dream team with Dina at right wing, Ovie as goalkeeper, and me at center midfield, perfectly arranged to stop Hillcrest's messy-but-powerful offense and brutally organized defense.

But Hillcrest—Leticia especially—is ready for us. Leticia's got a thin frame, but she's nearly six feet tall, so any shot we take is nothing more than a leap away from her nearest limb. And she makes every move count, holding the game steady at a 0–0 tie even as we approach the start of the second half.

It crosses my mind that this might be decided by penalty kicks if things don't get interesting soon, just as their offense makes a break for our goal. They're headed straight for Ovie, the potential first goal of the game pressuring everyone on both teams to surge that way.

I notice their left back lingering though. I slink toward her instead of helping my team, watching from an uncomfortable distance as the play unfolds. They could use my support, but if you want something done right, you have to do it yourself, so our goals may be up to me.

Red jerseys pass the ball like a pinball machine, dizzying our defenders. Our team is fast, but every time we're set to steal the ball, another red shirt breaks free from our sea of blue and the ball darts their way magnetically. A childlike voice in me begs to run back, help out, and let offense take over if we manage to turn it around. But I have to stay put or I forfeit the possibility of pulling off this perfect play. They'll manage fine on their own, and so will I.

Finally, probably just as tired of the dillydallying as we

are, a red shirt takes a shot from the top of the box. Ovie isn't as tall as Leticia, but she's spry and saves it like nothing.

Before I even finish shouting the second syllable of her name, her body swivels my way and she punts the ball straight to me.

The crowd on our side roars when I ditch the left back, rivaled in volume by my teammates and Coach shouting my name and red shirts hollering to get back. Dad's gravelly voice pierces through everything, more warning than cheer.

I tune them all out until the noise is nothing but a minor buzz. The combination of my panting and the rhythmic tap of my right foot against the ball as I dribble forward is all I need to stay grounded.

Leticia crouches, preparing to stop me. But I know her, I've studied her every move for years. No one scores on her one-on-one from this distance. She's too tall, too fast, and there's no way to trick her with a misdirected cross when you're alone. So I keep going, closer and closer. It's a risk, I know, but a calculated one.

She starts to catch on to my plan to force her out of the net, shifting her weight as she swiftly considers the pros and cons of leaning into it. I'm no better off, running out of time to draw her out if she does and space to set up a decent shot if she doesn't.

Out of the corner of my eye, I see movement.

Dina is perfectly aligned to shoot if I cross the ball over to her. Leticia probably wouldn't even have time to react, still favoring the right side of the field I'm barreling down.

But I got this far on my own. It's between us now, it has to be.

I can't mess this up I need to get this right there could be scouts in the crowd and Dad is watching and if he sees me mess this up I'll never—

I'm on the ground.

My face skids against the fake grass, neck bending at an awful angle as the friction keeps me from sliding farther than a few inches. My thighs and cheek sting from the rush of hot plastic turf against my skin. I hear the swish of the ball soaring away and then a whistle, realizing a second later that the whistle is for me.

I prop myself up on my elbow and look around, cringing at the ensuing pain. All the other players are taking a knee, including Leticia from a few inches away.

"You all right, Seven?" the ref asks, kneeling to look me in the eye.

"What happened?" I croak, belatedly realizing that the air got knocked out of me on impact.

"I stole the ball," Leticia says behind me, voice amused.

I roll over to properly face her. "You tripped me."

The ref makes a noise. "It was all ball. She didn't touch you."

"Your momentum got the best of you," Leticia says. "Tripped over the ball and your own feet." The ref gives her a look of warning. Leticia schools her face into an innocent smile.

The ref turns back to me. "Are you hurt?"

A quick glance and I see Coach on the sidelines, ready to come check on me if I don't get up in a few seconds. The pain of my fall starts to fade as embarrassment takes over. I had a perfect opportunity to score, a run with no defense to stop me, an open teammate to cross to. And I fucked it all up.

I don't dare look to Dad in the stands.

"I'm good," I say, and start to sit up, twisting my neck to test the damage. I wince, but the ache will fade. Scattered applause rewards me for my efforts as the other players stand. The age-old tradition of congratulating someone on not injuring themself irreparably. How charming.

"No shame in falling for me," Leticia says, leaning down to offer me a gloved hand. "Just maybe try focusing on the net and not me next time."

I look up at her, gloriously backed by the sun and bright blue sky. She's probably drowning in Division I offers already. She's got nothing real riding on this game. She's walking away from today, whether her team wins or loses, as the victor.

I deserved that goal, and now I don't even have a penalty kick as a consolation for her fouling and embarrassing me. Even after tripping me, she gets to be the noble one offering me a supportive hand.

Meanwhile I've got to go home to Dad, who'll be cooking up a lecture for me even if we manage to win this. Maybe if I'm lucky, he won't bring Mami into it, telling me she would've been ashamed to see me play so poorly. It's his usual speech though, and I don't exactly have a history of being lucky.

Unlike Leticia.

I take her hand, but instead of using it to brace my ascent, I embrace my anger and tug her down. Hard.

She falls onto my chest, knocking the wind out of me a second time. For a moment, she's caging me in, long brown arms on either side of my head as she pushes herself up, too stunned to speak. Her face is only inches from mine, our heavy breaths stirring the hair that's escaped our makeshift headbands.

The moment breaks.

"What the hell!" she yells, scrambling off. "What's your problem?"

I sit up, adrenaline flooding my senses. "I'm looking right at her."

Suddenly we're both standing and she gets in my face again, nearly touching our foreheads together, before bumping me back with her shoulder. Always watching those precious goalie hands. I, on the other hand, am about to lunge for that ridiculous, pretty face of hers when someone grabs me around the waist.

Dina drags me away, and the ref, who has apparently been yelling at us this whole time, lifts two yellow cards into the air.

My veins burn. "You're fucking kidding me! She trips me and you do nothing, but I accidentally pull her down and get carded?"

The ref scoffs at me. "You're calling that little stunt an accident?"

"Funny, I didn't think after that last fucking call of yours that you'd be wise enough to identify bullshit. I love witnessing character development."

Dina yanks my arm sharply, a warning. But it's too late.

"How's this for a call?" The ref lifts a second yellow, quickly followed by a red card, and waves both at me. "You're out of the game."

Dina drops my arm. "Fuck."

Minutes ago, the air was buzzing with excitement over my play. Now it's replaced by the din of disappointed teammates, an angry coach, and parents too far away to hear what I said to earn a red.

I take one look at Coach's stoic face on the sidelines. She's shaking her head at her clipboard as she rearranges the lineup to account for one less player.

Dina storms away from me, cursing, while the ref sets the ball back up. Leticia returned to her post already, tightening her gloves.

Everyone trickles into formation so the ball can resume play. But I don't want to watch this shit unravel without me from the sidelines. I don't even remember leaving the field. One minute I'm in the sun, the next I'm curled up on a bench in the locker room, hearing the final whistle blow and knowing that it's over. It's all over.

THREE

I LISTEN TO A MUFFLED VERSION of the post-loss speech from Coach's office, where I squirreled away to avoid the team. The second I stepped off the field, I knew we were going to lose. Doesn't make the confirmation any easier though.

Game highlights from the Colombia Women's National Team kept me company for the past hour after I showered and changed, but I put my phone away when I hear Coach tell Ovie she'll meet her in the parking lot after grabbing something from her office.

Coach stands in the doorway for a second, staring at me slumped in the seat across from her desk, before she closes the door behind her and sits down. She doesn't look particularly surprised to see me in here.

I tug on my hoodie's drawstrings out of habit. "Look, you don't have to say it. I already know I fucked up."

"Oh okay. Then you should just be on your way then." She gestures dramatically to the closed door. "No need to sit around and listen to my lecture if you're already so self-aware, right?"

"I get the feeling I'm going to make this much worse for myself if I say yes."

She rubs at her temples. "What you did out there was selfish, not to mention reckless. For your team, for your own health and future. I just—I can't believe you would do something that senseless." She laughs without humor. "Actually, given your track record lately, I can."

"Look, Leticia is the one who—"

"She took a knee when you fell and offered you a hand when you were ready to get back up."

"It was totally a foul."

She arches a single eyebrow at me. I sigh.

"I took a risk making you captain this year. I knew there would be backlash at every turn when I became the varsity coach." Coach ran JV for a handful of years, taking the team to state playoffs every season since she started. The old white guy reminiscing over his college soccer days who coached varsity could barely get us back-to-back wins. I made varsity as a freshman and played under him for two years, and there's no competition between who gets the job done better now that they swapped teams. Our streak this year proves that. "Still, I believed in you and I believed you could handle the pressure and responsibility. Even as a junior and even when I had people like Sarah's mom breathing down my neck, waiting for me to give her a reason to complain to the school board."

I don't hold my tongue. "Did people like Sarah's mom hate that you made a *junior* captain or that you made *me* captain?" The unspoken words—that I'm queer, that my mom wasn't born here, that I've never shied away from being proud of those things—hang in the air. Alongside the fact that people were only breathing down her neck in the first place because she's a Black woman from Nigeria.

Coach hesitates long enough that we both know the answer. "That's not the point. You proved me wrong today. You showed up late to the game after a night of partying—" The surprise must show on my face. "You think I couldn't smell you from a mile away?"

"It was team bonding," I try half-heartedly.

She squints at me. "I overheard girls complaining about relentless drills on loose sand."

"Bonding over their hatred of me is still bonding."

She takes a long, deep breath. I realize what she's going to say the second before she opens her mouth to say it.

"Coach. You can't."

"As of right now, I'm not appointing you captain next year."

You can see something awful barreling toward you, brace yourself for it, and still get crushed by it nonetheless. Years of soccer and living under Dad's roof, especially after losing Mami to a swift battle with cancer, have taught me that much.

"This is so unfair!" I jump out of my seat. "I make *one* mistake and all my hard work just goes down the drain?"

"Valentina, this is the cherry on top of a lot of selfish

behavior lately." She leans back in her chair and ticks off her fingers. "Threatening to lengthen the practices I let you run if girls don't perform drills exactly the way you like, discouraging players from trying out new positions if it challenges your role as center mid, encouraging them to prioritize games over studying and homework. You just admitted that you know they bond over their frustration with you." She drops her hand. "You pretending this is an isolated incident only proves my point."

"I'm team captain and easily our best scorer," I remind her. "Aren't I supposed to be tough on the girls? I know better than they do."

"You acted selfishly and partially cost us this game."

"If I don't matter at least *marginally* more than the other girls, why do my actions alone bear so much weight on whether we won or lost?"

The disappointment on her face is almost enough to make me take it back. But this is bullshit, and I tell her exactly that.

"I can't look like I'm rewarding this type of behavior. Nepotism allegations were already trickling in because of how close you and Ovie are. After this stunt, I can't justify keeping you as captain when you're obviously not invested in the well-being of this team."

"So who is going to replace me?" My voice turns sour. "Is Sarah going to be a super senior?"

She hesitates. "I'm considering Dina, among others."

"Oh yeah, pick your daughter's girlfriend. That'll help with the nepotism accusations." I yank my bag off the floor and ignore the pinch of regret at my harshness. It's her ass on the line too, but I'm the only one being punished right now. Maybe tomorrow I'll sympathize with her situation, knowing she's far more scrutinized than I am, but after losing playoffs and being captain in one clean sweep, I'm a little preoccupied with my own jeopardized future at the moment.

Shit, what the fuck am I going to tell Dad?

"Whatever, I don't need this."

"Valentina, wait—"

"I'm going home. The season is over, so as of right now, you're not my coach and not in charge of me."

I'm halfway out the door when she calls my name again. I pause, my adrenaline-induced rebelliousness overpowered by my longtime respect for this woman. Not enough to turn around and face her though.

"I'm speaking to you as a parent who cares about you and your future, not as your coach, when I say you need to reexamine your priorities. You weren't always like this." I hear the frown in her tone. Her emphasis on being a parent isn't lost on me either. "Figure out whether you're willing to keep losing yourself in the pursuit of winning."

FOUR

DINA SHOOTS ME A STIFF TEXT that she's getting a ride home with Ovie and Coach. All the better, really, since I don't need the two of them to double down on Coach's lecture. Ovie may let it slide since she's already pretty locked-in with Pepperdine, but Dina's college plans were banking on us winning playoffs this year, same as mine. If I'd just crossed to her, or not let Leticia get in my head, maybe the game would've ended that way.

The gratitude I feel over being able to drive myself home instead of riding with Dad and my brothers is endless. I need the few minutes of solitary silence to brace myself, but they fly by.

As I fidget with my key ring and cross the front yard, I realize the end of soccer season means the end of unlimited access to the minivan. I bet Jorge will be ecstatic now that he's sixteen and has his permit.

Speaking of, he's on the front porch, scribbling away at his sad boy poetry. He doesn't look up at me, even when I block his sunlight.

"Nice game."

I take a swig of water. "Shouldn't you be off mulling over the symbolism of a sunset or something?"

"Your insults are as shitty and uncreative as that goal you tried to score," he says dryly. I want to kick him.

But I'm already on Dad's shit list for causing a fight during a playoff game and jeopardizing my entire athletic and educational future—not that I'm ever *not* on Dad's shit list—so I settle for knocking over Jorge's cup of guanábana juice as I march up the steps.

"At least you made one decent kick today!" Jorge shouts after me as I slam the door. I lock it for good measure.

I consider slipping off to my room to stave off the lecture, but I'd rather just get the inevitable over with. You'd almost think I'd be numb to it by now.

Dad is in the backyard with Matteo, showing him how to kick a soccer ball properly. Top or side of the foot, never directly with your toes.

"Looking good there, futbolista," I say to my little brother as the ball ricochets off his tiny foot.

"A few more years and he'll be taking your place as the player of the family," Dad says as he chases down Matteo's stray ball. I swallow the sting of the comment.

"Can I join your team, Vale?" Matteo asks. I melt a little, the day's horrors washing away for just a moment.

"Unfortunately, her team won't be playing any more games for a while," Dad tells him, still not looking at me.

"Why don't you go get your cleats and I'll run through some drills with you?" I ask Matteo. He squeals and zips inside.

I watch him and speak without thinking. "Mami always said he'd be an amazing soccer player someday with how hard he kicked during her pregnancy."

Dad stiffens at the mention of Mami, and even with how disastrous today has been, I know mentioning her will be my biggest fuckup.

"Well, at least someone will make her memory proud," he replies, stepping past me to grab a glass of water off the patio table.

I take a deep breath. "I didn't mean to mess up."

He smiles unkindly from behind his drink. "Really? You're getting so good at it, I'm starting to think it must be intentional."

"Dad—" I start, with no idea what I'll say next.

"*You* lost that game," he interrupts. And it's fucked-up that, not for the first time, I wish Mami were here to give him some perspective. She also played soccer growing up, the only difference between them being that Dad was Mami's first love, but soccer was always Dad's. "Tell me, what exactly did Ortiz say to you that was more important than winning?"

This. The old there's-no-excuse-to-fight-someone-during-a-game argument.

Dad has played soccer all his life, still plays in an adult league during the fall, and never once fought during a game. After a game? In the parking lot or behind a gas station or anywhere where cops and coaches and refs couldn't see? The man fought like a boxer. He even taught me how to punch without breaking my hand after some boy cleated me on purpose during a random game at the park a few years ago, the closest to bonding that we get.

Never give the refs a reason to throw you out, he always says, *because they will.* And to be fair, they did.

Even outside legit games, in his eyes the greatest revenge you can get on an asshole who cares more about soccer than human decency is beating them. Bold stance from a conventionally attractive, nondisabled, white, cishet dude. If he only knew some of the things girls have said to me over the years. I'm sure Mami had it even worse. I never got to ask her.

I can't really defend myself with that argument here though. Leticia is an asshole, but not a bigot.

"So, what did she say?" he asks again. And I realize this is the first phase of my punishment.

"She made fun of my bad play," I mutter as quietly as possible.

"Speak up."

I lock my jaw and look him in the eye. "She made fun of my bad play."

"Right." He nods, a bitter smile on his face. "And that was worth throwing away all those potential scholarships and all the hours I've spent supporting you." Scoffing, he takes it home. "Your mom would be *so* proud."

He walks inside, everything about his demeanor calm and collected. If I so much as mention a happy memory of Mami, he flinches. But he can invoke her hypothetical disappointment in me at any turn, no sweat.

I walk over to one of the little goals Dad bought Matteo for his fourth birthday last year. We used to have one full-sized goal for me to practice on, but it was replaced when Matteo finally took to soccer. The ball finds its way under my foot, and I roll it absently back and forth.

When Mami first got pregnant with me, the doctors told her I would be a boy. So my parents, in an atrocious display of gender conformity, prepared for the arrival of their little male soccer player. They bought everything for me in shades of bright blue adorned with soccer balls.

And then I was born and they realized the doctors made a mistake. Well, sort of. I mean, I hate the story because it implies that the surprise of me being born with a uterus and vagina and whatnot meant there was no way I was the boy they were expecting. Which I'm not. But not because of my body parts.

My parents, young newlyweds still paying off Mami's nursing school and the start of Dad's landscaping business, couldn't afford to just buy me all new *everything* though. So I was entrenched in soccer and "boy things" from a young age. Which I didn't mind, of course. Because gender is made-up and I love soccer. But I wasn't meant to be the soccer kid, I was meant to be the soccer *boy*.

Then Jorge came along within a year of me, making us Irish twins according to Grandpa Green, and tada! Dad had his glorious soccer son.

Except Jorge *loathes* soccer. He tried playing a few seasons during elementary school, even miserably returning to it in middle school to appease Dad and stave off the family speculation that he was gay. I lessened the pressure there when I came out during Mami's treatments but, as always, I get the feeling he and I have a different set of standards in Dad's eyes.

The point is, Jorge hated soccer and Dad could tell.

No matter, because eventually Mami got pregnant with Matteo, so Dad had his soccer son fantasy intact once again, even if Mami's stage four breast cancer diagnosis came on the tail end of this realized dream.

I'm prepared to wallow in remembering the months of hospital visits and doctor's appointments and watching my mom fade away before my preteen eyes, but then Matteo zooms back outside wearing cleats and an old Colombian World Cup jersey of mine that swallows his body. Mami passed when he was far too young to form memories of her, but the way he clings to his Colombian heritage feels like he still knows her somehow.

He charges toward me and kicks the ball out from under my feet, wildly missing the goal as the toe of his cleat sends his shot into the brick wall surrounding our yard.

"Now you try," he says sweetly as I fetch the ball.

I indulge him and kick off my slides before tapping the ball just a touch ahead, an instinctual move to set up a shot without having to step back first. I swing and it slams into the net, tumbling the kiddie goal over.

Matteo screams and claps. "Teach me how to do that!"

I'm desperate to bail on my minutes-old promise to run drills with him. The desire to hide away in my room, licking my wounds and looking at old photos of Mami, is far more appealing than this. Anything to fuel the self-pity, I guess.

But his hopeful smile stops me.

If he's going to grow up under the weight of Dad's expectations, mostly without Jorge and me once we're out of the house and never looking back, I better at least prepare him to meet them. Odds are, even as the favorite kid, it won't be all hugs and encouraging smiles forever once Dad's run out of emotional punching bags. "All right. Watch me."

He stares as I set up the ball again, his big, brown eyes wide with wonder. And it aches, trying to think of the last time I looked that happy playing soccer.

FIVE

THE LAST DAY OF JUNIOR YEAR arrives as unceremoniously as the past three weeks since playoffs have. Anger still simmers beneath the surface of every interaction I have with my teammates. They sit with me at lunch and reply to texts about finals and study guides, but I know it's because of the team's hierarchy rather than any real friendship. Coach didn't tell everyone about her plan to boot me off my captain's throne, so maybe I can ride out this false loyalty until preseason, when it's clear someone else will be taking my place.

The bell rings, dismissing me from the fifth-period biology final I finished with only minutes to spare. I have no qualms about my grades. I'll pass, but I won't be bringing home anything to hang on the fridge, not that As would impress Dad anyway. Soccer is my ticket to a good college. Or at least that was the plan.

I've been contacted by a few Division I and II coaches since sophomore year, but if any of them were at playoffs, I can kiss those offers goodbye. It's already been radio silence from

Arizona State and Cal State Fullerton since then. It wouldn't be so bad if I had a full season ahead to shake off the rough impression before college apps go out in the fall, but I don't. At this point, I'd settle for playing Division III in the middle of Alaska if it'll get me out of the house and onto a college team without a copious amount of student debt or relying on Dad.

I head to the field, unofficially free from eleventh grade. Now that finals and the season are over, and our usual sixth-period training time isn't needed for studying, the team voted to bring food for a celebratory end-of-year potluck. Understandably, I don't feel particularly celebratory.

I step past the benchwarmers already sharing a bag of Twizzlers and talking about the hottest guys on the boys' team. Far away from everyone else at the top of the bleachers, I pull out the paper bag of empanadas I snagged from my uncle's restaurant, where I work part-time. They're cold now, but still tasty.

Dina and Ovie clamber up the steps when they arrive. Soccer is sort of the foundation for our friendship, so my fuckup at playoffs struck a nerve. Ovie moved on within forty-eight hours, which was basically an eternity for an Ovie grudge, and Dina swore she didn't care anymore after a week, but I can't ignore the permeating sense that they feel shackled to me. Like my mere presence bogs them down, but they're sticking by me out of some sort of obligation.

Ovie pulls out a Tupperware of Coach's famous jollof rice and a few spoons. "Mom gave me a smaller container to split with y'all."

"Wouldn't want my feral germs to contaminate the one for everyone else," I reply.

"Ugh, enough with the self-pity," Dina sighs, plopping down beside me and taking a spoon from Ovie. "You're acting like everyone is giving you the cold shoulder."

I poke her. "I guess this feels room temperature."

She cracks a smile.

"I actually have a proposition for you," Ovie starts, taking a bite of rice and passing me the container and a spoon before continuing. "One that I think will cheer you up."

"We're going to go slash Leticia's tires?" I shovel the delicious rice into my mouth.

"Close. Remember how much we loved Camp All-Stars as kids?"

I pause my chewing. "You're joking."

Dina sighs. "She really isn't."

"What, you want to be counselors for middle schoolers?" I ask.

"Worse," Dina says.

Ovie smiles sheepishly. "I want us to be campers."

"Ovie."

She throws her hands up. "What else are we going to do all summer?"

"Wallow in more self-pity," I suggest.

"Slashing Leticia's tires actually sounded pretty promising," Dina adds.

"Come on, we had so much fun there growing up! And that was when it was only three weeks at the start of summer for the U14-and-under session. Just think of it at this age for U16 through U18! Fresh air in our lungs. Co-captaining our own teams. Two months of freedom and low-stakes games."

Dina tilts her head, considering. "Months away from home, surrounded by nature in a cabin with my girlfriend?" She eyes Ovie, up and down, which somehow, even after years of them being together, still makes Ovie's dark eyes slide away, bashful. "I guess I'm listening."

"Cool, so while you two enjoy getting devoured by mosquitos during your glorified honeymoon, I will happily spend my summer with ESPN and air-conditioning," I reply.

"Spending all summer being mad about us losing isn't going to change the fact that Leticia and her team beat us, fair and square," Ovie says, uncharacteristically blunt.

"Hiding away with your family won't make you feel any better either," Dina adds. "And it's getting old."

I know for a fact that being stuck at home with my family all summer isn't going to do my happiness any favors. I don't admit this though. My friends don't exactly know just how strained my relationship with my dad is. Talking about it sounds so embarrassing.

I sigh. "I'm not even sure my dad would sign off on it. He barely let me go as a kid when I could at least promise it would teach me independence and make me a better player. But there's no way he's buying the idea I'll learn anything there that I don't already know. Not to mention the fees with college apps and tuition around the corner."

Ovie pulls out her phone and leans over Dina to hand it to me. "I thought you might say that."

A job application takes up the screen. "I'm going to work in the camp cafeteria?"

"You've got plenty of experience working at your uncle's restaurant." She grabs an empanada. "And players who work on the grounds get a major discount on enrollment fees."

"You're a genius, you know that?" Dina says. Ovie perks up and kisses her girlfriend on the cheek. I fake a gag.

At a discounted rate, I could easily pay to attend with what I've saved up from working. "Okay. Let's say I do agree to go to camp this year," I start. Ovie already looks ready to burst. "Please just promise me one thing."

"Anything!"

"If we share a cabin, you two save all of this"—I motion to their current position, tangled up in each other—"for when I'm on a run."

Dina scoffs good-naturedly and Ovie all but launches herself at me in excitement before going off about everything we need to do before the deadline for camper applications in a few days.

I'm already regretting this a little bit. The idea of a summer away from playing soccer, away from reminders of Coach and playoffs and Leticia, was the only thing that kept me going these past few weeks. But I can never really escape my thoughts, and the alternative of being stuck at home with Dad and his constant disappointment, without my best friends to hide out with, makes the decision an easy one.

Guess there are worse ways I could spend my summer.

SIX

I CRAM ONE MORE JACKET INTO my bag. Summer in the Valley means running shorts and tank tops, ripped jeans if I'm feeling risky. But if my memories of Santa Cruz summers serve me right, I'll need warm clothes for the mornings and evenings. The cabins aren't the most insulated and, unlike Ovie and Dina, I don't expect to have a cuddle-buddy to keep me warm on the colder nights. Plus, I grew up with a Bogotá-born mom, so I have ingrained in me the knowledge to always bring a jacket wherever I go.

Which reminds me to dig under my bed for the box I keep my most beloved item in. Dina got me a napkin with Megan Rapinoe's autograph on it when her parents took her to a USWNT game for her birthday a few years ago, but this has even that beat.

Mami's old soccer jacket is folded delicately between sheets of tissue paper. Abuelo gave it to me for my fourteenth birthday, my first one without Mami, but I've hardly taken it out of this box since then, let alone worn it. Not only does

Dad's reaction to anything Mami-adjacent dissuade me, I'm terrified of ruining it.

Because of this, the dark purple fabric hasn't faded and the white embroidery on the front and back, all done by Abuela, is still pretty intact. I doubt I'll actually wear it at camp, but the thought of being miles away from it all summer makes me itch, so I succumb to rearranging my meticulously packed luggage to make room for it.

Before I can finish, there's a light knock at my door. Slowly, Matteo pushes it open, peering out from behind it.

"¿Qué necesitas, mijo?" I ask him. "We already said goodbye last night."

"I told you I'd be awake," he yawns, rubbing at his eye. He's a bit of an early bird, but 6:00 a.m. is pushing it for a summer weekend.

He stumbles over to where I'm crouched by my bed and falls into my arms, hugging my chest in his little soccer ball–printed pajamas. I give him a kiss on the head, brushing out his hair a bit. He and Jorge take after Mami, with their tanner complexions and wavy, dark brown hair. My paler skin tone and straight black hair are more Dad.

"What's this?" Matteo asks, poking at the jacket folded on the bed.

I pull him into my lap, sitting crisscross-applesauce, and hold the jacket up.

"Who is Cielo?" he asks, reading and pronouncing the name perfectly.

"That's Mami, remember?" I reply, a little heartbroken.

It's normal for a young kid to forget that his mom isn't named "Mom," but he probably knows that Dad is Jack. "This was hers when she played soccer at my age."

"Oh," he says. I can't tell if it's wonder in his voice or sleepiness. "Was she good?"

At this, I smile. "Abuelo says she was okay. She *loved* playing though, even if she wasn't the best."

"You're the best." He snuggles closer to me and looks up. "Just like Daddy."

"Yeah, two peas in a pod," Jorge says in my doorway, startling me. He's just as disheveled as Matteo, glasses crooked on his face.

"Why are you awake?" I ask as Matteo scrambles off my lap and goes to hug Jorge, even though they share a room and he probably saw him two minutes ago.

"Some people don't know how to be quiet this early in the morning," he says, and picks up Matteo to prop against his hip. "At least Dad does us the courtesy of slipping out quietly."

I wasn't sure if Dad would see me off or already be out on a site visit, fulfilling his landscaping duties. Guess this saves me the trouble of deciding what to say to him after weeks of nothing but silence occasionally punctured by jabs referencing past games and my lack of training since the season ended. The longest conversation we had was when I asked him about camp, but after hearing I'd be paying for it myself and all he had to do was sign the permission slip, he had no objections. He made a comment under his breath about wasting tuition money, but I didn't rise to the bait and took the lack of a significant lecture as enough of a win.

My phone dings with a text from Ovie. "Well, good news for you." I stand and fold Mami's jacket back up. "My friends are here and I'll be out of your hair for the next two months."

Matteo's lip quivers. "Can we come visit you?"

"Maybe if you go see Abuelo up in Merced, he can drive you," I tell him, though I doubt at Abuelo's age he'd want to endure the car ride.

I zip up my bag and my brothers follow me to the front door. I give Matteo a tight hug, besos, and promises to call often. He runs back to his room before I go, claiming that watching me walk out the door will make him too sad. It's enough to almost make me want to stay.

"Well, see ya." I salute Jorge and step outside.

"Wait," he says. I turn around. "I might drive up to Abuelo's next weekend to help him go through some old boxes." Abuela died last year and Abuelo still hasn't gotten around to packing up her stuff. Our tío always says he'll go help, but the restaurant and my primos keep him pretty busy. Jorge and I have talked about going before, but Dad vetoed it as a family trip. Abuelo and Dad were never too fond of each other, and with Mami gone, their only reason for civility is us.

"Best of luck with the cobwebs," I say.

He rolls his eyes. "I'm telling you because he still has a lot of Mami's old stuff lying around. I know you love that jacket of hers, so I can keep an eye out for any of her other soccer gear, if you want."

I'm stunned by the gesture. Jorge and I aren't on terrible terms, but we've never been particularly close. When Mami died, a small part of me thought maybe it would bond us, but the grief seemed to drive a wedge. He turned to books and art and I ran myself into the ground with soccer.

"I'd like that," I finally manage. "Thanks."

He nods awkwardly, then shuts the door behind me.

I walk down the driveway to Dina's car in lingering surprise, but my friends' energy and their blasting music shift my mood quickly.

"And where are we heading today, Miss Castillo-Green?" Dina asks in a posh accent while I chuck my bag in the trunk.

"Anywhere but here." I hop in the back, trying to hide the earnestness in my voice. If my friends hear it, they don't say anything. Dina just puts the car into drive, and takes us away.

SEVEN

CAMP ALL-STARS IS JUST LIKE I remember it. Well, mostly.

I hit my growth spurt absurdly young; shooting up to five seven before we'd even made it to high school. Ovie didn't hit her growth spurt until a couple of years later, bringing her from Dina's barely five feet to my height. Dina, evidently, never hit hers.

So the trees still tower over us, but their tops don't disappear into the clouds like in my memories. Their magic seems a little faded.

Camp All-Stars occupies a sectioned-off area of the Santa Cruz forest, with the cabins and buildings all nestled between the redwoods, and the fields spread out across various clearings. It's a little past noon, but the air droops with residual morning dew and a promise of summer sprinkling. The thick fog has mostly cleared by now, allowing a proper view of the miles and miles of trees surrounding us. The magic may have faded, but the beauty sure hasn't.

We hike up the thick wooden stairs leading to the main office, where groups of girls are already trickling in. I look around for familiar faces as we shuffle into one of the lines formed behind a pair of card tables, but a lot of change happens between ages twelve and seventeen, so it's a little hopeless until I get to the front.

"Marley?"

The white girl with twin brown braids looks up from the table's rosters, her heavily freckled face twisted in confusion. A second, and then, "Valentina!" She throws her tall, lanky body around me, nearly dragging me down onto the table. "It's been so long, oh my gosh, I didn't know you were coming back to camp!"

She releases me and I smile at my old friend. Marley started at camp the last year Dina, Ovie, and I came. She wanted to start playing at home during fall season, but her small town near Fresno refused to let a trans girl play in the girls' league, as counterintuitive as that sounds. Lola and Juanita, the couple behind Camp All-Stars, welcomed her with open arms, and so did the three of us as experienced players.

"Ovie talked me and Dina into it," I tell her, stepping aside so she can see them behind me. She runs around the table and hugs them too, her squeals of excitement stirring up nostalgia for my childhood summers.

"Okay, okay. We *have* to catch up, but let me get y'all checked in first." Marley scurries back to her table. "Papers?"

We hand her all our forms in one go, a sloppy pile of stapled and paper-clipped documents promising our parents won't sue the camp if we fall off a cliff or break our legs during a game.

"Perfect!" She flips through and makes sure everything is in order, then scans over a long list on another clipboard. "Valentina Castillo-Green, check! Ovie Opara, check! And Adina Samat, check! You're all in Cabin Five together, as requested. You'll have three other girls with you though. Aaand you're good to go!" She hands us our little key rings. "Oh, wait, Valentina, it says here you're working in the kitchen?"

"Vale is fine, Marley," I remind her.

She smiles. "Right, I remember the Vale-like-kale mistakes when we were kids." People who don't know Spanish will almost exclusively pronounce Vale like "kale" instead of like "Val-aye" if they read it before hearing it aloud.

"Fun times," I deadpan. "But yeah, do I need to go check in at the kitchen?"

"Yeah, but it's moved since you guys came here. Actually . . ." She checks the delicate silver watch on her wrist. "My volunteer shift ended a few minutes ago. I can walk you there if you want?"

"Sounds good," I tell her. She calls some girl over to swap places with her, and then grabs a long gray cardigan before darting around the tables to lead us out.

"We can take your stuff to the cabin," Dina offers, reaching for my bag. "Squirrel bladder over here might explode if we don't get her to a bathroom soon." Ovie squirms beside her, legs twisted awkwardly.

"Go ahead. I don't want your soiled laundry on my conscience."

Dina rolls her eyes and adjusts our combined bags on her shoulders before taking Ovie's hand and dragging her away. Marley looks pointedly at their joined hands, then back at me, raising a dark, perfectly shaped eyebrow.

"Is that new?" she asks as we start walking in the opposite direction.

"Them being a couple or them being queer?"

She laughs. "Either, or."

"Ovie's bi and Dina's pan." Ovie's known she was queer as long as I've known her, but Dina came out after Halloween our freshman year. Ovie dressed as a fairy princess in this sparkly, gauzy dress, and let's just say there was a correlation between the costume and Dina realizing she likes girls. "They started dating the summer before tenth grade and have been together since."

"Awwwww. So cute!" Marley's bright blue eyes shine brighter, a twinkle glowing in each. I forgot how much she reminds me of Ovie—all Bambi-like and romantic about the world. "And what about you?" She stops to retie her shoes outside of a much smaller cabin than the one we just left. The wood is darker, like it's newly built.

"What about me?"

"Do you have anyone waiting on the bleachers for you back at home?" she asks, smiling sweetly up at me.

I've always been bad at this part of being sapphic, the part where I'm meant to know if a girl is flirting with me. The way most men are taught to flirt is so painstakingly obvious and I'm usually so painstakingly uninterested that it makes it hard to use that experience to navigate relationships with other genders. That and the idea of someone wanting to date me is a relatively foreign concept. Romantically, I guess it's anyone's game, but sexually, I'm almost universally apathetic.

I clear my throat. "Nope. You?"

Her cheeks flush. "My boyfriend and I started dating back in February; let me show you a picture! We actually met at a soccer game!" She hands me her phone before finishing with her shoes.

I flip through the photos, careful not to go too far so I don't accidentally snoop. Her boyfriend looks nice, tall and muscular with light brown skin and a buzzed haircut. In every photo, his hands are wrapped around her waist and she's smiling so hard, her eyes are nearly closed. It's enough to warm even my heart.

I'm startled when the phone starts ringing, the screen flashing with a new photo of this boyfriend and *Babe <3*.

"It's like he knew I was talking about him!" she says, pleased, as I hand her phone back. "We planned to talk after my shift, but I'll call him back in a few."

"No, you should answer," I insist. I'm not a romantic by any means, but even I'd hate to stand in the way of this sweetness.

She pops back off the ground, already answering the call. I really didn't have to tell her twice. "Caf's just a few cabins down that way." She waves vaguely to her right and starts walking away. "There should be a line already forming for lunch, so just follow the noise."

I salute her, equal parts relieved and disappointed to be alone again. Ovie was right: Being here already feels better than the first three weeks of summer I spent sitting around moping did. But there's an almost uncanny-valley nature to returning, like revisiting a tweaked version of my memories. Last time I was here, I was a kid. I still played defense, still tried to befriend every teammate, and still hoped for the day Dad would be proud of me, *still* believing that day would come. Not to mention, Mami was alive. The differences stack up, forming an opaque wall between me and who I was before the worst moments of my life.

I try to shake out of it and check my phone for cell service. The bars are shit—Marley's gotta have a different provider than me—but it's enough to shoot Jorge a text saying I made it here in one piece, hoping he can pass that information on to Dad. I hit send and turn to find the kitchen, when a familiar voice in the distance stops me in my tracks.

Like a coward, I duck under the stairs and pray that I'm wrong. I look between the slats of wood and see her, crimson team jacket and scowl harsh against the peaceful woods.

Leticia is on the phone, walking toward this cabin. Her long legs and arms are on full display in a pair of unhemmed black denim shorts and a black tank top, with her jacket tied loosely around her waist. I've never seen her calves not covered by long soccer socks.

She should be miles away, playing tournaments and

practicing with her club team. She shouldn't be *here*, dressed like *that*, already ruining my plan to escape from what happened the last time I saw her. I blink, willing her to disappear, but it's useless.

"Sí, sí, yes, Mom. Voy a hacerlo right now. I'm literally almost to the nurse's cabin. Yes, I'll make sure everyone knows so they don't break me." She winces, holding the phone away from her face for a second as she pauses on the steps. She's right above me. "I'm sorry—no, I'm taking this seriously, trust me. No te preocupes. Okay, I'm here, I have to go."

When she drops her hand to put her phone away, I realize it's wrapped in gauze a few shades lighter than her skin.

I wait until I hear the nurse's door shut behind her to leave my hiding spot and start jogging away, the entire time thinking: What is Leticia doing here, what the fuck happened to her wrist, and did me tugging her down during our game have anything to do with it?

EIGHT

AFTER A GOOD THIRTY MINUTES SPENT introducing myself to the kitchen staff, composed of three adult women and one local UCSC student, I'm given my schedule. I'll work mostly evenings to avoid interfering with games and practices, but I don't start until next week, so I have a minute to adjust to camp.

By the time I stumble my way through the final staff greeting, mentally running their names back and forth in my head so I don't forget them—realizing I'll have to do that all summer once I meet my team—the cafeteria has filled with bodies and chatter. I get in line for some salad and a serving of mac and cheese, hoping it isn't as stale as the congealed texture implies. Dina, Ovie, and Marley have already secured a table, waving at me from the far corner of the room.

"Perfect location for scouting familiar faces, right?" Ovie asks, dark eyes roaming the crowd.

"Or scoping out the competition," Dina jokes, alluding to the tournament we now get to participate in as U16/U18 players. "Though I guess we're already looking at it since you insisted on co-captaining your own team."

"There was no guarantee I'd be on your guys' team even if I decided not to apply as a co-captain," I say. "But forget about all of that, you'll never guess who I saw earlier."

"Who?" Dina asks, shoveling mac and cheese into her mouth. "Wait, was it that blond chick you used to have a crush on? What was her name again?"

"I have no idea who you're talking about."

"Sophia," Ovie says.

"Sophie," I correct, then blush. Ovie suppresses a grin. "Whatever, I doubt she even attends camp anymore. Who I actually saw was—"

"Leticia!" Marley shouts, standing up and waving across the room.

Dina chokes on her mac and cheese and Ovie drops her napkin. I whirl around to see Leticia carrying a tray of food and staring straight at us.

Marley keeps waving. "Come sit!"

Leticia's eyes widen as they flicker from Marley, to a still-choking Dina, to Ovie, before settling on me. She turns away and walks across the cafeteria to an empty table.

"That was weird," Marley says, sitting back down.

"You're friends with Leticia?" Dina asks once she catches her breath. "Since when?"

"We were on a team together two summers ago!" Marley replies, either blissfully unaware of the disgust on our faces or intentionally ignoring it. "We were cabinmates too! She couldn't come last summer, but I was so excited when she told me she was coming this year." Her smile weakens. "I wonder why she's sitting over there though. I texted her earlier that I'd save her a seat at lunch."

I try to picture it: sweet, innocent Marley befriending the she-devil incarnate. The math doesn't add up. "Why the hell is she here now?"

Marley's face twists. She's finally caught on. "You two still have that weird rivalry or whatever?"

"Or whatever all right," Dina mutters.

"Why is she here?" I ask Marley again, avoiding her question. "Wait, I watched her go into the nurse's cabin. Do you know what's wrong with her wrist?"

A smile breaks out on Dina's face. "You *watched* her?"

"Don't make it sound creepy," I say. "She happened to show up as I was passing by."

"So she saw you too, right? That whole deer-caught-in-the-headlights look she just gave was for show?"

"That's not important." I turn to Marley. "Her team qualified for nationals and she plays club. She should be preparing for summer tournaments right now. What gives?"

Marley bites her lip, scratching off some of her glittery lip gloss. "She sprained her wrist a few weeks ago. The ligament or whatever is all messed up and she basically can't play goalie at all while it heals or she risks damaging it permanently."

A few weeks ago means that it could've been from our

game. But she seemed fine at the time? Pissed, but definitely not injured. Maybe she was just putting on a brave show, but I'm missing something.

"Vale, stop daydreaming about Leticia," Dina says, waving her hand in front of my face. I smack it away, which makes her smile. "Aw, don't tell me you're worried about her."

I roll my eyes. "Please. This is good news for us next year."

"*Vale*," Ovie scolds.

"What? You're going to tell me you aren't thinking the same thing?" I look to Dina for backup, but her eyes are glued to her salad, avoiding mine. "Her team doesn't have a goalie sub that's even half as good as her, so they're fucked if her wrist doesn't heal right. The Tigers are our biggest competition in California, but without her, we have a real shot at beating them at next year's playoffs, if they even make it that far."

"She's *hurt*. This isn't something to celebrate," Ovie says. Marley pushes her food around her plate.

"I mean—" Dina starts. I shoot her a hopeful look while Ovie turns her disappointment from me to her girlfriend. "Look, I'm not saying I'm *happy* that she's hurt. But Vale has a point. Leticia was mediocre in other positions as kids, and she's spent the past few years perfecting being a goalie. If we play even half as good next year as we did this year, we've basically got playoffs in the bag."

Marley stands, taking her tray with her. "I'm going to go sit with Leticia and make sure she's okay. And by the way, Vale, Sophie is still a camper here."

I don't have time to react to this news before Ovie also starts to get up. "I'm going to go call my mom and let her know we made it here all right." She piles unused napkins onto her barely eaten lunch and walks away briskly.

"And then there were two," Dina says, watching Ovie leave. We eat the rest of our food in a weighted silence.

I sneak a peek at Leticia and Marley before we exit. I find Leticia's eyes waiting for me, glaring past a cheerfully chatting Marley. The contrast between them is surreal.

I turn and follow Dina out of the cafeteria, shaking off the intensity that could only be hatred in Leticia's eyes.

NINE

HOURS LATER, WE'VE ALL CHANGED FOR orientation and I pretend to be very interested in the laces of my sneakers while Dina and Ovie have a hushed conversation outside. I only catch bits and pieces about sportsmanship and positive energy, but nothing about me. Well, at least explicitly. Once they're done, Dina shouts for me to hurry up and makes some crack about being fashionably late. I roll my eyes and join them.

Dina and Ovie put more effort into their outfits tonight than they usually do back home, at least when the three of us hang out. Though the fact that we usually hang out after games, practices, and workouts is probably relevant. Dina pairs a leather jacket with dark jeans and gray boots, while Ovie wears an oversized lavender sweater under a pair of long blue overalls.

I, on the other hand, throw on a white Colombian women's national team jersey and black jeans. I'm not here to impress anyone.

But we're halfway to the campfire when Marley's comment

from earlier is confirmed, and I see Sophie Grayson for the first time since I was twelve years old.

Okay, that's kind of a lie. I do peruse her social media on occasion, never hitting that follow button for fear she doesn't remember me. When I was twelve and didn't realize I had a massive crush on her, it was fine to spend my free time mulling over her pretty smile and long lashes and tinkling laugh. You know, as totally undoubtedly heterosexual girls do. But I'm seventeen now and have known I'm queer for a few years. I don't make a habit of crushing on straight girls.

However, the way Sophie's face lights up when she sees me, Dina, and Ovie walking toward her raises the question of whether some habits are worth picking up for a trial run.

"Valentina?" Sophie says, jogging closer and abandoning the two tall brunettes she was standing with. Her light blond curls bounce as she approaches, her pink lips breaking into a smile. "Oh my gosh, Ovie! And Adina! This is wild! I had no idea you guys were coming back to camp this year."

"Surprise," Dina deadpans.

Sophie hugs each of us, me last. Her fruity perfume makes me feel useless.

"Come on, we should hurry before they start announcing the teams," Sophie says. "This is your guys' first year playing competitively at camp, right?" U14 and below still assigns teams, but is more focused on training than on the tournament.

I fall into step beside her. Dina and Ovie subtly hang back, bless them. "Yeah, but we play high school. So, you know, we're prepared."

Sophie cocks an eyebrow at me, the fading sunlight catching on the lightest strands. "It's still pretty intense."

I suppress a snort. "It's *summer camp.*"

She gives me a crooked smile that makes my stomach somersault. "Yeah, but a lot of the girls here are still pretty good. Camp is cheaper than private training, so they come to stay in practice." I glance at Ovie and Dina, who seem just as surprised as I am that camp won't be some walk in the park where we reign supreme over the other players. Sophie picks up on our shock and laughs, shaking her head. "Welcome back, ladies. Let's catch up later."

She blazes ahead of us as we enter the clearing where the campfire is already roaring. Girls are bathed in its orange glow from where they sit on scattered logs and benches.

Despite the weirdness at lunch, Marley waves us over from one of the logs right next to the fire, where her long legs are stretched out to reserve the space.

"Thanks," I tell Marley as we sit. She's changed since earlier, now wearing a summery blue dress under her gray cardigan, clearly chilly as she rubs her shins.

"I see you found Sophie," she says, inclining her head toward Sophie and those brunettes she was walking with before. Wisps of smoke blur their faces from across the fire.

"Oooh, are we gossiping about Vale's crush on Sophie?" Dina leans over, dragging Ovie—whose arm is around Dina's shoulder—with her.

"I hear Sophie and her longtime boyfriend just broke

up," Marley says, before I can defend myself. "If that means anything to you."

I laugh. God, this camp really does bring out the middle school in us. "That tells me very little about her interest in women. So no, it does not."

Dina nudges me and stage-whispers, "Speaking of your love life, am I allowed to joke about you being in love with Leticia in front of Marley, seeing as they're besties?"

My eyes widen in an expression meant to convey *Shut the fuck up*, but it's too late. Marley's mouth curls into a mischievous smile, and it's clear she's ecstatic about being let in on this cursed joke.

Dina's smug face looks ready to push it further, before she's interrupted by a woman standing up on a log. The slight wrinkles in Juanita's brown skin are exaggerated by the firelight. She tugs her co-owner and wife, Lola, whose smooth dark skin shows no sign of aging, up beside her.

The crowd's chatter drops to a murmur and both women smile. "We didn't even have to threaten you with mandatory morning practices to get you to settle down," Juanita says. The kind of laughter that only follows bad jokes made by adults you love echoes in the open space. "Welcome to the opening night of Camp All-Stars' combined U16 and U18 summer season!" Cheers erupt all around us, Marley's the loudest.

"I see both new and old faces here tonight," Lola says, her dark eyes locking on me and my friends for a second. "Now, as many of you know, we're splitting you off into teams co-captained by your peers. Every Friday you'll compete in a game against another team and earn one point if you win; there are no ties here. After the seventh week of camp, points will be tallied and final games will be determined based on everyone's rankings. The two teams that racked up the most points over the summer will compete in the final game for the entire camp to watch. Regardless of your score walking into that game, whoever wins walks out as the victor of the summer tournament." She pauses, leaving every girl around me on the edge of their seat, eyes wide and smiles wider.

I don't get it. I mean, I love winning on principle alone, obviously. But the energy buzzing around us is as if we're being told we have a chance to compete in the World Cup, rather than some cheesy camp tournament that'll probably have plastic trophies as the grand prize.

"We have a big surprise this year," Lola continues. "For the past few summers, we've invited college scouts to the final games." I sit up immediately. "Last year we managed to entice a few into attending, and it was so successful that this year, we've got scouts from at least twenty different colleges planning to come. Most of them are Division Two or Three, but there will be a few Division One coaches attending the last game."

My stomach bottoms out as girls start cheering and clapping. I spin around so quickly that my face almost smacks into Dina's. "Did you know about this?" I ask Ovie.

"You think I could've kept this a secret? I wouldn't have

made my whole argument 'Camp will be better than sitting at home' if I knew there would be recruiters coming."

"This is serious now," Dina says numbly. "That coach from Long Beach still hasn't gotten back to me, and if I can wow them in one of these games instead of just riding off last season—"

"Babe, calm down." Ovie takes her hand and places it in her lap. "We don't even know what scouts are attending yet." She looks back and forth between us. "We'll figure it out."

The sinking feeling in my stomach worsens. We all signed up as co-captains thinking the end goal wasn't this serious. I wanted to win, of course, but not as much as I now do. And the two best players that I know here aren't even going to be on my team.

Juanita runs through a few more announcements regarding camp regulations. No drinking, no drugs, no sneaking out after curfew or leaving camp grounds without permission, no inappropriate behavior with other campers. Read: *Please don't have sex, because your parents will hate us if you get caught.* The usual.

I can hardly focus on her words though. My mind just keeps screaming, *This is how you can still secure your future.* It sounds an awful lot like Dad's voice.

"Now, we've printed out your team rosters for you, which we created based on everyone's applications, but to make things easier, we'll call out the captains first so you know where to stand to meet your team," Lola says. "After that, feel free to stay and socialize, or you can head to bed. Captains, you should start planning your first practices once you've got everyone together."

"Well, there goes my bright idea," I say under my breath.

"What idea?" Dina asks, leaning closer as Lola and Juanita start calling off the sets of captains.

"Ginny Hawk and Emily Hawk!" Lola's voice bellows.

I lean closer to my friends. "I was hoping team captains could still drop out, so you could quit and Ovie and I could captain our team together. Though we might still be able to talk to Lola and Juanita about it if we explain the situation."

Dina's face curdles. "What situation?"

"Well, we have to win . . ." I look between them, puzzled by their faces. "Guys, we weren't prepared for the girls here to actually be good, or for there to be real stakes involved. Our best shot is being on the same team." Granted, we haven't seen the proof of our peers' skills in action yet. But I doubt D-I scouts would come out for nothing.

"Christina Holmes and Stacey Cubillos!" Lola shouts in the distance.

"I don't get why that means *I* have to drop out of being a captain," Dina says, voice colder than I've ever heard it before. "*You* can try quitting and ask to be put on *our* team."

"Yeah, we'd still all be together." Ovie tries for a smile.

I don't budge. "Dina, you've never even captained a team before. Ovie at least has experience learning from Coach." How are they not getting this? "And I think you're familiar with my résumé."

Dina coughs out a bitter laugh. "Oh yeah, trust me. I am.

Need I remind you how our last game under your leadership went?"

"Caitlin Aarons and Kaylee Aarons!" Lola's voice is drowned out by my pounding heartbeat.

"We had a great season, or are we suddenly forgetting all of that because of one game?" I reply, defensive and having to work overtime to make sure my voice doesn't crack. I'm used to my mistakes being held against me at home, but not with my friends. Not like this.

Ovie steps in. "Look, Vale, I get that you're accustomed to being captain. But you can't just ask Dina to quit for you."

"Especially after I'm the reason we lost the game that ruined her chances of impressing that Long Beach scout, right?"

"I mean," Dina says, looking almost remorseful. "Yeah."

I flinch. I set up the shot for her, I just didn't think she'd take it. "That's not fair."

"And neither is asking me to step aside for your fragile ego."

"Adina Samat and Ovie Opara!" Lola calls.

Dina marches off the second Lola finishes saying their names.

"I've got to—" Ovie stumbles, pointing to Dina. It's moments like this when I hate that our group went from a trio to me being their third wheel. We can say we're all friends as much as we want, but since they got together, their loyalty will always be to each other.

"Go ahead," I say, waving her off.

Either fire smoke is getting in my eyes or I actually might

be at risk of crying right now. So fucking ridiculous. Even here, miles away from home, I can't escape this feeling of doing wrong at every turn no matter how hard I try otherwise.

But . . . what if I don't even need them to win? Most of these girls are apparently as good as we are. I just need a killer team and a co-captain who won't get in my way. I can do this. This is so doable. This is how I get my future back. This is how I fix everything.

"And the last set of co-captains"—Lola's voice breaks through my thoughts—"Valentina Castillo-Green and Leticia Ortiz!"

Well. Fuck.

TEN

MARLEY COMES BARRELING TOWARD ME. "VALE! Look! I'm on your and Leticia's team!" She waves around her paper like an award. "Isn't that perfect?"

"Yeah, fantastic," I reply, distractedly trying to find Leticia in the crowd. The rest of our team is lined up behind me, but she's the one I need to talk to. Finally, I spot her in the distance. "I'll be right back. Stay with the troops."

I jog after Leticia, shouting her name. I catch up easily and block her path when she tries to sidestep me. For someone with legs as long as hers, she isn't particularly fast.

I take a deep breath. "Look, we can talk to Lola and Juanita about this and have someone swap with us."

She crosses her arms. "I'm not asking to swap."

"Fine, whatever, I'll ask. It'll be like we never—"

"No. We're not swapping," she says. We're far from the fire now, so her face is mostly shadows.

"And why the hell not?" My anger gives way just long

enough to notice how closely she's holding her wrist to her chest. "Is it because of that?" I motion to her injury, letting my frustration shield my guilt. "Did I do that?"

She exhales sharply through her nose, an almost silent laugh. "I'm sure you wish this was your fault, but you don't pull that hard."

My concern melts away. "Okay, so what's your deal then?"

"You do realize that just because you didn't injure me doesn't mean I'm not still pissed about the last time we saw each other, right?" she asks incredulously.

I could apologize, but we both know I wouldn't mean it. "Isn't that all the more reason to not want to work with me all summer?"

"Nope."

Once again, Leticia is standing in the way of my success. Only this time, it's not just one goal or game, it's my entire future.

"Why are you doing this?" I ask. But I feel like I'm asking her as much as I'm asking the universe.

She smirks. "Because I know the only thing you'd love to do more than make it to that final game is beat me. Can't do that if we're on the same team now, can you?" She starts walking away before I can think of anything clever to reply.

Well, at least anything more clever than, "You're the *worst*!"

She tosses a salute over her shoulder, continuing on her way. "See you at practice, captain!"

Dammit, dammit, dammit.

The next morning I wake up at seven o'clock. I slept with headphones in so my alarm wouldn't wake anyone else, especially Ovie and Dina. Even if we hadn't ended last night the way we did, there are three other girls in our cabin, all of whom ended up on Ovie and Dina's team, and I'd rather not piss them off too.

I slip out of bed and head for the cafeteria.

I could've stopped to change into something other than my now smoke-soaked jersey from last night and the pair of leggings I slept in, but I doubt many girls will be awake straight away. After my confrontation with Leticia, I went back to the campfire just long enough to tell my team to meet at the fields at nine sharp. Then I went to bed before I had the chance to dwell on the nightmare that's become my life.

The cafeteria is already halfway filled though. Ponytails and braids and brightly patterned leggings shuffle around the room. I really need to stop underestimating everyone here.

Once I've snagged a serving of scrambled eggs, hash browns, and a few sausage links, I spot Sophie sitting with those brunettes from last night. There's an empty table beside them that I could walk toward in the hope that Sophie might invite me over, but it's too early to start playing mind games. I suppress my anxiety, head directly for her table, and sit.

"Morning," I say casually, immediately digging into my food.

"We were actually saving that seat for someone," one of the brunettes says.

"Oh." I wish I could disappear. "Sorry, I'll just—"

"She's kidding." Sophie tugs me back down, and my wrist burns where she touched me.

"Totally," the brunette says with a smile. But her voice betrays her.

"This is Cate and Kaylee," Sophie says, motioning to the brunette with the charming sense of humor first and then the nearly identical brunette beside her. "They're cousins who've been coming to camp for a few years now."

They're both white, with slim noses and eyes equally as dark as their brown hair. But Cate's hair is short, stopping just above her chin, while Kaylee's is long enough that she's probably sitting on some of it.

"A pleasure," Kaylee says, barely looking up from her sausage-covered plate.

"You disappeared last night," Sophie says, even though she's the one who walked away from me once we got to the campfire. "I didn't get to see your face after the big reveal."

"Did you know scouts were coming this year?"

She shrugs. "Some came last year and the year before, but hardly any were D-One, and the few that were came as a favor to Juanita and Lola. But a lot of the best girls ended up getting drafted onto college teams and I guess word spread."

"But this place was a joke just a few years ago," I say without thinking.

Cate and Kaylee both poorly hide their snickers.

"I've been coming here every summer since I was nine." Sophie pauses to bite her wheat toast. "Maybe the junior camp session was a joke, but at this age?" She punctuates the sentiment with another bite.

"There are always a few weaker players each year though," Cate says, looking me up and down. "We can't *actually* all be stars, you know?"

"Right." Adding two more girls to my shit list here, I guess.

And speaking of shit lists, Leticia enters the cafeteria, Marley in tow.

"God, not those two," Kaylee says after turning to see who I'm noticeably staring at. "How one of the worst players befriended one of the best is beyond me. I'm just glad I don't have to captain that train wreck again."

I ignore the dig at Marley. I've already decided I hate these girls, but maybe they can give me some intel. "You guys are captains?" I finally take a bite of scrambled eggs, and they taste as rubbery as they look.

"Of course," Cate says, sounding insulted. "We're not going to jeopardize our chances of getting noticed by scouts by playing under someone else. You can't control who's on your team, but you can control who controls the team itself."

Marley waves and smiles when she catches my eye, but drops her hand when she sees Cate and Kaylee watching.

"Word of advice," Cate starts, pulling my attention back

to the table. "Stick her in whatever empty position you've got. I say this as someone who had to deal with her cluttering our team last year."

The help makes me suspicious. "You already memorized who's on my team?"

Cate's face freezes as she realizes her mistake. "We like to know what we'll be up against."

"And who we do or . . ." Kaylee takes her turn to scan me slowly, "*don't* need to be worried about." Then she gives me the fakest smile I've ever seen in my life.

I smile back at her tenfold, then watch while Dina and Ovie take a seat with Marley and Leticia. Ovie jumps straight into introducing herself, but Dina just gives a polite nod, ever the loyal Raven, even when she's pissed at me.

After breakfast, I go back to our cabin to change for practice. Mami's jacket calls to me from my bag, but it's too hot out, even if I were willing to risk dirtying it.

My T-shirt is halfway over my head when Dina and Ovie return with Marley. My first thought is that according to Cate and Kaylee, I need to brace myself for how bad Marley might be. My second thought is that I'm probably expected to apologize to Dina now.

"Hey, D?" I call. She looks up from her unzipped bag. "Good luck today—not that you need it! Just, you're going to be a great captain."

Dina squints at my comment. But after a beat, she offers an olive branch. "Did you know Leticia doesn't actually trap her meals in a web before eating them? There weren't even any human organs on her plate."

"I'll believe it when I see it," I reply, tugging off my sweats and on a pair of running shorts.

"You *could* see it, you know," Marley says, taking a seat on Ovie's bed while the rest of us keep changing. She's already geared up for practice, cleats and everything. Someone has to tell her she should stick to slides when not playing so she doesn't wear down her spikes. "If you just talked to Leticia, I bet you'd like her."

"Believe me, I have talked to her. That's *why* I dislike her."

"Well, the way you talk *about* her doesn't sound like the Letty I know," Marley replies. Dina gags.

"Yeah, well, it's bullshit that 'Letty' won't even consider swapping teams lest she waste a chance to piss me off." I sit across from Marley on my bunkmates' bed.

"At least you can use this time to suss out Leticia's weaknesses." Dina sits to put on her cleats. "You'll get to see how she plays outside of the goal, up close and personal. It's like the ultimate man-on-the-inside moment." Ovie nods along as she changes pants. "Besides, what would you even say to Lola and Juanita to explain the swap request. 'Hey, sorry I can't captain a team with my soul mate, I'll be too distracted by her luscious locks and killer calves to pay attention to the game'?"

I throw a sock at her. "I can't wait to beat your team."

Ovie finishes pulling a tank top on. "'Killer calves, huh?"

Dina sticks her tongue out. "She's got nothing on you, babe."

"If you two need me, I'll be barfing outside," I say.

Dina rolls her eyes. "If it's really such a big deal, you could just tell them about the fight. I doubt they'd want you two working together if they knew."

My eyes dart to Marley. She stills, but doesn't show any clear sign of knowing what happened at playoffs. "I don't exactly want to advertise my big fuckup. And they'd probably tell me to use this opportunity to bury the hatchet."

Ovie joins Dina on her bed. "Is that such a bad thing?"

"Uh, yeah. How am I supposed to crush her team next year if we aren't mortal enemies?"

Dina snorts as Ovie frowns. "By being good?" Ovie suggests. "It doesn't always have to be so personal."

But I think of Dad's disappointed face after playoffs and the other, albeit few, games that I've lost over the years. Soccer has always been personal, just as much an extension of my worth as anything else about me. Besides "the gift of life," the sport is the greatest gift my parents ever gave me. Knowing Mami played it too, even if she was never as intense about it as Dad and I are, makes it even more precious.

Soccer and I have a messy enough history; I won't let Leticia completely wreck my future with it too.

"Enough Leticia talk," Ovie says. "We should get going."

"I don't think Vale will ever run out of things to say about 'Letty,' but you're right," Dina says, jumping up and clapping her hands. "Off to the fields we go." She gives me a sly smile. "Good luck with your wife."

ELEVEN

I SNAGGED ONE OF THE ISOLATED fields buried in the thick trees for our first practice so we wouldn't have to share space. Brilliantly, I didn't get anyone's number last night before bailing, so more than once I call a passing girl over only to find out she's not on my team. Love starting off the day with some light humiliation.

Leticia is the last to find us, wearing that ugly bright red Tigers jacket around her waist again. Seeing her in general pisses me off, but I'm relieved she at least came. The last thing I needed was to go on a wild goose chase looking for her.

"This is a sweet gesture and all," Leticia says as I approach her. "But you don't need to escort me into practice."

"We have to talk about our game plan." I hand her a plain black notebook. "I figure I'll focus on checking out who is best for forward or midfield positions and you can focus on defense. We can compare notes after practice."

Her lips quirk as she stares at the book. "Someone is taking captaining seriously."

"One of us has to."

"Remind me again who won the game between us?" she asks. I roll my eyes and head toward our team, sensing her follow.

The girls are all stretching and chatting around the goal, but quiet down when we approach. For a second, I'm terrified I don't know what I'm doing, that maybe the Ravens were right to hate me as a captain, but I count to seven quickly in my head and let the years of soccer take over.

"I'm Valentina, one of your co-captains. Let me go over our roster and make sure everyone made it." I pull out the folded paper from my notebook. "Well, I know Marley is here." Marley beams from the ground while I run through the remaining players. *Kiko Aioki, Gloria DiMartino, Hayley Griffin, Bethany Kauffman, Rani Nasar, Anita Ortega, Natalia Rodrigues, Claire Torres.* Names I will try to memorize later on. Thankfully, everyone came.

"You didn't call me," Leticia stage-whispers.

"I was hoping I could manifest your absence."

"You seemed awfully relieved when I showed up a minute ago, but if that's your story."

I'm about to rebut, when I realize our entire team is staring at us. Everyone but Marley looks confused.

"We may or may not already know each other," I tell them. It doesn't make it less awkward. I take a deep breath. "This is Leticia, your other co-captain." Leticia gives a little wave. "Great, we're all introduced. Has everyone stretched?" I receive some mumbled agreements. "Let's start off with two laps around the field."

While the girls get moving, I watch. I don't even know what for yet, but it feels like the right thing to do. Leticia jogs after them, but I stop her. "Keep your eyes peeled. We need to know what we're working with."

She rolls her eyes, but doesn't protest as we join them. We're at the end of the second lap when I realize she is no longer beside me.

At first, I think she's being petty and intentionally running slow to piss me off. But her light brown face is tinged pink and her curls are matted to her head with sweat as she pulls in last. I put a pin in that observation.

Everyone signed up as offense, defense, or midfield, but their specific preferred positions aren't listed beyond that. I know I'll play center mid and assume Leticia will pick one of the center defense positions—either stopper, who steps up to shut down the other team's offense before they reach the goal, or sweeper, the last line of defense before the goalie, who sweeps up any mess that gets through. But I need to know who'll be on my sides at midfield, playing offense and defense wherever needed, and who'll be our hotshot striker, ready to shoot goals crossed over to them by the left and right offensive wings.

We only have eleven girls on the team, so we won't have any subs during games. We can get away with having one less defender if need be, but other than that we're going to be running a tight ship.

"We're going to scrimmage for a bit. It'll loosen us up and show me how you play." I wait a beat for Leticia to protest. When she doesn't, I stare down at the roster full of names my brain's already jumbled up. "Um, why don't we have me with Bethany, Rani, Kiko, and Claire. Marley, Hayley, Anita, Natalia, and Gloria can go with Leticia." I realize I don't have any flimsy pinny jerseys to give them yet. Leticia and I still have to pick up our captains' bags full of supplies—cones, extra balls, jerseys, whistles. "Try your best to remember who's on your team."

With a few shrugs, the girls split off and I set my notebook down by the goal.

"Giving yourself the smaller team was noble," Leticia says, tossing her notebook on top of mine. "Or overly confident."

"You look ready to pass out, so I figured I'd do you a favor."

We exchange tight smiles, then join our team.

There's good news. And there's bad news.

The good news is that Leticia and the Tigers are screwed next year if she doesn't heal properly because she sucks outside of the goal. Despite her years of experience as a right back before being a keeper, she insisted on playing left wing. Sure, she can kick and pass like no one's business, but she's useless the second she has to dribble more than a step or two and has no running stamina. The Ravens now have our best chance in years at winning state.

By the time our thirty-minute scrimmage ends—tied—I'm almost pleased enough to be distracted from the bad news:

Our entire team *also* sucks.

Don't get me wrong. I've played on some rough AYSO

teams before. You always have one or two kids with no experience, no raw talent. It's fine, genuinely. Soccer is my life, but it doesn't have to be everyone's, especially in a general league. Whatever.

But those teams didn't hold sway over whether or not I get to play in front of college scouts. This team does. And it's a bad team.

I'd excuse half the fuckups as girls being unfamiliar with each other and the lack of pinnies distinguishing our makeshift teams only adding to the confusion. But it was almost surreal watching some of them play.

The defenders let themselves be juked out over and over and over again. The forwards were shooting goals with their toes, directly at the goalies. The only girl who actually wanted to be a goalie, Gloria, couldn't catch the ball to save her life. Both she and Kiko, who played goalie for my team, punted the ball a wobbling three feet each time they attempted it.

And Marley, sweet, innocent Marley, who insisted on playing offense with Leticia, cannot kick or steal or dribble or pass. Point-blank.

I don't know what to say when it's all over. I can't even falsely muster up words of confidence or gratitude; my anxiety is already spiraling. It must show on my face, but Leticia doesn't step in.

Marley, bless her heart, does. "Well, that was a fun start!"

The girls smile, nodding along. It's nightmarish to me. They don't even realize how bad they were.

"I think that's enough practice for today," I manage to

get out. I don't even know where to start with drills or position swaps or training. I've never been handed such a task.

"Oh okay," Marley says, clearly confused but keeping the pep in her voice. "Should we start a group chat? So everyone knows where to meet next time?" Leticia hands over the notebook I gave her and Marley passes it around until everyone's written their numbers down.

Once they've finished and left, it's just me, Marley, and Leticia.

"Kiko and Hayley said they were going to grab lunch. We can probably go catch up with them if y'all are hungry?" Marley suggests. Leticia nods and yanks her bag onto her shoulder with her good hand.

I stop her. "Can we talk for a minute first?"

"Do I have a choice?"

I smile, close-lipped. "No."

Leticia looks at Marley over my shoulder. "Go ahead, Mars. I'll meet you there in a few."

Marley's eyes assess whether or not we're about to kill each other, but eventually she shrugs and skips off.

I wait until she's out of earshot before turning back to Leticia. "We're supremely fucked."

"I think you're being a bit dramatic." With her thumb hooked over her bag strap, hip cocked to bear her weight, she's the picture of nonchalance. It makes me see red.

"Are you serious? I don't even know where to start with training, they're so awful. All of them. You *saw* them be awful. Hell, you were pretty awful yourself and—"

"Oh-kay," she interrupts, hands raised. "I don't know how you run your Raven shit, but I'm washing my hands of you right now." She brushes past me, bumping my shoulder.

"Where are you going? We have a million things to do! Figure out plans, plays, when our next practice will be?" She keeps walking, picking up her pace the louder and more frantic my voice gets. "We haven't even discussed our lineup!"

She spins around, walking backward, and shrugs exaggeratedly. "Maybe you shouldn't have ended practice early then!"

My hands clench at my sides. Counting to seven can't fix this. I don't know if anything can.

I avoid everyone for the next few hours, doing my best to decide who should play what based on the limited time I spent watching them today. If I thought it would even remotely help, I'd hunt down Leticia and ask for her input, but at this point I don't think my blood pressure could handle her presence.

But, like I summoned her from the depths of hell with my thoughts, I look up from my scribbling to see her walking by my cabin, phone pressed to her ear. She's so distressed she doesn't even notice me.

"Yeah, I know. Well, she just gets like this sometimes. No—no, I'm not trying to defend her. But she is my friend too, it's just—" Leticia cuts herself off when she catches my eye. She stills on the path, a few feet away from me, and I swear if I didn't know better, I'd say she looks vulnerable.

"Can I help you?" She finally breaks the silence. "No, not you," she adds into the phone.

"You could be a dear and go get our coach bags from Lola and Juanita's office."

"That sounds an awful lot like a favor that would make your life easier, which isn't high on my list of priorities right now," she replies.

"But pissing me off seems higher than dealing with whatever that is," I say, nodding to her phone.

She looks at it in surprise, like she'd forgotten it was there. Lifting it to her ear quickly, she starts walking away again. "Sorry about that. No, it was nothing."

Great. I'm nothing now.

Sighing, I get up from the steps and wince at my aching back. I won't survive this summer if I fuck up my muscles crouched over a notebook for hours, so I head into the cabin to run through some stretches and lie down for a bit.

I know I should get the team bags before the office closes for the day or I'll hate myself more than usual in the morning. But when I finally get out of bed an hour later and open the cabin door, one of the two bags is already sitting on the top step, a torn page from the notebook I gave Leticia sticking out of the side pocket.

I pluck it and read the neat handwriting. *Don't say I never did anything for you.*

Even though I know she can't see me, I hide any show of amusement from my face and toss the bag into the cabin before going back to strategizing.

TWELVE

FRIDAY ROLLS AROUND AFTER A WEEK of unproductive practices, bringing with it the first games of the season. The excitement is palpable as Dina, Ovie, and I head into the cafeteria. If people aren't buzzing about the impending matches, they're sighing in relief over a morning off from practice.

"So when are you going to start sporting a hairnet?" Dina asks me as we slide out of line, our trays full of the usual scrambled eggs and sausages.

"I start next week." We sit at an empty table, the chatter around us muffling our words. "They wanted to give me a second to adjust before throwing me in the deep fryer."

"Was that . . . a joke?" Dina asks, leaning in to inspect me. "I think she's even smiling."

I push her away. "Shut up."

"You smiled once, you'll do it again."

"Speaking of," Ovie starts, "how are you feeling about your team now?"

I shrug as I chew my food, pretending to be calmer than I

am. I had to fight my frustration-induced desire to end practice early every day this week. The team isn't getting any better, so whatever fraction of me hoped to chalk up their shortcomings to first-day jitters was quickly snuffed out.

"For all I know, other teams are worse than us," I downplay it. "I tried to scope out the competition's practices, but there was no way to do it without looking like a creep. And to everyone's complete and utter surprise, Leticia is still being no help." The more I stress about our team, the more Leticia lays back.

"Don't let Marley hear you dragging her bestie," Dina warns with a smirk.

"I seriously don't get how the two of them could possibly be friends. Marley is like sugar and rainbows incarnate, and I'm pretty sure Leticia's ancestry could be traced back to Satan himself."

"Actually, I'm pretty sure she's Cuban," Ovie offers. "She's got the flag in her Insta bio."

"You follow her on Instagram?" Dina and I ask at the same time.

Ovie looks back and forth between us. "She followed me last night after Marley tagged us in her story. Did she not follow y'all?"

Dina and I exchange a look.

"Keep your enemies close, I guess," Dina says, dramatically sipping her orange juice.

Then Juanita and Lola enter the cafeteria and everyone freezes. Juanita pays it no mind, fluffing her curls as she walks, but Lola pauses to smile and wave around. Lucky for us, Juanita is the one holding the first matches sheet. She pins it to the bulletin board, bows with a self-satisfied flourish, and leaves.

Frenzy ensues while all the girls rush the paper. Ovie and Dina are hot on my trail while we shove our way through the crowd. I throw a few soft elbows, but nothing that would get me a yellow card, until I get to the front.

Valentina Castillo-Green & Leticia Ortiz vs. Claudia Gong & Ky Li

I sigh in relief, unaware until now that I was worried I'd be playing Dina and Ovie's team first. By the looks on their faces, they're experiencing the opposite. They're playing against Cate and Kaylee.

We fight our way out of the crowd. Once we're clear of the noise and sit back down, we discuss.

"We're going to lose," Ovie says, sulkily pushing sausage around with her fork. "Our defense is great, but our offense hasn't clicked yet and we know Cate and Kaylee's team has some of the best forwards at camp."

"How do you know that?" I interrupt the pity party.

"We asked around about players yesterday," Dina says without looking at me. It's clear this was a plan they hatched together, a plan that didn't involve me even though they know I'm floundering on my own. Though I guess I have been minimizing it when we talk.

The silence only lasts for a second before Dina breaks it, turning to her girlfriend. "We've got you in the goal at least."

"Even if I stop every ball, it won't matter if we can't score," Ovie replies.

"We'll figure it out," Dina says. She scoots closer to Ovie and wraps her arm around her.

"I'm going to go find Leticia," I say. They wave me goodbye without looking as I remove myself from third-wheeling.

Leticia is, predictably, sitting with Marley on the other side of the cafeteria. Neither of them looks like they got up to check the list.

"We're playing against Gong and Li, you know them?" I say by way of greeting and sit down.

"Oh, Ky is the sweetest!" Marley says. "She makes the cutest friendship bracelets for her teams every year."

"That's . . . nice." I look at Leticia. "Are they any good?"

"A lot of people here are," she replies, sipping her water.

"That's it?" I ask. "Do you know *anything* about their team?"

She smirks over her water glass. "They've got eleven players on it."

I take a deep breath. "I don't have the energy for *this*." I gesture vaguely at her. "Be at the fields twenty minutes early so we can pass out jersey numbers. If you're late, I'm setting your jersey on fire."

"If you want me to play shirtless, all you have to do is ask," she replies without missing a beat.

I leave before I can see her undoubtedly satisfied smile.

Avoiding my friends for the rest of the afternoon, I show up to the main fields thirty minutes before our scheduled game.

I set up camp behind one of the goals, watching the first game while I wait for my team to arrive. Normally when I watch soccer, I'm able to home in on every player and pick apart their strategy. But either the past week of watching a talentless team or the anxiety over knowing they're *my* talentless team is getting to me, because all I see are bodies zooming around a field.

I feel someone walk up beside me.

"Sorry, they don't have a six-six-six jersey," I say without looking away from the game. "Maybe you can put in a custom order."

"Cute," Leticia says, dropping her bag next to mine.

We approach the mound of dark purple jerseys. It isn't the worst color, but I was sort of hoping I'd get to see Leticia in blue. Watching her sport Raven colors would've almost made this entire thing feel worth it.

We reach for the uniforms at the same time, our hands brushing. I flinch and snatch my hand back, which, of course, makes her laugh.

"Don't worry, talent isn't contagious," she says, leaning in. Her hair is pushed back from her face with a headband, showcasing the few freckles dotted along her forehead, nose, and cheeks. And her eyes seem more vibrant than usual, dark but saturated. I haven't seen her face this up close in years, and I don't even realize I'm staring until her smirk deepens.

She grabs number thirteen from the pile, same as she wears on the Tigers. Following suit, I grab number seven and slip it on over my sports bra.

We wait in silence as our team trickles in and everyone starts stretching. I'm surprised Marley didn't show up early with Leticia, but when she finally does, I understand why.

Marley's long brown hair is done up in twin French braids, each one tied off with purple ribbons that match the glitter on her cheeks. She races over, a whirlwind of excitement. "Woo! First game, who is excited?"

A few girls give her minor smiles. She seems to deflate, so I reach out for a high five at the same time Leticia does.

"Double captain high fives!" Marley cheers. "That's gotta be a good omen."

Leticia and I exchange a look. This moment of support for our mutual friend solidifies for me that we're on the same team. That she's supposed to be my ally now.

It's disgusting.

When it comes time for the coin toss, Leticia and I walk to midfield. The two co-captains for the other team are decorated in bright red, with matching hearts painted on their cheeks.

"Do you have an agenda against all red teams?" Leticia asks under her breath, making me realize I'm scowling.

"It's instinct," I reply. "But the visual will make it easier to forget I'm not allowed to score on you." The ref approaches us before Leticia can say anything else, but I catch a flash of a smirk out of the corner of my eye.

"Heads or tails?" the ref asks.

"Heads," I reply at the same time Leticia says, "Tails."

I glare at her. "Heads," I repeat.

The coin soars through the air before the ref catches it and slaps it over on the back of their hand. The tails side glints at me mockingly in the afternoon light.

“We’ll stick with starting on this side,” one of the two red captains says sweetly, motioning to her practicing team behind her. I almost feel bad about how much I want to crush them.

I jog over to my position at center mid before Leticia can sass me about the coin toss. Claire and Kiko flank me. Neither is great at defense, but they can run and shoot well enough. Marley stuck with right wing, to my immense displeasure, but at least Leticia doesn’t join her on offense and instead takes sweeper like we agreed upon yesterday, the closest she can get to being goalie without strapping on the gloves.

The whistle blows as I’m still mentally running over who is where one last time, but the game is happening, so my mind clears away all that other shit.

Leticia steals the ball from a red forward so quickly that the girl only realizes it’s not under her feet after Leticia’s already passed it up to Marley. Marley, who *flinches* as she stops the ball fully before taking a step back to kick it. To no one.

“Marley, what the fuck?” I shout.

The ref spins around. I doubt they’re paid enough to warrant glaring at me like that.

I rush forward and manage to intercept a pass. I’m drowning in a sea of red and find no purple around me, so I’m forced to bob and weave until I get an opening.

Marley calls my name, but I shoot for the goal instead of passing. It skims the goalie’s fingertips and for a second I think she’s got it, but then the ball keeps going until it slams into the back of the net.

Cheers erupt, not just from our team, but from the sidelines as well. I try not to notice Sophie as she whistles in celebration.

We set the ball back at the center line and it hits me for the first time since I returned to camp that maybe, just maybe, my team has a chance here. It's an invigorating sensation being on the road toward victory, slow waves of optimism rolling over you, the image of your happiness when this is all over feeling like a prophecy and not a pipe dream. After days of misery over believing I'll be co-captaining the worst team at camp, I suddenly feel a sliver of hope pierce my pessimism. For this game, for every one that follows, and for my future.

My dad once told me hope is for people who aren't prepared enough to guarantee their successes. *If you're relying on hope during a game*, he'd tell me, *you're no longer relying on skill.* And who wants to win if you didn't earn it?

I did.

We lost. Bad. Worse than any other game I've lost in the fifteen years I've been playing soccer. By the middle of the second half, I wanted a mercy loss for the first time in my life, just to put me out of my misery.

After our one—yes, our *one*, only, solitary goal—the other team managed to score . . . *sixteen* times. I didn't even know it was possible to score that many goals in a match at this age. Maybe little kids like Matteo wobbling around on a field without any real comprehension of the game could manage that by some stroke of luck, but we're nearly adults.

Almost every time we seemed close to scoring again, one of my teammates would end up being off-sides. And I was right to think Gloria doesn't belong in the goal. My first confirmation was when she stepped *away* from the first ball that came soaring at her. Leticia did her best to help—I think. Her forehead is red with how many times she tried to head away the higher shots. Which is at least a consolation prize for me. The other three girls on defense, whose names I could probably never forget after screaming them so many times—Hayley, Anita, and Rani—rushed the red's offense with no strategy and maximum energy straight away. By the fifth goal, they'd run out of fuel. The wonderful perk of playing with no subs.

I don't stick around after the game to talk to anyone. I barely managed to make it through the tradition of high-fiving the other team before booking it to my cabin to rip off my sweaty clothes and trade them for shorts, a hoodie, and sneakers. I stare at Mami's jacket for a second before deciding it's still too precious to wear out.

Without a plan in mind, I head for the trees, as far as I can get from the rest of the world. As if the universe is trying to punish me further, my phone starts ringing. At first I worry it'll be Dina or Ovie wondering how my game went, or Marley asking where *I* went, but the name on the screen is worse than all three combined.

"Hi, Dad," I say as evenly as I can manage.

"Did you win your game?" he asks without greeting, the first words he's said to me in weeks, let alone since I got here.

I debate lying for a few seconds. It's not like he would know the difference. But I don't have much to lose these days. And it feels safer to be honest at this distance. "We lost by a lot."

He doesn't say anything at first. I can hear Matteo yelling something in the background. For a beat, I miss being home. At least I don't have any false hope about being anything other than a failure there.

Finally, "Who's co-captaining your team?"

Guess he actually read that paperwork about camp. I swallow down my anxiety and try to stop my hands from shaking so much. "Leticia Ortiz."

"Well. I'm sure you could learn a thing or two from her," he says, clearing his throat.

"She's rubbing off on me already."

He makes a noncommittal *hm*. "Matteo wants to say hi."

Just like that, the phone is passed to Matteo, who immediately asks what color my team is, if I've made friends yet, if I've seen any wild animals at camp. He ends with begging me to let him visit.

The idea of seeing Matteo right now makes me want to cry. I'm feeling lonelier and more out of my element by the moment, and his childish, unconditional love is needed. But I think of how little Dad had to say to me, how quickly I'm losing any chance to prove I'm not a lost cause. I can't have anyone here making me weak, making me think that this is, in fact, the best I can do. I know I can do better.

By next game, I'll prove it.

THIRTEEN

I MOVE UP OUR NEXT TEAM practice from Monday afternoon to Saturday morning, using the group chat to tell everyone that we'll be working throughout the weekend. The general unspoken rule of camp seems to be that weekday practices are mandatory to attend if your captain arranges them. Weekends are less strict.

While everyone was celebrating opening games at another campfire party last night, I was running over drills and plays by myself to prep for today's practice. But when I get to the fields at a quarter to eight, the only people there are Marley and Leticia.

"Where is everyone?" I ask.

"Sleeping, probably," Leticia says, eyes closed as she lies on her back with her arms crossed behind her head.

Marley tries her best to hide a yawn while she picks at the grass beside Leticia. "They'll be here soon," she says, chipper even at this hour. "We saw a few girls at the caf."

I nudge Leticia with my cleat. "You didn't make sure our players were coming?"

She cracks one eye open, squinting up at me. "Oh, I'm sorry, was I meant to forcibly remove them from their breakfasts?" Her head falls back, eyes shut once again. "Violence is your tactic, not mine."

"I'm not a violent person."

"Could've fooled me."

"I feel that changing by the second though."

She smiles sleepily.

I sit down and start stretching. Marley follows suit and eventually Leticia does too. After fifteen minutes, Kiko and Anita show up, claiming Claire said she'd come once she called her boyfriend. Fifteen minutes after that, our horrible goalie, Gloria, joins us. I give it another ten before any remaining hope leaves my body.

"This is it?" I ask, looking at the small crowd of us. They blink back at me, unsure of what to say. "We don't even have enough to do a basic scrimmage."

"We could practice more shooting drills!" Marley suggests, her excitement unnecessary but somehow the only thing keeping me from screaming. "Gloria, do you want to practice catching the ball?"

Gloria looks like she'd rather do anything else, but she follows Marley and Kiko over to the goal, dribbling one of the five balls I lugged over. I watch her footwork, cleaner than I would've guessed from her sloppy keeper performance.

Claire taps me on the shoulder. "I was actually hoping to leave early to FaceTime my boyfriend." Her tan cheeks are sunburned from our practices, but they seem extra flushed right now.

"Seriously? You're leaving already? Didn't you just show up late because you were talking to him?"

"Let her go," Leticia calls from the ground, where she's resumed her relaxation.

I glare at Leticia. Her shut eyes protect her from my wrath. "I don't take suggestions from unconscious people."

Leticia sits up on her elbows and stares me directly in the eye as she dismisses Claire. "Go talk to your boyfriend. Soccer will be here tomorrow."

Claire leaves without waiting for a third opinion.

I turn away and watch Gloria protect her face from a kick Marley makes directly at her. My sigh wants to be a scream.

Leticia stands beside me. "She technically saved that."

"None of this is funny to me, okay?"

She rolls her eyes. "Wouldn't have guessed, given what a darling sense of humor you have."

I clench my jaw and face her. "And you would know so much about me, right?"

Her head tilts in challenge. "I know you don't see it."

"See what?" My eyes can't help but track the bits of grass that ended up in her hair. My hand twitches with the most horrifying desire to free them.

"That they're having fun," she says, nodding to the girls.

I look at them and see the following: Marley kicks the ball with her toes, even when she has the time and space to back up and use the upper side of her foot. Gloria crouches when the ball goes above her head. Her only effective stops happen with her feet. When she punts the ball back to Kiko, Kiko stops it easily without freezing it entirely. She's fluid with the ball and gets around Marley with ease before burying a shot in the net with her left foot. Moments later, she scores another clean goal using her right foot this time. She's ambidextrous, but with her feet. If I weren't so married to center midfield, I might just—

Leticia waves her hand over my eyes. I smack it away quickly, earning me an amused laugh. "Fun doesn't require that much analysis," she says, reading my thoughts.

I look at them again, still seeing nothing but success or failure. Then Marley trips over her own feet and breaks out laughing, a hearty sound free of worry. Kiko grins when she scores another goal. Gloria looks pleased when she manages to punt the ball past Kiko, who tries to stop it with her head.

Whatever I felt watching Matteo that afternoon after we lost playoffs comes back to me, but worse. These girls aren't some little kids who've yet to realize their best isn't going to be good enough for long. These girls are here to compete; they're here because they supposedly care about this game. Even if they aren't experts or don't aspire to be professionals someday, they signed up to spend their summer playing soccer for two months straight. That means something.

But none of them look like they're carrying the burden

of yesterday's loss as they run, unconcerned about anything other than enjoying themselves.

They seem free. They seem happy.

I almost don't recognize it as soccer.

"Fun doesn't win games," I tell Leticia, trying to look as unaffected as possible.

"You never look like you're having fun when you're playing, and we lost our last game. In case you forgot." She walks backward to join the girls. "Maybe *fun* is worth a shot."

Dina and Ovie are lying in Ovie's bunk when I get back from my post-practice shower. They look up from whatever movie they're watching on Dina's iPad.

"Oh hey," Ovie says, sitting up. Yellow scrunchies wrap around her twin hair puffs, matching the one on Dina's wrist. Even if I hadn't seen their uniforms earlier this week, it wouldn't be hard to guess their team color.

"Hey." I drop my dirty practice clothes into the laundry bag hanging off my bunk railing, then sit on the bed below mine. I should really learn the girl who sleeps here's name with how often I've been using her bed as a chair.

"How was practice?" Ovie asks.

"We're getting there."

Dina smiles. "How's Leticia?"

I fall back onto the mattress, sighing.

"Guessing that wasn't a sigh of lovesickness," Ovie says. I glare at her, which causes the both of them to start giggling.

"She's just so . . ." I curl my fingers together and shake an invisible ball of anger in between my hands. "I don't know how Marley does it. I can barely handle being around her for a few hours."

"You think the two of them are a thing?" Dina asks abruptly. Ovie elbows her. "Hey! We're all thinking it! Why else would Marley be so defensive about her all the time?"

"Friends can still be defensive," I reply, feeling defensive myself all of a sudden. Over what, I'm not sure. "Besides, you'd do the same if someone was talking shit about me, right?"

"Depends on what they say. Maybe I'd agree with them," Dina says, sticking her tongue out. She and Ovie laugh it off, but their teasing hits different this time.

At least with Dad I know the default is disappointment and the exception is pride. With my friends lately, I'm struggling to work out which is which. My brain operates on a binary when it comes to people's opinions of me: They either hate me or they don't. I'm worrying about which side my friends are leaning toward.

Ovie notices my discomfort, refocusing the subject. "Marley has a boyfriend who she's head over heels in love with. She and Leticia are just weirdly matched besties."

"They're weirdly matched all right. They're practically opposites," Dina says.

"We're sorta opposites," Ovie says, nudging her.

Dina nestles against Ovie's shoulder. "Bad argument to make if you're convinced they aren't together."

I don't want to hear any more of this for some reason. Talking shit about Leticia being annoying and a wrench in my future is one thing. Speculating about her and Marley being involved makes me itchy.

"I'm hungry," I declare, sitting up too fast and immediately slamming my forehead into the bunk above me.

"Holy shit." Ovie drops from her bed. "Vale, are you okay?"

I clutch my throbbing forehead, feeling a bruise already forming. "Fucking peachy."

Hours after returning from the nurse's office, fresh bandage slapped on my thankfully not concussed forehead, I'm sitting outside my cabin, jotting down as many notes as I can about our players. Lucky for me, my bangs cover the bandage, which covers the massive nasty, purple bruise. So the only people who bore witness to my pain were Nurse Wu, Dina, and Ovie.

I'm trying to read my own chicken scratch from our first practice when a shadow covers me.

I look up and see Sophie hovering, one hand on her hip and the other holding her phone. "I didn't know we had homework here."

I wave my notes. "Extra credit."

She sits beside me, leaving only a sliver of space between us. Not that I'm tracking that amount of space. I am grateful I showered after practice though, smelling like the vanilla body wash I stole from Ovie.

Sophie leans over. "What're you working on?"

"Notes about my team," I confess. "About what we can

improve on." I don't tell her that when I sat down to get started, I nearly wrote *EVERYTHING* and called it a day.

"What a professional captain." She nudges my shoulder. "Very impressive."

"Well, my team certainly isn't."

"Ooh, do tell." She types something on her phone. "Sorry, just replying to Cate and Kaylee asking where I am. I swear it's like if I'm not spending every second practicing, they're on my ass for it." She sets it down on her lap. "You were saying?"

"Are they really that bad?" I mean, I know *I* don't like them. But I thought Sophie considered them friends. And I don't like many people anyway.

"They want to win the whole camp tournament this year, once and for all," she says, tucking a strand of white-blond hair behind her ear. "They made it to the final game last year only to lose to a team captained by girls who got recruited by D-One colleges. So I get why they're so desperate, but I came here to get away from all that. This place has the thrill of competitive soccer without all the stakes. That's why I love it so much."

I wish I could say the same, I almost tell her. The stakes here feel higher than they ever were at home. And at least then I had Dina and Ovie, and even Coach, to bear the brunt of it alongside me, even if Dad and our teammates were breathing down my neck. Here I feel like I'm doing it all on my own. "Makes sense," I say instead, choosing to continue bearing the weight.

"But you were talking about your team. You're co-captaining with Leticia, right?"

"Unfortunately." I laugh. "I know this must sound annoying if your captains are always on your ass, but Leticia couldn't care less about our team. I don't get why she even applied to be a captain if all she wants to do is sit back and leave everything to me." Though I imagine her nonchalance is her way of spiting me. I think of her and her *fun* and want to throw my notebook. "And don't even get me started on the other girls."

"You said Marley was on your team, right? I thought you two were friends."

"We are! I just—I thought this place was a joke before coming back. Now that I get that's not the case, I don't understand how she still sucks so badly when she's been here this long."

"I'm happy we've exceeded your expectations." Sophie laughs. "I know Marley's skills can leave a bit to be desired, but your whole team can't be *that* bad."

"Did you see our game on Friday?" I ask.

"Just the first few minutes."

"It was brutal." I drop my face into my hands, wincing when I accidentally touch my forehead. "There's no way we have a chance placing in the tournament at this rate."

"Okay, here's what we're going to do," Sophie says, pulling me back up. "You tell me about your players' weaknesses and I'll tell you what I know about their strengths. Most of the girls on your team have come for at least one other summer, so I'm sure I've got something good to say about each of them."

I hesitate. "Why help me?"

"Call it evening out the playing field." She smiles brightly.

"But I have to ask that you don't tell anyone about it. Cate and Kaylee would *kill* me if they knew I was helping you. And I don't want everyone coming to me for advice on their players."

"So this is a top secret, exclusive offer?" I ask, trying to keep the flirtation out of my voice.

"Sure, let's call it that."

So I decide to bear a little less of the weight. The more I talk about my teammates, recounting their horrible plays and athletic shortcomings, the better I expect to feel. Back home, this is all Dad and I would do after a good game. We'd sit down, him with a beer and me with a cool glass of Colombiana, and we'd dissect the flaws of everyone around me. It was the only time I knew he didn't just think the worst of me, because he was thinking the worst of everyone else too. So I followed his lead. And if we made it to the end of the evening without turning our scrutiny onto me, I knew he was proud. He didn't even have to say it; the lack of criticism was enough for me.

But after I've finished saying every shitty thing I can think of about my team, I don't feel any better. I don't feel like anyone's proud of me.

I feel like my dad.

FOURTEEN

OUR NEXT PRACTICE ON SUNDAY AFTERNOON only goes marginally better. At least this time the entire team shows up. I pick up on a few more important things, that Bethany manages to steal the ball from anyone she defends against despite settling for left wing and Hayley never loses steam switching between shooting and defending, even when she signed up for right back.

Sophie didn't end up telling me much about my team, since I spent most of our time together complaining rather than listening, but she got this much right: Because most of these girls play for fun, they've never had to care about whether or not their positions are right for them.

But sacrifices must be made if I—we—are going to have any chance making it to that final game. There are only six remaining games between us and it, so we can't afford to lose many more.

After practice, I shower, change, and set out to make my

own sacrifice. Captains should be good role models for their team, after all.

Leticia is juggling a ball by herself on one of the main fields when I find her. Her hair looks darker than normal, and when I get closer, I realize it's wet. Did she shower already and come back to keep practicing? She may be annoying, but she's usually not illogical. Her phone lies on the grass beside her, headphones splayed out, so maybe she was on another weird call.

There's no way she doesn't see me, but her eyes stay glued to the ball bouncing off her feet and knees.

I clear my throat. "We need to talk."

"You breaking up with me, Princesa?"

I rub at my temples. "We both know that this isn't working."

She snorts, still juggling. "I was joking about the breakup."

I reach out and snatch the ball midair. "*Our team* isn't working. *Us as co-captains* isn't working."

She plants her hands on her hips. "Tell me something I don't know."

"Fine." It's as good an opening as I'm going to get, even if she's being sarcastic. "I need us to win this tournament or at least make it to the final game if I want to secure a decent college recruitment and scholarship."

She scoffs. "You're captain of one of the top teams in the state."

"Was."

"What?"

I force the words out. "I *was* captain. As of right now, my spot is going to Dina. Or one of the leeches who have been waiting for me to screw up since day one."

"Gee, when you talk about your teammates like that, I wonder why they aren't begging you to keep valiantly leading them."

"Look, you're captain of *the* best high school team in the state." The compliment surprises her. Surprises me too. "If we take this seriously, together, and treat this team the way we treat our teams back home, we might actually have a chance at winning it all."

"The team back home that you just called leeches? Doesn't sound like you had the best strategy with them."

I take a deep breath and break the dam that kept me from admitting the one truth that pains me even more than admitting I lost my captain spot. "I need you, okay? I can't do this without you."

Her eyes widen and I swear she takes a step back. She lets the words settle, the quiet of the empty field pressing in.

Finally, she blinks. "I'll help you under two conditions." She ticks them off. "One: You beg."

"I beg your pardon?"

"Close. But not quite what I had in mind."

I roll my eyes. "What, you want me to grovel? Hands and knees—the whole deal?"

"I was just thinking a sincere 'please' would do, but I actually like the sound of all of that."

I don't have much, but I still have my dignity. Well, at

least most of it. "Whatever, I'm sure there's plenty of scholarships out there for girls with mediocre kitchen experience that I can apply for." I drop the ball and make it halfway across the field before she shouts for me to wait.

I spin around as she jogs over, carrying the ball and her phone. "An apology."

"Okay." I cross my arms. "I'm waiting."

A laugh escapes her mouth. "*You* apologize to *me*. No groveling needed."

"And what am I apologizing for, exactly?"

She cocks her head. "Tackling me during that game would be a good place to start."

"I didn't *tackle* you," I correct. "And they say guy soccer players are dramatic."

"Tackled, yanked, fought. Pick your verb. I'm flexible."

"You sure you don't just want me to do the groveling thing?" I try. She crosses her arms. "Fine." I take a deep breath, suppressing every ounce of pride I inherited from my father and channeling my mother. "Leticia Ortiz, I am deeply, deeply sorry for . . . tugging on your arm. Resulting in you falling. On top of me." She clears her throat, waving me on. "It is truly my deepest regret in life. Could I relive those moments, I would just accept your helping hand and proceed to kick your shitty team's ass with honor and sportsmanship."

She's fighting a smile. "Close enough."

I sigh. "So we're good? You'll take this seriously?"

"Ah, ah, ah. I did say I have *two* conditions."

"All right, Satan, what else do you want?"

She straightens, emphasizing the margin of height she has over me. I wish I were still wearing my cleats. "I want you to train me to play as a forward."

"I'm not a forward."

Her posture droops with annoyance. "I know *that*. But you were one before landing on center midfield, which means you know your way around that territory. And you played defense when we were younger, so you know how to make the switch." She lifts her injured wrist. "I can't exactly play goalie right now. I need to find a backup position if this doesn't heal right."

It's an easy enough bargain. With Dina and Ovie spending all their time together, I could use something to keep me busy outside of my kitchen duties. But something about this doesn't feel right. "Why switch from defense to offense? And why not just train with a club team or private coach over the summer?"

"I didn't realize this exchange of favors required a thesis statement," she says, and I sort of regret telling her about losing my captainship just on principle of her being an ass. She tucks the ball and her phone under one arm and offers me her uninjured hand. "Do we have a deal?"

It feels a little like making a deal with the devil, gaining her short-term help with this team but potentially losing my long-term advantage against her next year. But I'm desperate, and who doesn't sell a bit of their soul for success anyway?

Her hand envelops mine, our palms warm and slightly damp pressed together.

"You've got yourself a deal."

My first shift in the kitchen is both less and more chaotic than I expected.

On the one hand, after spending the past several days in a continued state of panic, stress, self-deprecation, and comparing myself to the worst parts of my father, any distraction is a welcomed one. On the other hand, athletes are ruthless, and cooking for a mass of them, all of whom are my age and have no reason to even pretend to respect me, is hell.

For the most part, they're impatient or ungrateful, but not outright cruel. I always empathized with the cafeteria staff at school, years of helping out at the restaurant priming me to recognize the efforts made by people in the service industry, but after tonight, I make a mental note to buy them all presents for the holidays.

A few of my teammates smile when I serve them, but no one tries to talk to me. That is, not until Cate and Kaylee get in the busy line.

"How very groundbreaking for you to be an athlete and a server," Cate says as I lump a pile of mashed potatoes onto her tray. "Extra gravy on mine. But only get it on one side of the potatoes."

I do my best to follow her illogical request. Not because I respect her or give two shits about whether her potatoes are properly gravied, but because the sooner I finish, the sooner she gets out of my face and I can keep the packed line moving.

"Pour my gravy into four little pockets in the potatoes," Kaylee says once I pass Cate's tray over the counter.

I take a handful of seconds to calm myself. "Does that mean you'd like me to make *four little pockets* in your potatoes for you?"

Kaylee sighs with pleasure. "Well, I'm not going to do it myself, now, am I? You're the one getting paid here." Her tone is sickly sweet.

I'm ready to tell her what tiny little pockets of hers she can shove these mashed potatoes into when Sophie steps up, and I spot Leticia and Marley right behind her.

Sophie shoots me a quick smile. "Come on, Kay, we've got to eat fast if you want to watch a movie before lights out." I can't tell if this is a rescue mission or not.

I hand Kaylee her tray, gravy sloppily poured into four messy pockets, and give her a smile that I hope conveys how much her customer satisfaction truly means to me. She rolls her eyes and keeps moving along, Sophie in tow.

I'm still watching her walk away, her long, blond ponytail swishing hypnotically back and forth, when someone clears their throat at me.

"Didn't know you were working in the cafeteria," Leticia says, swiftly handing me her tray.

"Make any jokes and I'll spit in your food."

She grins. "Don't threaten me with a good time. No gravy, please."

Once I finish slopping her mashed potatoes, giving her extra since I notice she's got nothing else on her tray, I see her eyes have latched intently onto Sophie, who is chatting with Kaylee and Cate at the soda dispenser.

Guess it's my turn to startle her out of staring. "Jealousy doesn't look good on you," I say. Sophie, Kaylee, and Cate are likely our biggest competition here. Leticia probably knows this as much as I do, but I'm not the one glaring them down and making that calculation obvious.

Her gaze swings around to me. "Everything looks good on me." She grabs her tray out of my hands. "And I'm not jealous. I was checking her out."

She leaves without waiting for Marley, heading toward their usual corner in the caf. Marley steps up to me, a small smile on her face.

"You didn't know Leticia was a lesbian?" she says as tauntingly as a sweetheart like her can manage.

"I try to avoid cluttering my brain with useless information about Leticia," I reply, handing over her food. But now the fact is churning over in my head, stuffing itself between all the crevices and folds of my brain.

Leticia is gay. Leticia likes girls.

Feasibly, but purely hypothetically, I could date Leticia and Leticia could date me.

"I don't know," Marley sing-songs, not noticing my wandering thoughts. "Dina's right. For someone who hates her, you do seem to talk about her a lot."

I point across the room. "Leave before I kick you out of my restaurant."

Marley's smile blooms, but she obliges, giggling as she leaves.

I survive the rest of my shift, thanking the staffers who were cooking and washing dishes all night on my way out. I throw away my gloves and hairnet on the walk back to my cabin, trying to distract myself with anything I can think of. The way the sunlight hits Sophie's eyes. How Rani found herself a sports hijab that somehow perfectly matches our jersey color. Kiko's glorious goals in practice. The ache in my lower back, the throbbing in my calves. My dad, as a general concept.

It's no use though. Because the only thing my useless brain has latched onto is the fact that Leticia and I actually have something in common outside of soccer: We both like girls.

Dina can never find out.

FIFTEEN

I REALIZE, WAITING OUTSIDE LETICIA'S CABIN at seven in the morning the next day, that I hardly know what I'm getting myself into.

It's cold and gloomy out, the sky gray behind the trees clustered above us, but I know I'll be grateful for the lack of baggy sweats weighing me down once we get started. Still, I feel exposed and like I'm pissing Mami's memory off by wearing nothing but a black sports bra and matching running shorts.

Leticia comes out, still wearing that cursed red jacket. Other than that, she's got on roughly the same outfit that I do. She yawns and uses a stretchy headband to push her short curls out of her face.

Without saying anything to me, she grabs one of her ankles and stretches her long leg back so far, the flat of her foot is nearly touching her lower back.

I clear my throat. "I work most weeknights in the cafeteria and I'd like some free time in the afternoons between practice and work to relax, so most of our training is going to have to be early in the morning."

She switches legs. "Mornings are fine. I don't exactly want word to spread that I need *you* to train me."

"I'm trying not to take that as an insult."

"Try all you want."

I blow out a breath and stretch my own legs. "I'm thinking one lap around the entire camp to start. We can work our way up to doing the hiking trails, but they've got a lot of steep bits and I don't want us tripping or getting shin splints."

"Wouldn't want to miss any of our precious tournament games," she coos.

I drop my ankle. "Look, I need you to take this seriously. I have a lot riding on this."

"Cálmate, Princesa," she says. Her voice is just as condescending in Spanish as it is in English. "I promised I'd help, and I will."

I smile. "Glad to hear it, because we're going to be organizing everyone into new positions while we run." Feeling limber enough, I take off. My ponytail swings wildly behind me, the crisp morning air sharp on my face.

It takes Leticia a moment to catch up. "We're going to do that *now*?"

"We've only got four practices until our next game, so we need to decide on new positions before we meet with the team this afternoon. Plus, welcome to the world of breath control."

She squints at me. "I think you just like hearing yourself talk."

"When I'm in conversation with such wonderful company as yourself, can you really blame me?"

"I'm actively fighting the urge to trip you right now," she puffs out between breaths.

We leave behind the final cabin, heading toward the fields. Dew flicks off the grass and onto my calves as we match running pace. It's still early enough that I can see Leticia's breath fogging around her, a cloud she blazes through as soon as it appears.

"We need a goalie," she says first, already panting. I look away from her just in time to stop myself from tripping over a root. "I'm obviously out of service, but I've got someone in mind."

"Please share with the class."

"Marley."

I stop running. She makes it a few steps ahead of me before she pauses. "You can't possibly be tired already." She holds her hands above her head and takes a deep breath, clearly the only one of us who is actually winded. "You're making this a little too easy for me; you know that, right?"

I ignore the bait. "You think Marley would be a good goalie? Marley, as in the girl who flinches when we pass her the ball?"

"I don't do stationary debates."

I bite back a comment about all our past "debates" being relatively stationary and keep running. "So?"

"Marley's super tall and she's sprightly as hell. Yes, she needs to work on not being so terrified of the ball. But she's quick and observant. Being goalie doesn't require the same skills playing upfield does."

"Tell me something I don't know." I steal her line from yesterday.

She smiles wickedly. "Your face gets all pink when you run."

I scoff, cursing Dad's genes. "Goalie is your territory. If you really think she's got what it takes, then I guess there's no harm in trying it out." I take my turn. "Gloria's no use in the goal, but I think she might be suited to take over Marley's spot on offense. She backed away from the ball too quickly on defense and doesn't take the best shots, but she kicks powerfully, and I bet she could get some killer crosses in there as a wing."

"Hm, interesting."

"What?"

"Just digesting how it feels to agree on something with you. It's a little disorienting."

"Trust me, I know the feeling," I reply, then continue. "I think Kiko and Hayley should play mid with me. Kiko dominates with either foot, is fast, has good stamina, and can defend well. Same goes for Hayley; plus, no one can intercept her passes in practice." I swallow the instinct to blame that on our team's shortcomings instead of Hayley's talents. "Anyone look good for defense?"

"I think Bethany could be our stopper," she says, slowing the pace a bit. "I'm a messy forward still, so I'll stick to sweeper for the time being. If Bethany acts as the first line of defense before me, I'd feel better about being able to lay back to keep Marley and the goal protected."

Hearing her admit she's struggling with her new positions feels weirdly intimate. "All right, your call."

"Wow, is this what it's like to have you trust me and my judgment? I feel all tingly inside."

"That tingling is just the lack of oxygen reaching your brain. Need me to slow down?"

She rolls her eyes but doesn't have the energy to retort. I'm seconds away from leaving her in the dust, but decide to choose peace today and slow my pace. It's the closest thing to mercy I ever intend to show her.

"Okay, girls, gather up," I shout to the team once Claire arrives, the last to make it to practice. "You were all there on Friday. You saw how poorly we played." I catch Kiko and Anita exchange an uncomfortable glance.

"I think what she means," Leticia says, stepping in, "is that there's lots of room for improvement here."

"Right, sure," I say. "The thing is, you all signed up with certain position preferences that we"—I motion to Leticia and myself—"don't think necessarily suit you, so we're going to switch things up."

More uncomfortable glances are exchanged.

Leticia steps in again. "How about we make you all a deal?"

"Are deals your go-to for socialization?" I mutter. For once, it's her turn to ignore my snappy comment.

"If we don't win at least one of our next two games, you can go back to whatever position you want."

"What are you doing?" I murmur to her as the girls consider. I thought the deal would be something like *Give it your best shot and we'll buy Popsicles after the game!* Captains don't negotiate their power; they make the calls and the team listens.

"What if we want the positions you play?" Bethany asks sharply. I sense someone is hungry for center mid.

"Well, I wouldn't go *that* far—"

"Even our positions are up for grabs," Leticia interrupts me, raising her eyebrows as if to say, *You asked for my help.* And I hate it—I hate it *so* much—but she's right.

"Yeah." I swallow my own rising panic. "What she said." But because I can't help it, I add, "You have to give it a real effort though. No intentionally slacking off just so you can go back to how it was before. And trust me, we'll know if you're actually trying." Which is a lie, seeing how poorly they play when apparently giving it their best.

The tension lessens as we go down the lineup we created, even though we move basically everyone's positions around. There's more than one look of confusion, especially when switching girls as drastically as we have Marley and Gloria, but no one makes any outright complaints.

We send everyone on a lap around the field to warm up, the two of us still plenty warm from our earlier run. Marley hangs back, looking uncertain about approaching us.

"You guys really want me to play goalie?" she asks, fear widening her already huge eyes.

"I wouldn't pass on my legacy to just anyone," Leticia says. "You've got this. And you'll be trained by the best." She gives an exaggerated bow. "Go catch up with the pack."

Leticia watches like a proud parent as Marley jets off, and I wonder how someone who has only ever made me feel feral could bring someone else that much peace of mind.

She catches me staring. "What?"

"Nothing."

"She's going to be great. You'll see."

"I'm not . . . that's not what I was thinking about." She lifts an eyebrow, waiting. "You're good at that, that's all." I gesture toward Marley, who is galloping after the other girls. "Motivating people."

Her eyes darken curiously. "Careful, Princesa." She tosses me a ball. "That almost sounded like a compliment."

Our first practice as a newly united front goes . . . better. Substantially better. Not only is Leticia genuinely good at rallying the girls and convincing them to try out these new positions, she manages to go several hours without making a single obnoxious comment about or to me. It's like a Christmas miracle in late June.

I finish pulling my hoodie on as Dina and Ovie burst into the cabin, reeking of grass and sweat.

"And did you see that save Emmina made in the last few minutes?" Dina shouts excitedly at her girlfriend.

"Ugh, chef's kiss," Ovie says, kissing her fingertips.

"How about captain's kiss?" Dina says, stepping forward. Ovie giggles.

I step out from behind my bunk, shielding my eyes. "Okay, okay, best friend present. Please keep your clothes on."

"Come on, Vale," Dina says, wrapping an arm around Ovie and giving me a wicked grin. "Nothing you haven't seen before."

Ovie and I synchronously roll our eyes. "Sounds like your team is coming together," I say.

"Yeah, we won't let one loss knock us down," Dina says, taking a seat on her bed. "Who would've thought I could actually hang as a captain?"

Her tone is joking, but I hear the underlying prod nonetheless. "I'm happy for y'all."

"Oh, by the way, my mom says hi," Ovie starts. "She asked about you and your team earlier when she called me."

"And what did you say?" I reply, already defensive. Dina tenses, noticing.

Ovie blinks. "I told her you and Leticia seem like you've got a promising team going? And that you're working really hard despite some hiccups."

I smile, knowing it doesn't reach my eyes. "Yeah . . . sounds about right."

Ovie and Dina exchange a look. I let myself remember who's likely taking my place in the captain's seat when we're back at school in the fall. Dina will be captain, Ovie will be the star goalie heading off to Pepperdine dating her, and

I'll be . . . there. The pathetic friend fallen from grace, who they'll tolerate until graduation before leaving her behind.

I mutter something akin to a goodbye and leave for my shift, feeling both like I've spared us the discomfort of acknowledging whatever is going on between us and like I'm only making it worse the longer I pretend it's not there.

SIXTEEN

"ANY REASON WE'RE THIS FAR APART?" Leticia shouts from midfield while I stand right outside the box. "I promise I don't bite unless asked!"

We're up early again the next day, the sunlight barely peeking over the trees, and I can tell that the opportunity to sass me is the only thing keeping Leticia awake at the moment.

"You need to learn how to dribble the ball!"

Leticia looks behind her, then points to herself. "I'm sorry, you must have me confused with someone else! Hi, I'm Leticia Linda Ortiz, captain of the top team in the state—your words, not mine—and longtime player in one of the most competitive club leagues in the country, nice to see you again!"

I didn't know her middle name was Linda. I hate that the translation suits her. "You asked for my help! You've spent too much time in the goal and forgot how to make your way down an entire field with the ball at your feet. A skill you *shockingly* may need as a wing."

"Some of us try passing to teammates instead of taking the ball all the way to the goal by ourselves! Fun concept called cooperation!"

I'm not going to roll my eyes, I'm not going to roll my eyes. Swiftly, I kick the nearest ball to her. It soars down the field, one of those beautifully satisfying *swoosh* sounds punctuating its arc.

The way she receives the ball is so smooth, equal parts calculated and instinctual. To be fair, she's had a lot of practice stopping balls I kick her way.

"Try to get around me to the goal!"

Leticia keeps the ball close at first, soft taps that don't hitch her stride but don't get so out of her range that a defender closer than I am could easily swoop in. But by the time we reach each other, she's falling behind her own kicks, trying to match speed and control, and failing miserably.

My ankle easily hooks around the ball and I sidestep her. Turning around, we're in our usual positions on the field, with her back to the net and me facing her.

I plant my foot on the ball. "Déjà vu."

"I seem to remember you falling on your face before," she says. "If you really want to rehash old times."

"Aw, deflection is a very humanizing look on you."

"You have a real way with teaching." She cracks her neck. "I feel so inspired."

I consider lecturing her on the importance of honing this skill, but I doubt it'd do anything other than annoy her. What actually motivates Leticia *Linda* Ortiz?

"Get the ball past me and into the goal within the next hour and I'll let you name the team."

She arches an eyebrow. "*Anything* I want?"

"Within reason."

Rolling the ball backward and resuming her spot at midfield, she chuckles villainously. "Our bounds of reason are very different, Princesa. But game on."

I feel like I'm going to regret this in an hour.

Generally speaking, I have regrets. I regret fighting Leticia before mouthing off at the ref during playoffs. I regret insinuating Dina can't be a captain. Existentially, I sort of regret being born as my father's daughter. And now? I regret promising Leticia she could name the team if she got the ball past me.

"All right, Purple Princesses," Leticia says, calling our team together after they've all warmed up. Anita and Bethany groan at the name, but girls like Marley, Kiko, and Claire are amused. I think most of them assume it's an attempt at irony, picking a name we probably would've chosen back in U8, and not Leticia's attempt to make me as miserable as possible at all times.

I take over. "We're focusing on crosses today. Even if you aren't playing offense, it's a reliable way to assist a goal, so you should all practice it. Marley, you're up in the net."

Marley straps on the hefty goalie gloves Leticia loaned her, the bright red detailing a mockery to me. "You got it, boss!" She smiles, wobbly, clearly nervous despite Leticia's pep talk yesterday.

I take my mark. "All right, everyone watch Leticia and me run through the drill! We might not get it perfect, but you'll get a good idea of what we're looking for."

I nod and she takes off. I kick the ball to her, slightly ahead to match her pace. By the time she receives it, I'm at the top of the box.

With one clean sweep, she sends the ball spiraling my way. It's almost sinful how easily I tip it in. A gentle redirection with my foot and it's soaring into the upper left of the net, above Marley's head.

The girls in line cheer for us, but all I can feel is my hammering heart. Leticia is new to playing right wing, but that was a flawless cross. It's like she knew where I'd be before even I did.

"I thought you said you weren't going to get it perfect!" Kiko shouts good-naturedly from the line, hands cupped around her mouth. The other girls laugh and Leticia and I shakily join them.

But our eyes meet as she jogs back to her line and I know it's not just me. What just happened between us was too natural, too perfect, for two girls who hate each other.

SEVENTEEN

OUR FIRST WEEK OF INTENSE PRACTICES flies by and before I know it, it's game day and I'm panicking. Now that names are in, I see we're playing a team called the Clovers. Marley says we're pretty evenly matched, but I can't tell if that's a compliment to us or an insult to them. I really should've been scouting instead of pouting after last week's game.

We've got the earliest playing slot, which doesn't give me much time to prepare. Marley, Dina, and Ovie watch me devour my food and leave, none of them commenting on my weirdness, which I'm both grateful for and bothered by.

Outside of the caf, girls are already in their uniforms, buzzing with excitement. I can't go a few steps before walking past another conversation about how today's games are where it *really* starts counting. It makes it hard to breathe.

Before I realize it, I'm running. I don't know where, or why, but I need to move. I need to give my body a reason other than my own thoughts to suffocate.

It works at first but I can only run so fast for so long in this state, especially in my socks and slides. Distantly, I know I need to preserve my strength for the game, but it takes me nearly tripping over a stray tree root to finally stop.

Then I'm on the ground and gasping for air.

What am I going to say to Dad if we lose this game? What am I going to do next? Swap everyone's positions again? Keep hammering them into these new roles and hope Leticia and I were right to mix everything up?

God, I should've just signed up to be a normal camper on a team where our victory doesn't feel like it's all up to me. One where my own personal failings don't feel reflected in everyone else's. One where I don't feel so damn alone.

I don't even realize I'm sitting against a tree near the bathrooms until I hear a toilet flush. It shakes me out of my thoughts momentarily, but my body is still in panic mode. My lungs are shaky and tight in my heaving chest.

I try to hide around the other side of the tree as I hear someone leaving the bathroom, but I can only get my body to move so fast right now. It's no use. I hear their footsteps stop before I see them, and when I look up, it feels like the universe is punishing me again.

Leticia crouches down in front of me. "Are you okay?"

I must look even worse than I feel. I choke on my breath. "I'm fantastic."

I tuck my head between my knees. I don't need seven seconds to panic. I need seven seconds to relax.

1. The bark underneath my ass
2. My socks bunched up around my toes
3. A cooling bead of sweat dripping down my neck
4. My bangs plastered against my forehead
5. My dry throat
6. My chapped lips
7. Leticia's warm palm

After a second longer, I find the strength to sit up. Leticia takes her hand off my knee, and it's only then that I register she'd been rubbing small circles on it.

"Really worried Bethany is going to come for your midfield spot, aren't you?" she jokes hesitantly.

I manage a laugh. "Once she realizes how much aggression she can let out playing stopper, she'll be defending her position on the roster more than she will on the field."

She smiles as she stands, scratching the back of her neck with the same hand that was rubbing my skin in comfort only moments ago. The sun hangs low behind her, sparks of light bursting around her silhouette. "Team is warming up. Game starts in twenty." Guess I was running for longer than I thought. "You ready for this?"

"Doesn't really matter if I am or not, does it?"

She nudges me with her cleat. "I could always cause a distraction that gets the game postponed. Unrelated, but do you know what the state fine for starting a forest fire is?"

I crack a smile. "As noble as destroying the environment

on my behalf is, I'd rather not have to bail you out from jail."

"I'm touched you'd even consider it." This must feel as much like flirting to her as it does to me, because she clears her throat and looks away. "Well, I'd offer you a hand up, but that didn't work out too well for me last time."

There she is. "Go get the girls ready while I change."

While I run to my cabin to get my gear, I find myself smiling.

We're ten minutes into the game and it's still 0–0.

The Clovers have had more opportunities than us, but Leticia and Bethany are there every time to clean up whatever slips by Rani and Natalia. Marley hasn't had to save a goal yet and I'd like to keep it that way.

Hayley passes the ball up to Gloria, but a Clover collides with her before she can do anything more than receive it. Lola calls a foul and gives us a free kick that may as well be a corner with the angle it's at. I tell Kiko to take it, but before she goes, I whisper a trick play to her that we went over this week, praying she can pull it off.

She gives me a cunning smile, shaking her ponytail over her shoulder. "Ready when you are, captain."

I race over to Anita and remind her what to do. Her smile matches Kiko's, and she nods right before we hear the whistle blow.

Kiko runs toward the ball, angled like she's going to kick high and hard at the goal, but instead kicks it low to Anita outside the box. Anita heads straight for it and the Clovers move to match her swing, pushing to defend the right side.

But at the last second, she steps over the ball, still running in the same direction so it takes the disoriented defense a second to realize I swooped in behind her, wide open to shoot.

The ball soars into the upper left corner, barely sliding in under the top post.

It takes me a second to even realize it's a goal. I scored a goal. *We* scored a goal.

"Holy shit!" Kiko screams, running over to tackle me in a hug. "It worked!"

"It worked," I repeat, almost numbly. But I don't just mean the goal. I mean us.

My brain is rushing to optimistic conclusions, hopeful feelings. But I shut it down fast. The game is still early; this doesn't mean anything.

"Let's see if we can make it work again," I tell Kiko.

By halftime, we're up 2–1. But the whole team is exhausted.

I'm guzzling lukewarm yellow Gatorade like my life depends on it, the neon juice dripping down the sides of my mouth and onto the collar of my uniform. Last game I was too distracted by my misery over being crushed so brutally to notice how much it sucks to play without subs.

"Offense, you're doing great," Leticia says, filling in for me while I continue chugging. I make a mental note to never run off my anxiety right before a game ever again if I'd like to keep my lungs from popping. "They're going to apply even more pressure this half to try to overtake the score, so brace yourselves, defense. You especially, Marley."

Marley freezes in the middle of retying her French braid with a sparkly purple bow. "Sorry about that goal, by the way." She winces, guilt painted as clearly across her face as her freckles.

My throat stops feeling like sandpaper and I finally catch my breath. "They completed a perfect cross. No shame in missing that," I say. Marley smiles, looking adequately consoled. It boosts my already high spirits. "Leticia is right though."

"First time for everything," Leticia says. Kiko and Anita laugh, having caught on to our dynamic by now. Natalia and Rani still look unsure about whether we genuinely hate each other or not.

Lola blows her whistle, calling halftime to an end. I finish off my drink as I hear another whistle, this one coming straight from someone's lips, and look up to see Sophie walking over with Cate and Kaylee in tow.

They're in spotless white uniforms, their hair pushed back with matching white prewrap.

"Go Princesses!" Sophie shouts, cupping her hands around her mouth. Cate and Kaylee exchange an annoyed look.

I smile, hoping my already flushed face hides my blush.

"Valentina!" Leticia shouts behind me. I spin around. "We've got a game to play. Talk to your cheerleader later."

"Did you actually just call me 'Valentina'?"

Leticia opens her mouth to reply but stops. She didn't

realize she did. "Well, the princess nickname is getting a little too popular for my taste." She nods to Sophie, who is now sitting on the sidelines with her captains.

Something about this afternoon and hearing Leticia use my real name makes me bold. "If I accuse you of being jealous again, are you going to blame it on being gay this time too?"

Leticia rolls her eyes, already running backward to her position, fighting a smile. "Just play the fucking game."

Five minutes left and we're desperately clinging to our lead. The Clovers haven't scored again, but neither have we, and fear that we might let this victory slip through our hands shakes me every time the ball gets away from us.

"Push up!" I shout to our defenders as Kiko passes the ball up to Hayley.

"No, hang back!" Leticia yells in response. The part of me that played defense for years agrees with her. As long as we keep the Clovers from scoring again, we win.

But the bigger part of me that was raised by my dad says otherwise. *Rush after Hayley and Kiko, secure another goal, prove you don't have to win by margins but by miles.*

Scoring for our team feels more in my control than keeping Clovers from scoring. I have to do something about this panic, so I listen to Dad instead of myself and Leticia.

Even our defense follows my lead as we continue down the field, leaving only Leticia and Bethany hanging back.

Claire passes to me, but I'm too far to shoot. Kiko and

Hayley are close to the net, but so are all the Clovers marking them.

I curve around the defenders and try to find a clear shot. Right as I maneuver past the last girl in my way, I hear Anita calling me from the top of the box.

I hesitate for a split second, weighing whether or not I can trust Anita to make the goal if I pass to her instead of shooting it myself, when a flash of green comes barreling toward me.

I take the shot quickly—messily—hoping Anita can carry it through if I miss.

The goalie catches it midair, an easy save. Then she punts it toward our goal.

My body is aching as I run back to defend, miserable and hot and soaked with sweat. I'm pummeling the grass with my cleats, sending chunks of it flying behind me. But it's no use.

Our defense has been working nonstop since the second half started, so the Clovers dodge a huffing Bethany with ease. Leticia is my last hope.

Then the Clover does what I couldn't and passes to her teammate, who kicks it straight past Marley in the lower corner.

It's a beautiful, heartbreaking goal. The same kind Anita could've made if I'd passed to her.

The game is tied now and there's probably seconds left on the clock. If we've got a play in motion, we can score before they'll call it. But I don't feel the fire I normally do in a game like this, the burst of desperate fuel.

I feel tired. And weak. And foolish for thinking that a little shift in our positions could actually make a difference. That *I* could make a difference, or at least a positive one, when all I seem capable of is making the same mistakes over and over again.

The whistle blows and we're on our way to the Clover goal. It's all a haze though. My legs don't feel like my own and my eyes can't read any of the moving bodies in a coherent way. Where I should see players, I see blobs of green and purple darting around the field.

I barely realize Kiko misses a shot at the goal. Lola's whistle knocks me out of my daze, but only enough to register that we're going to penalty kicks. I sit down with the rest of the team while Marley and the Clover goalie get situated by the same net. Each team will get five chances to score on the other team's goalie, and whoever makes the most at the end of it takes the game. If it's still tied, we go until it isn't.

"Who's going to shoot?" Leticia asks me.

Numbly, I try to shake my head out of this fog. "Me, Kiko, Anita, Hayley, and Claire," I recite without feeling.

"I've, uh, never done penalty kicks before," Claire admits.

"It's just like shooting on Marley in practice," Leticia says, a lie if I've ever heard one. In practice, our entire future for the summer isn't on the line.

"All right, first up from the Princesses!" Lola shouts as the Clover goalie takes her mark.

I go up to get it over with. Even in my state, I know how to take a penalty. That's the upside of growing up with Dad, I guess. When all you're used to hearing when playing is yelling, critiques, and the stressful echoes of parental disappointment, you learn how to shoot under pressure. Learn to swim in a storm and you'll never drown when you're thrown in the deep end.

Lola blows her whistle and I move. Right foot, upper right corner. Perfect swish as the ball snaps against the net.

My team cheers and Leticia tries to catch my eye, but I ignore them as I sit and watch Marley swap places with the Clover goalie. She tightens the straps on her gloves and drops into a crouch, looking like she's poorly balancing on the edge of a surfboard.

Whistle blows, Clover runs, Marley leaps. And she catches the ball.

Leticia and Kiko scream beside me. Marley is smiling so wide you'd think she just saved the game-winning goal. It's like they don't get where this is going.

But I do. That's the other upside of growing up with Dad. The losses hurt, but they don't surprise me.

Kiko takes her shot, scores. That's two to zero.

The Clovers score on Marley. Two to one.

Claire kicks it straight at the goalie. They save it, big surprise. Clovers score on Marley. Two to two. Anita takes a good shot, but the goalie uses the tips of her fingers to knock it away. Clovers score on Marley. Two to three. Hayley almost misses the net altogether, she shoots so high. The Clovers score. Two to four.

We don't need to go any longer; we've lost. Shocker.

I brush past my team. I don't stay to console Marley, I don't stop to cheer anyone up, I don't stick around to congratulate the Clovers. A good player would do all of that. And maybe that's exactly why I don't.

The worst part is, it would be easy to give in to the voice in my head. The one that sounds like Dad's, but I know is mine. Blame Marley, blame Claire, blame Anita, blame Hayley. Blame Leticia for not training them hard enough, for not caring sooner, for winning playoffs and landing me in this desperate position.

But I can't, not yet. All I can think is that I should've crossed to Anita. I should've passed the ball. Me, the common denominator in this game and last week's. On this team and on the Ravens. Always me.

Now *that* is Dad's voice.

EIGHTEEN

WHEN I GET BACK FROM MY early morning run the next day, I'm surprised to find Leticia sitting outside of my cabin with Ovie.

Ovie's nimble fingers are weaving in and out of Leticia's short curls, French braiding one half of her hair against her scalp.

"Traitor," I accuse Ovie by way of greeting, before taking a swig of Gatorade.

"You're on the same team," Ovie replies without looking up from her work.

"If she keeps drinking piss-colored Gatorade, we may not be," Leticia says, nodding to the electric-yellow bottle in my hand. Ovie frowns as Leticia's movement messes up the braid.

"Well, what you define as good taste is *super* important to me and I'd love to hear more about it, but I do need to change. So if you two will excuse me." I step between them, making Ovie drop her handiwork before she can fix it.

"I actually came here to see you," Leticia says, tipping her head up at me. Her throat is exposed in the early morning light, long and lean.

"You saw me," I reply, and walk into the cabin, letting the door slam behind me.

"Is she always this bright and sunny in the morning?" Leticia's muffled voice asks Ovie behind the door. As if we hadn't spent every morning of the past week running together.

"Just feel lucky you missed her bed head," Ovie replies.

I grab a change of clothes and stumble back out, toward the showers.

Leticia chases after me. "Wait up, Princesa, we need to talk."

I almost throw her breakup joke back at her, but my heart isn't in it. "Then talk," I say without turning around or slowing down.

"You bailed after yesterday's game. I thought we were meant to be dissecting our plays and analyzing our efficiency, or whatever you said at that first practice."

"Oh yeah, you sound *really* serious about this."

She grabs my wrist and spins me around to face her, but doesn't stop moving forward, so we end up a hair's width apart. She swallows. For the briefest of seconds, I wish she had confronted me after my shower when I don't smell like hot garbage. Or that the light freckles on her face weren't so clear this close.

We both step back at the same time, but I speak first. "I don't see the point in any of that now."

"You've certainly changed your tune since last week."

I shrug, trying not to show how defeated I feel. "We gave it a shot; we still lost."

"Yeah, in *penalty kicks*," she says incredulously.

"Losing is still losing."

She shakes her head at me, brows furrowed. "What is with you? This isn't you."

I laugh. "Oh, so now you know me?"

"I guess not. The Valentina I knew was a pain in my ass because she refused to give up even when the clock and score and odds were against her. Not because she's a quitter." She crosses her arms. "But now it makes sense why my team always beat yours. You just don't want to work hard."

"Are you kidding me?" My skin burns. "I've been working like hell to make this team better! And I run myself into the ground during the school year to keep the Ravens at the top of their game while balancing homework, the restaurant, *and* babysitting my brother."

"Maybe that's who you used to be, but you seem to be giving up pretty quickly. Even without the homework or the brother around to keep you down. So sad to see how the mighty have fallen."

"Oh fuck you."

She pouts at me. "Does the truth hurt?"

"No, because it's not the truth. I haven't given up on shit."

"Then I guess I'll see you bright and early tomorrow for our run."

"Then I guess you will!"

"Don't be late."

"I won't be."

Leticia's lips only give the slightest twitch of a smile before she struts off. Leaving me, panting and death-gripping my clothes against my chest, only barely realizing I walked straight into that.

NINETEEN

AFTER TEN MINUTES OF WAITING OUTSIDE of Leticia's cabin, I finally succumb to calling her a third time.

I hear the phone ringing inside, loud enough to wake her but hopefully not her whole cabin. The only reason I'm not banging the door down is because the last thing I need is to piss off a bunch of athletes this early on a Sunday morning, including Marley, Kiko, and Anita, who bunk with her.

I hear mumbling inside, then Leticia answers my call. And immediately hangs up. Granted, it is six in the morning.

I gently knock on the door and it swings open. Leticia's curls are a mess, with half of them sticking up and the other half flat against her head. It's clear what side she sleeps on.

"Why," is all she moans.

"You were sluggish in the second half." I stretch my arms over my head. "Cardio could help with that. Also you were the one who reverse-psychologied me into this run." The early morning wake-up is my revenge.

The door is slammed in my face. I'll give her five minutes before I knock again.

I walk out of earshot and stare at my phone. I avoided Dad's call after Friday's game, but if I squeeze it in now I will at least have Leticia as an excuse to hang up pretty quickly. He's always up at this hour anyway, aggressively being a morning person.

He answers on the second ring. "You finally decided to call me back."

"Yeah, sorry, I've been a little busy. Camp has bee—"

"Did you win on Friday?" he interrupts.

I hesitate. "No."

"How much?"

"Tied, then lost in penalties."

"Did you make yours?"

"Of course, I always do." We've spent enough hours practicing them for him to know this.

"Don't get so defensive, it was just a question. I'm not the bad guy for wanting to know how my daughter is playing." He takes a deep breath. "Especially when this is starting to sound like a waste of your summer."

"I swear it's not," I say, but feel unsure myself. If I tell him about the scouts, he'll be on my ass even more than before, but if I don't, he'll still think this was a bad idea. Neither sounds particularly pleasant.

"I have to go get breakfast started for Matteo," he says before I can decide whether or not to tell him.

It's a lie. Matteo is an early bird, but not this early. "Tell him I say hi. Jorge too."

Dad scoffs at that. I guess Jorge and I aren't the closest, but I'd hardly considered my request scoff-worthy.

"Have a good week. Hopefully your next game doesn't go so poorly; you can play better than this."

And then he hangs up, leaving the child in me desperate to wring a compliment out of his last comment.

Leticia sneaks up on me. "That your boyfriend calling?"

I spin around. Her hair is yanked back with a headband and the bags under her eyes are almost as dark as her running clothes. It's puzzling seeing her this sleepy. Makes her look a little too human for my liking, like all her rough edges are softened by the morning light.

I shove my phone into the waistband of my shorts. "How do you know it wasn't my girlfriend?"

She coughs out a laugh. It strikes me that she may not have known I was queer either. "Did you wake me up this early to talk about your love life?" she asks, like she didn't bring it up. "We could've done that over breakfast."

"I'll add that to our itinerary." I feel oddly compelled to clarify. "But given that I'm single, there won't be much to discuss."

She stretches her neck, twisting her head side to side. "Guess that makes sense, with how much you've been drooling over Sophie."

I bend my knee and pull my ankle against my butt. "You're the one who called her hot last week."

"I said I was checking her out."

"Which you only do when you think someone is hot."

She leans into a leg lunge. "Maybe I was assessing."

"And your conclusion?"

She switches her legs. "She's hot."

Funny. I don't feel as accomplished as I thought I would after getting her to admit that.

"Doesn't mean anything though," she adds, standing up from her lunge. "I think plenty of girls are hot." She flicks her gaze over me quickly, then tilts her head. "All warmed up?"

I start running in lieu of answering. I'm not sure I could speak even if I tried.

After our run, I have enough time to go over corner kick drills with Leticia before work.

"It's just like crossing," I tell her as I set down the ball. "Only stationary. And you're starting from out of bounds. And you don't have to kick it to the goal if someone is open elsewhere."

"So . . . not like crossing," she says.

"Whatever, just practice kicking it to me."

I spend the next hour shifting from spot to spot—top of the box, the closest post, the farthest post, etc.—so she can get a feel for various angles and distances. By the end of it all, I'm more exhausted than I was by the run. But meeting her kicks and knocking each and every one of them into an empty goal feels oddly thrilling. It's simple and relatively easy, but it reminds me of the basics of soccer. Like I'm a kid again.

"That's weird," Leticia says as we sit to hydrate. "You're smiling."

"That's not weird. I smile all the time."

"Wouldn't hurt to do it a bit more."

"That's a generally frowned-upon thing to say to a girl." I lean back on my elbows. "Are you trying to tell me you like my smile or something?"

She rolls her eyes and sips her Gatorade. "Or something."

I chug half of my water, then toss it into my bag. "All right, I've got to go shower before I get sweaty and greasy all over again in the kitchen."

"Can I ask why you're working in the cafeteria?" she says as she tugs off her cleats. "Captaining and playing nonstop wasn't enough to keep you busy?"

"I know you're a private school kid, but some of us have to work to pay for things, Leticia." I stand and swing my bag over my shoulder. "It's called capitalism."

"Not a fan. And one of my moms works at my school, so I'm a scholarship kid first and foremost," she replies, leaning back in the grass so she can look up at me. "I'm just surprised your parents would let you sign up for so much. My moms have been on my ass about not overdoing it here, especially with my wrist." She wiggles her fingers. "They don't really get the soccer obsession thing though."

"Well, my dad gets the soccer obsession thing a little too well," I admit, tucking away the facts that she's probably not as rich as I assumed and that she has two moms into my mental Leticia folder.

"And your mom? Or other parent? I of all people shouldn't be assuming, I guess," she laughs.

This awkward conversation. I guess if I didn't know she has two moms, there's no way she'd know I have a dead one. Still, losing my mom was such a monumental shift in my life that it continues to gut me when I talk to someone new about it. Like they should feel the loss in the world, the absence of someone beautiful, even if they never met her.

"My mom died when I was thirteen," I tell her plainly, because if there's one person I've never had to sugarcoat things with, it's Leticia.

Leticia sits up. "I'm sorry."

I don't know why I feel a little disappointed by the pitying look on her face. I don't want to be pitied. I don't want to see how heartbreaking my loss was through the eyes of someone who never even knew her.

"It's been a few years now. I'm fine," I tell her. "I'm going to be late to work though." I start walking away before she can say something kind or apologize again.

"Wait."

I turn around slowly, bracing myself for the usual empty platitudes.

She walks over. "Your mom played, didn't she?"

"How'd you know that?"

She looks at her cleats. "The way you play, I don't know how to explain it."

I crack a smile. "I thought I look like I'm not having fun when I play."

"You do," she laughs. "But you also look like you're trying to honor something. Or someone."

Mami and I never really bonded over soccer the way Dad and I do—if you can even call our relationship with the sport "bonding." But it does matter to me that she played when she was younger. That of all the parts of her I think I'm missing—her patience and kindness and beauty—at least we share soccer. I always loved it, but never more than after she died.

I didn't think anyone ever noticed that love in the way I play. I don't think I even noticed it myself.

"You pay a lot of attention to me when we play against each other, huh?" I tease, because I don't know how to process this.

"Don't flatter yourself."

"I don't have to." I grin. "You already did."

TWENTY

MY FIRST FULL WEEKEND OF WORKING as well as training leaves me sore and drained. I spend more time with my coworkers at least. Mainly Maria, the kind older woman who wouldn't stop bragging about her kids while I helped her with dinner prep, and Eli, the UCSC student majoring in computer science who actually managed to make their classes sound interesting. So I didn't suffer alone.

Monday poses a new problem though. We've lost two games already, and if we lose another, I don't see us having any chance of making it to the final tournament game. Leticia's voice rings through my head as I push our team hard on Monday and Tuesday. The things she said to reverse-psychology me into not giving up, her comments about how I play.

Normally, her existence motivates me to do well so I can crush her. Now I feel compelled to do well so I can prove her right about me.

We make the most of the daylight and practice from almost sunrise to sunset. If it weren't for my dinner shifts, I'd probably make us play through the night. Offense runs shooting, crossing, and penalty drills on Marley. Defense practices stealing the ball from each other. Midfield does all of the above. We jog through camp, switching pace constantly so everyone gets used to shifting gears at a moment's notice when a play demands it. It pains me, but I even spend an hour on Tuesday making sure everyone can do throw-ins without lifting their feet up.

In the Princesses' defense, it's not until Wednesday morning that they start to show signs of losing steam. While other teams are off taking bonding trips to the beach and having picnics in the forest, we're on our third long practice of the week. Everyone looks exhausted, sore, and like they'd rather decapitate me than run another drill. We've spent the past hour practicing heading, so my neck is ready to give out either way.

Leticia pulls me aside. "We're losing them."

"You're right." She smiles, so I push on before she can get an annoying comment in. "But we need the practice or we're going to lose our games too. If what Sophie told me is true—"

"Disputably reliable source," she interrupts.

I glare at her before continuing. "If what she, Dina, Ovie, *and* Marley have told me is true, we need all the practice we can get. Imagine what would happen if we go up against Cate and Kaylee this week." Leticia shudders. I only half think it's a joke. "The team will be crushed and their faith in our plan will be gone."

"I think I have an idea," she says, looking at our miserable team as they chug neon-colored electrolytes. "Do you trust me?"

"Not for a second."

"For a millisecond?"

"Maybe. On a good day."

"Works for me."

Leticia walks over to the girls, clapping loudly. "I've got a fun idea for practice today."

"Does it involve taking a group nap?" Kiko whines, dropping her flushed face onto Marley's shoulder.

"I like Kiko's idea," Marley says. She pats Kiko's damp hair. "Kiko is smart."

I shoot Leticia a desperate glance.

"We're going to scrimmage ourselves again," she starts, and is immediately met with groans and complaints. We played two long scrimmages yesterday, one to open and one to close practice. "Hold on, hold on. Here's the fun part: You can only touch the ball with your nondominant foot." Kiko raises her hand. "Just pick one if you have even control with both." Kiko lowers her hand.

I pull Leticia aside as Marley takes over distributing the white pinnies to half of the team. "This doesn't sound like a very efficient use of our time."

She gives me a look. "They're tired and unhappy. Tired and unhappy doesn't win games," she adds, stealing and changing my line from last week. "It's good practice for them to use both feet and, more importantly, it's *fun*."

"Fine." I walk over to Marley and grab a pinny. "But if we play Cate and Kaylee this week, you're in the goal, fucked-up wrist and all."

Leticia smirks. "I'd like to see you try to enforce that threat."

I'm pretty shit with my left foot, a fact made apparent five minutes into our scrimmage. Claire sits out because her asthma is acting up and I haven't reached the level of desperation that warrants killing my players, so we have even teams this time.

I'm grateful that Leticia is on the other team. I'm due a good rivalry moment, especially if she keeps proving herself so disorientingly helpful. You don't spend years hating someone for them to start becoming one of the few people keeping you afloat.

Sadly, being terrible at shooting and dribbling with only my left foot turns out to be just as big a problem as you'd expect in a game like this. I fumble passes and shoot over the net, mistakes I rarely, if ever, make these days. The other girls giggle their way through the messy scrimmage, Kiko the only one of us who thrives. I know we're meant to be having fun, but I don't get what's fun about being bad at something I should be brilliant at.

My team eventually loses, unable to score even with Gloria reprising her role as temporary goalie for Letica's team.

No one else takes the loss like a loss though. Anita and Rani laugh and recount the hilarious missteps that happened only minutes ago while Hayley and Bethany pester Kiko for tips on training both feet. I strip off my gear in silence.

Before everyone leaves, Leticia grabs their attention. "Take tomorrow off. No practice." Loud cheers interrupt her. Gloria even whistles. "All right, all right. Try to get some workouts in if you can manage. But rest up for Friday."

My mouth falls open while the team merrily walks away. I push past them toward Leticia, who is packing the pinnies away in her team bag.

"What the hell?" I say. "We can't afford to take time off, let alone before a game."

She beckons with her hand. I sigh and strip off my pinny, handing it to her harshly.

"You said it yourself earlier; we're screwed if we're up against Cate and Kaylee this week. Probably Dina and Ovie too." It feels weird hearing her say my best friends' names, even if they've talked several times now. Leticia is supposed to be our enemy, but these days I see her more than I do them. "No amount of practice between now and Friday will drastically change our odds. But if they take tomorrow off to recharge, we still have a good chance against other teams." I brace myself to argue. "Think of how tired they were during last week's game. They need the rest or they'll burn out."

I hate that I find myself agreeing with her. "You still shouldn't make calls like that without talking to me first. We're co-captains; we make decisions together."

"You're right." She lifts her hands in exaggerated surrender. "My bad."

"Just don't do it again."

"Oh." She stands, swinging her team bag over her left shoulder with ease. Years of playing goalie gave her strong upper arms. "Well, I can't promise that."

I shake out of staring at her arms. "Excuse me?"

She's already backing away. "Sorry. Too much fun watching you get pissed off. I only have so many ways to do that when we're playing for the same team." She winks, then turns and leaves.

God, this summer can't end fast enough.

I've got some downtime before my shift that could be spent running or going over my practice notes. But it's been too long since I've heard Matteo's voice, so I call Jorge, poking at my forehead bruise while I wait for him to answer.

"You butt-dialed me," he says the second the call connects.

"Ha ha."

A pause. "Wait, did you actually mean to call me?"

"Yes, but I'm calling for the smaller, cuter version of you."

He snorts. "Yeah, like Matteo is anything but a mini-Dad. He's been begging for you to come home and teach him more *fancy soccer moves.*"

I slouch in bed and toy with one of the sleeves of Mami's jacket, splayed out across my chest. It feels almost like hugging her. "If Matteo wants me around, he's the exact opposite of Dad."

"Yeah, well, Dad's not exactly crazy about me either right now," he says. "Anyway, I'm not with Matteo, I'm at Abuelo's."

Now I can hear the familiar din of a soccer game in Spanish in the background. "Damn, still? How much stuff did Abuela even have?" He's too silent, not joining in on our usual sibling banter. "Jorge, ¿qué pasa?"

He sighs. "Dad and I got into it over something before I left for Abuelo's. It was just supposed to be a weekend visit, but after that I decided to make it a summerlong one."

"Wait, what?" There's no way Dad wouldn't drive up to Abuelo's and drag Jorge home. "What was the argument about?"

"It was nothing, forget it."

"Jorge," I push.

My brother sighs. "He wanted me to enroll in a soccer program for the summer. Said it would get me out of the house and help me finally make some friends." He laughs bitterly. "Would you be surprised that he didn't like my answer? I even got the classic 'Your mom would be so disappointed to see you wasting your potential like this.' As if I ever showed potential in soccer."

"Yeah, he loves using that one," I say numbly. You'd think living in the same household would mean I know he pulls the same shit on my brother as he does on me, but this is the first I've heard of Dad knocking Jorge down with that exact line. I thought he saved the particularly cruel words just for me. Most of the time Dad is just disinterested in Jorge, which probably stings in its own right. "Well, you spend half your time at the library and the other half at the park with your nose in a book. You get out plenty," I add, unfamiliarly defending him. I don't touch the subject of friends though.

"You know what he means."

"Yeah," I say, the words carrying more meaning than words should be able to. "I do."

I may not be the soccer star son Dad wanted, but at least

I am *a* soccer star. Not anymore, I guess. But Matteo isn't filling the void enough for him. Jorge has to compensate for me now too.

Or maybe I had been compensating for him.

Sophie catches me by surprise on my way to work, shouting as she jogs over.

"Hey, stranger, where are you off to?"

"Getting a quick bite in before fulfilling my exciting duties as dishpig for the evening," I tell her.

"Mind if I walk you there?" Her smile looks like the type of challenge that gets girls like me in trouble. "You can tell me how it's going in the kitchen."

"It's nothing special, but it pays the bills."

That earns me a laugh. "I get what you mean. I worked in Lola and Juanita's office last summer. They seriously need to switch to all digital files. They just have boxes and boxes of paperwork sitting around in there."

"You're not working this summer?"

"Nah." She scrunches her nose. "Just needed something to add to college apps, you know how it is. But it was *not* worth the paper cuts."

I laugh along stiffly, unsure how to reply since me being here was contingent on me working in the caf. It leaves us awkwardly silent for a moment as we trek down the gravel.

"So I saw you and Leticia jogging yesterday morning," she says, swinging her arms as she walks.

"We've just been working on cardio together."

"I thought I saw you two out on the fields too," she adds. "But I didn't see your team anywhere."

"You seem to see a lot," I reply, sensing a question lurking around the corner.

"You said you two didn't get along, that's all." She shrugs. "I thought you weren't a good fit as co-captains, so I was surprised to see you working together so much."

I kick a twig off the path. "Have to put aside our differences to win, you know?"

"Well, that's great. It would've sucked to spend all summer stuck with a captain you can't get along with."

It's one thing for me to notice I haven't hated Leticia as much lately. It's a whole other thing to hear someone else has noticed it. God forbid Leticia realizes. "Oh, don't get me wrong. I still can't stand her."

She smiles coyly. "Good to know." She backs away before I can get out a reply. "Well, I gotta go call home. I'll see you later."

I wave her off, feeling a little like I just failed a test I didn't know I was taking.

When I get in the caf, I see Marley and Leticia sitting in the corner. I consider joining them for a split second before remembering that would mean actually conversing with Leticia. I only have half an hour before my shift, so I do myself the favor of sitting alone.

But a few minutes into devouring my chewy pasta and soggy chicken salad, Kiko and Anita join me.

"Valentina, you seem like you have some semblance of

taste. Help me out here," Kiko starts, plopping her tray and body down. "Anita is trying to convince me that strapped shin guards are better than strapless."

Anita points her fork at Kiko. "Everyone hates on the straps because they remind them of childhood. But when someone's cleat runs into the side of your leg and sends that shin guard slipping, you'll wish you had some straps." She lifts her leg up, revealing an aged scar stretching across her shin, the light line contrasting sharply with her dark skin. "This is from an AYSO game against a team that acted like we were competing in the Olympics."

"Is soccer even in the Olympics?" Kiko asks, mouth full of pasta.

"Um, yeah," I insert, shocked she doesn't know this. Besides me and Leticia, she's probably the best on the team since she switched positions, but I get the feeling she's more of a natural than an experienced player.

Kiko rolls her eyes and stabs her salad. "Whatever. That's still barely a scratch."

Anita laughs. "Keep this sassing in mind next time it's between me passing the ball to you or passing to Valentina."

"You're supposed to be striking, not passing," Kiko sasses her again, unfazed by the threat.

"Vale," I offer. They both look at me, confused. "You can call me Vale."

They test it out, Anita's pronunciation of the nickname better than Kiko's. It's clear she speaks Spanish, which makes sense since she's got a Dominican flag pinned on her soccer bag.

Silence settles over us as we eat our food. Anita and Kiko make eyes over their meals. At first, I think they're flirting and rue whatever it is about me that gives off perpetual third-wheel vibes. But when Kiko tilts her head slightly my way, I realize, almost with a start, that they're working out how to talk to me right now. Like they're trying to be my friends.

"I, uh, I kinda miss strapped shin guards," I say. Which is a fucking lie.

But it makes Anita laugh and gloat while Kiko flips her off. And then the next debate is brought to the table: real headbands or tied prewrap. Kiko is team prewrap, but Anita is team headband. They turn to me, smiling in anticipation, and I feel something I didn't even realize was missing from our team. Something I haven't experienced since I was a kid: the wonderfully strange, temporarily intense friendships that come with recreational league sports teams.

"I'm not just saying this to avoid starting a civil war among the midfielders," I say, as I take a stab at my salad. "But, I'm team prewrap."

Now it's Kiko's turn to gloat and Anita's turn to flip the both of us off. As they continue the debate, citing efficiency with certain hair textures and densities to support their claims, I take a sip of water to hide my smile.

TWENTY-ONE

THE NEXT MORNING, I WEAR ROUGHLY the same thing I have worn on all of my and Leticia's runs. It's chillier out than normal, but I chalk it up to June gloom bleeding into July.

When Leticia emerges, she's in leggings and, to my disgust but not surprise, her red team jacket. It's slightly unzipped, so I see a baggy T-shirt instead of her usual sports bra beneath it.

"You're going to burn up in that," I say at the same time she says, "You're going to freeze in that."

We stare at each other.

She points to the sky. "Those clouds aren't for decoration."

"It's not going to rain. I checked the weather report last night."

"Well, I checked this morning."

"Not everything has to be a competition."

"So you're not competing to get hypothermia before me?" she asks. I roll my eyes. "It's not too late to go grab a jacket from your cabin." She looks at my bare legs. "Or pants."

"Leticia, do I detect . . . *concern* in your voice?"

"Forget it." She plants her foot on the side of her cabin, way higher than should be humanly possible, and tightens the laces on her running shoes. "When you catch a cold, I won't be the one spoon-feeding you chicken soup."

"But I *am* still being spoon-fed chicken soup by someone at some point?" I ask. She runs her tongue over her teeth and sets off jogging, not even waiting to finish her normal stretching routine. I scoff and chase after her.

Unfortunately, my jokes about her concern for me stop being funny fifteen minutes into our run when it starts pouring. I really shouldn't be surprised by it at this point—inconvenient, shitty things happen to me. Maybe if I had a better sense of humor, I'd be laughing right now.

We were heading for the hiking trails when the downpour hit. Through the sheets of rain, we managed to find an old storage shed, just bordering one of the hidden fields. There's no way we'd make it back to our cabins at this point without being thoroughly drenched.

Though, as I take a seat against one wall of the incredibly tiny shed, shivering and brushing droplets from my bangs out of my face, I do suppose I'm a little beyond that point.

"So . . . ," Leticia starts, looking damp, but ultimately pretty warm in comparison to me. That obnoxious jacket of hers is apparently water-resistant, along with her leggings. "Are you going to make me say it or . . ."

"I'm not saying it."

"You *could* just say it and save us both the time and energy of arguing."

I glare at her. Given that I look like a wet dog—my ponytail drooping over my bare back like a pathetic, sad tail, and my bangs plastered to my forehead as water dribbles into my eyes—I don't think it does much to intimidate her. "No."

"Okay. Guess it's up to me." She takes a seat against the opposite wall. "I told you so."

I groan. "We're going to be stuck here for a while until this lets up, unless you want us both to go out with pneumonia. I think it would work in our mutual best interests if we spent that time in silence."

She purses her lips. "You don't want to talk strategy?"

I can't tell if she's mocking me or not. A foreign feeling with her. "I'd like a single moment of peace." I shut my eyes and lean my head against the old wood, unconcerned about the splinters that'll probably end up in my hair.

A few stray droplets make it in through gaps in the weathered roof, sprinkling the floor. Oddly enough, it reminds me of a few months ago when an away game got canceled because of the rain, so Dad took me to get something to eat. My teammates all hung out at Dina's, playing truth or dare and sharing a couple cans of beer that they managed to smuggle out of her garage. But Dad and I just sat in his car, rain pattering down around us, sipping hot chocolate and nibbling on sandwiches. We didn't talk about soccer at all. It felt almost like we were both relieved we didn't have to.

"That's not true, you know." Leticia's voice startles me. I

felt calm for the first time in weeks, so it only seems right that her voice should be the thing that disrupts that.

Something tells me that, for once, if I were to ignore her, she would leave me be. But now my thoughts are swarming, every other conversation Dad and I have had over the past couple of years coming in to replace the one good memory I can seem to find. So I need the distraction. "What isn't true?"

I hear her move closer to me, the rain dulling both our voices. I crack my eyes open.

"The whole thing about being in the rain making you sick. It's not true."

"Yes it is," I tell her. Mami instilled the belief in me from a young age. The amount of times I got lectured in a flurry of Spanglish for trying to make it out of the house in winter wearing nothing but a T-shirt and shorts is uncountable. It punctures me like a needle when I remember I'll never hear those warnings again, even years out from her death. Sometimes, on days like today, I think I avoid wearing a jacket just to spite the world, to prove that I was robbed of the person who would've reminded me to grab one.

"Not really." Her eyes are darker than normal in this minimal light. "Cold weather can lower the strength of your immune system. But a lot of people get sick in the fall and winter because they spend so much time indoors surrounded by other people who *also* have lowered immune systems. The proximity to people is what makes them sick, not the weather. The weather is more like a prompter."

I can't help it. "The weather assists the goal."

She laughs and it's breathy, far softer than I'd expect of her. "I thought you didn't want to talk about soccer." She tilts her head lazily toward me. The droplets of rain decorating her black hair look like stardust.

I swallow. "I don't."

She stares for a beat longer, her eyes tracing the rain-carved tracks down my face. When her gaze reaches my lips, she looks away. It's only then that I notice she's no longer smiling. "Why do you even play?"

"I'm sorry?"

"Soccer," she says. "Why do you play soccer?"

"Are you seriously trying to have a philosophical conversation with me in the rain? About why I play soccer?"

She scoffs. "Fine, I'll come up with more health facts if you prefer. I've got plenty from my ER nurse mom."

Well, now I feel defensive. "Soccer is everything to me," I answer.

"Something can be everything to you and still not make you happy." With the rain enveloping the space around us, it feels like we've built a bubble that's slowly shrinking.

I'm almost embarrassed by how much I'm shaking from the cold, especially when it leads to me bumping her. I'm jolted by the brief sensation of her entire leg against mine.

She peels off her team jacket in one fluid movement. "Take this."

I eye the tragic piece of clothing. "I'd rather risk the hypothermia. Or the pneumonia. Or another lecture on how the rain doesn't actually make me sick."

"It's just a jacket," she says, but it's obvious that even she doesn't believe that.

It looks warm though.

I shake my head. "I'm good."

"Fine." She sets the jacket in the slight wedge of space between my feet and the wall she's got her back against, then exaggeratedly digs her hands into the tight pockets of her leggings.

"What are you doing?"

"Feeling around for a different colored jacket for you." She lifts her hands out and shakes them. "Shit. I've got nothing."

I sigh in annoyance at her ability to be an ass at every possible turn. "Put it back on."

"Never had someone ask me to put my clothes back on after I stripped for them. First time for everything."

Thankfully, my cheeks are already red from the cold. "We don't both need to freeze."

"I run hot," she says, snuggling her hands back in her pockets. "It's the Satanic blood coursing through me." She cocks her head, a challenge.

"So Marley doesn't know how to keep a secret," I note neutrally.

"I didn't know the way you felt about me was a secret," she says, smiling. "But Marley knows how to keep those if you ask nicely." Something in my face must show the way I interpret her. "Don't get jealous, Princesa. She's got a boyfriend. And she isn't really my type."

"I didn't know you had a type," I say, once again forcing neutrality into my voice. It's more difficult this time.

"Weirdly enough, I'm actually super into girls who get hypothermia. Don't want to get me all hot and bothered now, do you?" She nudges the jacket closer to me, using her right hand. The injured one.

"Tell me how you hurt your wrist and I'll wear the jacket."

"Oh, and *I'm* the one whose social interactions all revolve around deals?" She laughs. "You still haven't told me how you fucked up your face the other week."

I touch my forehead. The bruise is still healing, but I stopped wearing the bandage by our second game. "I got into a fight with a bunk bed."

"And lost, evidently."

"I didn't think you noticed it," I admit, brushing my wet bangs out.

"It was kind of hard to miss, Princesa. I thought I would spare you your dignity and not question it."

"You've never been particularly concerned about my dignity before."

"No, but apparently I care about your warmth." She looks down at the jacket. I don't budge. "Fine, whatever. I guess I sort of owe you a secret anyway."

That was suspiciously easy. "Why?"

"Because you told me about your whole captainhood situation. I believe in reciprocity."

"How romantic of you," I deadpan.

An arched eyebrow and quirked lips. "Don't tell me you're an unrequited love enthusiast?"

"Wouldn't know." I shrug, still shivering a bit. "Not much experience in that department." Admitting this to her feels weird in and of itself, so I leave out the fact that despite having a handful of crushes here and there—Sophie included—I haven't dated or even kissed anyone before. It doesn't really bother me, but people can get so weird about reaching certain relationship milestones by certain ages. Wait until they hear how uninterested I am in doing anything beyond kissing.

She picks up the jacket and drops it on my knees. It slides into my lap like a puddle of blood. I feel like a traitor just letting it touch me. "Welcome to your first romantic cliché: borrowing a jacket to keep warm. If you get mud on that, I kick your ass during our next game."

I lightly pick it up with the tips of my fingers, holding it like a dead animal. "Next game we play against each other or tomorrow's game?"

"Take your pick." She shrugs. "Jacket first, then story time."

She's enjoying watching me squirm, so I slip my arms into the sleeves and zip it up. You wouldn't know it from the outside, but the jacket is lined with smooth, soft fabric akin to fleece. I instantly feel warmer.

"Red looks good on you," she says. It doesn't feel like a compliment.

"I seem to remember you promising me a story."

She stares at her right wrist in her lap for a minute. Spots of the bandage are darkened by the rain. "I sorta wish I'd injured it during a game, to be honest," she finally says. "At least then maybe there'd be some glory in this."

"I could hurt you in a game, if you'd like."

"After seeing how guilty you looked thinking that you were responsible for this, I'm not sure I believe you," she says. I'm suddenly very interested in the stitching on this jacket's sleeves. "Anyway, you know any of the girls on my team back home besides me?"

"A few." I run their lineup through my head. I know their faces and numbers, but most of their names are lost to me.

"Our right mid. Becca," she says. I remember the girl immediately. She's petite, with spiky blond hair and a collection of ear piercings she has to cover with Band-Aids before every game. "She had a girlfriend this year, Wendy, who came to all our games and started hanging out with the team. After winning playoffs, Becca threw a party where both of them got pretty wasted and started arguing. It was messy and Becca said some things she shouldn't have, but it ended in a breakup that was a long time coming. Wendy still came to our practice the next week like she always did, but when everyone was leaving to go get food together, no one spoke to her." Leticia's voice gets tender. "All that time she'd spent with us, she mostly just spoke to Becca. But I realized that we were her only friends. She didn't have anyone else."

I remember how ostracized I felt by the team after our final game, how even Ovie and Dina were cold at first, and can't help but empathize with this girl I've never met. Even if the gentle way Leticia's talking about her makes me shift uncomfortably.

"So I told everyone I didn't want to go out because of a headache, and then I stayed behind and asked Wendy if she wanted to help me practice. We were just messing around—no, not like *that*." I school my expression. I hadn't even realized I'd reacted. "Well, okay, it wasn't like that at first. We ended up hanging out again the next day. And again after that." Her face is a jumble of conflicted feelings. "For two weeks I hid from Becca and the rest of my team that Wendy and I were spending almost every day together, even while knowing Becca had regrets about the breakup."

"So . . . you were dating?"

"No, I mean, I—I don't know. Maybe? You know how it is, a queer girl is nice to you and you have no idea whether it means she wants to be your friend or suck your face."

"I imagine there's at least one other option."

"Well, what does it mean when you're nice to me?"

My heartbeat trips over itself. "I'm never nice to you."

"Touché." Her smile falters when she remembers she's in the middle of her story. "One day after practice ended, the two of us were sitting on the field sharing some orange slices and out of nowhere, she kissed me. And I mean, I guess I kissed her back? It happened so fast and all of a sudden I was thinking about Becca and all the years we'd been friends and how sad she'd seemed since their breakup and I sorta freaked out. I tried to pull back but when I did, I landed on my wrist all wrong and . . ." She snaps with her left hand. "It was like my wrist just popped. Wendy drove me to the emergency room my mom was working at. She wanted to walk me in, but I begged her to leave because I was so embarrassed."

"Embarrassed about what?" I ask, trying to shove away the mental image of Leticia kissing this girl.

"I don't even know," she admits. "How badly my wrist hurt? Her kissing me and me reacting the way I did? It was a lot and I didn't know how to handle any of it. I'm not exactly a fan of being vulnerable."

"You're being vulnerable now," I say without thinking.

She stares at me for a second. "You don't count." But there is no coldness to her words. "The doctors told me it was a bad sprain and I was out of the goal for the foreseeable future until it heals." She spreads her hands out, laying all her cards on the table. "Just like that, my entire future potentially down the drain."

I don't know why I want to comfort her. "It'll probably heal fine."

"So you're a doctor now?" The bite in her words is back. It feels different than usual though, meaner somehow. The apology in her eyes says she heard it too. "Time will tell, I guess. Just gotta be careful and stick to my PT stretches."

I can't help it. "So, what happened with Wendy?"

She laughs bitterly. "That's the best part. After the hospital and a weekend of thinking things over, I tried to FaceTime her to talk about everything but she didn't answer. She texted me an hour later saying Becca showed up at her house and they got back together."

"Did she tell Becca—"

"That she and I had spent all that time together behind her back? Nope. I got the message loud and clear when she told me we probably shouldn't hang out or text as much. Of course she still calls me the second they have a fight." Her few mysterious phone calls make more sense now. "My whole team thinks I hurt myself practicing at home with my moms because I couldn't tell anyone the truth without exposing Wendy. So there." She splays her hands out. "How does it feel to be right?"

"Right about what?"

Her eyes harden. "About me being a shitty person. Satanic spawn." Her resolve is lost, whatever spark that normally lights up her smirk dampened by the storm in and outside of her. "Whatever other nicknames you and your friends call me to make you feel better about losing playoffs."

"I almost felt sorry for you until you brought up playoffs."

She cracks a smile at that at least. "I didn't tell you so you'd feel sorry for me."

"Why then?" I ask, then raise my hand to stop her. "And don't say it's because you owed me a secret. Or because you wanted to see me in this hideous jacket."

She wraps her arms around herself. "Because I was tired of keeping it to myself," she says softly. "Only my moms know the truth, and that's just because they wanted to know who drove me to the hospital."

"Why not tell Marley? You two seem so close."

She sighs. "Because she'd try to make me feel better about it."

"And that's a bad thing?"

"No, it's a Marley thing," she laughs sadly. "I guess I want to feel better, like generally speaking. But not about this. I shouldn't have hid hanging out with Wendy behind Becca's back, and now I have to live with that. And *this*." She lifts her wrist again. "I did a shitty thing. I don't need someone to absolve me of that." Smiling crookedly, she adds, "Plus, you already hate me, so there was no harm in telling you. Can't disappoint someone who already thinks the worst of you."

That's exactly why it's so hard to be around Ovie and Dina right now. They would console me if I told them I lost my captainhood, but I don't want someone to coddle or shield me from my mistakes. I also don't want someone to hold them over me every chance they get. I want someone to see all of me, including the worst parts that scare and remind me of Dad the most, and not look away. To not even want to.

Leticia is staring directly at me.

"Doesn't make me right though," I say. "I mean, to be clear, I *do* still think you're a nightmare." There's her smile again. I feel warmer, like the rain is miles away. "But I don't think making a shitty mistake makes you a bad person."

"What does it make me then?"

Our eyes both drift to the ceiling as the storm eases up. If we were smart, we'd head back to camp now in case it picks up again.

I stretch my legs out, settling in. When I glance over at Leticia, she can't seem to pull her gaze away from the beauty of sunlight seeping through the clouds and piercing the cracks in the roof, fighting its way to us.

I keep watching her, almost forgetting to answer her question. "Just a person."

When we eventually make our way back to camp, we match a steady jogging pace. When she starts to fall behind, I slow down. When I pause to tie my shoe, she stops to stretch her calves until I'm done.

We separate silently when we reach my cabin, me still wearing her jacket. She doesn't ask for it back.

I stand in the doorway, watching Leticia leave. My eyes are fixated on her, a constant dot on the horizon. Something to look forward to—even as she drifts farther away—knowing she'll be back.

TWENTY-TWO

I WEAR MY PURPLE JERSEY TO breakfast. It feels symbolic.

Dina and Ovie went on a morning stroll, so I enter the caf alone. Nodding to Maria behind the counter, I grab my food and take a seat closest to the game-schedule board. And then I wait.

My remotely peaceful energy is interrupted by Cate and Kaylee as they sit at the end of my table, as close as they can get to the board without looking like they're actually eating with me.

"Can you go tell your friends in the kitchen that these eggs taste like rubber?" Cate says, scowling at her food.

I grin tightly. "You could always walk over and tell them yourself."

Kaylee scoffs, then says under her breath, "Like anyone in there is smart enough to understand her."

My entire body tenses. "What did you just say?"

"Hey, girlies, how are we doing today?" Sophie interrupts, chipper as ever, as she sits in the space between her captains and me. She looks back and forth. "I'm getting the feeling that we're not doing great."

I lean past Sophie. "What the fuck did you say, Kaylee?"

Kaylee just smiles, clearly pleased. "I don't know what you're talking about."

Cate pats my hand. "You might want to calm down, Valentina. You wouldn't fight another team's captain, now, would you?" Her smile is a hideous thing, so bright and sunny and dangerous for people who don't look like her. "That would be *super* embarrassing."

I yank my hand away. Guess they know about playoffs now. Sophie scoots closer to me, nudging me down the bench as far as I can go.

"Don't worry about them," she says sweetly, like they were making casual banter and not a stereotypical, shitty-ass xenophobic comment and then taunting me over it.

I'm not embarrassed that I'm working in the kitchen to afford being here, I'm not embarrassed to speak Spanish with some of the staff, and I'm not embarrassed on behalf of the one or two who favor that over English. None of it correlates to intelligence, and assimilation and class-based superiority complexes aren't my aspirations anyway.

But I'm pissed that those things get twisted into insults. Years of rude-ass customers—most of them white—making comments about "imperfect" English or queries about documentation status to the waiters at my uncle's restaurant if there was so much as an extra ice cube in their drink. They didn't see people doing a job, they saw something to look down on. I've been on the receiving end of some of it, but my light skin and native English have always sheltered me from the worst of it.

All of this has me ready to push Sophie aside and take another verbal—or physical, who knows—swing at her captains, but then Lola and Juanita come strutting through the doors to hang up the schedule and the cousins rush the paper with everyone else.

I take my tray and storm outside as quickly as possible without spilling my food. I'm bursting through the doors when I nearly crash into someone who steadies my tray with one hand and my body with the other.

"Whoa, where's the fire?" Leticia asks. She lets go of my tray first, taking her sweet time to drop her hand from my hip. "Actually, it looks like it's in your eyes."

I try not to get flustered, letting my anger swallow whatever her touch is doing to my chest. "Please go check the schedule and tell me we're playing the Angels today."

"Since when did you have a death wish? You want to lose?"

"No, I want the chance to wait until Lola looks away so I can drive the heel of my cleats into Cate's and Kaylee's eye soc—"

"Okaayy," she interrupts, pulling me down the cafeteria steps. Once we reach a picnic bench between the caf and the cabins, she lets go of me and we sit down. "You want to explain to me why you're craving murder? More so than usual, at least."

I take a deep breath, feeling the heat in my lungs. I

explain what Kaylee said. Leticia's eyes light with a rage that matches my own.

"It would be a more efficient tactic if each of us took one of them out," she finally says. "It'd be uncaptainly of me to make you do all the dirty work."

I laugh, calming just a bit. Leticia's stomach growls and I push my nearly full tray toward her.

She plucks a grape, sucking it into her mouth with a satisfying pop. "Thanks." Her phone dings in her back pocket and she frowns when she reads the incoming text. "So are you more of a good news or a bad news kind of girl?"

I snatch a few grapes. "My life seems to be a series of bad news right now, so take your pick."

"Kiko texted. We're not playing Cate and Kaylee today."

I pause. "Is that the good news or the bad news?"

She presses her lips together. "We're playing Dina and Ovie's team."

"Well, shit," I reply, now knowing which is which.

The Purple Princesses gather around a goal thirty minutes before the game. Leticia and I have already been here for a bit, running over plays and double-checking our lineup. Surprisingly, I haven't passed out yet. But the day is still young.

The team must notice our worrying, since Marley takes it upon herself to lead them in a lap around the field and Kiko gets the drills started. I'm grateful for them, but I'm sure my grimace doesn't show it.

"They've got a weak offense," Leticia says, scribbling on

our whiteboard. "Their strongest players are Dina, Ovie, and their sweeper, but their only win, last week, was a close call because they struggle with scoring."

It doesn't matter how Leticia tries to pitch it. Our team is unprepared to go against the Daisies—Ovie named them—and that's not even getting into the weirdness of playing against my best friends. I'm used to antagonizing the other team, feeling no remorse about demolishing them because in my mind, they have to be the bad guys. It's why playing against Leticia and the Tigers was always substantially more energizing than any other game of the season. There was no room for second-guessing your aggression if they deserved it.

But this is Ovie and Dina. Regardless of our weirdness lately, they're my teammates come fall, and my brain can't register that they're on the other side now.

"You make it work for me. You can make it work for them," Leticia says, reading my silence. I raise an eyebrow. "You consider me a teammate right now, right?"

"Technically, yes." Though there is nothing technical about whatever our relationship is.

"Then you can treat them as opponents for an hour and a half," she says. She drops the whiteboard and stands. "You know how they play. Use that."

I sigh, and together we rally the team. We emphasize the importance of our offensive advantage in this game, reminding the girls to conserve their energy since this'll probably be a long one. And before I know it, Leticia and I are approaching the midfield line where Dina and Ovie are already standing.

"Fancy meeting you two here," Dina says with a wink. I'm hit with the horrible realization that I've never had to endure Dina and Ovie's teasing about me and Leticia *in front of* Leticia.

Ovie offers her hand to Leticia. "Good luck!"

Leticia's smile is hesitant, like she isn't sure if Ovie is fucking with her or being sincere. "Igualmente."

Ovie's Spanish is rusty but Dina cracks a smile as she shakes Leticia's hand and then turns to me. "Never thought I'd see you on the other side of the trenches, captain."

I tense at Dina's words. Leticia side-eyes me, clearly wondering if they know what she does about me not being captain in the fall. I get the strangest feeling that when she looks away, it's because she knows they don't. Like if Dina were really teasing me about it, Leticia would be bracing for a fight.

Ovie and I shake hands, then Lola walks over. She looks relaxed, probably figuring that given 75 percent of these captains are best friends, this game will go over smoothly. I hope she's right.

Dina calls heads and wins the toss. Leticia goes back to her place downfield and Ovie leaves for her goal. Dina and I linger.

"Best of luck," she says. It feels like an olive branch and a declaration of war, all at once.

It quickly becomes apparent that Leticia was right, a phrase that is becoming all too frequent in my day-to-day life. The Daisies' offense is meh, but their defense . . . well, I guess I get why Leticia hates our high school team so much.

Not only does Ovie block any and every ball that comes her way, she manages to steal it out from under Kiko's feet *twice*. Coach has been training her since she was a baby, Coach having played college soccer herself, and it's never been more evident than in this game.

I'm equal parts proud and annoyed.

By halftime, the score is still 0–0. Marley made some incredible saves, but our defense has been covering her pretty well regardless. Offense, on the other hand, is feeling the pressure.

"I don't know whether to congratulate her or challenge her to a duel," Kiko says of Ovie, recounting her stealing the ball away. "She's giving your reputation a run for your money, Ortiz."

Leticia raises two sweaty hands in surrender. "I've always been on the other side of the field from her, so I'll take your word for it."

Their praise warms my heart and scares me. It sounds an awful lot like the shit you say after losing a tough game, not what you say during it.

What we need is a goal, and an unexpected one at that. Leticia's comment inspires me.

"Leticia, we're putting you on offense."

Leticia halts her red Gatorade before her lips. "What? No, I've only been practicing for a few weeks," she says, looking suddenly, uncharacteristically terrified. "I'm not ready."

"Now you know how we felt," Bethany cracks good-naturedly. Marley gives a pointed nod of agreement.

"I can drop back if defense needs help," I tell Leticia,

knowing her mind is going to her instinctual place of protection. "But we need a good cross. You can do this."

"Almost sounds like you believe in me," she jokes.

"Because I do." This surprises both of us.

She blinks at me, calmer but confused, like I just pulled her hands away from picking at the flaws in this plan by holding them in my own, then nods. Oddly enough, it feels good to know I'm just as capable of settling her as I am of aggravating her.

The second half is immediate chaos, tilting our semblance of preparation off its axis. Claire isn't used to playing sweeper instead of Leticia, and her inexperience allows the Daisies' offense through time and time again, leaving me to scramble back to help. Only this time, with Dina and her striker already poised to shoot, I might be too late.

But then, miraculously, Marley jumps at the right second and catches the ball. Just like she did in practice with Leticia and me.

It was a bad shot kicked with haste. Somehow, despite knowing this, I find myself screaming at the top of my lungs.

Marley takes my cheers as a sign I'm open and punts the ball my way, shooting it across the blue sky with a height that would put Leticia Ortiz to shame. Though I'm sure she's smiling upfield.

The second it drops to my feet, I'm off toward the Daisies' goal. Dina appears in my periphery, but I know her moves. We learned them together.

"You and your girlfriend make a good team," Dina taunts, panting as she shuffles closer. We're both exhausted and losing steam.

"Right back at you."

She catches my unintentional admission before I do, cracking up as she swipes a foot at the ball. Despite my distracted thoughts, my body moves automatically and I pull back. But she's still in my way, smooth on her feet with a fluidity that helps her defend even when playing wing. I could try to rush past her, but I doubt I'd get far.

I briefly glance toward the goal, and in a crowd of girls, my eyes find Leticia with ease. Like she's just been waiting there for me to finally notice her, all I had to do was look up.

I shift like I'm going to break left and Dina pivots accordingly, expecting me to take this on by myself. But her slight step gives me enough space to instead move right and kick the ball straight past her to Leticia, essentially a cross at this angle.

Ovie is a brilliant goalie, probably the best I've ever seen. Even better than Leticia. But it's obvious she thought I would pass to someone else.

Leticia redirects my cross and the ball goes in.

The ball goes in.

Before I even know what's happening, I'm running toward Leticia and she's running toward me and we clash in a hug that spins us in a circle.

"You scored a goal!" I scream at her.

"I scored a goal!" she screams back.

We're still clutching each other, buzzing with energy, when I realize everyone has already moved back to their marks to start the next play. As I run to midfield, I catch Dina's eye. I expect her to be smirking, but instead she's looking at me like she doesn't recognize me.

Lola blows her whistle and the Daisies make a good run, but it's no use. Bethany shuts them down and then Lola's whistle is off again, signaling the end of the game and the start of our victories.

I should feel like something shifted just now, some unnamable magic that happens in a sport that requires so much reliance on other people knowing what to do and when to do it. *The final piece of our team has snapped into place, and we're ready now.* That's where my mind should be going.

But instead, as the adrenaline of our goal dissipates, I'm left terrified. Because starting to win means you finally have something to lose.

The team is a parade of excitement as we leave the fields. Marley and Kiko haven't stopped ranting about ways to celebrate, meanwhile Claire is asking Bethany how to know when to push up or hang back on defense, before a call from her boyfriend sends her running to her cabin. It seems widely accepted that Leticia will be playing wing more in the coming weeks.

I'm grateful that Dina and Ovie's team left for the cafeteria before I had to make up a reason for avoiding them. Their smiles and congrats looked sincere when we high-fived at the end of the game, but I don't know how much of it was for show. I don't think I'd be so cheery if they'd beat us.

Leticia sidles up next to me as the rest of the girls go on. Our slowed pace stretches the distance between us and them, until eventually they're far enough ahead that their words are nothing but noise.

"At risk of you, again, wrongly assuming that I like your smile, I want to say that you can probably squeeze one in before your shift starts."

I shake out of my stupor. "I don't work tonight."

"All the more reason to celebrate," she says, cocky grin and all. "You could lecture me for hesitating to swap positions; that type of thing usually brings a smile to your face. Or you could save that for next practice to embarrass me in front of the team. Just remember that everyone loves a hot martyr."

Without replying, I walk over to the nurse's cabin and sit on the steps. Leticia, reading my mood, follows suit silently.

I consider what I'm about to say before I say it. "We shouldn't have won that game."

"I can go ask them to change the score if you'd like."

I roll my eyes. "That goal was lucky."

Her left hand lands on her chest, mocking me. "This is more hurtful than the lecture I was sure you had in store for me."

"I'm sorry," I say, only realizing once the words are out that I actually mean them. "But it's true. It was a lucky cross after a lucky move that led to a lucky shot. We shouldn't have won."

She squints at me. "Are you normally like this after you play *my* team? Because if so, we should really start hanging out after games. I could use the ego boost."

"No you couldn't." I hate my mouth for smiling at her. She seems pleased by it, even as she flips me off. I feel marginally better, against my will.

When the smile settles though, my dissatisfaction remains. "But you agree with me, right? We didn't earn that. We're just putting off the inevitable next loss to believe otherwise. We weren't prepared to play them."

"You do realize soccer is at least a small percentage luck based, right?" she asks, riffling around in her bag. "You practice and prepare, but at the end of the day sometimes a good play just comes down to good luck."

"What a delightfully cheesy statement," I deadpan.

She looks up from her rummaging to glare at me. "Getting to know you, you're more pessimistic than I thought you'd be."

"Sorry to disappoint," I joke, but the sentiment feels all too familiar.

She pulls two bottles of Gatorade out of her bag, one yellow and one red, and offers them to me. I take the yellow.

"Do you actively work toward having bad taste or does it come naturally?" she asks.

I grin at her as I snap off the cap and take a long sip. "You've seen me drink yellow Gatorade at every practice for the past three weeks. Your disgust and shock should have lessened by now."

She shudders. I try not to think about why she would

have my favorite flavor of Gatorade in her bag if she hates it so much. I try not to watch her lips part as she drinks her own. I don't do well on either front.

Lucky for me, my phone starts ringing. The relief of the distraction disappears quickly as I realize there's only one person that would be calling me right now. I keep drinking, ignoring my phone as best I can.

Leticia, of course, hears it though. "Aren't you going to answer that?"

"It's probably my dad, so no."

"Is it inappropriate for me to tell you that I'm sensing I shouldn't be his biggest fan?" she asks. I make a face. "It's kind of hard to miss the way he yells at you when our teams play each other."

"He's not all bad," I defend, unsure exactly why I'm doing it. I guess when you only have one living parent left, you're more willing to swallow their bullshit. And despite what he does, I can't fight the ingrained feeling that I can't speak ill of my family. In my head, and maybe even aloud with Jorge, I can say whatever I want about my dad and the way he treats me. But the rest of the world isn't supposed to see so transparently what I deal with. Somehow, Leticia manages to see a lot about me that I try to hide from everyone else.

"So you're avoiding his call because . . . ?" she asks, not unkindly.

It feels safe to be honest right now. "Here is how it'll go if I answer: I'll tell him we won. He'll ask by how many goals. I'll tell him by one, that I assisted. He'll ask why we didn't score earlier, why I was assisting instead of shooting, why I'm wasting my summer here if I can't score a simple goal on a girl I've played with for years and should know like the back of my hand." I take another sip for my suddenly dry throat. I still can't believe I'm telling Leticia, of all people, about this. "As much fun as that sounds, I'll pass."

"If it helps, you could always blame your devilishly hot right wing for at least one of those things." She downs the rest of her bottle.

"I'm sure he'd love to hear all about a hot girl being the reason for his daughter disappointing him."

I can see her calculating whether she'd rather call me out for agreeing that she's hot or stick to my dad problems. When she doesn't start smirking, I know she's picked the latter. "He sounds like a dick."

"I'd cheers to that, but you're out of Gatorade."

Watching me, she pulls the bottle out of my hand, presses her mouth where mine was a second ago, and tips back her head. I watch the small movement of her throat as she swallows the last of the drink.

It suddenly feels imperative that I be anywhere but here.

"Not as bad as the color implies." She wipes her mouth and hands the bottle back. "We did earn that win, by the way. Regardless of what your dad would say."

My phone starts ringing again. I stare at it, conflicted.

"And not for nothing," Leticia starts as she stands, pulling her bag onto her shoulder. "But that was my first time scoring a goal since U12. Not much time to do that when you're in the goal." I open my mouth to respond, but she goes on. "Self-hatred tends to find collateral damage in team sports. Be careful whose successes you start blaming on luck."

For the first time since I decided as a kid that I didn't care about trying to be her friend anymore, I feel guilty for insulting Leticia. Worst of all, it was an insult I made without thinking, without aiming to take her down a peg or get her to shut up. It was an insult I made like it was fact, like an objective failure rather than just another dig in our personal rivalry.

My eyes dart between her retreating figure and Dad's call. Before I can decide between the two, Leticia is long gone and Dad's call has gone to voice mail.

Not for the first time this summer, I feel exactly like the father whose call I've ignored.

TWENTY-THREE

I CONTINUE TO IGNORE DAD, BUT I ignore most everyone else too. Dina and Ovie were still out by the time I crashed early on Friday night, and they spent their Saturday off at a local beach to celebrate some anniversary. I spent most of the day in our cabin, brushing up on highlight reels and strategies for next week's practices before work.

After knocking out early Saturday night, I wake up Sunday morning to the chatter of conversation. I sit up, rubbing my eyes.

"She's alive," Dina jokes. Once my vision clears, I see she's lying in her bunk with an arm wrapped around Ovie's shoulder. A quick look down and I see Marley's long legs stretched out, demurely crossed, from the bed below mine. And a brown pair of legs sitting wide-spread beside them.

I catch Dina's eye. She's smirking.

Leticia hooks an arm over the edge of my bunk and smiles up at me. "Good morning, Princesa."

My hands itch to fix my hair, which is inevitably a tangled

mess around my head. Leticia's eyes wander to it, confirming my suspicions with the twitch of her lips.

"We're talking about going to the beach again today," Ovie says, saving me from myself. The warmth in her smile says it's intentional. "There's this strip by a cliffside that was pretty empty yesterday. It would be fun to go in a big group and hang out, maybe play a few games for fun."

"I don't think 'playing games for fun' is in Valentina's vocabulary," Leticia says.

Dina laughs, pointing a finger at Leticia. "You know, when you're not blocking all of Vale's shots, I kinda like you."

"Hey, she doesn't block *all* my shots," I insist, but I'm ignored.

"What about when I'm scoring on your girlfriend?" Leticia tosses back at Dina.

Dina and Ovie both laugh this time.

I hate it. I hate all of this.

"I've got more drills to plan for practices this week," I say, to no one in particular. The awkward silence that descends afterward, however, comes from everyone.

Leticia stands. She's wearing ripped black denim shorts and a loose white tank top. Planting two hands on the edge of my bed, she leans in. "Nope. You're coming to the beach."

I see Dina and Ovie glance at each other from behind her.

"I have work to do," I insist.

"No, you have *fun* to do." Leticia leans back. "We'll invite the whole team, it can be a bonding day."

Marley claps and pulls out her phone to text everyone.

"We don't have the car space," I reply.

"I can fit five in my car," Dina says.

"Kiko has a minivan that can fit another eight," Marley adds.

Leticia tilts her head at me.

"Most of us are minors; we can't all just leave camp." I try to finger-comb my hair. "You two only got a free pass because Coach knows Lola and Juanita personally."

"Oh please," Dina says. "One of us can swing by their office before we go and make sure it's cool with them."

"Which it will be," Leticia punctuates.

"Okay, but—" I ready myself to throw another excuse out, but run into a mental wall.

Leticia heads for the door. "I'll grab snacks from the cafeteria and round up some of the girls. Y'all can finish getting ready." Everyone but me nods at her. With one foot out the open door, she looks back at me. "You know, I'm surprised you didn't lie about working a shift at the cafeteria today to get out of this."

I pause. "How would you have known if I was lying?"

Her smile falters a bit. I feel Dina, Ovie, and Marley watching us. "You must have mentioned your schedule to me."

"And you remembered it?"

"Guess I have a good memory." Then she's off, the door dropping shut behind her.

I glance at the pages of strategies and plays and drills spilling over my bed, then at my friends as they get ready. I check the time on my phone and see two more missed calls from Dad, and a surprising text from Jorge asking how I'm doing.

I'm not sure I'd know how to answer if I tried.

I ride in Dina's car with her and Ovie after watching Marley, Leticia, Hayley, Anita, and Gloria pile into Kiko's. The rest of the girls on our team were either busy (like Rani and Natalia, who'd already planned a movie marathon in their cabin) or uninterested (like Claire, who said she had to talk to her boyfriend, and Bethany, who said she hates sand).

The beach isn't too crowded for a Sunday afternoon in early July. While everyone else heads for the water, I sit off to the side and pull out my notebook. I never said I wouldn't work while I'm here.

I get about five minutes of peaceful scribbling done before a shadow blocks my sunlight.

"What exactly are you doing?"

I squint up at Leticia. A breeze ruffles my papers. "Going over my observations from Friday's game."

"You cannot be serious." She plops down on my towel, hipchecking me to scoot over even though there's plenty of space. Once she seems comfortable, she bends over to peer at my notes. I press them to my chest.

"Oh come on. How am I supposed to help if you don't let me see your thoughts?"

"I didn't ask for your help."

She squints at me. "You literally did."

She flexes her hand. I relent, passing them over.

Her eyes scan my chicken scratch. "You counted how many times your passes were intercepted?"

I try to grab the papers back. "It's just an estimate."

She leans away, out of reach. "You underlined your assist."

"It was our only goal."

"A lucky one, at that," she mocks.

"Okay, seriously, give them back. You're not even trying to be helpful."

She looks at me, then the papers. Then the water.

I make a face. "No."

She hands them back with a pout. "I was just thinking about it."

I tuck the papers and notebook into my hoodie's pocket and pull my folded knees to my chest.

"I'd ask where you learned to be that meticulous, but I feel like I know the answer." She leans back on her hands, then winces and sits up. She adjusts the wrap on her right wrist.

"My dad always expected me to have things to discuss after games. Guess it became a habit."

"So I have Mr. Castillo-Green to thank for whatever drills we'll be running this week. Good to know."

I almost don't say it. "It's just Green."

"Huh?"

"My dad didn't change his last name when he and my mom got married. He's just Green, but me and my brothers are Castillo-Green."

She cocks her head. "Wait, I just realized, why is your mom's last name first? Aren't you Colombian?"

A stray Frisbee comes soaring toward us. Leticia reaches up to grab it with her right hand, but seeing as that's her injured wrist, I quickly lean into her lap and messily catch it with both of mine.

Kiko runs over, sweaty in denim shorts, her white button-up floating open to reveal a red bikini underneath. "Sorry, captains."

I scramble off Leticia and hand Kiko the Frisbee. "No worries." She rejoins her game with Ovie and Anita.

I dust my sandy hands off on my bare thighs. "You really have to be more careful with your wrist," I tell Leticia.

"Valentina, is that *concern* I detect in *your* voice?" she asks, quoting me from our rainy run. "I thought you of all people would be praying that I hurt myself irreparably this summer."

"Well, I need you in one piece for the next few weeks. Then you can run free." Despite what I said at the start of camp, I don't love the idea of Leticia's goalie career being over anymore. Maybe it's selfish, but I'd like to beat her just once at her best.

She snorts a laugh as if she can read my thoughts. "Noted."

I watch the waves break on the shoreline, an explosion of white foam that smooths the sand back down every time it retreats. The sunlight sparkles all across it, almost obnoxious in its beauty. The moment is silent and peaceful, and somehow makes me think of Mami.

"My mom was born in Colombia but mostly grew up in

the US," I say. "You're right that it's traditional in Colombian culture to put the father's last name first. But my dad thought it would look silly that way, like we'd get bullied or something if our last name looked like Green Castle."

She cocks an eyebrow. "He knows the adjective goes second in Spanish, right? Your last name is quite literally Green Castle as is."

"I couldn't exactly advocate for myself as a newly born infant, but trust me, I know. Secretly, I think he just wanted the final word. Like our last names ending with his name meant people would assume 'Castillo' was a middle name and 'Green' was our real last name. It's happened enough times to me and my brothers to give it some merit, even with the addition of the nontraditional hyphen."

Leticia scoops sand into her palm. "Did your mom change her last name when they got married?"

"She did," I say, watching the sand trickle through her fingers. "I used to naively think that wasn't very feminist of her or whatever, but 'Castillo' is my abuelo's last name, so it's not like she wouldn't be using a man's name either way. And I like that we shared a new hybrid name, like I always have a piece of her."

"You would regardless," Leticia says, then cringes. "Sorry, I don't mean to overstep."

"Oh no, you wouldn't *dare* dream of ever offending me."

She nudges me with her shoulder. "Shut up. I just mean, you're her daughter. *You* are a piece of her."

"Yeah, I guess," I agree, drawing a heart in the sand with

my finger. "I'm a lot more like my dad, that's all. So I cling to whatever I have of hers."

"Well, your dad sounds like a riot, but I doubt you're actually that much like him." She draws a blobby arrow through my heart.

I look up at her. "Is it fucked up that it sounds like you're complimenting me when you say I'm not like my dad?"

She laughs. I'm struck by the realization that I like the way she smiles when she laughs, all toothy and wide. "Yeah, it's kinda fucked up. But I do mean it as a compliment."

"I guess I should wait until you actually meet him before I accept it."

"Wow, did you just invite me to meet your father?" She fans herself. "This is moving so fast, but I'm so flattered, Valentina."

I shove her, then freeze. She stops herself from falling over with her left hand, not hurting her right. I exhale. "It's weird that you keep calling me Valentina."

"Missing the exclusive use of 'Princesa'?"

"Oh please, I'd rather the identity crisis of being fully first-named."

She digs her toes in the sand. "Do you mind it?"

I shrug. "It's the name on my birth certificate."

She snorts. "Like I give a shit about that."

"I like my name," I admit. "But my dad picked it out and it just feels uncomfortably feminine sometimes, with the whole Spanish-word-ending-in-an-*a*-makes-it-feminine thing. I sorta like the implied neutrality of Vale. I'm a girl, and I like being one, but I do hate the baggage of what my dad expects of me compared to my brothers. Especially as a girl who plays soccer."

She's quiet for a second, eyes focused on her wiggling toes freeing themselves from the mound of sand she buried them under. "So do you want me to call you Vale? When I'm not calling you Princesa, of course. That's nonnegotiable."

I roll my eyes, tempted to shove her again but holding back on account of her wrist. "*You* can call me Valentina. I know the same baggage doesn't carry over when you say it."

Her dark eyes sparkle in the sunlight as she looks over at me. "Yeah, trust me, I'm a big fan of girls who play soccer."

Dina saves me from figuring out how the hell to respond to that when she runs over, soccer ball tucked under her arm. "Care for a rematch, ladies?"

"Won't be much of a rematch considering most of the girls here are on our team," Leticia says, getting up and brushing sand off her butt and the backs of her thighs. Not that I'm looking.

Dina's smile says she caught me. "What about a game of keep-away then? Me and Ortiz here against Ovie and Vale."

"I would be so honored," Leticia says. She looks down at me, grinning crookedly. "Princesa?"

I roll my eyes and get up too. "If I play, will you go back to calling me Valentina?"

"Not likely."

Leticia jogs off to ask Kiko and Marley if they want to

join us. I follow Dina closer to the water, where the sand won't be so hard to run on and we won't trample the families soaking in the sun.

Dina nudges me. "So she calls you Valentina now?"

"Don't start."

"Just an innocent observation," she says, though her smile is anything but.

Keep-away is as simple a game as it sounds. There aren't goals, there isn't even any real winner. Just keep the ball away from the other team as long as possible through pivoting and passing. To make things interesting, we decide you can only have the ball in your possession for ten seconds before you have to pass to someone on your team.

It ends up being me, Ovie, and Kiko against Dina, Marley, and Leticia. Stacked in our favor, if you ask me.

"Care to do the honors, babe?" Dina hands Ovie the ball.

"I'd be happy to." Ovie punts the ball into the water.

Leticia and I meet eyes for a second before we're both rushing the waves.

I kick off my shorts as I run, stripping away my T-shirt so all I'm in is my black bikini. Leticia, on the other hand, sprints into the water fully clothed, with her injured wrist high above her head.

"I'd tackle you if I didn't think soaking your wrap would be unsportsmanlike!" I shout, trudging my way over the waves as quickly as I can. The water is up to our thighs now.

"Since when do you care about sportsmanship?" she calls back, nearly falling face-first into the water when the sand gives out beneath her.

I make it to the ball first, only to realize I'm screwed. I can't use my hands, but the water is too high for me to stand and walk the ball against my chest back to shore.

I nudge it forward with my head as I swim.

Leticia just waits for me where the water is still low enough she can touch the bottom. Curse her for being taller. The ocean skims her chin, wetting the tips of her hair when a big wave comes in. Though she came to camp with it close-cropped, it's curling over her ears now. "What exactly is your game plan here?"

I wait for a second. Then I splash her, low enough to keep her raised wrist dry but hard enough that it soaks her face and hair.

"Hey!" she yells.

"You're the one who said I don't care about sportsmanship!" I shout over my shoulder.

Dina is waiting for me when I get to shore. "I guess you get a pass on the ten-second rule given that you looked like you were drowning."

"Generous," I reply, then kick the ball to Kiko.

The game is an absolute mess. I make some of the sloppiest passes I've made in years, stumbling over abandoned sandcastles and driftwood. My body is on fire from the running and dodging, but I'm also shivering in my soaked state.

Sweat mixes with salt water, sticky and cold against my skin. Grainy sand coats my toes and scrapes my feet when I kick the ball hard enough.

It's the most fun I've had playing something like soccer in years.

Ovie drags the ball back so it rolls on top of her foot, then taps it into the air before sending it flying my way in what's essentially a bicycle kick. Man, if she weren't such a killer goalie, she'd be a beast as a striker.

I stop the ball with my nearly bare chest, knowing it'll leave a red mark on my skin. Leticia runs my way, counting loudly with every step.

"One, two—"

"Those wet shorts aren't chafing?" I tease, floating the ball between my feet. I'm not one for tricks or fancy footwork, but I'm not usually one for smiling while playing either.

"Are you asking me to strip?" Leticia tsks. "Five, six . . ."

I take a page out of Ovie's book, pulling the ball back onto my foot and kicking it high enough that I can catch it with one knee. I juggle it back and forth between both of them for a second.

"Well, now you're just showing off," Leticia says with her hands on her hips. She doesn't seem to be looking at the ball though. "Eight, nine . . ."

"Ten," I say, letting the ball drop and passing it directly to her.

She stops the ball automatically, but her face is full of

confusion. Before she can even look down, let alone turn away from me, I charge her and steal it back.

"Distracted over there, Leticia?" Kiko shouts. Leticia flips her off but is biting down on a smile.

"I know there aren't winners in this game, but I think Vale just won," Ovie says before running over to Dina and jumping on her back. "Swim time?"

"I feel like I'm being seduced into surrendering," Dina says, grabbing at Ovie's thighs so she doesn't fall. "And it's working."

"Seems to be the tactic today," Leticia mutters.

Kiko plants her foot on the ball. "I could use a swim too." Her hair is flying out of her ponytail and her face is bright red. "Marley?"

"Gladly." Marley, in her pink tankini and matching shorts covered in yellow hearts, follows Kiko into the water. Dina jogs after them with Ovie gripping her shoulders, squealing as they hit the waves.

"You going?" Leticia nods toward them.

"Are you?" I nod to her wrist.

"I'll be *careful*." She backs away. "Coming?"

My throat burns from the running and laughing. "Let me get a drink first."

"All right," she says. I start to turn away. "By the way," she continues, so I turn back to face her. "Happiness looks good on you." And then she's gone, a blur of movement against the setting sun and crashing waves.

Now my throat is dry for a whole different reason.

I gather my discarded clothes and plop onto my towel. As I chug my sun-warmed water, I feel my phone buzz. The high of the game protects me from my usual fear when I see it's Dad calling. I don't immediately send it to voice mail. I have to face him eventually, and my chest feels so unburdened and happy, I convince myself I can handle this right now.

He starts speaking the second I answer, so I miss a few words as I lift my phone to my ear. "—calling me back? I called the camp to make sure you're all right and the woman said you're at the beach? You're meant to be training."

The water I just swallowed evaporates from my throat, alongside any sense of peace I'd been feeling. "I—a few of us just wanted to blow off steam. I was going to call you back toni—"

"Blow off steam from summer camp?" he asks. "Did you even win your game on Friday?"

At least this will calm him down, maybe make him a little proud. "Yeah, we did. We actually played D—"

"By how much?"

I try not to scream. "Well, it wasn't by a lot, but—"

His sigh cuts me off. "Valentina." Funny, how quickly he turned my name back into an insult, all on its own. "You can't just coast your way through wins. What was the score?"

I remember my talk with Leticia after the game, how well I predicted this reaction. And even though my dad is regularly like this, it feels worse right now. Maybe it's Leticia showing me other people can see he treats me poorly, maybe it's the knowledge that Jorge is hiding away at Abuelo's because it's gotten this bad for him too. Maybe I'm just tired.

"Twenty to zero, actually," I say. "It was a landslide. They nearly called a mercy win because the other team was so tired and hopeless. I scored every last one of those goals too. They're thinking of erecting a statue in my name."

I hate myself so much in this moment. I'm sure Dad shares the same sentiment.

"This is how you react to me showing interest in your summer? Sarcasm and mockery?" He scoffs. "Call me back next time. It could've been an emergency." His voice is tight. "And don't stay out too late."

The call ends before I can reply. I stare at the screen, feeling something akin to guilt for talking back. We did actually win though. I didn't fail. That should be enough for him.

But I know it isn't. He would kill to see the notes I took, all the mistakes I know I made. All the mistakes my team made too, a reflection of my inability to captain a team here any more than back home.

I watch Kiko and Marley battle in a splashing fight. Anita, Gloria, and Hayley are taking selfies on a shared towel, brainstorming a caption that'll be a clever play on our team name.

Leticia's head pops up from under a wave, her wrist raised comically high above her, and instantly shifts my way. Even from this far away, her expression when she sees me does something to my chest. She believes in me. So does our team.

I want it to be, but I don't know if that's enough for me.

TWENTY-FOUR

APPROACHING THE HALFWAY POINT OF THE summer, we need to crank up our focus or we'll lose momentum in whatever good we've managed thus far. Safe to say that waiting for a late Marley in the shivering Monday morning air while Leticia smacks her chicle isn't a great start.

"Sorry, sorry!" Marley sings as she runs over to our field, long legs goose bumped in neon-pink running shorts. She drops her bag and adjusts the bow at the end of her braid. "I forgot about this last-minute practice."

"Seeing as it was scheduled at nearly midnight last night, that's not very surprising," Leticia murmurs from the sideline.

"You need more practice defending penalty kicks," I tell Marley, ignoring Leticia. "I know it was last minute, but this is important. I expect you to be on time."

"Oh, calm your castle, Princesa," Leticia says, sitting up. "She was ten minutes late."

Finally I face Leticia. "She could've been on time if she ditched the makeup and glitter."

Marley raises her pointer finger. "'She' is also right here. Look, I'm sorry for being late, it won't happen again." Her finger sags. "But as for how I choose to get ready in the morning, if never exfoliating your face or moisturizing your legs makes you happy, all the power to you, Vale, genuinely. But let's not police how other girls get our gender euphoria, yeah?" With that, Marley spins away, her braid twirling behind her as she struts toward the goal and starts tugging on her gloves.

Leticia poorly holds back a laugh, then motions to my knees. "You really should do something about those."

"Go put your gear on," I snap. She rolls her eyes and goes to trade out her slides for cleats.

I approach Marley, swallowing hard. She's focused on her gloves, but seeing as they're fully strapped already, I'm guessing she's just avoiding eye contact with me.

I don't do apologies well, considering they're rarely given or accepted in my house. I try anyway. "Hey, I'm really sorry."

"It's fine, don't worry about it."

"No, it's not." I bite the inside of my cheek to ground my breathing. "How you choose to dress or do your hair and makeup or whatever isn't something I have a right to dictate. Especially when it looks this good." I motion to her sparkling cheekbones and she stifles a smile. It fills my strained lungs with relief. "I'm sorry. Won't happen again."

"And I won't be late again." She wiggles her gloved hands. "Believe it or not, I actually do want to get good."

"You're already good," I say, believing it and hoping she does too.

"It's just that every year I've gone to camp here, I've been slotted into whatever spare position the team needed. Even that team I played on with Leticia a few years ago tossed me around." Marley looks down at her cleats, mud caking their white and pink leather. "This is the first team I've ever been on where I feel like I'm actually being treated like a player and not a burden."

"You can thank her for that." I nod toward Leticia, who is picking at a knot in her laces with stubby fingernails. "She saw your potential and I would've been hopeless training a goalie."

Marley grins slowly. "Maybe she's not so bad when you get to know her, huh?"

I choke out a laugh. "Yeah, no, I still think she sucks."

Marley just grins, neither of us believing me this time.

An hour later, the rest of the team arrives for practice. We work on a new drill where Marley punts the ball as evenly as she can and then two girls, one from the left and one from the right, race to get to the ball first. Whoever steals it and maintains control for ten seconds wins. If you lose, you have to go again until you win. I may or may not have been inspired by yesterday.

I go up against Bethany. Predictably, I reach the ball first and box her out. She gets a good elbow in as she dances her way around me, her enthusiasm teetering on violence, but the aggression only motivates me further.

"One . . . two . . . two and a half," Leticia calls from her place in the left line.

"Are you kidding me?" I shout over Bethany's snarling. "You seemed plenty capable of counting properly yesterday!"

"Yeah, during the rare moments when she wasn't so distracted," Kiko adds quietly.

"Two and three quarters . . . ," Leticia continues.

My motivation is giving way to annoyance, so I dribble the ball and take a shot. Marley is close to catching it, but she wasn't prepared to defend right now, so it glides past her fingertips.

Leticia blows her whistle. "No winner! Both of you get back in line."

Bethany huffs and jogs back to the right side. I run over to the left line, where Leticia stands with her hands on her hips.

"The goal wasn't to score a goal," she says before I can get my complaint in, words garbled by the whistle still in her mouth.

I rub my arm. "I think she bruised me."

"On the bright side, your ego looks untouched." She flicks my bangs. My bruise underneath them is still a little green and yellow. "Forehead could use some more work."

I open my mouth, but she blows the whistle in my face before darting off for the ball against Kiko. The two of them duke it out for a few minutes as Kiko's footwork meets Leticia's defensive skills.

Eventually, Kiko starts waving the white scrunchie on her wrist in surrender. Leticia blows her whistle in agreement, and they shake hands.

I frown as Leticia jogs back to our line. "The goal wasn't

to give up either," I tell her. She blows the whistle and sends Claire and Gloria running. Next time we go to the beach, I'm throwing that whistle in the ocean.

"It's no fun for everyone else to watch Kiko and me fight for the ball for that long." She doesn't look at me, eyes trained on Claire and Gloria. "We'll go again in a different set."

"You're teaching them it's okay to give up."

At this, she glares at me. "They're not babies, we're all between fifteen and eighteen. I'm not going to shatter their belief that you fight for the ball for as long as it takes by cutting one drill short."

She blows the whistle again. I look up to see Gloria do a little dance while Claire lovingly rolls her eyes. Gloria heads for the sideline with Anita and Hayley, but I call after Claire when she follows her.

"You've gotta go again," I say.

"Actually, I was hoping to leave early?" Claire brushes away the hair escaping her ponytail. Her roots have grown in, pushing her bleached, orangey hair down. "I need to call my boyfriend and check in with him."

"'Check in'?" I ask in disbelief. "No, you can talk to him afterward, you still need to finish the drill."

Claire glances to her bag on the sideline, then back to me. "It's really important."

"So is winning, in case you forgot."

"*Valentina*," Leticia scolds. She steps closer to Claire and nods to the sideline. "Go ahead." Claire doesn't wait for Leticia to change her mind.

"Okay, seriously? She can't keep leaving practice to chat with her probably overbearing boyfriend," I say. "I think he can survive one afternoon without her calling to tell him what she's doing. It isn't healthy."

Leticia stares at me hard, her thick brows furrowed. "What happened at the beach?"

"What do you mean?"

"Yesterday you actually looked like you were enjoying playing soccer," Leticia says.

"Keep-away isn't technically soccer."

"It's soccer-adjacent," she says. "I thought maybe you'd mellowed out. But first this morning with Marley and now with Claire? You're back to dictator mode."

"I thought I was a princess," I reply, being difficult. She rolls her eyes. "Look, I'm not going to apologize for wanting to win. If you expect that to change, you clearly don't know me and have mistaken me for another girl you hate."

Leticia's expression is unreadable. "Yeah, this is all about me *not* knowing you." She scoffs and goes back to watching the girls, Bethany and Natalia this time. Another whistle blow and they're off to fight for the ball.

While I'm left to fight the feeling her words leave in my chest.

Another wonderful shift in the cafeteria drags on that night. Kiko and Gloria say hi as I serve them spaghetti and ask if they want meatballs on top. Kiko says yes, Gloria says no, my mind says it will shut down if I have to stand for one more second.

Because the universe has a sick sense of humor, that's right when Cate and Kaylee show up, sans Sophie.

They're both sweaty and flushed, clearly having just finished a run or practice, and the exhaustion in their eyes says they're equally as irritable as I am right now.

Cate glares at the pasta. "Is this vegan?"

I try not to pass out. "Yes."

Kaylee points at the meatballs in a separate pot. "Those don't look vegan."

"Most balls of animal flesh aren't." I smile like an asshole, mostly to give me something to focus on other than my exhausted legs. But as annoying as they are, I'm not going to fault them for dietary choices or restrictions. "I can give you the pasta without the meatballs. We have two separate tubs of sauce."

Both girls suck their teeth. "That won't do," Cate says. "You're serving both, so the pasta is clearly tainted."

"I'm using different serving spoons." I open and close my hands. "And I'm wearing gloves."

Kaylee ignores me, turning to Cate. "Maybe if she changed the gloves?"

Cate tilts her head. "Are the gloves vegan though?"

Suddenly, I feel like I'm not the asshole in this equation. "Are either of you even vegan? Both of you got extra servings of ice cream last week and you were complaining about the eggs the other day."

Cate gasps. "Should you really be talking back like this to your customers?"

"Customers? Wait, what are you even—" Cate's mouth twitches, like she's fighting a smile. I glance at Kaylee, who is doing a worse job at it. "You're fucking with me."

"We would never," Cate says.

"We take matters like this very seriously," Kaylee adds. "It would just be a shame if one of the captains that's miraculously improving her team was suddenly on probation for using her cafeteria job to intentionally target players whose teams she feels threatened by."

"Especially if she already had a reputation for fighting prior to camp." Cate pouts.

I feel sick to my stomach. Years of swallowing my anger under Dad's roof help steady my voice. "Would you like pasta, or not? And if so, how would you like it?"

They look at each other, satisfied, and drop their trays on the counter. Cate's voice is like fingers on a chalkboard. "I could actually go for some meat lover's pizza. I think we could order some before that local place closes." Kaylee nods in agreement and they leave, arms hooked, like they didn't just threaten me, my job, my place at camp, and my team.

My break comes an hour later, but I hardly feel the minutes pass. I'm still shaken by Cate and Kaylee's words, staring blankly at my pasta, when a tray lands in front of me.

"I would kill for some red pepper flakes right now," Leticia says before sitting down with a plate of meatball-less pasta. I stare at her as she takes a massive bite. She looks up at me midchew. "What?"

"You're sitting with me."

She swallows. "Astute observation. If this whole soccer thing doesn't work out, you could make a great private investigator."

In my already agitated state, I don't even have annoyance to spare for her. "I thought we were fighting," I say, feeling both like a child and like a needy girlfriend.

"I can kick you in your shins if you want. But not too hard, we have a game Friday. Which I'm sure you've forgotten about." When I don't crack a smile or even roll my eyes, she loses sarcastic steam. "You were a bit of a dick today, if that's what you want to hear. And I mean, more so than usual." The rush to get defensive bubbles to the surface before she adds, "That doesn't mean I'm not going to talk to you."

I pause. "But you're annoyed with me." In my house, that's grounds for weeks of silent treatment.

"I'm always annoyed with you," she says, smiling close-lipped, her mouth full of pasta. "Your proclivity for being annoying is part of your charm."

I scoff, nudging my food around my plate. "My dad called while we were at the beach."

She nods slowly and swallows. "Well, now *I* feel like a bit of a dick."

"Don't." I drop my fork and stare at it. "I'm just . . . dealing with a lot."

Leticia nudges my hand until I look up. "Encouraging the girls to keep improving doesn't have to come at the expense of letting them be proud of what they've already accomplished. And having fun. And calling their boyfriends."

"Is this your way of asking me to say you won that game against the Daisies for us? Because you can be proud about your goal. I give you my blessing."

She rolls her eyes. "*We* won us the game. It was our goal to be proud of. You can be proud of it too."

"Yeah, I'm not great at that."

"Maybe start with being proud of our team without qualifying it," she suggests.

"Would you believe me if I told you I'm not familiar with the idea of unqualified praise?"

"No, that sounds about right," she says. "You know, it's funny that you can seem like such a prideful person while actually being so hard on yourself." She takes a big bite of pasta and smiles at me smugly. Like she is both insulting me and empathizing with me. Like she gets what I'm going through, and also knows how hard it is for me to talk about it.

It makes me bold enough to reach over and wipe a bit of sauce off the side of her mouth with my thumb. It's probably the most tender thing I've ever done in my life. And though I barely graze her lips with the pad of my thumb, there's a satisfaction in feeling how soft they are.

Then I sit back, shocked at myself. Based on the way her mouth falls open after she swallows, she feels the same way.

Before either of us can say anything about it, Hayley and Bethany walk over and ask to join us.

"Uh, yeah, yeah, of course," I say, while throwing my unused napkins onto my unfinished plate of food. "I actually need to get back to work, so I should go, but you should sit and eat." I stand up quickly and nearly drop my tray.

Leticia just stares at me.

"Oh okay," Hayley says as she sits. "Have a good shift!"

"See you tomorrow at practice," Bethany adds.

"Thanks. Uh, bye," I tell them, refusing to look at Leticia before I turn away and rush back to the kitchen.

TWENTY-FIVE

TUESDAY MORNING, I TAKE A RADICAL approach to soccer.

Maybe what Leticia said had some merit. It's unfortunate that camp resides in some parallel universe in which she's becoming increasingly more correct about things and I'm compelled to do shit like gently wipe her face after she calls me a dick, but that's my reality right now.

I text Leticia that we're rain-checking our training this morning, but that I'll see her at practice later. She likes the message but doesn't reply, which doesn't give me much intel on where we stand after last night.

Then I text the rest of the team that we aren't having a normal practice today, and to show up to our usual field in normal clothes at noon. It takes some strategic bribing of Lola and Juanita, and by that I mean asking very nicely and promising to wash them when I'm done, but I scrounge up a couple of extra bedsheets and lay them out on the field. I have to sit and wait by myself for the next part, but by the time the team arrives, everything is here.

"What's all of this?" Anita asks as she and Kiko walk over, Anita in joggers and a tank top and Kiko in a mustard-colored romper.

I had to dip into the small chunk of my cafeteria paycheck I planned on pocketing, since most of it is going to pay for camp, but the hesitant smiles on their faces as they look at the pizza laid out across the sheets already make it worth it.

"Sit, eat. I'll explain when more of the team gets here."

They exchange a glance of uncertainty, which doesn't bode well for me, since they're two of the players I talk to the most. But after a beat, they sit down and flip open the nearest box of pizza.

Rani and Natalia look similarly skeptical when they walk up, Rani's floral hijab matching Natalia's floral stretch pants, but they dive into slices of the halal-friendly cheese within a few minutes. Bethany cracks a joke about this being a trap while Claire and Gloria serve themselves immediately. Hayley seems more disturbed by the pineapple on one of the pizzas than anything else.

Leticia and Marley are last, and I'm confused by the twinge of disappointment I feel when I realize there isn't room on my blanket for them.

Regardless, I jump up and face everyone. "We won on Friday." My voice feels too loud, especially as everyone quiets. Leticia watches me intently. "Not everyone could come to the beach on Sunday, so I thought we could celebrate today. Instead of practice."

"What's the catch?" Kiko asks, followed by Natalia's nervous laughter.

I try to smile. "No catch. Just a day to celebrate the win."

Gloria lifts a piece of pizza. "So we don't have to run deadlies after eating this?"

The replacement nickname for suicide sprints has stuck with the team. I don't have to try to smile this time. "No. No running, no playing. Unless you all want to. But you should probably take it easy unless you want to get sick."

They all cheer and dig in. Chatter and laughter takes over the silence that enveloped my words. The conversation drifts to past positions everyone's played and how comfortably they're adjusting to their new ones.

Kiko has played for years, but never on a seriously competitive team and never sticking to any position for too long. Her aloofness means all that raw talent has gone unstructured. I'll have to talk to her about trying out for her high school team when the summer is over, especially since she's only going into her junior year and could maybe swing a college scholarship out of it.

She confirms how good she is half an hour later, when she challenges Anita to a juggling contest. The rest of the girls except for me and Leticia join them, everyone breaking out the balls I packed just in case. They are soccer players at the end of the day.

I'm watching the joyful chaos unfold in front of my eyes when Leticia drops down next to me.

"I thought we weren't making big decisions like canceling practice without consulting each other," she says, picking a piece of bell pepper off my pizza and popping it into her mouth.

"I believe I said *you* weren't going to do that anymore." I tilt my head. "And then you disagreed."

"Touché."

We watch our girls in a sort of companionable silence. Given the weird note we ended last night on, I'm grateful for it. Marley is doing a hilariously bad job juggling the ball, with her knobby knees sending it spiraling away from her. Natalia, Rani, and Hayley are attempting to actually juggle the ball between the three of them, but keep accidentally kneeing it at Bethany, who is trying to tie Claire's hair back for her so she doesn't lose her stride. Gloria juggles the ball almost flawlessly with an impressive cadence, her short, thick legs acting as a drum for the ball's rhythm. Kiko is unsurprisingly thriving, even as Anita keeps trying to knock her ball away.

I pivot back to the abandoned conversation. "I've been wondering why you never played outside the net in high school," I say to Leticia.

She picks at the grass beside the blanket, slowly starting to stack it on my knee. I hold very still, careful not to do anything that would make her stop. For some reason. "I don't know. I played stopper as a kid, but it never clicked for me. I'd always get frustrated and want to just scoop up the ball."

I laugh. "Only you would be so stubborn you'd find the one position that lets you actually do that."

"Maybe I'm just a girl who knows what she wants." She wipes her hands together to clean off the grass and leans back onto her elbows. "So what about you? Why midfield? As far as I remember, you were a passably decent defender."

"Don't hurt yourself with all that praise."

She rolls her eyes. "You played defense, then offense, then mid. Unrelated, but do you have commitment issues?"

"It's called having range."

"And yet I've never seen you try out keeper."

"You've already corrupted Marley into becoming one of you, don't come for my soul next."

She shakes her head, smiling. "All right, so I'm a goalie because I have issues with authority figures telling me I can't use my hands. What's your damage?"

I set down my slice of pizza. "When I was a kid I loved protecting the goal on defense, but I wanted to score my own goals too. Then I played forward for a bit, but I missed helping defend. Either way I felt sorta useless, so freshman year I wrote center mid on my application for varsity."

She takes a sip of her soda. "Bold move."

"Yeah, well, the team sucked, needed a new right mid, and it was clear I at least kinda knew what I was doing on the field, so I got lucky. I wanted a distraction from the grief, so I trained nonstop with my dad, who also needed distracting." I fidget with my fingers, suddenly feeling exposed for accidentally taking her question this literally. Maybe the way I chose to grieve wasn't the healthiest, but it at least dulled the ache to pour everything into something more controllable than mortality. "Anyway, I found my home in center mid. I get to do it all there—defend, attack, assist."

She watches me from under hooded lids. The sun dances across the stretches of color in her irises. "You're always able to help."

I nod, feeling shy. "Whether the ball is in play on our side or theirs, someone needs me and I can do something about it."

"Hm." She stares at me for a beat longer.

I clear my throat. "So are you ever going to tell me why you're training to play forward instead of sticking with defense?"

She shrugs. "I got so used to being star goalie that I let myself forget the basics. I figured if I was going to face the mortifying ordeal of being a mediocre soccer player, I might as well dive straight into the deep end and try an entirely new position."

"That's . . . noble."

"Oh fuck off."

"No," I laugh, placing my hand on her knee. "I'm serious."

Leticia stares down at my hand. I snatch it back and we both pretend like it didn't happen.

"It's impressive, that's all," I quickly say. "You being willing to put in all this effort."

"I could say the same to you," she replies, tilting her head at our team, who've broken out into a scrimmage.

Throwing a pizza party to celebrate one win that came after two losses instead of practicing is exactly the kind of thing Dad would scoff at. But right now, looking over at Gloria and Rani playfully shoving each other aside for the ball, only to have it stolen from both of them by Kiko, leaving them erupting in laughter, makes me feel like this was one of my best moves so far.

Leticia laughs at Kiko running across the field hunched over, balancing the ball on her back. "Room for two more?" she shouts.

The ball falls off Kiko's back. Marley steals it and shoots at the undefended goal. She scores messily, a toe-kick if I've ever seen one, and slides into a celebratory pose on her knees.

She doesn't see an imperfect shot the way I do. She just sees a successful goal.

"We're down by one, but come on in!" Kiko shouts back to us.

"I'll join y'all, and Leticia can join the team that's winning!" I yell. I turn to Leticia. "You won't be much help to them anyway, right?"

"Oh, just you wait, Princesa," she says, a challenge sparking in her eyes.

Hours later, I don't even know the final score. It doesn't matter.

TWENTY-SIX

LETICIA PLANS TO RUN VARIOUS GOALIE drills with Marley for the rest of the week during practice, so she needs extra forward training with me on the side. Shifts at the cafeteria and our long practices are giving me nearly no time to breathe, but Leticia is going above and beyond what I initially asked of her, so it only feels fair that I do the same.

Plus, it's fun to start my mornings off by watching her miserably run deadlies back and forth across a field while I sit on the grass, sipping a cup of coffee I got from Maria in the kitchen.

"Enjoying the view?" Leticia shouts as she bends down to touch the midfield line and starts running back to the goal.

"You're doing great, champ!" I shout back with a thumbs-up.

She replies with an expressive finger gesture of her own.

I see Claire walking by out of the corner of my eye. She's just hanging up the phone when she notices me. I wave tentatively.

She leaves the path and comes over, waving to Leticia before plopping down beside me. It feels momentarily awkward, probably because the two of us hardly talk outside of her asking if she can leave practice to call her boyfriend.

"You two are up early," she says.

I tug at the sleeves of my hoodie. I almost wore Leticia's jacket today, but she's yet to ask for it back and I've yet to figure out why I don't want her to. "Captains' duties. Gotta prep Leticia to properly take over as a wing." Claire nods along. I clear my throat. "You're okay with this, right? You and Leticia swapping positions more permanently?"

She stretches her short legs. "Honestly, I already like being sweeper more than wing. I feel like I actually know what I'm doing back there, somehow. Bethany's definitely helping me find my footing."

"Good," I say. "I'm glad." I try not to stare at her phone in her hand, but she catches me looking. She slips it into her pocket.

"He's not an asshole, by the way," Claire says, looking pointedly down at her chubby fingers. Chipped purple nail polish clings to her thumb. "My boyfriend."

"Oh."

"I know what the girls on the team probably think with me calling him all the time. I heard Bethany and Hayley wondering about it the other day in the showers." She picks at a hair tie on her wrist.

"I—okay," I say.

"He's going through something pretty rough right now

and I want to be there for him. I care about soccer, I promise. But it's not a life or death situation for me." She seems to catch herself, her face freezing for a beat. I try not to move. "I'll just say cancer is a bitch. Especially for someone our age."

Suddenly, I'm twelve again and googling things like "stages of cancer" and "metastasizing" and "prayers for people who aren't sure they believe in God" on the way to soccer practice. I'm watching my dad, the proudest and most stubborn person I've ever met, be told there's nothing left to do. That there is no winning this.

I don't know what to say. A lump clogs my throat. "I'm sorry."

"Yeah, me too." She hugs her knees to her chest and watches Leticia for a second.

I'm still at a loss for words, but I try to find some. Maybe it's the few times I've broached the subject with Leticia now, but it feels easier to bring up than usual. Which still means it isn't easy at all. "Cancer is definitely a bitch." Claire tilts her head curiously. "My mom," I say, hoping it's explanation enough. Just in case, I add, "I was thirteen."

Her dark eyes soften. "I'm sorry. I wouldn't wish it on anyone."

I nod, feeling both vulnerable and seen. She hasn't lost her boyfriend, but she knows what it feels like to look at someone you love and see a clock ticking down, and that's more than most people understand.

"Thanks for telling me," I say. "You can leave practice as early as you need. Or skip them altogether if you'd like. No excuses necessary." My hand twitches to provide her some comfort, a hug or a pat on the shoulder at the very least. But I'm no good at this. I'm not the person who heals people, I'm usually the one hurting them.

But when Claire smiles, small and easy and more real than I've ever seen her do in any practice or game before, I guess I'm not so sure that's true about me.

TWENTY-SEVEN

WE WIN ANOTHER GAME.

It's so absurd, I almost don't realize we've won until Marley rushes over and envelops me in a hug after saving a last-minute goal that would've tied it.

We played against the Cheetos, a neon-orange team that makes me appreciate our purple color more than I did at the start of the summer. They scored quickly, two goals in the first thirty minutes. We'd started with Leticia on defense, but swapped her and Claire right after the second goal to go harder on offense. And it worked.

Leticia solidified her legacy as a wing. The years of split-second decisions in the goal prepared her for quick assessments. She finds an open party in the middle with no problem, especially when that open party happens to be me.

We win 3–2. Of the three goals we scored, two of them came from me and Leticia. The most effective dysfunctional partnership. The third came from Kiko and Anita, just as impressive a pair.

After those first two goals, something in Marley clicked. There were close calls, but she stopped overthinking things. Could she have done better? Of course. But it's a learning curve, so I don't shout or lecture. I guess I'm following my own learning curve.

Before we even finish cheering, high-fiving the other team, and stripping off our gear, I know I am celebrating with my team tonight. I won't take this away from them, or from me. Lucky streak or not, fuck it.

The Princesses have been eating and chatting in the caf for hours alongside Ovie and Dina's team, who also won their game. I'm in the middle of listening to Kiko rehash some story about busting her knee open while skateboarding when her eyes drift off to the corner of the room. I follow her gaze and spot Kaylee, Cate, and Sophie.

Sophie and I exchange waves, but when Kaylee and Cate turn around and spot me, Sophie drops her hand. Kiko scoffs.

"You ever play with them?" I ask Kiko, watching the trio sit with the rest of their team.

"Once, with Sophie," she says. Her mouth is curled sourly, an odd look for someone who is usually all laughs. "That girl certainly changed once those two got their claws in her."

I feel my brow furrow. "Sophie doesn't seem that different than when we were kids."

"All I'm saying is that Sophie and I were on a team my first year at camp, back in U14 before the whole tournament thing, and we were attached at the hip. I hadn't seen her play before then, but apparently she made a big enough improvement from the year before to catch their attention." She nods to Kaylee and Cate. "The last two weeks of camp they invited her to eat with them and gifted her extra hair ties and scrunchies and deodorants. Like, absolutely *showered* her with attention as if they were recruiters or something. Next summer she barely even looked at me."

"That doesn't sound like Sophie," I defend, even though I'm starting to notice cracks in the rose-colored glass I've boxed her in. "She's not an asshole like that."

"I'm not here to deny anyone's realities." Kiko purses her lips. "But even if she isn't, the people she chooses to hang out with are, so is there really a difference?"

Kiko gets up to refill her juice. I tune in to Anita and Rani's conversation about their lives back home. Anita's love of swimming and Rani's passion for sewing are genuinely interesting, but I can't stop sneaking glances over at Sophie in the corner of the room. A beam of light from the ceiling casts an angelic glow around her and her teammates, but the longer I stare, the harsher and faker it looks.

Back in the cabin that night, after Dina, Ovie, and I have all showered and changed, I find them sitting on the porch, watching the stars.

"There's our favorite temporary rival," Dina says as I sit down beside them.

"Hey, it's not my fault my team beat yours," I joke, nudging her. "I did offer to be your captain, if you really cared that badly about winning."

Dina stiffens and turns away. I guess I got so used to bantering with Leticia, I forgot that there are, in fact, lines I should be cautious about crossing. "I don't know if I congratulated you guys on your win yet though," I add.

"Thank you," Ovie says, pleased.

"The Clovers are a tough team," I go on, waiting for Dina to acknowledge me.

"Why, just because *you* lost to them?" Dina jokes, but there's that edge to her words again.

I sigh, and try to do better. "I'm sorry I brought up the captain thing again."

"You were just joking." Ovie tries to play Switzerland. "But Dina has been working really hard."

"And we've won just as many games as your team has," Dina points out.

I remember Coach's potential decision to make Dina captain. She's good at this apparently, maybe even better than me. Which shouldn't feel like a threat, and it isn't in general. But when I think about Dad hearing that I lost being captain to my best friend, which he absolutely will find out about once next season starts, all I can feel is panic.

"I should go sleep," I say, wanting to get away from them before I say the wrong thing again. At camp they're my competition, but back home no one from our team is going to tolerate—let alone hang out with—me if I'm no longer captain, so I'd like to at least not lose my only two friends in the process.

But when Dina scoffs in response and Ovie offers nothing more than a tight smile, I feel like that process has already begun.

TWENTY-EIGHT

DISTANCE FROM THE LAST GAME MAKES it harder for me not to pick at the flaws in our plays: Kiko's off-side offenses, Claire's hesitancy to push up, Hayley's sloppy throw-ins. Even Leticia botched a cross or two and is still struggling to take solid shots at the goal herself. Without the thrill of the girls celebrating around me, I'm drowning in bad habits.

Which is why I'm so on edge when Leticia doesn't show up for our one-on-one practice Sunday morning. I gave her Saturday off to help train Marley again, but by the end of the day I was regretting that call. The only thing that distracts me from my worst thoughts lately is her annoying voice. And the team, now that I think about it. Ironic, that the sources of my greatest anxiety here are also my greatest reliefs.

I burst into Leticia's cabin without knocking. It's past ten, so it's her cabinmates' faults if they're not awake already. "You were supposed to meet me at the fields fifteen minutes a—"

Leticia is sitting on her bed, phone in hand. From this angle I can see that she's on FaceTime, but can't see with whom.

"Hey," Leticia says, looking caught.

"Hi," I say tentatively.

"Hello!" a voice calls from the phone. Leticia closes her eyes and exhales.

"Am I interrupting something?" I ask. "Something more important than, say, practicing how not to shoot the ball over the net?"

Leticia checks the time at the top of her screen. "Shit."

"My fault! I called and distracted Letty," the phone says again. "Force of habit, talking her pretty ears off for hours on end."

I raise an eyebrow at Leticia. I didn't know anyone but Marley called her "Letty" unironically.

Leticia looks pained and faces the phone to me. "Valentina, this is my friend Wendy." *The girl who kissed and then ditched you,* I want to correct.

On the screen is a pale Asian girl, long brown hair hanging around her face while she eats a bowl of yogurt. She swallows and waves excitedly with her spoon. "Finally I meet the elusive longtime rival! I've only ever seen you from the stands. While booing you," she laughs, but it's without cruelty. She's even prettier than I expected she'd be.

I don't know how to play this. "Nice to meet you," I say, smiling to the best of my ability. "I'll let you two get back to it."

The screen door falls shut behind me, but moments later, Leticia comes fumbling through it. Her cleats hang from their laces in her hand and her socks droop down her calves. "I'm sorry I spaced. Wendy called and I—"

"Got caught up," I finish for her. "It's fine."

"You're not mad?"

I shrug. "No."

She squints at me. "I blew off our one-on-one practice to FaceTime someone . . . and you're not mad?"

"You didn't do it on purpose, so . . ."

She's still staring at me, dark brown eyes scrutinizing and confused.

"*What?* Do you want me to make you run extra deadlies or bench you or something? It can be arranged if that would make you feel better for wasting my time digitally flirting with some girl."

"Okay, yeah, this sounds more like you."

I take a deep breath. "I just thought you two weren't a thing anymore. That's all."

"We're not. We never technically were." She drops her cleats and runs her free hand through her loose curls. They've grown out so much since the start of the summer, they'll be grazing her shoulders in a few weeks at this rate. I wonder if they're as soft to the touch as they look. "I told you we still talk now and then."

I pause. "Did she call to talk about a fight with her girlfriend?"

"Yeah, I gue— Why are you making that face?"

"It just seems like she only reaches out when they have issues. Like she doesn't even try to talk to you otherwise."

"It's not like that."

"Then what is it like?" I ask.

"We're *friends.*"

"Are you *friends* when she and her girlfriend are getting along just fine?" I ask. Leticia opens her mouth and closes it again, looking away. Something in me softens. "Don't hold me to this, but you deserve better than being someone's second choice or backup every time something goes wrong with her actual girlfriend."

"What do I deserve then?"

I swallow. "What?"

She steps closer and looks down at me through her thick lashes. "If I deserve better than this, what do I deserve?"

It feels like a dare. And in the absence of my answer, the silence stretches, almost unbearable.

I'm unsure which one of us will break it, or if we'll just keep stubbornly staring into each other's eyes until we both pass out. But then I hear my name.

"Vale!" Sophie calls from a distance. She's with a pack of Angels, all decked out in their pristine white jerseys that must reek of bleach. There's no way they're staying that clean otherwise. She jogs over to us, either ignoring the tension between Leticia and me or completely oblivious to it. "Just the girl I wanted to see." I brighten while Leticia scoffs. "Mind if I borrow your co-captain for a second?" Sophie asks her.

"By all means," Leticia says. "I've already wasted enough of her time today." With that, she walks off.

I watch her for longer than I should with an audience, but Sophie doesn't seem to mind. Right, Sophie. "So, what's up?" I ask.

"I just thought we should chat," she says casually, as if she didn't pull me aside for this. "I heard your team won again on Friday."

"Yup," I say. "Second win in a row."

"We've yet to lose one," she says quickly, then seems to catch herself. "But with this second win you're currently tied with the Daisies, Razzberries, and Scarlet Fevers in qualifying points."

"Yeah, I think we're officially making a comeback," I reply, almost too earnestly.

"Sounds like it." She says it with a smile. But her words sound sharp, restrained. It's almost the same passive-aggressive tone that Cate and Kaylee use when they're bothering me at work. "I just thought I'd give you a few more tips, you know, about your players. Make sure you don't lose that standing while you're still on the rise."

"Oh. Um, that's cool of you, but I'm good. I've been working with the team a lot lately and think I've got it covered."

"You alone or . . . ?" She looks in the direction Leticia left.

"Turns out Leticia isn't the worst co-captain imaginable," I say, laughing but internally cringing at the awkwardness of this whole conversation.

"That's not how you felt a few weeks ago."

"Yeah, well, looks like things changed." I'm losing grip on my patience. As annoyed as I am at Leticia in this moment for . . . reasons, I still feel compelled to defend her and whatever our relationship has become.

"So you really don't want to know about your team's weaknesses? Because we've been keeping track of them." Now Sophie's gaze drifts over to her team. Cate and Kaylee catch us watching and give a tiny wave, bitter smiles tacked on. "And we've seen plenty."

There goes the last bit of sweetness.

"No thanks." I begin walking away. "But if you ever want to hear about *your* flaws, I'm starting to pick up on a few."

"So what did Soccer Barbie want?" Leticia asks when I find her at the field we were meant to meet at earlier. She's bouncing a ball between her knees.

"You should be practicing dribbling, not juggling," I scold. "And Marley would be pissed if she knew you were giving the title of Soccer Barbie to anyone but her."

She shrugs without looking up. "Marley isn't blonde; it doesn't work as well. And my coach wasn't here to help me."

"Gee, I wonder what waiting around for someone at this field feels like."

She loses control of the ball and it drops to the grass. "Point taken."

I sit down to stretch my legs. "Sophie said she wanted to help me spot our team's weaknesses, but I got a weird vibe." I downplay it, feeling embarrassed all of a sudden. "I think she was just trying to psych me out."

"Well, duh." Leticia sits across from me and pulls her legs into a butterfly stretch. "Why do you think she's been batting her lashes at you for weeks? She sees you as a threat."

I laugh, irritated. "Nice to know you think a hot girl needs an ulterior motive to talk to me."

"I don't think that," she corrects quickly, seriously. My annoyance dips for a second before she adds, "For instance, I'm talking to you right now."

I chuck a handful of grass at her.

"Hey!" She picks out the bits that stuck to her curls. "Look, I'm bagging on Sophie, not you. If the only times she talks to you are to shit on our team or to sit still and look pretty while her besties harass you, maybe it's time to take your own advice and realize you deserve better too."

I try to bite down on my smile. "So you're admitting you deserve better?"

Now it's her turn to chuck grass at me. "Shut up and finish stretching so we can practice. We've got a team of Angels to beat."

After hours of waiting for Leticia to make twenty perfect shots in the upper corners of the net in a row—no low shots, no hitting the post, no overshooting it—we lie back in the grass. I consider asking her about Wendy again, feeling both owed a response and like I'm overstepping some line, when my phone starts ringing.

"Is it my favorite member of the Castillo-Green household?" she asks as she pulls a bottle of yellow Gatorade out of her bag and passes it to me.

"How would I be calling myself?" I reply. She sticks her tongue out.

It's Jorge, actually. Which is weird, but I guess we have

texted a few times over the past couple of weeks since our phone call. I've been meaning to check in on him and his situation with Dad more often, but it keeps slipping my mind.

"To what do I owe the pleasure?" I say as I answer. Leticia looks at me in confusion and I mouth, *My brother* to her.

"Do you remember that time I caught you and Dina sneaking out the bottle of Aguardiente that Tío Raphael gave Dad for Nochebuena?" he says.

"No?"

He's quiet for a second. "Is now a good time to mention that I caught you and Dina sneaking out the bottle of Aguardiente that Tío Raphael gave Dad for Nochebuena?"

"All right, you heathen, what do you want?"

"He sounds like a pain in your ass," Leticia whispers to me. "I like him." She goes to take a sip of her red Gatorade, but I tip the bottle's bottom so it spills a little over her chin. "Hey!"

"Shh," I tell her. "I'm on the phone." She flips me off while I ask Jorge to repeat himself.

"Wait, are you on a date or something?" he asks.

My cheeks go hot. "What? No."

"You used your flirting voice," he says.

"I don't have a flirting voice," I say, and then realize my mistake when Leticia starts grinning, confused but amused.

"You used to use it with that babysitter Dad hired when Mami first died."

"She was hot, and I was thirteen and grieving. Leave adolescent me be and tell me why you're calling."

He remembers himself. "Right. I need to ask you for a favor."

"And that would be?"

"Dad's driving up to Abuelo's on Tuesday with Matteo and is spending the night here before going back home with some of Mami's old stuff. I mean, that's what he claims it's for, but I think he just wants to prove he could get me if he wanted to."

My heart sinks a little. I knew Jorge's temporary escape seemed too good to be true. "I'm sorry, dude. Do you think he's going to make you come home?"

"I don't think he'll make a big deal in front of Abuelo given how they feel about each other. I didn't even realize the full extent of Abuelo's disdain for Dad until now. Old age is making him very honest."

It should hurt me to know my mom's father dislikes my dad. It doesn't. "Well, that's good at least, but where does my favor come into this?"

"He wants to take me out to lunch before he leaves on Wednesday. But Matteo has been begging to see you and we're only a few hours away from your camp, so I thought maybe we'd feed two birds with one scone," he says, voice pleading. "Dad specifically said he wants it to be just a father-kids lunch, no Abuelo invited. I think I can use that and Matteo's excitement over being near you to get Dad to agree to drive over to Santa Cruz and include you in the lunch plans."

"You want me to come too?" The surprise is apparent in my voice. Jorge doesn't invite me to things. "Why?"

He pauses before speaking. "Because you make it easier to be around him. Matteo doesn't see it yet, but you do." He takes a deep breath. "I know you've got your own freedom going on there, but I don't want to face him alone."

Unease must show on my face, because Leticia brushes her knuckles against my knee.

You good? she mouths. I nod to her.

"Yeah, okay, I can come to lunch," I finally say. I don't want to see Dad anytime sooner than I need to, but I have to make an exception. Because my brother has never needed me before. Because I didn't know I made anything easier for anyone.

Jorge exhales loudly. It pinches my chest. "Thank you, Vale. Thank you."

"Of course," I say, wanting him to know I mean it.

"And you can invite a friend if you'd like," he adds. "Like the girl you're flirting with right now."

I snort. "Like she'd want to go." The words themselves wouldn't have clued Leticia in, but I look up at her right as I say them, drawing that confused grin back to her face. "All right, Jorge, I gotta go. I'll talk to you Wednesday."

We hang up and I pretend to be fascinated by my phone's wallpaper, which is Matteo clutching a massive blow-up soccer ball. Leticia clears her throat.

"So where do I not want to go?" she asks, batting her lashes. I don't know how I never noticed how pretty her eyes are before this summer. Rich, dark brown, and almost too big for her face.

"Huh?" I ask, after I realize I've been staring.

The corner of her mouth twitches. "Where. Do. I. Not. Want. To. Go?"

"How do you know I was talking about you?" I ask. She gives me a look. "Fine, whatever. My brother asked me to come to lunch with him, our baby brother, and our dad on Wednesday. I'm playing peacekeeper. Or bulletproof vest." I shrug. "I'll be there in solidarity. He said I could invite you."

Her mouth curves wider. "Did you tell your brother about me?"

"He already knows who you are," I say. When she looks more smug, I correct myself. "He knows vaguely about me having a rival on our rival team. Don't get so excited."

"Wouldn't dream of it," she says without dropping her smile one bit. "So what time are we going?"

"Excuse me?"

"Oh I'm sorry, do I need a formal invitation from you?" she teases. "I can wait for you to ask me properly. It can be like a promposal."

"You don't want to come to my family lunch."

"I do."

"You really don't."

"How else am I supposed to disprove your theory that you're like your dad?" she asks, crossing her arms. "Plus, you basically invited me to meet him at the beach last weekend."

"That was a figure of speech."

She rolls her eyes. "So are you uninviting me?"

I pause, trying to read her expression. "Do you actually want to come?"

"Do *you* want me to?" she asks casually.

Inexplicably, I find that I do want her there. I want to see her play with Matteo and deadpan with Jorge and silently judge my dad. If nothing else, the idea of spending more time with her, time outside of things specific to soccer and our team, gives me a warm feeling I refuse to look further into.

"I guess," I reply.

"Then I guess I'll come," she replies in the same apathetic tone.

I uncap my Gatorade again. "I'll text you the details when I have them."

She copies my movement. "Okay."

My eyes find hers as we both drink. And though it's hard to do while guzzling Gatorade, I notice both of us are smiling, small and gently. Like we have a secret neither is ready to share.

TWENTY-NINE

DAYS LATER, I FINISH TEXTING LETICIA the details for tomorrow's lunch with my family, which still feels surreal, and swing open the cabin door, hoping to squeeze a quick shower in before my dinner shift starts.

Dina and Ovie are hugging each other tightly in the middle of the cabin, peppering kisses on each other's faces. It's not an unusual sight, but the shininess in their eyes is.

They separate when they hear me come in and Dina waves her phone around, laughing in disbelief. "Long Beach's coach just called! They want me to have an overnight visit when camp is over, before school starts. He mentioned they're short on wings, so they'd love to see how I play with the girls." She starts squealing and throws her hands in the air. "Go Beach, bitches!"

"Holy shit, D, that's awesome," I say. After the weirdness of the other night, we've mostly avoided each other, but this news seems to warrant a ceasefire. I step forward to hug her but we pause, both noticing how sweaty I am at the same time.

"Oh, what the hell," she says, and pulls me into a hug.

Ovie kisses her long and hard when we step apart. "I'm so proud of you, babe."

I shield my eyes, but Dina smacks my hands away. "Get used to this because we're going to be spending the rest of summer celebrating me and my girl taking the SoCal soccer scene by storm," Dina cheers, picking up Ovie and spinning her in a circle.

Dina's been working toward this forever, and Long Beach is one of her dream schools. If this all works out, she can play soccer on scholarship, major in chemistry, and be close to her big Thai family. Everything she deserves.

Plus, Ovie's already set for Pepperdine's team and kinesiology program, so they'll both be local-ish to home, close enough to make long distance work as they follow their dreams.

They've secured the next steps in their incredible futures. I couldn't be happier for them. And yet the next thing out of my mouth is, "So are you still trying to win the tournament then?"

Dina freezes, then lowers Ovie. "Why?" she asks.

I swallow. "Well, you're one of the top teams now, but you don't need to impress the scouts anymore. And my team is just getting up there so—"

"Seriously, Vale?" Dina scoffs. "You can't go five minutes without making this about you?"

"No, I didn't mean—"

"You never do, do you?" she interrupts, crossing her arms. "It's like you're just programmed to turn *everything* into some contest you have to win. Something amazing happens to me, and you immediately start to wonder what that means for you."

I open my mouth to try to say something to take it back, to tell her I'm proud and know how much this means to her, how hard she's practiced and played for years to make this happen, how sorry I am that I keep doing this to her, but the words are lodged in my throat. I'm choking on equal parts guilt and regret.

"Whatever," Dina says, shaking her head. "Not that it's any of your business, but we're still going to play our best for the rest of the summer. Some of us play soccer because we like it, not just to boost our already massive egos."

With that, she storms out of the cabin.

I dare a glance at Ovie, who is focused on the floor. "You can go after her," I say. Knowing Ovie, she'll feel guilty picking sides, but she should be with Dina right now.

"I don't need your permission, captain," she says sharply, then looks surprised by her own words. "She's probably calling her parents. Or cooling off," she adds, softer.

I sit down on the bunk below mine. "I'm not trying to be like this."

She taps the toe of her sneaker against the floor. "Doesn't really matter if you're trying to or not when you keep knocking her down. Being our captain for a year doesn't give you the right to do that."

"Did your mom tell you?" I ask suddenly. Coach isn't one for gossip, especially when it comes to our private business, but Dina and I are two of the closest people in Ovie's life. I don't know if I'd blame her for sharing the news about our potentially shifting captain positions.

Ovie shakes her head. "She's booting you from being captain though, right?"

I nod. "How'd you guess?"

Ovie joins me on the bed. "I know my mom. She cares, but she isn't a pushover. And I know you. Since playoffs you've been more intense than usual. Which is sorta saying something."

"I just—I can't lose this," I say, hoping she knows what I mean. Soccer. Success. Doing one thing in my life at least marginally right. Since Mami died, the only thing I ever felt like I could control was how I play soccer. If I lose being captain and lose the tournament, what does that say about me? That the skill everyone attributes as my greatest still isn't good enough to secure a modicum of a future? That it doesn't matter how hard I try, I can't do anything to affect how my life will unfold?

"I know." She stands, moving for the door. "But in the meantime, you might lose us."

THIRTY

"SO IS THERE ANYTHING I SHOULD know before we head into the lion's den?" Leticia asks me Wednesday afternoon as we wait for our rideshare driver in the camp parking lot. I know we're standing a ridiculous distance apart, but when she walked out of her cabin smelling like citrus, wearing mascara and winged eyeliner, I think part of my brain short-circuited and distance is the only thing helping me regain consciousness. "Your dad's name? Favorite team? Messi or Ronaldo? Favorite color?"

I roll my eyes at the last one. "Jack, he goes hard for Irish and Colombian national teams on principle, LAFC over Galaxy—I don't agree, but that's neither here nor there—Ronaldo, anything but green." She gives me a sly look. "Apparently there were a lot of last-name jokes growing up."

"Who would ever make a joke about someone's last name?" she gasps. "What about stuff with you? Anything I'm not supposed to mention?"

I know what she's actually asking. "He knows I'm queer.

It's not his favorite thing about me, but it's not his least favorite either. Though I think he secretly hopes because I technically can like any gender, I'll happen to end up with a man."

"And what's the likelihood of that?" she asks, as if her looking the way she does right now isn't playing any role in who or what I might be into.

"Low, but not just because I think I lean more toward non-men." She waves me on. "Romantic relationships and I don't have the best history. Or any, really."

"Oh right, we covered this in the rain shed. Speaking of, am I ever getting my jacket back?"

"Oh look! There's our ride," I say, quickly jogging over. "Don't want to be late!"

Jorge picked out the restaurant, an innocuous diner off the side of the highway. He's definitely appealing to Dad's disinterest in food with any seasoning more flavorful than salt on it. The two of them and Matteo are already seated in a booth when Leticia and I step inside.

Dad looks up at us and I freeze, suddenly realizing this isn't some hypothetical, noble plan for my brother anymore. This is actually happening.

I didn't realize what a chokehold his presence has on me until now. The pressure is suffocating, but all he's done is glance at me. I've been away for long enough that my body forgot how to pretend this level of anxiety around him is normal.

Matteo springing out of his seat and running toward me,

screaming my name, is the only thing that gets me moving. I meet him halfway and scoop him into my arms.

"You're here!" he shouts joyfully.

"So are you!" I shout back, playfully mirroring his voice. "And you got bigger! What are you, seven now?"

He pouts as I set him back down. "No, solamente tengo cinco a—" He stops, noticing Leticia behind me. "¿Quién es?"

"Matteo," Dad calls from the table, prounouncing his name as *Muh*-teo instead of *Mah*-teo. "It's not polite to speak a different language when meeting someone new. She can't understand you."

Leticia takes a deep breath. I pray for her patience.

She steps around me and sticks a hand out to Matteo. "Hola, soy Leticia. Soy una amiga de tu hermana."

Matteo smiles at her, wide and toothy. "Hola, Leticia. Me llamo Matteo."

"Yo sé," she tells him, and winks.

Dad's frowning, but quiet. Maybe I'm here to protect Jorge, but I get the feeling Leticia is here to protect all of us.

We join them at the booth, Leticia and I sliding in beside Jorge while Dad and Matteo sit opposite us.

"How was the drive?" I ask, tugging my hands into my lap so I don't tear at my paper napkin. Matteo helps when he steals it for doodling with his pack of crayons.

"Long," Dad says, but there is more humor in his voice than usual.

"Pretty," Jorge says, nudging me slightly. When Dad isn't looking, he mouths, *Thank you for coming.* I nod.

"So, Valentina, are you going to introduce us to your friend?" Dad says, looking pointedly at Leticia.

"Oh, I'm sorry," Leticia starts before I can speak. "I didn't know you didn't understand Spanish." She reaches a hand across the table. "I'm Leticia. I'm co-captaining Valentina's team with her this summer."

Dad ignores Leticia's dig at his Spanish. He already knows who she is, and he obviously heard and understood her introduction to Matteo. He just didn't like not getting one himself. "Right, of course. You're an incredible player. Obviously I hate to see my daughter lose, but I understand why she does so often when she's playing against you."

My hands ball into fists. Just then, the waitress comes over to take our orders. Matteo gets chicken nuggets, Dad gets a steak, I get a chicken sandwich, and both Jorge and Leticia order veggie burgers.

"You don't need to order something cheap," Dad says to Leticia while the waitress is still standing next to us, even though her veggie burger costs two dollars more than my chicken sandwich. "It's my treat. Get a steak, if you'd like."

Leticia smiles, but I know enough about her by now to recognize this one as fake. "Thank you, sir." Then to the waitress, "I'm okay with the veggie burger."

Dad reaches out to stop the waitress again. "No, please, I insis—"

"She's vegetarian, Dad," I say. It doesn't feel like me who says it, but it must've been, because suddenly he's looking at me like he forgot I was even there.

But Leticia is looking at me with a different kind of wonder. "I never told you that."

"You never get meat in the caf. I put two and two together," I reply, unsure of when I even had this realization. Maybe it was just another detail about her I stored away without thinking much of it.

"Speaking of, how has working in the cafeteria been?" Jorge asks while Leticia sets the waitress free.

"Tough, but not bad. Some of the girls are rude, but it's nothing I haven't dealt with at the restaurant before," I tell him, relishing having a normal conversation with my brother.

Dad, of course, has to put a stop to it. "So, Leticia, do you have any ideas about where you'll be applying for college? With a track record like yours at a nice private school, I'm sure you've got plenty of options. Maybe you can help Valentina figure out where she might manage to get in."

The waitress comes back just in time to place waters in front of each of us. I assume Leticia will drop it and try talking about something else, maybe rope Matteo back into the conversation, but instead she takes a sip of water and smiles. "I bet Valentina will have plenty of choices."

"Surely not as many as you," he says sweetly. But I can tell he's losing some of his patience. "Don't get me wrong, of course I'm proud of her." It guts me that this is one of the few times I've heard him say that, and that I already know what's coming next. "But you know as well as I do that she had a bit of a disappointing season, so offers may be hard to come by."

"Weren't you undefeated?" Jorge interjects, only looking at me. I nod, but can't otherwise speak.

"Until Leticia's team beat them," Dad adds, his voice still so forcefully, fraudulently cheery. "That's my point here. Not that Valentina is a bad player, no, of course not, but that some players, like Leticia, are simply bett—"

"Your daughter is one of the best players I've ever seen," Leticia loudly interrupts.

The table goes silent.

Dad clears his throat. "Well, that's nice of you to think that," he says patronizingly.

"It really isn't," Leticia replies. "I'm just being honest. Trust me, it would be way more convenient for me if she sucked, but she doesn't. Playing against her always lives up to my high expectations, it's never been easy. I used to wish Valentina would disappoint me in a game, but I've yet to see it."

Dad's smile is strained, but smug. "Not even in the games your team has lost this summer? I hear you've been having a bit of a rough time."

Leticia presses her knee against mine under the table. "You can't win them all."

"What about when she fouled you at the end of the school year?" He tilts his head. "Surely that was disappointing."

Leticia shrugs and takes a sip of her water. I decide to follow her lead, feeling parched suddenly. "No. It was kind of hot."

I choke, a small burst of water escaping my mouth.

Dad's face is incredulous. "Pardon me?" he asks, while Jorge smacks my back.

Leticia smiles slowly. "I said it was kind of *not.* As in *not* disappointing. Sorry, I should learn to enunciate better." She turns to me. "You okay?"

I barely manage a nod.

Dad grimaces. He knows bullshit when he sees it, but he also knows when he's losing a fight, even if it's a rare occasion. "Right, of course."

I'm still having trouble catching my breath, which feels like it has less to do with choking on my water, and more to do with how pleased Leticia looks beside me, our legs still touching.

I don't even register the awkward silence until Jorge clears his throat. "So, Matteo, what are you drawing there, buddy?"

Matteo lifts the napkin up, showing us a blob of orange and black. "It's Leticia!"

Leticia holds back a laugh, voice pitched high by her amusement. "Wow, I look so beautiful. Thanks, buddy."

"You're welcome," he says shyly, then loudly whispers to me, "I like her."

I smile at him, but look at Leticia as I reply. "Yeah, me too."

Dad pays the bill at the counter while the rest of us wait outside. But he made sure to flip the receipt up so everyone could see the cost first before he insisted it was his treat.

Leticia and Matteo are playing with a tiny soccer ball Matteo brought with him. She chases him comically slowly around the empty lot, exaggerating her movements whenever he tries to juke her out or steal the ball back.

Jorge sidles up beside me. "Sorry for the bullshit in there.

I didn't mean to subject you to that when I asked you to come."

"I know," I reply, still watching Leticia and Matteo. "It's not your fault."

He clears his throat. "You ever think Mami would've shut him down if she were still around? Put a stop to all of his shit sooner?"

I don't know why the sudden mention of Mami doesn't make me go stock-still like it usually does. Maybe because with Jorge, the loss is something precious we share, not something I'm showing to someone in the hopes they don't poke at or shatter it. "Maybe? He was like this before she died though, even if it wasn't as bad as it is now. I don't know."

He makes a noncommittal noise, but leaves it at that.

I loved my mom, but she was a person, she was flawed. I've wondered before, in a way I didn't dare to as a kid, why she was even with him in the first place. My memories of her are full of kindness, empathy, generosity. But she was also quiet, sometimes to the point of meekness. And as fucked as it may be, sometimes I think I've convinced myself that if a life with Dad was fine for her, it should be fine for me too. I only have one parent now. I don't know if I'm allowed to be picky about him.

I guess I'm still staring at Leticia and Matteo as I think this over, because Jorge adds, "Leticia is pretty cute, by the way."

"Sorry, she's gay."

He side-eyes me. "You don't say."

I roll my eyes. "Go get Matteo before he falls in love with her too."

"Oh, sorry, am *I* the one who fell in love with her first?" he asks, smirking.

I shove my brother away. He joins Matteo and Leticia as Dad steps out of the diner and approaches me.

"You two seem to have patched things up since your behavior at playoffs," Dad says, bringing up the fight for the second time in the past hour. "That's admirable of her."

"Whatever it takes to win, right?" I reply, forcing myself to look at him.

His hair is going gray a bit at the roots, and the skin around his eyes is creasing, but not too badly for a white guy. Must help that he doesn't smile much.

When he's not right in front of me, I perpetually imagine him the way he looked when Mami first died. It's only been four years, but the loss aged him. Physically, that is. I think in all other areas, it trapped him in time.

"Well, I'll see you in a few weeks," Dad says, and pulls me into a hug. It's quick and loose, but I relish the embrace like a starved stray would a scrap of food. Like I don't know when more will come.

My goodbyes to my brothers last longer. I ask Jorge to keep me updated on his summer and text me when he gets back to Abuelo's. And I promise Matteo that I'll call more often, avoiding Dad's eyes when I say it.

Jorge offers to drive us back to camp before heading inland

again, but I don't want to deal with him analyzing me and Leticia the whole time, so I insist I can just get another rideshare. After my family leaves, Leticia and I wait in a far quieter companionship than we did on our way out of camp.

"I'm sorry," she finally says.

"For what?"

She kicks at gravel. "For arguing with your dad. I hope he didn't take anything out on you."

"He didn't, but even if he had, it wouldn't be your fault," I tell her honestly. Then swallow, my mouth suddenly dry. "Actually, I wanted to thank you for what you said. No one has ever really defended me to him like that."

She nods, almost to herself instead of me. "You don't need to thank me. I said what I said because I mean it, and I didn't like the way he was talking about you."

I press my lips down on a smile. "What, you're the only one who's allowed to talk shit about me?"

She rolls her eyes. "That's different."

"How?"

A pause, and her expression drops from teasing to tense. "You know how."

I feel bolder. "So you meant what you said? All of it?"

It was kind of hot.

She doesn't say anything; she just nods.

A car honks at us. Leticia and I spring back. I didn't even realize we'd both been leaning in.

A grown white woman with faded red hair leans out the

window. "Are you Valentina?" I notice the rideshare sticker on her windshield, and the license plate matches the one on my phone.

"That's me," I say, regretfully, and get in the back seat with Leticia.

Whatever was happening outside the diner dissipates in the ride, as our driver tells us all about her daughter winning prom queen last spring. We nod along, pretending we're listening. And pretending not to notice every time our knees bump together and we leave them there, touching for a few seconds before retreating.

THIRTY-ONE

IT'S BEEN A WEEK OF MORE intense practices and avoiding Dina and Ovie at all costs. Work keeps me out late, so they're both asleep by the time I get home. And I get up early to meet with Leticia, taking to dribbling balls while we run—which she just *loves*—and playing one-on-one when we finish. It's the best I've felt physically in years, but emotions are still fluctuating at every turn.

I encounter Leticia and Marley on their way into the caf on Friday morning. Leticia looks like she just rolled out of bed, curls a mess and face still sleepily swollen. It's unfair how sloppy still looks pretty on her. Marley, on the other hand, is the face of excitement, stripes of purple painted on her cheeks. She's been working her ass off this week, practicing in the goal with anyone and everyone who has the spare time. It doesn't seem like regular enthusiasm flooding her system anymore. I recognize it as the same hype I feel before a game I feel confident about.

"Think we'll finally get lucky this week and go against the Angels?" Leticia asks us as I swipe at a fly buzzing around my face.

"Lucky?" Marley says, confidence visibly dwindling. "They're undefeated; why would you want to play against them?"

"Simple." Leticia opens the door for us with an elaborate wave. "End that streak."

"Your teams have a pesky habit of doing that," I reply.

She smirks as we all take a seat with the rest of the team, who are already chowing down on their breakfasts. I barely get a few words in with Anita about her difficulty shooting at the right side of the net with her dominant foot when Lola enters the caf and pins the game schedule to the board. The chaos has died down each week, but seems to be picking up again as we move past the midway point of the summer.

"I'll go check," Kiko offers, jumping up with Natalia and Anita on her heels.

"Well, we know we can't be playing the Daisies, Clovers, Scarlet Fevers, or Cheetos," Leticia counts off on her fingers. "That leaves the Angels, Razzberries, and—"

"Nightmares," Anita finishes for her, Natalia and Kiko behind her. "Also, there was an announcement about another campfire party during week seven, the night before the final qualifying games."

"Party later, game first," I say, but I make a mental note to ask for that night off from work. "When do we play today?"

Anita sits back down. "Last game of the day."

"Sweet," Claire says, pulling out her phone.

"Boyfriend duties?" Kiko teases as she takes her seat and stabs at her eggs. Anita and Hayley start *Ooh*ing. Claire cringes.

"Hey, maybe we can watch some of the other games together as a team." I change the subject. "It'll help us prepare to play against the Angels and Razzberries."

"Sounds good to me!" Marley says, then her stomach lets out a deep growl. "Late game means not worrying about getting sick after a big breakfast for once." She leaves to get in line with some of the other girls.

I move to follow them too, but Leticia grabs my wrist and pulls me away.

"Where am I being taken?" I ask, but don't fight her. I've learned to pick my battles. Plus, I don't exactly hate the way it feels to have her hand on me.

"I need to double-check something."

"And that requires possession of my arm?"

She ignores me and heads toward the bulletin board. Her eyes scan the paper quickly. "I was right."

"About?" I look over her shoulder at the schedule, but don't notice anything glaring.

"We're tied with the Daisies and Scarlet Fevers for points right now, right?" she asks. I nod. "Well, look who's playing against each other this week."

My eyes find their names immediately this time. "Oh shit."

"Yeah," she says, laughing. "If we win today, we've got one less team to worry about competing against for that final game spot. We've already played both of them, so that just leaves—"

"The Razzberries and the Angels," I finish for her. "The only teams we've yet to play against. Wow."

"Right?" Her eyes drift down to her hand. We notice at the same time she's still holding my wrist.

We spring apart. "Okay, we just have to beat the Nightmares this week, then the Angels and Razzberries in the next two," I say. "No problem."

"You look ready to pass out."

"No, no, I'm great," I lie. Leticia sees right through it. "I just might need to sit down. And use an oxygen tank."

She grabs my wrist again and pulls me through the kitchen door.

"This is for employees only," I argue, but it's half-assed as I run out of air. My mind is whirring, already overwhelmed by the seemingly impossible challenge of winning three more games. Three more games against teams that are probably better prepared than we are, with players who haven't been playing catch-up all summer, with a co-captain who doesn't panic about their games every week.

"You're an employee," Leticia says, stepping around my coworker Eli washing dishes. They don't even bat an eye at us until Leticia turns back around and points. "Got any lemons back here?"

Dizzily, I watch Eli nod toward a crate in the corner of the room. Leticia drags me over, grabs a lemon, and bites into the skin.

"That's—not very sanitary," I say with difficulty, pressing a hand against my collapsing chest. My lungs squeeze. I try to focus on her scrunched-up expression as anxiety pounds the inside of my skull in time with my racing heart. Three more games, three more games, three more games. Losing any of them means we're done.

She spits the chunk of peel into her palm and then shoves the lemon in my face. "Bite it."

I try to take a deep breath, but the air scrapes like sandpaper and my skin feels too tight. All I can manage is shaking my head.

"I don't have cooties. Just trust me."

For some ridiculous reason I already do, and my brain is too cluttered to argue further, so I lean in, biting the exposed flesh. Immediately, my entire face pinches at the spark of sourness, a punch to my tastebuds.

"Blegh." I step back, wiping my forearm over my mouth. "That was disgusting, what the fuck?"

"Please don't vomit in the kitchen!" Eli yells from across the room. Leticia waves them off.

"Was this a prank or what?" I say as my tongue curls in on itself. "Because congrats, that was incredibly unpleasant."

Leticia rips a paper towel off a spare roll lying on the counter and hands it to me. I use it to rub the sourness off. "You're not panicking anymore," she says matter-of-factly.

I freeze. She's right. "How'd you do that?"

She tosses the lemon into the trash. "Old trick my mom mentioned once. Some therapists recommend patients with anxiety disorders eat sour candy when they feel an attack coming on. Something about the aggressive sourness takes over your instincts and can knock you out of the feeling. Holding an ice cube in your hand can work too."

"I've never heard of that."

She hesitates for a second, poking at the crate of remaining lemons. "That day by the bathrooms before our second game, were you having an anxiety attack?"

I pick at the paper towel. "Maybe? I just get shaky and out of breath like that sometimes. It happened occasionally when I was a kid, like when my mom first got diagnosed, but it's gotten worse over the years."

"That makes sense," she says, reminding me that she's met my dad already. "Well, I'm definitely not a therapist or anything, but you can talk to me about it sometime. If you want, or whatever."

"Thanks," I say softly. She nods.

I don't realize we're staring at each other until two pots loudly clang together.

"Vale!" Eli shouts. "Either put on an apron and clock in or go away."

"Sorry, we're leaving!"

They nod as Leticia and I go. I can't decide whether or not I'm grateful for the interruption.

THIRTY-TWO

WE WATCH THE ANGELS VS. RAZZBERRIES game before our own. The Angels win, which isn't a big surprise to me or anyone else. But it means their undefeated streak lives to see another day. The Razzberries put up a good fight though; the score was close until the end. A last-minute cross between Sophie and Kaylee saved the game from going to penalties.

Overall, both teams are killer. Either one we play next week will be a challenge, even with the insight Marley noted about Kaylee and Sophie almost always shooting in the left corner and Rani's point that Cate is easily their best defender. I try not to panic over whether or not we'll be able to handle them, at least not yet. Before we even get to weeks six and seven, we still have a game to win today.

The Nightmares are living up to their name.

For a team that's only won one game so far, you'd think they'd be easier to beat. But their offense is relentless, putting more pressure on Marley, Bethany, Claire, Rani, and Natalia than they're used to. Kiko and I drop back to help beef up the security, but it leaves Anita on her own to help out offense.

"We need to start scoring," I say to Kiko in passing as Marley sets up a goal kick. "You want to push up or hang back?"

"You go up, I'll hang back."

I dart away from her and the black uniforms surrounding us, finding a wedge of free space, and shout for Marley.

She sends the ball my way, an imperfect but much improved kick. I'm smiling as I receive it and move toward the Nightmares' goal.

I pass to Hayley, who narrowly dips around a Nightmare and gets it up to Leticia on the sideline. Someone's marking her closely, sidling up against her and forcing her down the line. I race to match their pace, hoping I can open myself in time before Leticia either loses the ball to the sideline or the Nightmare.

Luckily, she glances up and passes to me just before she would've crossed out of bounds.

I'm fast enough to get around the Nightmare defense and take a clear shot. No Princesses shout that they're open, so I go for it. The ball just barely slides past the keeper, giving us our first goal of the game.

I'm distracted by the thrill of scoring, cheering, and hugging Hayley, so it's only when Juanita blows her whistle and runs over to a crumpled figure on the other side of the field that I notice Leticia is down.

We're supposed to take a knee but I sprint over in a second, nearly pushing Juanita out of the way.

I drop down beside her, my eyes rushing over her body. "What's wrong? What happened?"

"Wrist," Leticia says, clutching her already injured hand to her chest. "That girl crashed into me as I passed the ball and my hand got squished between our bodies when we fell. I think I bent my wrist wrong." She attempts to flex her fingers and winces in pain. "Fuck."

I stand up. "Who was it? Who pushed her?"

"Valentina, it wasn't a foul," Juanita says calmly.

"Was it you?" I point to the nearest player in black. I should've been paying closer attention. She shakes her head quickly, looking to another girl beside her. "You?"

"Vale, it was an accident!" Anita calls from a few feet away, kneeling on the ground. "I saw the whole thing, they just fell into each other."

My eyes whirl back to the second girl. "So it *was* you." She opens her mouth but doesn't speak, confusion on her face. I take a step toward her. "You better hope you didn't h—" Something stops me.

Leticia's uninjured hand is wrapped around my ankle. "Princesa, look at me." My eyes shift from her hand to her face. "I'm okay."

She sits up, moving her hand a little more. Her next breath comes seething out between her teeth, but she manages to turn her wrist once.

"Leticia, we should have Nurse Wu look at that for you," Juanita says gently.

"We don't have any subs," Leticia says, like that has anything to do with her being injured. "I can play."

"No, you can't," I say, then turn to Juanita. "We can play down one girl."

"You and I both know we can't afford that," Leticia says, but I don't care that she's right. She stands up, brushing the grass off her shorts with her left hand. Girls around us clap politely.

"I can't let a girl play if she's injured," Juanita says gently. "It's a lawsuit waiting to happen, even if I didn't care about your health personally."

Leticia's eyes are ablaze. "I'm *good*, I promise. I'd sit out if I wasn't."

Juanita hesitates, then nods. She blows her whistle and moves toward the midfield line to start the game again.

Leticia walks past me, and now it's my turn to grab her, reaching for her shoulder. "If that doesn't heal properly, you're screwed for next year."

"Not giving my offensive skills much credit, now, are we?" She smiles. "Guess my trainer is a bit shit." I give her a look and her smile drops. "We've already lost two games. If we lose a third, we're kissing the final game in the tournament goodbye. Which means *you* would be screwed for next year." I open my mouth to protest, but Juanita is calling us over and the entire game is waiting. "Come on, Princesa, have a little faith." She winks and jogs off.

A few minutes later, the ball is back in play, but my thoughts aren't.

Bethany stops a Nightmare's shot, passing up to me. I receive the ball and run, trying to focus.

"Valentina!" Leticia calls, dodging the girl trying to mark her and giving me a perfect opening to pass.

I don't take it. I shift the opposite direction and pass to Gloria when she breaks away from a Nightmare. I get to the top of the box, but Anita is already open and has a better shot, so Gloria crosses it to her instead. Anita slams it past the goalie.

The two of them run toward each other for double high fives. A smile matching theirs takes over my face.

Until I turn to see Leticia frowning at me.

"What the hell?" she says. "I was open."

I look at her hand without meaning to. It swings by her side, fingers bent awkwardly like she's trying to keep her wrist as still as possible.

She rolls her eyes. "I don't shoot with my wrist."

I brush her off and walk toward midfield. "We scored, didn't we?"

Her gaze burns a hole in the back of my head the rest of the game.

We won. We're in the top three.

Marley made an incredible save in the final minutes of the game. Even though it wouldn't have cost us the win, seeing the look in her eyes—surprise, awe, joy—made it feel like she'd just saved the final penalty kick in a World Cup championship. I haven't been so happy to see someone catch a ball in years.

We talk briefly as a team after the game, but most of us

are starving, exhausted, disgusting, or a combination of all three, so I don't keep anyone long. Claire disappeared immediately, focused on her phone, giving me a small, knowing smile as she left.

I head straight for the showers, desperate to get the sweat off my skin and avoid anyone asking me questions I don't have answers to about some of my decisions post–Leticia's injury. Lucky for me, Marley dragged her off to Nurse Wu the second the game finished. But when I leave the showers, she's waiting for me outside the doors, leaning against the same tree she found me hyperventilating under weeks ago.

"Are you trying to walk me home?" I ask.

"Ew, no," Leticia says. She brushes splinters off her shorts, still in uniform. "But if you need me to protect you from getting mauled by a bear on your way back to your cabin, I suppose I could get the job done."

"There aren't really bears in this area."

"Okay, a turkey."

"I think I could take a turkey."

She steps closer and lifts up one of my washed arms like a limp noodle. I snatch it back.

"What I lack in upper body strength, I make up for in—"

"Sarcasm? A very hoodie-centered wardrobe? Horrible taste in Gatorade flavors?"

"You're lucky I'm not a violent turkey."

"And don't I know it."

When our laughter subsides, all that's left is a silence weighed down by the obvious words neither of us is saying.

"How's the wrist feeling?" I give in and motion to her hand, freshly wrapped.

She wiggles her fingers. "Just a little sore. Nurse Wu said I should ice and elevate it tonight, and keep an eye out for any swelling. But it doesn't seem like the sprain got any worse."

"Good, I'm glad," I say, then push myself. "What you did today . . . you didn't need to do that."

"What? Play spectacularly? Reinvent the game of soccer with my magical skill?" She grins. "It was nothing."

I roll my eyes, then blink away the faux annoyance. "You didn't need to keep playing with your wrist hurting."

Her eyes fall to her feet. "We couldn't risk the loss. I just did what anyone would do."

"But you did it for me." My heart starts pounding. "Team. Me team, *mi* team. Equipo. Spanglish brain fart."

The grin trickles back in. "Right."

"Thank you, that's all. For making sure this summer wasn't for nothing."

She pauses. "Is that what you think it'll be if we don't make it to that final game?"

I open my mouth to say *Yes, of course*. But then I slam it shut. Because the way she's looking at me right now, all dark eyes and dark curls and soft smile, it doesn't feel like nothing.

"No, you're right. This summer was great espionage for next year."

She laughs, dipping her head so her curls bounce around her face. "Of course. You've been an excellent spy. Really learned all my secrets."

"You've made the job pretty easy for me."

The silence returns, pulled taut. She breaks it this time. "So . . . that was interesting that you didn't pass to me for the rest of the game."

I start walking away, thinking maybe I can leave this behind if I do. "Thanks! I actually have to go call my dad, so—"

"Valentina—" She jogs after me. "If I say I'm good to play, I'm good. I don't need to be babied."

I face her. "Okay, won't happen again."

"All right." She nods. "Good."

I clear my throat and look down at my feet for about seven seconds before I can meet her eyes again. "Because if you get hurt like that again, I will drag you out of the game myself before I let you keep playing."

Her pupils seem to grow three sizes. "I'd like to see you try."

We're suddenly standing closer than we were seconds before. Against all better judgment, my eyes flicker to her mouth. Brownish-pink lips, defined and plump, creeping into a smile.

There are no rideshare drivers out here, no shouting Eli, no distractions or excuses. It's just us.

I step back, nearly tripping on myself. "Well, thank you for protecting me from the turkeys and bears, but I think I can find my way home just fine from here."

Her head shakes just slightly, like she's leaving a trance. "Right, no problem. I just thought it would be unfortunate if you were mauled right as I started to not hate you a little bit."

"Leticia Ortiz, did you just confess that you're in love with me?"

She turns around and starts walking away, flipping me off over her shoulder in the process. "Goodnight, Valentina."

"The sun hasn't even set yet!" I shout, the ease with which I can tease her growing as the distance between us does.

She doesn't bring her finger down. But her arm wobbles as she walks away, her laughter shaking her body and echoing against the chirping crickets and faint sounds of girls chattering in the distance.

I walk home, only realizing once I'm right outside our cabin that I have no idea whether Dina and Ovie are already inside. Or what I would say if they were.

I flick on the light to see empty beds. They're probably getting dinner.

I wait for the relief I should be feeling to hit me. They were at the game earlier; they probably saw how I reacted to Leticia's injury. If we were still talking, if they were here, they would tease me nonstop about it. The fact that we aren't talking isn't great, but the fact that they aren't here to tease me should be.

So I don't know why I sit up for an hour, waiting for my friends to come home, like they could still somehow catch me and Leticia in the act. The act of what, I don't know. But by the time I crash, alone and unteased with my hand wrapped around her jacket that I've kept hidden under my pillow for weeks now, all I can think about is Leticia not totally hating me. And me wondering how I ever hated her.

THIRTY-THREE

LETICIA AND I RARELY SPOT PEOPLE when running through the hiking trails. Though Santa Cruz is popular for this sort of thing, ours are out of the way since they zigzag through the hills surrounding camp. Today, we hit the goldmine though.

Leticia doesn't initially notice the black lab yanking their owner over to us as we're taking a cooldown stroll during a decline, but when she does, something flips.

"Ohhhh, perrito!" she coos, immediately crouching to greet the dog. The owner, who looks around our age, maybe older, laughs and stops to catch her breath.

"Tú eres el más precioso, ¿sí? Oh, sí sí sí," Leticia continues.

She cups the dog's face and swings their ears back and forth, going gentler with her right hand. I haven't asked how her wrist feels since the postgame nurse visit. I'm more distracted by the fact that her voice has risen ten octaves and she's currently whispering to a puppy in Spanish.

"I don't think they can understand you," I tell her as I

crouch down and give the dog a few pats myself, adjusting their rainbow collar that's embroidered to say I LOVE MY MOM.

"All puppies speak Spanish," Leticia says, voice still sugary sweet. I feel like I'm hallucinating. Even with Matteo, she wasn't this cute. "Hablas español, ¿sí?"

"Well," the owner laughs from above. I almost forgot she was there. "She actually sorta does? Only because of my girlfriend."

"See?" Leticia says, glancing at me before focusing back on the dog. "¿Cómo te llamas?"

"Oh, I know this one," the owner says. "This is Hamlet. Her name is also courtesy of my girlfriend."

"Good name," I say, pretending like I remember a single thing about the play from English class. I barely step back in time to dodge Hamlet's tongue going for my cheek.

"Good taste in humans too," Leticia notes.

We let them pass, saying goodbye to Hamlet. And without agreeing to, we don't start running again when we reach the end of the steep bit.

"So you're a dog person," I note.

"Don't shoehorn me in anywhere," Leticia replies. Her arm swings at her side, almost brushing my hand. "My cat would be very hurt by your assessment."

"Does this cat have a name?"

She goes quiet, but keeps walking. I try to catch her eye, then realize she's intently avoiding it.

"Oh, how bad is it?"

"Just know that I got her when I was eleven, okay?"

"And we all know how bad your judgment was at eleven," I say without thinking. That catches her attention, but she looks confused. "Oh come on. That's when we met and you decided to despise my existence for no reason."

Her brows furrow and her head tilts to the side. "I'm sorry, are we rewriting history today?"

"I'm not rewriting anything," I say, taking a moment to retie my ponytail. "You hated me that first year."

She shakes her head incredulously. "No I didn't. I thought we were cool until next summer when it was clear *you* hated *me*."

My eyes bulge out of my head. "How were we cool? You ignored me ninety percent of the time!"

"You roll your eyes at half the things I say to you now," she says. "I was doing you a favor."

It takes a great deal of effort not to roll my eyes. "You practically ran away from me after our last game of the summer."

She flinches. "No, I—you caught me off guard, that's it."

"'That's it'?" I ask. "You acted like I was a nuisance, and then the next year it was like, I don't know."

"Like we were enemies," she finishes for me, looking lost in thought.

Parents are always invited to the final games of the summer, but most kids don't want theirs to come because it means less time to say goodbye to friends. Dad didn't care whether I wanted him there or not, he needed to see if camp had been worth the time and money. The only thing was, I didn't know he'd come.

We lost our final game, pretty badly too. But I was still cocooned in the comfort of a summer spent playing with my best and new friends, so it didn't faze me. Then after the game, I tried to help Leticia take her pulse when she was checking it in the wrong place, she reacted the way she did, I realized we weren't going to be friends, and Dad found me shortly after. I didn't get to properly say goodbye to anyone, let alone Leticia. The entire car ride home I was chewed out for playing so poorly after I was supposed to be improving.

I found out later from Jorge that Dad and Mami had been arguing about something before he'd come to get me, hence his intense reaction. Nowadays I wouldn't be surprised by it, but back then it was a shock to be yelled at that aggressively, one of the first times he really treated me as badly as he does now. I guess I associated that with Leticia.

The only reason I even got to go to camp the next summer was because Mami received a bonus the previous year and it was easier to have me out of the house as they dealt with newly born Matteo. But the real reason I wanted to go back was to make up for that shitty last day, to prove something to Dad or Leticia or myself.

And by the time I came home from that summer, Mami had the diagnosis.

Leticia pulls me out of my thoughts. "I wasn't the best at making friends as a kid."

"You were a jerk."

She scrunches her face. "I was *shy*. Being invited to go do things and talk with new people made me nervous."

"You do remember yelling at me multiple times in our games back then, right? That was basically the only time you did speak to me."

She gives me a look. "It's different on the field. You know that." I shrug in agreement. "But off the field, I didn't have soccer as a prop. Even now, do you see me crawling with friends?" She spins in a slow circle with her arms out. "There's a reason I jumped at the chance to spend so much time with Wendy."

She hasn't mentioned Wendy since the day I walked in on their call. I can't tell if that's a good or bad thing. "You have Marley, which still doesn't make sense to me."

She shoulders me and we keep moving. "Marley does most of the talking. Plus, it's not exactly hard to be her friend."

"Fair," I say, trying to keep my voice steady when our hands brush again.

"And I mean, she knows what it can be like here. Back home most people are cool with the non-cishet shit, but girls come to camp from around the state and not everyone is super excited to share a bathroom or cabin with a lesbian. Marley gets that in a slightly different way."

"It's sweet," I admit. "That y'all are there for each other like that." I know I've felt the same way with Dina and Ovie at times. "Though while we're talking about growing up, I just realized I've never asked you the most cliché of questions—and it's not 'Why do you play soccer?'"

Now it's her turn to roll her eyes at me. "Go on."

"How'd you know you weren't straight?" I ask. "It's an annoying question sometimes but—"

"But 'we live in a society,' and not everyone knows right away?" she finishes for me. "Nothing exciting for me. Thought I was straight as a kid, realized I had a crush on a girl when I was like twelve, chalked up the childhood to comp-het, and the rest is history." She shrugs. "I grew up with two moms and their gay college roommate's sperm donation to thank for my existence. 'Lesbian' was always a welcome word in my house."

The story suits Leticia. She's good at adjusting and reflecting. I'm not surprised it happened so simply for her, not because her life seems easy, but because she seems so capable of embracing change instead of fighting it.

"What about you?" she says, interrupting me waxing poetic in my head.

"Oh right." I collect myself. "Similarish story? I already had inklings, but then we did this trust exercise during a theater unit in eighth grade where we had to be blindfolded and let someone hold our hand as they led us around the room. I was supposed to be partnered with some boy, but he made a sarcastic joke about cooties, so the teacher swapped me to be with a girl. At the end of class, I recognized that I liked the intimacy of the hand-holding and would've regardless of my partner's gender. I also realized intimacy was different for me than other people." I hardly talk about being on the asexual spectrum with anyone, but it feels safe with her. "I didn't have the words for it yet, especially when the differences between romantic and sexual attraction came into play, but time and research helped me figure out the whole queer-ace thing."

"And staring at Sophie across a soccer field probably helped."

I shove her, sending us both stumbling into a tree. She catches herself, leaving me pushed up against her. I quickly move away, adjusting my shorts and shirt even though they're not out of place.

"So, you noticed the crush back then?" I ask her.

Leticia's eyes flicker across my face. She should be smirking right now, making this a joke, but she isn't. She's just looking at me. "It was kind of hard to miss."

I clear my throat and keep walking, hearing her follow me after a second. "Speaking of back then, does what we said earlier mean our entire rivalry was all in our heads?"

"Oh absolutely not," she laughs as she catches up to me. I like the way our strides align, her long legs taking smaller steps to match mine. "You're still a nightmare and I will be destroying you come next year."

"Okay, good." I swipe away an invisible line of sweat on my forehead. "Would really be a shame if I wasted all these years hating you for nothing."

"I can give you a few more reasons if you need some." She flicks at my bangs. "Would admitting I named my cat 'Punt' suffice?"

"Oh." I stop walking again. "You did not."

"I told you I was eleven! I just started learning how to be a goalie and thought it was cute."

I click my tongue and reach up to pat her on the cheek. "That's the dorkiest thing I've ever heard."

She swats me away. "Oh bite me."

"Maybe if you ask nicely," I reply without thinking.

She looks impressed, trying to hold back a grin. And failing miserably at it.

I busy myself with counting the trees in my line of vision. I feel less flustered once I get to seven. "Well, I guess it's just nice we haven't grown out of the rivalry."

She looks down at me, making a big show of the few inches of height separating us. "I don't think you've grown out of anything."

"Fuck you," I laugh. "I'm practically five-eight."

"On a good day, I bet."

I stick my tongue out at her. "Bad days too."

"And what's today?"

"What?"

She smiles sideways at me. "A good day or a bad day?"

I match her smile, feeling my heart pick up pace. "The absolute worst."

The first I really see of Dina and Ovie in days comes when they stop by for dinner on Tuesday night.

I nearly run into the back room to bribe Eli to switch stations with me, but the two of them have already spotted me and are headed for the counter. Plus, Eli hasn't let me forget about my and Leticia's lemon-biting ordeal, so I'd rather avoid them too.

"White or brown rice?" I ask Dina and Ovie when they step up with their trays.

"White, please," Ovie says, polite to the point of distant.

"Brown," Dina says neutrally.

I scoop both their servings in silence.

Marley follows behind them, giving the three of us a questioning glance.

"White or brown rice?" I ask her as Dina and Ovie walk down the line.

"What's going on with you three?" she asks, setting her tray down for me.

"Gossip isn't on the menu."

She frowns. "White rice."

"Excellent choice." I slide her tray back over and watch as she joins Dina and Ovie.

Once or twice, I catch the three of them looking over. And though none of their faces give anything away, I feel like I'm being dissected. Things are good with me and Marley, great even. But I think back to the horrible things I said about her to Sophie weeks ago. Suddenly all I can think about is any and every moment I've messed up with her, commenting on her dressing up for practice included, and then all of the ways I've messed up with Dina and Ovie lately too. It's a long, self-hating list that wraps around my throat and squeezes.

When Eli steps out to ask if the trays need refills, I offer to wash the dishes for the rest of the week if they take over serving. I can't handle being watched right now.

THIRTY-FOUR

I STEAL THE BALL FROM UNDER Leticia's feet for the third time in ten minutes. We've been practicing for half an hour since we let the girls break for lunch.

She's mastered keeping the ball away from one defender when staying in place or heading toward the goal, but when she has to double back and maneuver around the field to find someone who is open, she starts to trip up on herself.

"Come on." I pass her the ball. "Again."

"Why can't I just pass to you if I'm in a tricky spot?" she whines.

"I won't always be there to pass to." I put my hands on my hips and stretch back until I hear my spine crack.

"What if I ask you really, *really* nicely to always be open?" she asks, batting her eyes comically. It gets the effect across nonetheless.

"I'll do my best," I placate her. "But just in case, you should be working on this. There's a reason that girl on

Friday was able to drive you all the way down the line before she crashed into you."

She narrows her eyes, blowing hair out of her face. "I liked you better when you were all concerned about me being hurt."

"You never like me. Now don't let me get the ball."

She nods once, a frown still on her face, and starts moving.

But as soon as I get close to her, instead of shifting away from me like she's supposed to, she abandons the ball and scoops me up in her arms, tossing me over her shoulder.

"Leticia!" I smack her back as she clings to my waist and thighs. "This is not the drill!"

She shrugs, shifting me with the movement. "You said to not let you get the ball." She keeps walking off the field, carrying me without faltering.

"Is this your idea of a trust exercise?"

"Consider it weight lifting."

"I don't think they recommend that for people with sprained wrists."

"Oh good, we're going back to you being concerned about me."

All the blood is rushing to my head. Which is precisely what I'll blame for my hot face. I'm so exhausted from practice and work, I give in and sag my body. "Fine. I'm taking a nap."

"You're supposed to be annoyed with me, not fall asleep on me," she says, then drops me gently by our bags. We both take a seat and drink from our Gatorade bottles for a few minutes, catching our breaths.

After the tomfoolery, she's being suspiciously quiet. "You good?" I ask. She nods loosely, not meeting my eyes. I nudge her with my cleat. "What's up?"

"I'm mulling over your possibly correct assessment of my remaining flaws as a wing."

"Those were a lot of fancy words just to tell me I'm right."

"I'm concerned for your GPA if you think those were fancy words."

I move like I'm going to throw my Gatorade at her. Instead of flinching, she opens her mouth.

"Seriously?" I ask.

"What? The flavor is growing on me."

I put one hand under her chin and pour Gatorade into her mouth, waterfall-style.

She wipes her mouth. "Scared of my cooties?"

"You're not nearly as good at deflection as you think you are."

She groans and leans back on her uninjured hand. "It's been weeks and I'm still falling short as a wing."

"You're great at crossing, good at staying open, and—friendly reminder—you've only been at this position for a few weeks," I argue. "You're not going to be perfect."

"But I was in the goal."

"Aren't we feeling proud today?" I tease. She smiles slightly, but it doesn't stick.

"What am I going to do if fall rolls around and my wrist

still isn't the way it used to be?" She holds her wrapped wrist carefully with her left hand. "PT can only do so much."

I scoot closer. "On the small chance that happens, you keep training as a wing and wait for me to kick your ass when our teams play each other." This time when she smiles, it lasts for longer than a blink of an eye. I soak it in before it slips away again.

"And when my friends on my team see me as a mediocre wing and not the superstar goalie they knew before?" she asks softly.

I blow my wet bangs off my sweaty forehead, pretending to think about it. "I don't know. I guess they might have to like you for your personality?"

She smirks, tilting her head. "And what personality might that be?"

"I guess some people could possibly, in a certain light, see you as mildly funny. And the tiniest bit intelligent. I've seen one or two moments that could maybe convince a jury you're a good friend."

"Don't strain yourself with all that praise."

"Oh, don't worry, this is purely hypothetical," I say. "It's not like *I* could relate to any of those observations."

"Oh, of course not." She smiles, but it's not as full as it could be.

I bump her knee. "You're a good player, goalie or not. You work hard, you help out when your teammates are in a tough spot, you motivate others. Even if you're not the same player you were before, you're trying, and that's more than most people could say in your position. Your team back home will see that too."

Slowly, her smile grows. "Are these purely hypothetical observations too?"

"Absolutely," I lie.

She reaches her hand out for my yellow Gatorade. I relent and pass it over. "Man, look at how you're corrupting me. I used to hate this flavor."

"And now?" I ask, daring to meet her eye.

She licks her lips after taking another sip. "Hypothetically, I can see how some people could like it."

After running through the same drill a few more times, we find the girls in the caf, still not back from their lunch break. Kiko and Anita are laughing over something Marley is saying, but Rani spots us and freezes midbite.

"Having fun, ladies?" I ask as Leticia and I slide into seats at their table.

"We were just about to head back," Kiko claims, trying not to grin.

"Uh-huh." I wave it away and drop my head to the table. "You earned the break. We'll start up again in an hour or so."

Kiko pokes me. "Did someone replace Vale?"

"Ha ha," I say, my voice muffled.

Leticia slaps her palms on the table. "Well, since we're already here, I'm getting food. Princesa, you joining me?"

I turn my head and reach for her, exhaustion skewing my

voice to a whine. "Get me something? This table is so nice and cool. Good place for a nap. Better than your back."

At that last comment, I catch Kiko's glance to Anita, who just laughs and shakes her head. If I weren't already face-down, I would be now.

Leticia just pats my head. "Sure thing, Sleeping Beauty."

As she leaves, I sit up. Marley gives me a pointed look over her water, but I ignore her, only to find my eyes meeting Dina's and Ovie's across the room. They must have seen me with Leticia, because despite our fight, despite our weirdness, I see a ghost of a smile on each of their faces.

THIRTY-FIVE

WE KEEP TRAINING. HARDER, LONGER, TOUGHER. I didn't think it was possible to push ourselves more than we already have been, but we do.

More than once during the week, I catch girls working out outside of practice. Leticia and I run into Kiko and Hayley doing the same hiking trail as us one morning. Marley and Gloria practice penalty kicks together. Rani and Natalia swap defending on each other, building up offensive skills too as a result. Claire leaves practice early almost every day, but when I'm finishing up in the caf at night, sometimes I spot her and Anita outside her cabin, playing one-on-one games, using the trees as goalposts.

Of course, Leticia and I are not exempt from the increased training. But we meander more on our walks. Take more frequent breaks during our shooting drills. Get distracted when she's meant to be keeping the ball away from me. Accidentally, we end up talking about things that aren't soccer. College majors we'd possibly be interested in, food we miss eating back home, anecdotes about our families and friends. She's an only child who laments growing up without siblings, blaming this for her childhood shyness and blaming me being an eldest daughter for my controllingness.

My mind mulls over what we could be outside of camp, months from now when the team isn't forcing us together anymore. Disturbingly, I imagine us taking Matteo to the park, me and Leticia laughing over his goofy kicks and correcting him lightly between barbs while Jorge reads under a tree.

Suffice to say, it's been a long week.

But somehow none of us look or feel exhausted by Friday. And somehow, when we win our game against the Razzberries, I'm not surprised by the outcome.

It was a tight game, even after preparing ourselves by watching them last week against the Angels. They played dirty, hooking ankles and jutting their elbows out when going shoulder to shoulder for the ball. Miraculously, I bit my tongue and didn't sass the volunteer ref the entire game for not making the right calls.

We barely won, 2-1 score, but every goal came in the first half, so it was more about clinging to the lead than anything else. Staying tight on defense, falling back to protect instead of going for a demolishing glory. When the final whistle blew, I felt myself sag with relief, and something loosened in my chest. Caring makes it so much harder. It also makes the victories that much sweeter.

Someone suggests we go to the beach after the game

since it's still early enough that we'd be back long before sunset. Lola gives us her blessing when we ask for permission, completely missing that we're all cramming into Kiko's one car. What she doesn't know won't hurt her.

"All right, Tanaka here only fits eight, so two of you need to lap up," Kiko says once we've all showered, changed, and gathered back at her car. Only Claire didn't come, saying she needed to call her boyfriend. When the team started cracking jokes, I immediately diverted the topic to snacks and Claire mouthed a quick *Thank you* before running off.

"Did you seriously name your car after a *Haikyuu!!* character?" Anita laughs.

Kiko grins. "You're officially delegated to share a seat." Anita rolls her eyes, but gets in, pulling Natalia onto her lap.

Marley takes shotgun and Bethany declares that she deserves her own seat for enduring her hatred of sand so we have a legal adult, even though Lola let us go to the beach last time without one.

I don't care if I have to sit on someone's lap or vice versa. Until the only two people who aren't seated are me and Leticia.

She eyes me from head to toe. "I'll crush you."

"You're not that much taller than me."

"So you *want* me to sit in your lap?"

I push her forward. "Just get in the car."

We sit in the middle row, behind Marley. I try to keep myself very still as Kiko hits every single pothole, bump, and sharp turn these roads have to offer.

The tires bounce over roots bubbling under the road, sending me and Natalia flopping onto Rani in the middle seat. Leticia pulls me back into her lap by my waist, leaving one arm wrapped around it and the other resting on my knee.

"I think you missed one of those rocks back there, Kiko," Anita deadpans. "Do you want to drive back and run over it? I don't think Vale and Natalia were concussed enough."

"Oh hush," Kiko says to her via the rearview mirror. "I'm sorry, darlings!" she adds to me and Natalia. But the smirk on her face and the fact that Marley keeps trying to discreetly film Leticia clutching me in her lap tells me otherwise. I'm going to fight both of them.

When we get to the beach, I practically jump out of the car, embarrassed over the pools of sweat gathered where my and Leticia's skin were touching. She doesn't seem flustered at all though, getting out slowly and helping Hayley, Gloria, and Bethany free themselves from their cramped position in the way back.

I run into the ocean with Kiko and Marley before letting myself think about why seeing her unbothered bothers me so much.

After an hour of splashing around in the waves, some of us drift back to our towels, baking in the sun as salt water dries off our legs.

"Man, I miss going to the beach every day in the summer," Gloria says, wiggling contently. "My little brothers love it, and as long as I'm technically babysitting them, my parents don't mind us going."

"I miss getting ice cream at this little shop by my house," Marley adds, closing her eyes against the sunlight like she's picturing the taste. "I could eat their cotton-candy flavor every day for the rest of my life."

"You're going to make me crave the mangonadas with extra chamoy and Tajín I normally get on the corner by my house," Leticia says, falling back on her blanket. "What I'd give to be eating one right now."

"My sisters and I have little reading parties at the park by my house on summer weekends," Rani says softly from beside me. "We set up a picnic blanket with snacks from the store and just read under the trees for hours."

Then it's my turn, I guess, but I don't know what to say. I run a line through the sand with my finger. "Sounds like you've all got a lot you're missing from back home."

Bethany props up on her elbows from a few blankets down. Her heart-shaped sunglasses slide down the bridge of her wide nose. "I had a falling out with a bunch of friends at the end of the year, so I'm not missing shit. I'm glad I'm here surrounded by people I actually like instead of spending the summer before college all alone in my room."

"Yeah," Marley toes me playfully. "Cotton-candy flavored ice cream has nothing on our sweet victories."

I swat her away, barely registering Bethany's admission that she likes us. "That was so cheesy."

"She's right though," Rani says, sitting up straighter.

"Maybe I'll try adding soccer to the weekend plans now that I actually feel like a real player."

My heart pinches a little. "You do?" She nods, and I notice the other girls looking similarly proud.

"Same here," Bethany adds. "I'm hoping my college has intramural soccer. I've played on and off for a year with family and friends, but this is the first time I feel confident enough to actually sign up for something like that."

"That's . . . I'm glad," I say, voice strained. Because this team means something to them, what we've done here means something. And I wasn't prepared to know that.

"What about you though, Vale?" Gloria asks. "Have you been missing anything this summer?"

I look at each of them in the conversation, then to Natalia, Hayley, Anita, and Kiko having a splash fight in the waves. Then, as always, my eyes find Leticia's, warm and bright in the sunlight.

"Not really."

THIRTY-SIX

AFTER BASKING IN THE VAST HOPEFULNESS of our victory and beach celebration, this week's practices give me emotional whiplash. Half the team is pumped, thinking we've got our last qualifying game in the bag. The other half realized sometime over the weekend that the Angels are the team we're playing in said game.

The slowly developing optimist in me says we have a chance. If we could accomplish what we have so far this summer, there's nothing saying we can't beat the Angels. The veteran pessimist in me just laughs.

"You've got to watch those crosses, Rani!" I shout as Gloria gets the ball past her to Kiko. Marley catches Kiko's lazy shot. "And Kiko, it doesn't do anyone any favors to hold back in practice!"

"It does my burning lungs a few favors," she jokes, keeling over to catch her breath.

We've been going at it for days now, trying to keep the girls distracted with the hard work. Kiko's humor helps.

"I don't see why we're still doing this," Claire says from downfield. "It's not like we have a chance of winning on Friday. We've peaked already."

I sigh, having heard this argument for three days in a row now. Though Claire is being unusually stubborn about it today. "Practicing less wouldn't exactly help our odds then, would it?"

Claire huffs and turns away, but I think she knows I'm right.

We run through the play a few more times before breaking for a drink. Leticia jogs over to me and I pass her my Gatorade.

"We're losing them again," she says, reminding me of earlier this summer. She takes a sip and passes it back to me.

"We're a different team now."

Natalia and Gloria smile over a video from last week's game on Kiko's phone. Rani directs Marley toward the eyelash stuck on her cheek while discussing defense strategy. Anita braids Hayley's hair back, using a tie from Bethany, and jokes about how much Hayley's throw-ins have improved.

They're tired and sweaty, sure. But they see the end to these means, most of them believing it's in our reach. They're an actual team now, friends even.

"Tell that to the nonbelievers," Leticia says, lightly turning my chin. I focus on what she's showing me—Claire viciously typing on her phone—and not the tingling sensation where her fingers brushed my skin, feather-light.

Claire's energy matches the scowl on Bethany's face and

the slight sag in Hayley's posture. They've been the most vocal about our rough chances, but I also overheard Natalia agreeing with Claire's pessimism at dinner yesterday.

"It's our job to keep them going even when they're ready to give up, right?" I ask Leticia. She, like me, seems to flip-flop in her confidence. We've been leaning on each other to maintain some balance of hope, letting the other have moments of panic when it's hard to keep believing.

"As long as the pushing is motivational, not draining," Leticia says, a warning in her voice.

"When have I ever been one to push?"

"Do you want an itemized list? I could do alphabetical order or chronological, your pick."

"Paying close attention to me, huh?"

"Shut up." She bumps my hip. "We've got this. Just because the Angels haven't lost yet doesn't mean it's impossible to beat them. Undefeated streaks don't last forever." She winks. "As you know."

"Cute." I bump her back. "Let's get back to work."

I'm the last to leave the caf after my shift ends. It's pitch black out, the surrounding mountains thick with shadowed trees that melt into the sky.

I tug off my hairnet, exhausted and desperately in need of a shower. I thought reeking of sweat and grass was bad, but fryer grease and dirty dish soap take the cake. I flinch at my own stench, then at the sniffling that echoes from one of the cabins tucked away in darkness.

"Hello?" I call, and step toward the noise, realizing how I've just fallen into being a cliché. Guess Dad's genes won out in dictating how I'd behave in a horror movie.

"It's just me," the voice says. I quickly recognize it as Claire's.

My eyes adjust to the dark and slowly process her outline. She's sitting on a bench outside her cabin wearing a baggy hoodie, wiping at her eyes and cheeks, which shine in the minimal moonlight.

"Oh shit, are you okay?" I walk over and sit beside her. Closer up, I can see her face is puffy and red. "Did something happen with—"

Her voice hitches as she speaks. "My boyfriend, yeah." My stomach plummets; I'm picturing the worst. It looks just like me, aged thirteen, hugging an unmoving Jorge while Dad punches a hole in the wall and a doctor threatens to call security.

Claire catches the terror in my eyes. "No, no, he's okay. Well, he's still in treatment. Nothing has worsened."

"So . . ."

She laughs bitterly, throwing up her hands. "He broke up with me on Friday, after the game. While you were all at the beach."

"Why?"

"He feels like he's holding me back. I thought maybe I'd been overwhelming him, calling every day and checking in. But he said it just makes him sad. We've been friends most our lives, before we even started dating, and I hate being away while he's going through this." She sighs shakily. "He's worried I'm shaping my whole life around him. And that if this round of treatment doesn't work, it'll break me."

I don't do this well. But I move closer and put an arm around her shoulder. She softens into the touch, but I go rigid with worry that I'm going to mess this up.

"I'm really sorry, Claire," I say.

"The ironic thing," she begins, shifting off me. I pull my arm back, following her lead. "—is that this summer is the closest I've gotten in forever to focusing on something other than him."

"Really?"

She nods, a whisper of a smile appearing on her face. "My parents made me sign up because they were worried about me spending too much time sulking around the hospital. I told them I'd go, but didn't expect to, like, actually try or care." She pulls at her sleeves. "But now I really give a shit about our team."

"Even if we don't have a chance at winning on Friday?" I tease lightly.

She snorts. "I guess I haven't been the biggest team player this week. It just felt like I'm losing two important things at once: him and the tournament."

"I didn't realize the team and our games meant so much to you."

"I don't think I did either." Her smile widens. "I love him more, of course, but you guys are up there."

And it strikes me as odd, that we're the thing that matters

to her, not soccer itself. I threw myself into soccer once Mami died, taking an already passionate love for the sport to something all-consuming. Worked my way up to varsity as a freshman, to center mid as a sophomore, to captain as a junior. Sure, my team hated me and my only friends remained the two I already had, who hardly knew anything about my home life other than the dead mom I never talked about. Sure, I drifted from Jorge and only bonded with Matteo over soccer. Sure, Dad and I became nothing more than an unofficial coach and player. But I was good at something I had control over. And if I couldn't have love—my mom's, my dad's, my peers'—well, at least I could have control.

But people like Claire and Marley, like our team in general, they like soccer because of how it makes them feel when they're playing. Not because of how it makes them feel all the time.

I look at the key in my hand. I know that nothing can truly heal cancer-related pain, but being alone doesn't help either. "There's leftover ice cream from tonight's dinner. It expires in two days, so I was going to toss it tomorrow. Want some?"

The tension leaves her shoulders. "That'd be really nice."

We head back toward the caf, Claire gently telling me about how she and her boyfriend first met and started dating. I don't even notice until an hour later, when I'm washing our empty bowls as Claire sleepily waits against one of the walls for me, that I'm not exhausted anymore. I feel good, but still like me.

THIRTY-SEVEN

THE NIGHT OF THE CAMPFIRE PARTY, I'm antsy my entire shift. It feels silly to be this excited to hang out with the same people I have all summer, but something about the idea of it being a *party* where we're hanging out as *friends*, instead of just as teammates, sets off butterflies in my stomach. Not that I'd ever admit that to anyone.

The kitchen is closing early and I already asked for the night off, leaving just Maria, one of my older coworkers, to finish up with the dishes. I'm hanging my apron when I hear her turn the corner, whispering into her phone.

"Yo sé, mija. Seras increíble. Lo siento, lo siento." She rubs at her forehead with a gloved hand, before peeling the glove off and tossing it on the floor. "Voy a verte en la mañana. Sí, sí. Bueno, besitos." She hangs up and her entire body droops, like a puppet whose strings have been cut.

"¿Usted está bien?" I ask, startling her. She grasps her chest before sighing when she realizes it's just me.

"You scared me," she says, then smiles, undoubtedly

because I've used "usted" with her again after she's told me several times I don't need to be so formal. But it feels important that she knows I respect her. "Sí, estoy bien. Mi hija tiene un concierto en la escuela esta noche pero no puedo asistir porque necesito lavar los platos del almuerzo y la cena."

"¿Alguien más puede hacerlo?" I ask. The staff is small, but surely someone else can come in to wash the dishes so she can go to her daughter's concert.

"Nadie." Her forced smile is tugged down by a clear desire to cry. "Está bien. No te preocupes."

She picks her discarded glove off the floor and moves to throw it out. Dad has come to every game I've played my entire life, except for the ones played here. But he's never attended any of Jorge's art shows. I can't tell which one of us is worse off for it.

What I wouldn't do for my dad to be as proud of me as Maria sounded on the phone. What I wouldn't do for my mom to be able to come see me play, just one more time.

"You should go," I tell her. "Puedo trabajar esta noche."

"Pero . . . la fiesta."

I wave it off. "No quiero ir," I lie.

She stares at me, her eyes beginning to water. She doesn't want to let me do this for her. I know the feeling.

"It's okay," I tell her. "Be with your daughter."

Her eyes are still wet, but her face crinkles into a brilliant smile. She envelops me in a hug, her papery skin warm and soft around me. I swallow the lump in my throat. Missing Mami stabs through my heart.

“Gracias, Valentina,” she says when she finally pulls back, still gripping my shoulders. “Tienes un corazón muy, muy fuerte.”

You have a very, very strong heart.

I'm grateful when she leaves, rushing to strip off her kitchen clothes. It would be too hard for me to ignore the tear falling down my cheek if she were to see it too.

I sing to myself as I rinse off another tray and add it to the stack. The cafeteria was all but empty last I checked, but dinner tonight was a self-serve salad station and most girls ate early to prep for the campfire, so I don't worry about anyone missing me out there.

“Do you take song requests?” a familiar voice calls from the other room. Wiping my hands quickly on the towel folded over the edge of my apron pocket, I step out to see Leticia leaning over the counter.

I've obviously seen her in non-soccer clothes before, but never like this.

Her lips are painted a red so dark, it's nearly black, which shines the way her damp curls do. Even in the shitty caf lighting, I can tell she's got glitter on her cheeks and eyes, with lashes so long their tips tap against her thick eyebrows as she blinks at me. She's decked out in ripped dark gray boyfriend jeans with matching silver chains dangling from her neck and belt loops, brushing against her thighs. It's tied together by her platform Doc Martens and a tight black tank top that shows off what her sports bra normally compresses.

"I can spin around if you'd like to get a better look," she says, startling me out of my staring.

"Hope you're not planning on going through airport security anytime soon," I reply, poorly trying to nudge away the shared knowledge that I was, in fact, blatantly checking her out.

Leticia smirks. She's letting me off the hook and wants me to know it. "Why aren't you getting ready for the campfire? Unless cafeteria chic is your style." She motions to my soggy apron. "You pull it off nicely, but Marley will probably throw a fit. She insisted I go all out, and I doubt you're exempt from that."

I jab my thumb behind me. "I have an entire day's worth of dishes to wash."

"What?" Her brows furrow, pushing down on her long lashes. "I thought you had tonight off for the party."

"I did," I say, looking down as I twist my towel. I hope I sound more aloof than I look. "I'm covering for someone else's shift. No big deal."

She looks at me with the same expression she throws my way when I cheer on Marley, or cover for Claire, or praise Kiko for a good play. It's less rare these days, but the tenderness in her eyes feels precious in a way I'm scared to examine closely.

I clear my throat, wanting to scare the look away. It makes me light-headed to be on the receiving end of it, an unspoken admiration I'm not used to. "Anyway, this is fortunate for you. I've been told I'm very seductive near campfire. Nearly impossible to resist me."

She presses her lips together. Her dark, shiny lips. "Is that so?"

"You might even start to not hate me a little bit."

"Not ever letting me live that one down, are you?"

"Maybe if I bring it up enough, the hatred will come back." I gasp. "Do I dare test the theory?"

When our mutual laughter settles, there's just me, already missing this conversation and the rush I get when we go back and forth like this, like when she crosses the ball to me, already knowing I'll be there. And there's her, thumbs in her pockets, staring at me like she's realizing how much she doesn't want that hatred to come back either.

Finally, "Well, as per usual, you're wrong."

"I'd ask about what, but I get the feeling you're about to tell me."

"Careful, being right about *that* doesn't negate being wrong about the other thing," she says. "You being stuck in the kitchen is actually deeply unfortunate for me." My lungs do a weird pause, like a ball just knocked the wind out of me. She pulls a hair tie off her wrist and starts gathering her curls into the world's shortest ponytail. She couldn't even tie it into one at the start of the summer. "Because I'm going to help you wash those dishes. And I'm not the only one." Before I can even reply, or even react for that matter, she turns around. "Hey, Marley!"

I lean over the counter to see Marley eating with Kiko, Anita, Claire, and Bethany. All of them are dressed up in various glittery tops or patterned pants, picking at salads.

"We need some help over here, hurry up with that food!"

Leticia shouts. Without question, they start scarfing down the last of their meals, the few other girls in the caf staring at them and us like we've lost it.

"What are you doing?" I ask Leticia.

She smiles wickedly at me. It looks different than it has for all the years I've known her, like I'm in on whatever joke she's telling, rather than the target of it. "Gathering some allies. You're going to the party."

I swallow back my gratitude, stepping into my father's skin. "You don't have to do that. I'm paid to be here. More importantly, I volunteered to do this tonight."

"And now we've volunteered too," she retorts, already moving around the counter to join me. "And don't worry, this isn't some deal or about me doing you any favors."

"So why help?" I ask, suspicious.

"Simple," she says, tucking a stray strand of hair behind my ear. As she walks backward into the kitchen, a single curl escapes her ponytail and I want to return the favor. "Need to test if your campfire theory is true. You know how much I love to prove you wrong."

I tell the team not to wait for me to change, but Leticia and Marley insist. My stomach goes haywire the way it does before a game as I swap out my caf gear and stare at the basic clothes I packed. Counting them in groups of seven won't help me here.

Marley, like the goddess she is, pops her head in after ten minutes. "You okay?" Her eyes are covered as she wanders in, feeling her way around.

"You can look. All you'll see is that I have no sense of fashion." I'm crouched on the floor in a sports bra and leggings, piles of Under Armour, hoodies, and running shorts spread across my lap.

"Oh, love, I know." She walks over, nudging the clothes aside, and pats me on the head. "I think I've got something that would work for you in my cabin. One sec."

She darts out, shouting to Leticia that she'll be right back.

"Knock knock?" Leticia calls to me as I wait.

"Come on in."

She finds me on the floor, surrounded by my athletic gear.

"Don't dress too fancy now, Princesa." She kicks one of my stray socks and sits on Ovie's bed.

"Not all of us packed for a fashion show."

She presses a hand to her chest. "Did you just call me a model? How you flatter me."

I throw the matching sock at her. "Keep it up and a cleat is coming your way next."

Then Marley bursts through the door, carrying clothes in her long arms. "Leticia, you're not supposed to be in here, you'll ruin the surprise!"

Leticia snorts. "This isn't our wedding day, Mars, what surprise?"

Marley winks. "You'll see." She pulls Leticia off the bed and starts pushing her out the door. "Give us ten minutes."

Once Leticia is gone, Marley gives me a long-sleeved black mesh top and forest-green, Dad-ish cargo pants that

I'm convinced will look hideous before I put them on. I feel a surge of fresh love for her as I turn away to change. Washing the dishes with me was a kindness I couldn't comprehend but could still convince my brain to attribute to team motivation and bonding. Loyalty to a captain, like the girls back home. But I can't excuse my way out of this generosity. She is just being a good friend.

Lucky for the both of us, we're roughly the same chest size. But the pants are too long on me, so I have to cuff them a few times over. She says this makes me look gayer, which we both agree is a good thing. I slip on my dirty black Converses.

"Are the shoes nonnegotiable?" Marley asks, a slight pinch to her face.

"Yes, but I'll indulge you in some mascara."

She squeals, pulling a tube out from her pocket and handing me a mirror to look at while she applies it. Allegedly it distracts the eye, but I still blink and flinch my way through the whole ordeal.

But as I stare at my reflection—thick brows, nearly black eyes and blacker hair, mole sitting below my normally scowling mouth—I wonder what the girls saw when they looked at me tonight. I wonder what Leticia will see when I step outside.

But more than anything else, I wonder what I'm seeing as I stare back at myself.

My hand and Leticia's brush lightly against each other as we walk. Marley pays it no mind, or pretends not to, as she tries to walk and take a selfie to send to her boyfriend at the same time. We hear the girls before we see them, noisy shadows against the blazing campfire. It looks like we're the last people here, minus Lola and Juanita, who promised to come and check on things every half hour.

"Thirsty?" I ask Leticia, needing to do something with my hands other than skim the edges of hers.

"Anything but yellow Gatorade."

Marley walks with me over to the table of drinks. I imagine someone will try to spike their punch or soda, but I'm not about to get thrown out of camp for a misdemeanor. I grab Leticia and myself each a can of Coke.

I turn around and Marley is gone, replaced by Sophie. "Oh hey."

"Hey," she says. With the fire behind her, her face is backlit, making it hard to read her expression. We haven't spoken since that weirdness the other day. "When I saw you washing dishes in the cafeteria earlier, I wasn't sure you were going to make it tonight."

"My team pulled through for me." I raise one of the sodas in the direction of my friends. Marley, who wandered her way back without me, is racing Kiko to see who can chug their Sprite faster.

Sophie scratches the back of her neck, eyes darting around the party. "How nice."

"You okay?" I ask, concerned despite her shittiness lately. The fire lights up her contorted face as she looks around.

Without meeting my eye, she nods. "Yeah. Yeah, I'm great. Um, have you seen Cate or Kaylee?"

"No, sorry. I just got here."

"If you see them, can you tell them to find me? Right away?"

I nod, but I can't help it. "Are you sure you're okay?"

Her mouth droops to a frown. "Yeah. Yeah, I have to—" She motions vaguely in the opposite direction and leaves, pushing girls out of her way.

Leticia walks over while I'm still watching Sophie stumble her way through the dark. "What was that about?"

I take a risk. "Nothing to get jealous over."

She rolls her eyes and takes the unopened Coke from my hand. "You wish." Her eyes stay trained on mine from over the rim of the can as she sips.

I look away from Leticia's fiery gaze to the real fire. But it lingers, as warm on my cheeks as the flames.

She watches me watch the other girls for a minute, and then I feel her hand brush against mine again. It's a gentle touch, almost unnoticeable, but my entire body freezes. I'm worried that if I move, I'll scare her off.

I guess missing a shot is better than never taking one at all.

My palm turns outward and my fingers slip through hers. Then we're holding hands, just like that. And it's everything, in a way few things can ever hope to be.

A light tug and I turn to her. She knocks her head to the

side—a question—motioning to the strip of path between the trees that would lead us away from the group. I give a nod, squeezing her hand, and pray for my sake that Dina and Ovie aren't watching us somewhere in the distance as I let Leticia guide me.

We walk in silence, the emptiness thick in comparison to the comfortable quiet we've descended into on our runs through these same paths over the past few weeks. When we come across a cluster of rocks, we sit down without speaking.

"So, it pains me to admit this, but it seems like you were right," she finally says. Her words should have shattered the quiet between us, something that felt so fragile just moments before. Instead, they feel like a gentle crack releasing the pressure.

I sip my soda, still unable to look at her. "About?"

She tugs on my hand again, the tiniest of movements. I look up at her, and she smiles just as subtly. "The thing about you by a fire."

Something loosens. Whatever anxiety that wouldn't let me enjoy this moments ago weakens. "Hmm, that's not ringing any bells. Could you be more specific?"

Her smile grows wider as she sets down her soda. "You know what? Come to think of it, I don't remember the details. It probably wasn't that important anyway."

"Sounded pretty important." I set mine down too.

"If only one of us could remember." She leans closer.

"If only." I lean closer.

Her now free hand comes up and softly brushes aside my bangs. "Hm, your bruise is all healed up."

"Disappointed?"

"No, I didn't expect it to still be there."

I swallow. "Then why'd you check?"

She drops my bangs and they flutter against my forehead, gentle as her voice. "I just needed an excuse to touch your face."

It's the easiest move I've ever made, natural and inevitable and reciprocated. We lean in at the same moment, our mouths a breath apart, our foreheads and noses touching lightly. Her hand cups my face, like it was always meant to, and our lips just graze each other's, sending a shiver up my spine.

I've never been a romantic about the idea of my first kiss, but I don't think anyone in the history of all time has had a better one than this.

I'm reaching up to bury my hands in her curls like I've never even dared to let myself dream of doing, when there's a sudden uproar of noise from afar.

We separate and turn toward the campfire. We glance back at the same time, the regret at moving apart clear on both of our faces. But the noise doesn't quiet, and soon I hear something that makes my stomach flip.

"Is that Valentina?" someone asks. The voices are far away and unclear, but my name trickles in and out of the crowd.

"We should—" Leticia starts.

"Yeah," I finish.

When we reach the fire again, everyone's eyes find me quickly. My anxiety ramps up to an all-time high as the chatter quiets, and I'd run for the trees if I could convince my legs to do anything but shake beneath me. I want Leticia to grab my hand and take me away from here, but she looks just as frozen in confusion as I am.

It's Marley's voice that breaks the silence as she marches toward us. "Do you really wish I wasn't on your team?"

"What?"

My eyes dart to the phone in her hand. Quickly, I notice that everyone else also has their phones open. On the nearest screen, I see my face from an awkward angle. It's not just an unflattering photo though, it's a video. One I have no recollection of taking.

Kiko steps up besides Marley. "How could you say that shit about us? After all the work we've put in and all your talk about our improvements?" She shakes her head, furious. "And you had the audacity to tell me you think I'm good enough to play back home, like you weren't lying through your teeth about believing in us the whole time."

Gloria appears beside her before I can reply, Hayley and Anita close behind. "We've been working our assess off for weeks. Sorry we don't measure up to whatever bullshit teams you normally play on."

"I don't—" My throat feels like it's collapsing. I'm surrounded by a mob of girls waiting for me to say something to fix whatever it is I did, but I have no idea where any of this is even coming from. "What are you guys talking about?"

Marley shoves her phone in my face and presses play on whatever video of me it seems everyone was sent.

The phone is filming from a weird angle, almost like it's in my lap but slightly off to the side. I come in and out of shot randomly, but slowly the camera is shifted my way. I'm so focused on the weirdness of it that I almost don't recognize what I'm saying.

"God, I still just can't believe what an absolute mess of a player Marley is. The girl couldn't score a goal to save her life, let alone dribble the ball for a consecutive five seconds without tripping over it. She's spent years at this camp and she's still *that* bad? It's practically an accomplishment to fail so spectacularly. The things I'd do to get her off my team . . ." My stomach turns at the look of sick relief on my face. The me in the video turns to her right, closer to the camera, but the video skips, because a second later, I'm facing forward again. "This one girl, Claire, left like five minutes into practice to go call her boyfriend, after already showing up late because they were talking. Like they're not some high school couple that'll break up in a few weeks when he gets bored of her being gone all summer." I look up to meet Claire's eyes as the video goes on, but she's turning into Kiko's protective arms. "Kiko has all this energy but doesn't know where to direct it other than cracking jokes no one cares about every five minutes when we're trying to focus. And you'd think Gloria has a fear of soccer balls the way she runs away every time one gets even remotely close—"

My ears start buzzing. Like my body is trying to protect me from hearing whatever it is I say next. It doesn't matter though, I suddenly remember it all.

Calling Bethany the worst shooter I've seen in years, blaming Anita for lazy passes my little brother could intercept, mercilessly berating Hayley for lifting her feet every time she did a throw-in. Rani's too shy to fight for the ball, so she might as well pass it to the other team if she wants to be so polite. Natalia hits the ball with her hand more than she manages to with her feet.

Every terrible thing I said about my teammates to Sophie weeks ago, here on-screen for everyone to see. Sophie isn't in it, of course, because she was never supposed to be. That must've been the plan the whole time.

It doesn't matter. Sophie pressed record, but I'm the one who opened my mouth. I'm the one that did this.

Finally, as my tirade is ending, the me in the video brushes back her bangs. It's a pointless detail to focus on, but I see my forehead is freshly bandaged up, since this was recorded the day I bruised it. I feel a blend of jealousy and sadness for this version of me who has no idea what further pain she'll endure and cause.

"Believe it or not, none of them are even close to being the worst person on the team. No, that title goes to Leticia. Not to be a bitch, but if she was going to sprain something, couldn't it have been her ankle? Or a bad break that would bench her for the whole year?" Leticia takes a step away from me. The space she occupied beside me goes cold, alongside the spot on my cheek where her hand was resting just minutes ago.

"If I wasn't so desperate to make it to that final game, I

would quit now and cut my losses," past me says. "With these embarrassments as my teammates, I'm never gonna have a shot at winning."

And then the video ends.

Whatever silence befell the campfire before is nothing compared to this. Slowly, a few whispers start trickling in. Phrases like "What a bitch" and "I can't believe she hates her team that much" slip in and out of my awareness. My eyes stay stuck on the girls in front of me. Leticia has joined them, standing beside Marley.

The grip my anxiety has on me is ironclad, but my regret is stronger. "I can explain—"

"Don't," Marley says. Her voice is hollow, bitter. There is no sweetness left. I took it all from her. "Just don't."

My voice, however, breaks. "Please, I didn't mea—"

"I can't believe you let me think you were actually proud of us," she interrupts, her words slicing through mine. "Proud of *me*."

My heart sinks to the bottom of my chest. "Marley—"

Kiko steps in front of her. "You've said enough. Let us *embarrassments* get out of your hair."

Kiko leads Marley away, and slowly the rest of the girls follow. I try to open my mouth, to protest against what they heard me say, promise that was weeks ago and I was wrong to say it even then. But I can't do it, my mouth and empty lungs won't let me.

Leticia hangs back, doing nothing but stare at me. With the flames flickering beside her, one eye is bright and full of reflected fire. The anguish on that side is plain to see. But the other side is cold, shadows melding over her features.

"Leticia?" Bethany calls over her shoulder. Natalia and Rani stall for a moment beside her.

I know what it's like to be stared down by Leticia Ortiz when she hates you, sees you as the enemy. But this isn't that, it's worse. Her anger now doesn't come from a place of hatred. It comes from a place of disappointment, the one thing she swore I'd never been.

Her shoulders sink. Just when I thought I already knew everything about her, I learn what she looks like when she's heartbroken.

And then she's gone, walking away with the rest of the team I let down.

No one else leaves the campfire, but it's obvious I'm not wanted here. I'm not sure I'm wanted anywhere.

Somehow, I make it back to our cabin. Ovie and Dina aren't inside, probably off somewhere in the forest making out, since I didn't see them by the fire. Not that they'd have come to my defense if they'd been there. Not that I'd deserve it.

I crawl into bed, still wearing Marley's clothing, the smell of ash clinging to every inch of fabric. My blankets aren't enough to warm me, so I reach under my pillow and feel for Mami's jacket. Leticia's is beside it. They're right here, but the safe places they represent are lost to me forever.

Choking on smoke and tears, I fall asleep.

THIRTY-EIGHT

I WAKE UP THE NEXT MORNING with a jolt. Ovie and Dina are in my face, clinging to the edge of my bed while standing on the one below it. I owe my bunkmate an apology for how we've used her bed all summer, but that's a long list to add to at the moment.

Ovie smiles apologetically. "We were going to let you sleep in, but it's nearly noon and you should eat something before your game." Dina drops down from the edge first.

I sit up, rubbing my eyes, which've crusted over with dried tears. I must look like a mess, but it can't compete with how I feel. By the time my vision clears, my friends are sitting on Ovie's bunk and staring up at me. "What time does my team play?"

"Not until two," Ovie says. My body relaxes, but theirs don't.

"I guess you guys saw it," I say, because I get the feeling I'm meant to be leading this conversation.

"We were off on our own when it was sent out to everyone,

but yeah," Ovie says. She wrings her hands in her lap. "It was pretty bad, Vale."

I hug my pillow. "I know . . ."

"But?" Dina says.

"But what?" I reply.

"I was priming you for whatever excuse you were about to give to explain why you said all that shit."

And there it is.

Rushing to the surface is the instinct to defend myself and my words. Even now, I know what I said about their skill set wasn't entirely untrue. But I think of the look on Marley's face. On Kiko's and Claire's and, oh god, Leticia's. And the urge dies out.

There's a difference between criticism that's constructive and criticism that's cruel. The problem with living your entire life sitting on one side of that line is never really knowing what the other side looks like.

"Nope." I squeeze my pillow tighter. "No excuse. I fucked up."

Dina looks surprised to hear me admit this. I feel the same.

I pull my phone out from under my pillow. No one has texted or called me, which is both a relief and a disappointment. No one, other than whoever sent the video last night. I was so caught up in everything that went down, I hadn't even noticed I'd been sent it too. I don't recognize the number though.

"You should come get some food in you before your

game," Dina says as they stand. Her tone is gentle in a way I'm not worthy of right now.

"I think I'm going to stay here. I should call my dad," I lie. Their eyes flicker in a moment of mutual disbelief, making me briefly think that maybe they actually do understand the extent of how shitty my relationship with him is. But then they let it go and head out with a promise to bring me back some fruit, leaving me to the silence of the empty cabin.

It feels fitting that after all this, the team we're playing is Cate and Kaylee's. Maybe I'd laugh if I couldn't still feel the tear tracks etched into my cheeks.

I consider actually calling Dad for a second, but I don't think my heart could handle it. I know it's wishful thinking to believe Mami could solve all of this for me if she were alive, but the yearning to have her come fix my life remains.

I crawl out of bed and swap Marley's borrowed clothing for a pair of running shorts and a sports bra. Within minutes, I'm deep in the forest, jogging to the pulsing volume of my music turned up full blast.

I'm so used to having Leticia beside me that, several times, I catch myself turning to point out a pretty patch of flowers or cool cloud. Every time, the realization she's not here makes my heart ache.

My lungs burn, but it's the good kind of pain. The kind that numbs the rest of the world for a moment. I can almost pretend it really is just me out here. No one else in these trees to judge me. No one else to let down. No one else to hurt.

I want to keep running and never stop, but my phone dings

with some email coupon for 25 percent off athleisure, and it reminds me to check the time. I've got an hour until my game.

I could just disappear into the trees. Maybe I could run my way back to SoCal. It would take a few days, sure, but at least I'd be wrapped up in the familiar feeling of disappointing my family instead of this web of hurting people who actually believed in me for once. Dad's been using the line that Mami would be disappointed in me with reckless abandon since she died. Today, I believe he's right.

Somehow my feet bring me back to my empty cabin and my body changes into my uniform. I use Ovie's mirror to tie my hair up. My bangs are pressed to my skin, slick with sweat, and my cheeks are bright red. Just last night I was staring in this mirror, trying to work out what I, and everyone around me, saw when they looked at me.

I see it now. A disappointment. A failure. The villain of her own story. Foolishly, I'd started to think maybe I was wrong to expect that was all there was to me. Maybe I could be a good leader, a teacher, a teammate. Someone who empathized with others, someone who helped people believe in themselves. Someone who could be loved. What a joke.

I force myself to grab my captain's bag and head to the fields. I can't run away from this, not when my team could still be counting on me. I pass a few girls on the way, all of whom stop to stare at me, but I keep going.

The Angels are already warming up. Cate and Kaylee count off their jumping jacks with efficiency. The only one who's offbeat is Sophie. She looks nearly as shitty as I do.

My side of the field, however, is almost empty. Rani, Hayley, and Natalia sit in a little circle by the goal, picking at grass. Hayley spots me first, whispering before the other two turn to watch me walk over.

"Hey," I say, testing the waters.

"I'm pretty sure this is it," Natalia says evenly.

"What?" I take a step back without meaning to. "No one else is coming?"

"No one else besides me," Leticia says, appearing from nowhere. I turn around to face her but she walks past me, dropping her bag by the goal.

"Can you really blame them?" Hayley asks. "After watching that video, I'm not sure I want to be here either. Me or my shitty throw-ins."

"Hayley, I'm so—"

She stops me with a raised hand. "We can't play with this many girls anyway. You might as well just go tell Juanita we concede."

"But—" I start, cutting myself off this time. *But if we don't win this game, we don't make it to the final game.* "Then it's all over."

"We probably would've lost," Natalia says, still picking at the grass. "It's not like we really had a chance." I know I'm responsible for the hurt in her voice.

I walk over to Leticia, who is retying her cleats for what looks like the third time. "You know we need to win this game."

"Why do you think I'm here?" She looks up, jaw clenched.

"I tried to convince the other girls to come, but what you said in that video?" She stands, facing me head-on. "You're not the only one here trying to prove her worst thoughts about herself wrong."

My eyes go to her sprained wrist. She didn't know if she'd be a good enough player outside of the goal. She didn't know who she would be if she lost soccer due to her injury. And the girl in the video last night, *me*, someone she trusted to share that with, said she wished Leticia had been hurt even worse.

I open my mouth, but Juanita blows her whistle, calling for the captains to come meet her. I shoot a desperate look in her direction before facing Leticia again. She's gathering up her gear. "What are you doing?"

"We can't play with only five girls," she says. For a second, it looks like she actually feels sorry for me. "It's over, Valentina."

I don't know if she means the game, this team, us, or all three.

Without feeling, I go tell Juanita that we forfeit. She doesn't ask any questions, which is how I know she's seen the video too. The look in her eyes as she watches me walk away confirms it for me. I'd recognize disappointment anywhere.

THIRTY-NINE

DAD CALLS. I LET IT RING. Jorge calls. I send it to voice mail.

Despite this, Jorge texts me a photo of Mami when she was my age, wearing the same jacket that I've kept tucked under my pillow all summer. The same jacket I refuse to touch or wear or do anything with other than hide away. She didn't realize how precious it would become to her daughter someday. Or how neglected.

I stare at the photo for a solid five minutes before turning my phone off.

I started playing soccer competitively at two years old. But it was in my blood long before that, pumping through Mami's and Dad's veins before I was even a whisper of a possibility. Playing this sport was always my destiny.

I've broken bones, sprained ankles. I chipped a tooth on a goalpost when I was ten. Once, a girl kicked me in the head, still swinging after I'd fallen to where the ball had been a moment before, and stars burst behind my eyes a second before the pain followed. None of that mattered; it was worth every ounce of agony to feel like I was a part of something bigger than just me.

Still, I've known my whole life that no matter what I do, I'll never be the kid my dad wanted. I'll never be the flawless athletic son he prayed and waited for. And though nothing could ever compare to losing Mami, her death and Dad's expectations were out of my control.

This wasn't. Earning these girls' trust and faith only to shatter it the moment we needed it most is all me.

The day and night float by me. Dina and Ovie sneak me a grilled cheese from the caf, but other than that and telling me the Angels and Scarlet Fevers are playing the final tournament game next week, they leave me to myself. Which is good, all things considered. The fewer people around me, the fewer people I can hurt.

When I wake up early Saturday morning, I crawl out of bed before anyone else is up. I do one of the only things I'm good at: I put on leggings and a sports bra, plug my earbuds in, blast my music, and run.

I loop around the trails Leticia and I had previously covered, and then a few we hadn't, until I end up back on our usual route. My phone dings when I've hit my third mile.

I stop and plant my hands on my thighs, listening to my screaming lungs and legs for once. Sucking air in, I regret the last mile more than I thought I would. But I know my limits, and I've only skimmed their surface.

Something brushes my shoulder and I whirl around.

Leticia stares at me, panting, eyes wide. She starts talking, but my music swallows her words.

I yank out an earbud. "What?"

"Have you been holding back on our runs?" She exhales, dropping her hands to her knees and cursing. "It took me forever to catch up to you."

Her tone is airy, playful even, despite the hyperventilating. It reminds me of who we were before. Or I guess, after? Our relationship has gone through so many different stages, I'm not sure I've ever really known what we are. By the time I thought I'd begun to figure it out, I wrecked it.

"What are you doing here?" I ask, vaguely concerned over just how winded she is.

"You had a bandage on your forehead in the video," she says, not answering me and still catching her breath. "But you only wore one for a few days and then had a nasty bruise for a while. And some of the comments you made were about the girls' old positions. That video was from weeks ago."

"First week of camp." I pull out my other earbud.

She nods, standing straight. "I figured it had to have been around then. And no one on our team was on the other side of that camera, seeing as you shit on all of us—"

"Leticia."

"And I doubt your best friends would throw you under the bus like this, even if you've been fighting lately," she continues. "Taking into account the fact that you're generally an antisocial person and assuming it wasn't, like, Lola or Juanita, you had to have been talking to—"

"Leticia."

She stares at me intensely. "It was Sophie, right?"

"Yeah," I sigh.

"I'm surprised no one else has worked it ou—wait, where are you going?"

I've already turned away from her. "I'm finishing my run. And then I'm going to go back to my cabin, shower, work, then call and beg Jorge to come get me tomorrow."

"You're kidding," she says, circling me so we're facing each other again. "You're going to let Sophie and those Angel freaks get away with this?"

"Get away with what? Sophie recorded me saying shit I shouldn't have thought—let alone *said*—and now it's out in the world. She didn't force me to do it."

She shakes her head. "Seriously? You're not even the slightest bit pissed about this? They set you up, Valentina. We can still go to Lola and Juanita and—"

"And tell them what? Tell them that I openly and easily shit-talked my entire team? That I berated their skill, their efforts—fucking hell—I made fun of Claire's relationship without knowing a single thing about her situation! I made fun of your *injury*! I'm surprised they haven't sent me packing already." My hands clench at my sides. "You can just go, okay? You don't owe me anything, especially not now. Take this victory and go call Wendy—"

"What does Wendy have to do with any of this? I haven't even talked to her in weeks," she interrupts. I've shown my cards. "And how is this a victory for me?"

"I proved you and everyone else right. I'm just the arrogant girl who only cares about winning and doesn't think about who I hurt to do so. Including you."

"Do you honestly think that's how I see you?" She asks this like a challenge, her eyes on fire. "That video threw me off and it took until realizing it was weeks old to figure out why. I've watched you instill pride into these girls who previously thought they'd never be good enough for anyone to care about them. I've listened to the way you talk about them, and that girl in the video? That wasn't you. It *isn't* you."

My throat tightens. "You're wrong. It's who I've always been."

She shakes her head at me, almost pleading. "I wouldn't have spent these past two months with you if that was true."

"Oh *come on*." Everything in my head is screaming. I'm so angry all of a sudden, so mad she'd dare try to tell me that this isn't my fault. "You spent all that time with me because you needed my help. We made a deal, don't pretend you were doing me any favors."

She pauses, hand in front of her mouth, before she speaks. When she does, her voice comes out gentler than I've ever heard it, like a sigh. Like a breath she's held in too long. "Valentina, I didn't need you to train me."

"Yes, you did. That's why you helped me. That's the *only* reason."

"No, it's not," she says. "I mean, yes, I did want to try out new positions in case my wrist doesn't heal properly in time for next season. But I didn't need you to teach me." She laughs to herself. "Or at least I didn't think I did until you proved yourself to actually be a very helpful trainer."

"I—I don't understand," I say, overwhelmed with the most unfamiliar feeling. "You *hated* me. I had to beg you to agree to take the team seriously. Why would you force yourself to spend that much time with me if you didn't even need my help?"

"I lied."

"I got that much, bu—"

"No," she interrupts. "When I said how I knew I was a lesbian, I lied." She sighs, smiling sadly. "When I was a kid, I didn't know how to check my pulse. I saw other girls doing it after running laps or during halftime, but I guess I was putting my finger in the wrong place. I knew my heart was racing, but when I felt for it, there was barely anything there. I thought maybe something was wrong with me and I didn't want to admit it to anyone, so I just kept pretending I could feel it." She sounds out of breath. "And then one day, a girl who I'd spent all summer nervously avoiding, even though she was trying her best to become my friend, saw me checking my pulse wrong. But she didn't laugh at me or even explain my mistake, she just reached out and moved my hand to the right place. She hardly even touched me." Her voice breaks. "It scared me, that because of her I felt my heartbeat for the first time."

The day Leticia stormed off. The day I accepted that she'd never want to be my friend and I should stop trying to impress her. The day my dad told me maybe I wasn't cut out to play soccer anymore and the whole ride home from camp I thought no one would ever see me as anything other than useless.

"That was me," I whisper, like a secret.

"It was you," she says. "It was you, and that was how I knew. And then you came back the next summer like I was your enemy, and it became our whole thing." She runs a hand through her hair and laughs, sadly. "I tried *really* hard to over the years, but I meant it when I said I never hated you, Valentina."

I don't know what to say. I thought I was difficult to love, not to hate.

"I—I can't," is all I get out before I start running again. I don't even know why, but I have to get away from her, her kindness, her forgiveness, her earnestness. Her ability to crumble the walls of self-hate I've done nothing but nurture my entire life.

She calls after me, but she doesn't follow.

I run the fourth mile.

Exhausted, I'm splayed out on a bench hidden behind the last field when my phone starts ringing. Automatically, I go to hit ignore. But then I see the name.

I rub at my throbbing temple while I answer. "Valentina's going through a crisis and can't come to the phone right now."

"Hello to you too," Jorge laughs. "Wanted to warn you that I just got off the phone with Dad and he's going to pick us both up after the final game at your camp. Asked me if I knew how your last game went."

"You can tell him we forfeited because my team realized I'm a massive bitch and just as much of a failure as he's always thought I am. And that I'd rather walk all the way home than have him drive me back."

A pause. "I absolutely won't be the one to tell him all of that."

We both laugh, a brief moment of shared sibling trauma. Then Jorge clears his throat. "You do realize he doesn't actually think you're a failure though, right?"

"It's a miracle I haven't passed out from how much I've run this morning. I really don't have the energy to debate a solid fact with you. If you're really itching for it, we can debate something easier. Like the existence of gravity. Or whether Coke is better than Colombiana."

"They're both colas, Valentina," he whines. "No one but you can taste a difference."

"God, maybe I'm really not the family failure. Next thing you're gonna tell me Grandma Green's meat loaf is basically carne asada."

I can practically hear him roll his eyes at me. "You've always been Dad's soccer prodigy. You think he gives a crap about me or my writing?"

"I don't," I reply bluntly. "Matteo is the favorite, obviously. But then it's you, *then* me. If we had a dog, I'm sure they'd rank above me too."

He sighs. "Look, I just called to make sure you were still breathing after ignoring all my other calls and texts, and since you're practically panting into the phone you sound so out of breath, I will take that as a yes. But seriously, if Dad sees anyone as a failure in our house, it's me."

"Disgraced queer daughter whose mere birth ruined his dream of a first-born soccer-playing son?"

"Gay writer who cried every time he was stuffed into a soccer uniform and who's *literally* the first-born son of the house?"

He's never shared what I've always had an inkling about. "If you ever plan on telling him, I can show up wearing a rainbow shirt and make out with a girl in the background to take the pressure off." Pathetically, I picture Leticia as the girl.

He laughs and it feels like I take my first real breath all morning. "Deal." Then he goes quiet. "I used to think you had it easier than me. I guess I resented you for being the athlete I wasn't, but it's not like that's ever really saved you from him."

It hurts my heart to know my little brother has felt the same anger and pain as me. I don't picture him on the other side of the line as he is now, sixteen and dry-humored and witty. I picture him as a kid, a twelve-year-old whose mom just died and whose dad has never truly accepted him. "Maybe it doesn't have to be a competition of which one of us is the bigger disappointment," I say. "I'm willing to settle for a tie."

"Every bone in your body is competitive, what gives?"

I can't believe we're actually having this conversation. "I'm tired of being like this, like him. Always picking at flaws, always somehow expecting the best and worst of myself at once and taking it out on the people around me." And then I admit the hardest truth I've ever had to. "I don't think I've been a very good person since Mami died."

He lets that sit there for a second. "Whatever you did to make your team hate you, it doesn't make the stuff Dad says right. It's always been about him, not us. He's never known how to say sorry, even before Mami died. I don't think he even knows what being sorry feels like. You're a pain in the ass, but you clearly do.

"But you don't have to be like him, Vale. Just because Mami is gone doesn't mean he's all you have left." His voice breaks a little, like he's telling himself this as much as he's telling me. "You can't change what happened, but you can change this. You don't have to be like him if you don't want to."

We hang up and I sit there, drenched in sweat, tearing up. This whole summer, every time I felt like my father, it was after I did something cruel. After I complained about my teammates and insulted Leticia's goal and acted like a tyrant instead of a captain.

The idea of making anyone else feel the way he's made me feel terrifies me more than my chances of playing college soccer rushing down the drain does. I can't do much to change the latter right now, but I can change the former. At the very least, I don't have to disappoint myself by never trying not to.

I get up and start running again.

FORTY

AFTER MY RUN AND A HOT shower yesterday, I worked a long shift in the caf. I'd hoped I'd run into my teammates, but I was stuck washing dishes in the back. I considered texting the group chat and asking them to meet up, but I was already exhausted and needed a fresh night of sleep to clear my head.

But as I make my way up the steps into the caf on Sunday morning, I hear my name.

"Valentina!" Cate shouts. I turn around and descend the last step so we're on even ground. Alongside her is Kaylee, but no Sophie. "Could you give me a few pointers for motivational speeches? I'm working on what to say to the girls on Friday before our big game and I know that no one does team spirit like you."

Gritting my teeth, I hold my ground. "You have a natural gift for instilling happiness in those around you. I'm sure you'll work something out."

Kaylee gasps. "I didn't realize you were capable of complimenting anyone but yourself."

I've gotten so used to covering up my insecurities; it feels treacherous to let them out, like I'll drown myself in them if I do. But keeping them inside does nothing but convince myself they're all I am. "I'm not going to pretend like what I did wasn't shitty. My intention was never to hurt my teammates, but I still did and I won't hide from that."

"You know I was joking about the motivational speech thing, right?" Cate says.

"Whatever," I reply. It's not my job to teach them that they're assholes. I turn to walk away, but of course they don't want to let me off that easy.

"You should be grateful that video came out when it did," Kaylee says. "It would've been even more embarrassing if your team actually tried to play us. We did you a favor."

I face them slowly, absorbing the unintentional confession. "I don't know who would've won that game if you hadn't sent the video to everyone. But I know this: Those girls, *my* teammates, they play with more heart and soul than y'all ever have. You know why? Because they actually have hearts and souls. The only thing you two care about is yourselves. I regret my cruelty, but you bask in yours."

Both girls swallow, their jaws tight.

I'm on a roll now though. If I could do it all over, I know what I'd say on that video this time around. So I say it now. "You warned me about Marley, but she embodies the spirit of teamwork, of caring about and believing in others. She never played goalie in her life and she has *thrived* at it because all she needed was someone to see her potential. Kiko has more natural talent than anyone I've ever met; it's actually absurd to me that she isn't running this entire camp. Claire is brave enough to go back and forth from right wing to sweeper at the drop of a hat even though those positions couldn't be more different and she's new to both of them." I can't stop. My heart feels stronger than it ever has before. *I* feel stronger. "Anita takes shots with the confidence and precision of a seasoned player. Hayley would rather pass out than let a teammate go more than a second without someone open to pass to. Gloria could execute a perfect cross with her eyes closed. Rani and Natalia are some of the nicest girls I've ever met, but I'd be scared shitless if they were standing between me and a goal. Bethany's a powerhouse who protects the net like it's her own home."

I step closer, inches away from Cate's and Kaylee's faces. "And the next time someone asks me why I play soccer, I'll tell them it's because people like Leticia play it. And it would be a waste of a lifetime to never know what it's like to be on the same field as her. Whether she's playing with or against me, watching her is a goddamn miracle.

"You didn't leak that video because we're bad or even because you hate me. You did it because for the first time you realized those girls were more than people to look down on to make you feel good about yourselves. And trust me, I get that, but nothing I said in that video made me feel good about myself. It didn't fix my shit left foot or how I overthink clear shots or selfishly hog the ball when I'm too scared to trust anyone else." I shake my head. "It made me weak, and the same goes for y'all."

They're stunned into silence. Either because what I said actually resonated, or because that was probably one of the most painfully earnest speeches anyone has ever given at a soccer camp, which is really saying something.

Finally, Cate opens her mouth. "Unless you want us to go to Juanita and Lola right now and report you for harassment, you should walk away." But then her eyes snag on something behind me.

A group of girls make their way down the steps. I was so caught up in this confrontation, I didn't see or hear any of them before now. But they're not just any girls, they're *my* girls.

"Testifying against you two sounds like a dream come true," Kiko says as she reaches us. Marley, Anita, and Hayley flank her. "So just say the word, and we can call that meeting."

"It's kind of pathetic that you'd defend her after what she said about all of you," Cate says, but the venom in her voice doesn't have the same bite.

"And it's kind of ironic for you to call other people pathetic," Marley says. Leticia taught her well.

"Whatever," Kaylee says, tugging on Cate's sleeve. "I'd say 'See you at the finals' but we all know that isn't happening anymore." She turns, her cousin following after her.

Once they're gone, it's just me and my teammates. "Hey," I say, trying to meet their eyes.

"Hey," Kiko replies. She looks down at her sneakers.

"Did you mean what you said?" Anita asks, the first to look me in the eye. "About how we play?"

I didn't know they heard all that. I realize suddenly that

their lack of eye contact isn't anger. They look . . . bashful. Bashful, but fighting not to be.

"I did," I say. "Every last word."

"Now I kinda wish we hadn't ditched on Friday," Kiko jokes, nodding toward where the cousins walked off. "We could've crushed them."

"Speak for yourself," Hayley says, nudging her. "Some of us still went."

"Yeah, yeah, whatever," Kiko laughs.

"You really think we play with heart and soul?" Marley interjects.

Something warms in my chest. "More than any other team I've been on," I reply. "I'm really, really sorry for what I said about each of you in that video. You deserved better."

I expect the apprehension to return, but all of them seem to soften at once.

"We were talking about it over dinner last night," Hayley starts, "and you weren't totally wrong about us."

"We did need more discipline and training," Kiko adds. "You and Leticia helped us with that."

Hearing Leticia's name stings. "Still, I shouldn't have said what I did, especially not the way I did." And then I say something I hadn't even realized until then. "Even if you hadn't improved and we lost every game, you wouldn't have deserved that cruelty."

This, more than anything else, aches to admit. Because it means that even if I sucked at soccer my entire life, I wouldn't deserve Dad's cruelty either.

I was a kid when my mom died. I learned too young that too much of life is out of our control. Turning to soccer to cope, making that the one thing I *could* control, wasn't the healthiest decision. I can see that now; I realized it weeks ago.

But it's only now that I realize I became that for Dad. I was the thing he could still control, the closest thing to Mami left in this world. It went beyond the hours I spent practicing in an attempt to meet his always shifting expectations. He found a way to control how I felt about soccer, the people around me, and worst of all, myself.

I didn't deserve it, any of it. I never have.

"Thanks," Kiko says. The other girls nod along. It shakes me out of my childhood, and reminds me that yes, so much of life is outside of our control, but how I act toward the people around me doesn't need to be.

I swallow, taking them even talking to me this long as a victory. "I should head to work now."

"Right," Hayley says. The group of them step aside, but then Kiko reaches out.

"We were going to go play some scrimmages for fun. You could join us when your shift is over?"

I look at the other girls. Their smiles are small, a little stiff, but they're not the looks they gave me at the campfire. They're tentative, trying.

The hope in my chest swells, but it comes crashing when I think about facing Leticia again. She came to me, trying to help make things right; meanwhile I basically spat in her face, then ran away when she told me how she felt about me.

I don't know how to be on the receiving end of love like hers. Though I guess I have been for weeks without realizing it. Years, actually.

"I've got a few more stops to make on my apology tour first," I tell them. "But thank you. Really."

I watch them head toward the fields. And it may be my imagination, but they look fired up again. Like the heart and soul I saw in them has come back with a vengeance, tournament or not. I hope to feel that way too one day. Maybe I still can.

I spend hours tracking down the rest of the girls once work is over. By nighttime, I am all but dragging myself to bed.

Not everyone accepted my apologies outright. Natalia and Rani were grateful for my words, but didn't want to talk for long. Gloria didn't seem much happier when I left her than she did when I showed up, and Bethany said she needed more time to cool off.

Forgiveness wasn't the point though. The point was saying sorry and letting them decide how they feel from there.

I'm exhausted, but I still haven't found Claire, and no one has seen her all day. I have an idea though, and head back to the cafeteria a few minutes before closing.

Claire is there, sitting in the back corner eating ice cream. She doesn't look up from her bowl, even when I sit down across from her.

"How does that fare against the freezer-burnt stuff we had?" I ask.

She shoves a spoonful into her mouth and makes me wait for her to swallow before answering. "Tastes better, but isn't doing much for my mood."

"How's your—how is he?" I risk asking.

Her shoulders soften. "He's good. We've talked since the breakup. I actually told him about our team before the campfire party. He said he was really proud of me." She stabs at her ice cream. "Wait until he hears that we're not making it to the final game like I thought we might."

"But you said we didn't stand a chance at beating the Angels."

She shrugs. "Maybe I had decent captains who taught me to believe in us and myself."

"One of them really let you down though, didn't she?"

"Yeah, she did."

"Leticia has a habit of doing that."

At this, she laughs. But when she finally looks up at me, her eyes are a little red. "You said some pretty fucked-up stuff in that video. I didn't want to compare insults with anyone, but mine felt the most personal." She twists her mouth. "Okay, maybe Leticia's was a tad more personal."

"I'm so sorry, Claire," I say, fidgeting with my hands in my lap. "I was out of line with everyone, but what I said about you and your boyfriend . . . it was never any of my business. I didn't know about your situation, but after what happened with my mom and all the stuff I missed as a kid because of it, I should've known better than to judge."

"Yeah . . ." She takes another bite, thinking. "But you

were also there when it counted." I jolt with surprise. "I mean, fuck you for being an ass about my relationship when you'd barely known me for like a week. But you eased up, you covered for me when other girls teased, and you were there for me after the breakup. Plus, Marley texted me what you said about us earlier." She twirls her spoon. "I think that's why the video hurt so much. You've been this amazing friend and mentor for us. Finding out you thought those things felt like a betrayal."

It aches to hear someone call me an amazing friend and mentor. It doesn't feel right, like a lie I should be correcting. "I became the player I am because someone trained me," I say, careful to choose my words. "But I was also trained to look at soccer a very specific way. Messing up wasn't just a mistake, it meant something was wrong with you as a person. The day of the video, I leaned into that, thinking it would help." I sigh. "You guys weren't the only ones who had a lot to learn about soccer this summer."

Claire fiddles with her empty bowl. "So, when you assumed the worst of my relationship . . ."

My throat feels tight. "Let's just say I know what it's like to have someone constantly on your case, making you check in just to tear you down. I think I projected." She nods.

Claire gets up and I follow her to the dirty dish stack. Eli nods at me from the kitchen window as I pass and Maria gives me a smile. I think they're some of the only people I've ever met who've liked me despite never seeing me play soccer.

"Did you really go around apologizing to the team all day?" she asks when we get outside.

"Yeah, I guess. It didn't feel right just sending a mass text saying 'My bad for being a dick, see y'all next summer.'"

She laughs, shaking her head. "Well, it sounds you've outgrown whoever trained you to see soccer the way you did. Even if you meant what you said in the video, I don't think that girl would've gone through the trouble of making amends with everyone she hurt."

I open my mouth to deny it, to ask her not to give me grace where I don't deserve it. But I freeze, wondering if the desire stems from me knowing that I don't need praise after messing up so badly, or from something in me still thinking I'm not allowed to believe I could be a good person.

When I get back to the cabin, I flop into bed, not even caring that it's been hours since I showered. I'm nibbling on an apple left over from when Dina and Ovie snuck me food yesterday as they come through the door, badly singing along to whatever's playing in their shared headphones.

"You're already in bed?" Dina asks, yanking out her music.

"But looking suspiciously chipper," Ovie adds, squinting at me. "We ran into Marley earlier and she told us about your apology."

I stretch my arms over my head, sitting up. "Yeah, well, before we talk about that, I owe you guys one too." They exchange a look, but don't sit down yet. "Ovie, I'm sorry for putting you in a weird position by causing all this tension between us." Ovie nods in acknowledgment. "And D, I'm really sorry for how I've treated you this summer."

Dina smiles small, almost awkwardly. "Ovie filled me in on what happened with Coach. About you no longer being captain," she says. "That bites."

"Yeah, it does. But I shouldn't have taken it out on you."

She picks at the skin around her nails, voice quiet. "Why did you then? You've been *a lot* at times as our captain, but you've never tried to knock me down like you have this summer. We used to be good friends, but something changed."

Our friendship began with soccer, but I don't want it to end there. "I don't think I realized I was even doing it for this reason, and it's not an excuse, but Coach wanting you to replace me—"

"Wait, what?" Dina interrupts, then turns to Ovie. "Did you know about that part?" Ovie shakes her head in confusion. "Vale, I don't want to be captain."

"What? Why not? You wanted to be one here."

She laughs. "Yeah, because it's just camp. But I don't like coming up with plays and organizing practices, something I definitely learned this summer." She points her thumb at Ovie. "You have no idea how much Ovie had to do on my behalf to keep our team afloat."

Ovie tilts her head sheepishly. "Turns out I love planning," she says, pleased.

Dina kisses her cheek gratefully, then looks at me. "I'm flattered Coach thought of me, but I like playing wing and minding my business. I won't accept her offer if she picks me."

Oddly enough, this doesn't make me feel relieved. Because it was never about Dina in the first place, it was about me feeling like I'd let someone down, again. "Guess we'll see what happens come fall then."

"Guess so," she says. "But if it's any consolation, the other day Marley told us about how you've been captaining your team and it sounds like you've found your groove again. I mean, I was trying to talk shit about you—don't look at me like that, you made my college recruitment about you—but all Marley could talk about was how well you'd led the Princesses to victory."

"Until now," I sigh.

Realization dawns on Ovie's face. "Oh my gosh. You've been all weird because the tournament was your last chance to impress college scouts if you're no longer the Ravens' captain." I nod. "Oh, Vale." Even Dina can't look me in the eye.

"I'll figure it out," I say, trying to brush aside my still dwindling future. "That doesn't matter right now. What matters is that I'm sorry for being so selfish lately. I'm proud of you, both of you." I look between them. "I'm lucky to have you as teammates, but I'm luckier to have you as friends."

"Aw," Dina coos, turning to Ovie. "The spirit of sportsmanship made her a softie."

"Shut up," I laugh, and climb off my bed to exchange hugs with them. It's a small talk, but enough. And maybe, down the line, I can talk to them more about what's been going on at home. Not to excuse myself, but to explain everything better. Leticia showed me I'm capable of doing that.

"So you really apologized to *all* of your teammates?" Dina asks, reading my mind as I crawl back into my bed.

"I feel like co-captains don't count as teammates," I reply, knowing what she's really asking. They both roll their eyes at me.

"You two need to kiss and make up already. It's no fun watching you hate each other if you're not bickering with homoerotic undertones." Dina reaches into her bag on the floor and pulls out her reusable bottle.

Her words remind me of the night of the campfire, how soft Leticia's lips felt against mine for the briefest of seconds before the video was sent out.

"Holy shit," Ovie says, staring at my face. I try to school my features. Dina looks at her in confusion as she takes a long sip of water. "You two actually kissed, didn't you?"

I wait a beat. "I mean, *technically*, yes, but it lasted like a split second before we got interrupted by that video."

Dina spits water all over the floor.

"Seriously, Dina?" I say at the same time Ovie shouts, "Babe, gross!"

"I'm *sorry*," Dina says, wiping the water dribbling down her chin. "You and *whomst* got interrupted doing *what*?"

I rub at my temples. "It's . . . a long story."

"We've got nothing but time, baby girl!" Dina shouts, kicking off her shoes and settling onto her bed. "This is like Christmas morning for me."

"You're insufferable."

Dina cocks her head. "Are you flirting with me?" She looks to Ovie. "That sounds like something she'd say to Leticia and now that we *know* she was flirting with her—"

My pillow hits her in the face, cutting her off. "Hey! Is violence another one of your methods?"

Ovie smacks her girlfriend's leg. "Shut up so she can tell us the details."

The two of them stare at me like little schoolchildren waiting for story time. I'd gotten so used to them being involved in every facet of my life, from practice to games to classes, that their absence in the past few weeks of it feels tangible now in a way I hadn't noticed before.

I tell myself there's not actually that much to share. But I think back to the early weeks of camp, every small moment between Leticia and me that turned our fire toward each other into a different kind of warmth. When it comes down to it, I'm not exactly sure when things began to change. But I know a good place to start.

"So," I say, and their smiles immediately grow wider and giddier. I hold back my eye roll. "One morning, when the weather forecast completely lied to me about the chance of it raining later, Leticia and I went for a run . . ."

FORTY-ONE

EARLY THE NEXT MORNING, I WAKE up to a soft knock. I slip out of bed as quietly as possible and open the cabin door to find a small note pasted outside.

Valentina, please report to the front office at 8:00 a.m. for an important meeting.

–Juanita & Lola

"What's that?" Ovie asks sleepily, rubbing at her eyes as she sits up in bed.

"Love letter from a co-captain?" Dina asks, only half-conscious.

"Juanita and Lola want to see me," I whisper as I tiptoe back to bed.

"Does it say why?" Ovie whispers back.

I shake my head, but her face tells me she's thinking the same thing I am. I know Juanita saw the video somehow, and I assume she's shown Lola already, but maybe they were waiting the weekend to work out my punishment. There's only a few days left of camp, but they could still send me home early and suspend me from returning.

I crawl back into bed, hoping to get some sleep before I have to go meet them. But I end up spending the next hour staring up at the ceiling, bracing myself.

When I walk into Lola and Juanita's office, I'm prepared to say goodbye to camp. Or as prepared as I can be. It'll suck not getting to spend these final days mending whatever I can with my team and playing one final game alongside them, but I understand why Juanita and Lola would want me gone. I fought Coach on staying captain back home; I won't make that mistake twice.

Lola greets me, her smile dimmer than usual. I can feel the disappointment radiating off her as she leads me into a room with two chairs in front of a large desk. Juanita sits behind the desk, typing away at a laptop with glasses perched on her nose, and Marley sits in one of the two chairs before her.

"Marley was early," Juanita says, closing her laptop and setting her glasses aside. She nods to Lola, who leaves the room and shuts the door behind her. "Marley alerted me to some bullying that's been happening at camp, and I thought we should discuss it together."

"I'm so sorry," I interrupt. Juanita's mouth falls open, but the words burst out of me. "I didn't mean what I said—well, I mean, I knew my team needed help, but the way I said it was so wrong and I didn't realize I was being recorded, but that doesn't matter because at the end of the day I still was the one who hurt everyone and I want to take account—" Juanita raises a hand, silencing me.

"Vale, this isn't about what you said in that video."

I look at Marley, who is smiling in reserved amusement. "It isn't?" I ask.

Juanita sighs. "Please take a seat." I do, and she stares at the arch her hands form on the desk as she collects her thoughts. "I did see the video. And it did disappoint me to hear you talking about your teammates like that. It wasn't very captainly of you." I fight the urge to look away from her heavy gaze. "Many of the girls on your team have been coming here for years. And though they've always loved the sport, I've never seen them as happy as they've been this summer. What you and Leticia did by taking them seriously, building their strengths and showing them that they mattered just as much as the girls who come here between club seasons and working with expensive coaches, it changed the way they see themselves as players."

I open my mouth to object to the compliment, but she raises her hand again. "We do, however, need to talk about what you're here for today." I startle at a knock on the door. "Send them in," Juanita says.

Lola steps inside, followed by Cate and Kaylee. They must finally be following through on their threats to lie about me harassing and poisoning them. Maybe this is my true punishment, facing the consequences for bullying I didn't commit to make up for the cruelty I did.

Juanita clears her throat. "Ladies, we've called you all

here because Marley brought it to my attention that Kaylee and Caitlin admitted to stealing private information from this office in order to text the whole camp a video of Valentina that was filmed without her awareness."

"What?" Cate, Kaylee, and I say at the same time. I spin around to see their flushed and angry faces.

"We've received complaints over the years from various girls on your teams about some"—Juanita pauses, clearly struggling to contain her anger—"*questionable* things you've said about other players. But with your long history here and your family's generous donations, we hoped our small talks with you would solve the issues." She leans back in her chair. "Would you girls care to tell me how you got the phone numbers of every single girl at camp?"

Kaylee sputters out half-formed sentences while Cate steps forward. "This has got to be some kind of joke. If anyone has been harassing anyone, it's her." She points one manicured hand at me. Someone painted a tiny angel wing on her nail. "Valentina has repeatedly threatened my cousin and me, and we've been *terrified* of saying anything."

Juanita rubs at her temples. "Girls, I'll ask again, how did you get everyone's numbers?"

Marley finally speaks up. "I got a new number right before coming to camp. The only people here who had it were the front office or on my team, and none of them gave it to you. Unless Vale here has something to share."

I raise my hands. "Not me." I turn to Cate and Kaylee. "I never even wondered how you'd texted all of us."

"We didn't though," Cate says. "You can compare our numbers to the one that sent out the video. It wasn't us."

"There are plenty of apps that let you send texts from a fake number," Marley says, spinning around in her chair to face them. "Me and a bunch of girls on my team heard you admit you sent it."

"That's not evidence," Kaylee says.

"Did you get sent the video?" I ask. Their faces go white. "Or were you the only girls at camp who didn't?"

At once, they both shift their expressions. "I can't believe you'd accuse us of something so awful," Kaylee says, still forcing her face into her impression of a frown. Cate wipes at an invisible tear.

Juanita doesn't look like she's buying it, but a part of me knows that another person probably would. At another camp, they'd likely get away with this.

Lola steps forward and places a hand on each of their shoulders. "Well, there's no need to get emotional, girls." Their faces quirk into grins behind their hands. I feel sick. "If you are so sure you weren't responsible, then you won't mind Juanita and I starting an investigation into who stole the phone number files from our office. Or, you could leave camp willingly and save us all the trouble of looking into that. Because we'd of course have to make it public information to any inquiring college coaches if you were involved in stealing other minors' private information."

This time when their eyes begin to well, it seems genuine.

Lola pats their backs. "We're going to be making some calls to your parents this afternoon while we get started on finding out who was behind all of this."

Juanita looks to me. "Vale and Marley, could you step out so we can talk to Kaylee and Caitlin? Marley, you're free to go, but I'd like to talk to Vale when we're done here."

"You good to wait alone?" Marley asks me, yawning, when we get outside.

"Yeah, go back to bed," I tell her with a smile. "And thank you. You didn't need to tell Juanita and Lola about what Cate and Kaylee did."

Marley shrugs. "They've treated a lot of people poorly for years now, me included. This is just the first time they didn't cover their tracks." I nod along. "And they went after my captain, so you know I had to do something."

I hug her immediately, despite my usual awkward hesitation with stuff like this. "I'm really glad you ended up on my team," I say.

I feel her smile against the top of my head. "Me too, Vale." She lets me go. "But now that I'm a star goalie, you might not be able to afford me next summer."

I laugh and roll my eyes. "I'm starting to understand how you and Leticia ended up being friends."

"You're lucky I'm desperate to go back to bed, or I'd be telling you that you need to talk to her." She lifts her hand when I open my mouth to protest. "I don't want to hear it, I really do need sleep. But if I see you at lunch later . . ."

She makes a *V* with her fingers, pointing it at her eyes, then mine, before walking away.

I wait outside the office, letting my thoughts run wild about what it is Juanita and Lola still have to say to me. But I'm not alone with them for too long, because a few minutes after Marley leaves, I look up and watch Sophie approach me.

She doesn't look like she's been sleeping.

"It was you, wasn't it?' I ask her, firmness in my voice but no fire. "You worked in Juanita and Lola's office last year. You knew where they keep all our records."

She opens her mouth as if to deny it, but just looks away.

"I thought we were friends," I say, hating how hurt I sound. Weeks ago, I'd abandoned most falsehoods I had about Sophie being the same person she was when we were kids, but I never thought she'd stoop to this. The preteen in me who had a huge crush on her once upon a time is heart-broken. "This whole time you were playing me."

"You were a threat," she says, voice small. "It wasn't my idea, but when Cate and Kaylee knew we'd been friends, they ask me to record you talking about your team. They thought you'd just reveal stuff about your game plans or whatever. I didn't expect you to say what you did." At least she has the guts to look ashamed. "I didn't mean to hurt you. I considered stopping them, if that counts for anything."

I don't even know what to say to that non-apology. But the door to Lola and Juanita's office bangs open before I can mull it over.

"You bitch," Cate says. She charges down the stairs, Kaylee close behind. "You *lost*. This isn't how soccer works."

I hear my dad's voice, telling me not to let what they'd said and done off the field get to me. He taught me that the best way to beat girls like them is to beat them in a game, prove I'm better.

But maybe I don't want to prove that I'm good enough all the time. Whether on or off the field, I'm tired of hinging my entire self-worth on his standards, even when he isn't around. It's not as easy as flipping a switch to change the way my brain's been programmed by his parenting, but today, it can be as easy as not taking the blame for someone else's mistakes.

"You're the ones who made it personal," I say, looking at the three of them. "You're great players, I can't deny that, but you're shitty people first and foremost."

Cate looks ready to lunge at me, but Kaylee stops her when her phone starts ringing. She checks the screen with haunted eyes. "It's my dad."

Maybe they're worried that this'll disappoint their parents; maybe their parents will just be disappointed they got caught. The apple doesn't fall far from the tree when it comes to pulling shit like this, but shaking off the legacy of our parents' worst traits isn't a cakewalk. I'd know.

Still, I don't spare them another look as I head back into the office.

"You wanted to see me again?" I ask Juanita from the doorway.

"Yes, come in." She motions to the seat I sat in earlier. I take it. "We're just waiting on—"

Leticia steps in the doorway with Lola. "What's up?" she asks, moments before noticing me. The split second she spends looking at me is enough to kick-start my heartbeat.

"You might want to sit down," Juanita says as Lola steps around to join her behind the desk. Leticia hesitantly sits in the other chair, like she's making a concentrated effort not to accidentally brush against me, even from a foot away.

"Cate and Kaylee admitted that Sophie was the one who stole the files from our office," Lola says, confirming what I already know. Leticia doesn't look surprised by this update either, but she was the first to figure out who filmed it. "I can't in good conscience let the three of them play in the final tournament game at the end of the week, but there aren't enough girls remaining on their team to compete without them. It wouldn't be fair to knock the Angels out of the tournament entirely though, especially since they've been undefeated all summer. And we could borrow players from other teams to play with them, but there's no way to arrange that fairly without also jeopardizing those teams and their games."

"Um, what does this have to do with us?" Leticia asks Lola. It's clear she's trying not to be a smartass, but this rant has me wondering the exact same thing.

"The Angels were meant to play against the Scarlet Fevers to determine the summer champion. I'll have to talk to both of them before we make any final decisions—because candidly, this is *very* unorthodox and requires the complication of another team playing twice so everyone has a match to determine final rankings—but how would you feel about dividing the remaining eight players on the Angels between your team and the Scarlet Fevers? Four girls transferred onto each team. That way we still have a final game without punishing the Angels as a whole for what their captains and teammate did. It's a messy solution, but it seems like the best option, all things considered."

"Holy shit," I whisper. "Are you saying . . ."

Juanita smiles. "I know it's short notice, but you've still got a few days to prepare yourselves. The Purple Princesses are competing in the final game of the summer."

FORTY-TWO

LETICIA AND I LEAVE THE OFFICE together. My mind is still in a haze, so I almost don't realize when she starts walking away.

"Leticia, wait," I say. She stops but doesn't turn around. "I'm sorry for running off the other day."

She shoots me a thumbs-up over her shoulder. "Cool. See you at practice tomorrow."

"Please, just let me—"

She spins around and it's like I'm seeing her for the first time. Her strong arms, her shining, dark eyes. The way her freckles warm her light brown skin and her curls reflect the sunlight in their every dip and fold. I've thought she was beautiful a million times this summer, probably a million times before it too, but this is the first time I've ever truly let myself appreciate the observation in its entirety. Because it's about more than just her appearance.

It's her quick wit and sharp mind. The way she was too shy to befriend me when we were kids but too protective over the people she cares about to let my dad berate me unchallenged now. Her desire to be good and kind, hidden under layers of snark and nonchalance. The bravery to know her entire relationship with soccer may be forever changed, and to still wake up every day and try to reshape it into something different, but just as good.

This girl I've known for a good chunk of my life who's been everything from my enemy to my ally to my best friend. I've only just begun to understand her. And somehow, at some point, I irrevocably fell for her too.

Her lips, full and softly curved, droop into a frown. "We really don't have to do this, okay? I promise it's fine, we're good. I'll see you at practice tomorrow."

I let her go. Partially because I'm a coward who is scared to face the real possibility that I might not be able to fix whatever we are. Partially because I'm a coward who is only beginning to realize and admit to feeling something she did long before me.

Even though saving the reveal for our casual Tuesday practice sounds temptingly dramatic, I opt for texting the team that we're having an emergency meeting at dinner so I can tell them then. This summer has been a lot of intense training and pushing ourselves nonstop, but up until this morning we all thought our chance to compete in the final game of the tournament was long gone. I wouldn't blame the girls if they decide they don't want to work their asses off every day anymore, even with this new development, so telling them comes before anything else.

Everyone but Leticia replies to the text, so I don't expect

her to show up. But she and Marley are the first two to arrive, heading straight for the food line before sitting down with me.

"So what's with the cryptic text?" Marley asks as she sits and takes a bite of a potato wedge. "Does it have to do with whatever Juanita and Lola wanted to talk about after I left?"

I glance at Leticia. "You didn't tell her yet?"

She shrugs, staring down at her salad. "I thought you'd want to be the one to do it." Her voice isn't cold. If anything, she sounds like she's trying not to seem like she did me a favor.

Marley looks back and forth between us curiously, but keeps chewing without comment. The three of us wait in silence for the rest of the team.

When Rani and Natalia are the last to join our crammed table, everyone's eyes turn to me. I stand up.

"So, we got some big news this morning," I say, looking to Leticia in the hopes she will join me in my little speech. I expect her to just roll her eyes and keep eating, but instead she rolls her eyes and stands up.

"Cate, Kaylee, and Sophie are suspended from camp, which means the Angels don't have enough players anymore," Leticia says. "The evil has been defeated."

I explain Lola's plan to everyone. They're quiet and attentive, but don't give me much reaction beyond that.

"So that leaves us with the decision of whether or not we still want to try to win this whole thing," I say. "And I know it's been a long, hard summer, so I get it if y'all would rather spend the next week relaxing and—" I stop when Kiko raises her hand. "Um, yes, Kiko?"

"Do you still have notes from our first game against the Scarlet Fevers? The ones you took after we played the Cheetos really helped me realize how much I'd been slacking on defense, so I want to see where I could improve for Friday."

"Wait, does that mean—"

Bethany raises her hand but doesn't wait for me to call on her to speak. "I was playing a totally different position in that game, but I want to see the notes too."

I'm shocked. "So y'all—"

"We were all playing different positions, Bethany," Anita points out.

"Oh gosh, I was still a *forward*," Marley says with disgust. Gloria and Anita give her a look. "No offense." They all laugh at the accidental pun.

Leticia whistles sharply. The table immediately goes silent.

"Thank you," I whisper. She inclines her head slightly in response. I face the team. "So we're doing this? We're trying to win?"

Claire laughs. "We didn't spend all summer training for nothing." The others nod in agreement.

"Is that what it would be though?" I ask, maybe too seriously. I feel Leticia's eyes on me. "Would this summer have been for nothing if we don't win?"

"No," Leticia answers, before anyone else can. She clears her throat, like she didn't mean to speak. "But we should start talking game plan." She sits back down and pulls out that notebook I gave her weeks ago. It's full of notes and plays. I thought she'd thrown it out.

The team crowds her as she starts ripping and passing out pages. Kiko and Anita fight over one of them while Natalia and Rani scoot off to the side, motioning Bethany and Claire to join their defense huddle. Gloria and Leticia discuss crossing with Hayley, all three of them trying to get Kiko and Anita to stop bickering and listen.

I'm the only one still standing when Marley nudges me.

"You joining us, captain?" she asks.

It might be the last week I ever hear someone call me that title. Even if we lose, I know one thing that gives this summer meaning: feeling like I actually deserve the title of captain, but knowing it doesn't define my future anymore.

I look at these girls, Leticia in particular, and know being captain is the least rewarding part of being here.

Jorge shoots me a text in the middle of Wednesday's practice. I guzzle Gatorade and open it up, stepping away from the team.

I'm confirming that you know Dad is still driving up for your game.

I sigh. In the chaos of this week, I forgot about Jorge mentioning it during our last call.

In another life, maybe the cancer didn't take Mami from us. Maybe the experience made my dad softer, kinder. More appreciative of the people around him. And maybe I wouldn't have become an outlet for his rage at losing control.

Or maybe she lived and then realized what a shitty person he could be and she divorced him and got full custody and I never had to see his face again. And I spent the rest of my life having a loving parent who was proud of me and never made me feel the way he does.

I could play this game forever, imagining a life where my mom didn't die and because of it, my life was perfect. It was the catalyst for so much pain and hurt, it's easy to think that without it, I'd also be without pain and hurt.

But I live in this life, this world. I have a dead mom and a shit dad and a lot of stuff I should start talking to a therapist about.

I also have Jorge, a brother I'm learning to recognize as an ally, not a competitor. I have Matteo, someone who loves me deeply and unconditionally. I have Dina and Ovie, who are willing to call me out on my shit but not give up on me as I learn to be better. I have a whole team of players who along the way became friends—Marley, Claire, and Kiko especially. Lots of people who believe in me, even when I screw up, teaching me that I deserve the kind of love I was starved for during the years I needed it most.

I look up from my phone and see Leticia reaching into her bag for a Gatorade. She has two inside, one yellow and one red. She pulls the yellow out and sets it beside my bag carefully, making sure the girls aren't watching her. But I am, of course I am.

Maybe I still have her too.

thanks, I text Jorge back. *good looking out*

It's no problem, he replies. I smile at the shift in our sibling dynamic.

And then he adds, *Try not to foul anyone this time around.*

FORTY-THREE

THE GAME CAME FASTER THAN I thought possible. After days of practicing harder than we have all summer, I feel ready. Whether it's to win or to lose, I don't know. But I'm ready to play.

Practicing with four new players was weird, but we adjusted as quickly as we could to our new left wing, right midfield, left back, and stopper. They're good players too. Not just because they play well with a ball under their feet, but because they play well with our girls beside them.

I wait for Kiko to finish her turn in our shooting warm-up before calling the girls in.

Everyone sits, hydrating and stretching. Leticia stands off to the side, watching me.

"All right Princesses, how are we feeling?"

The faces they make back at me aren't full of anger or distrust, but they aren't full of confidence either. For a second, I want to turn to Leticia to motivate them. She was always so much better at this kind of thing. But if I'm truly going to make amends and step up for this final game as captain, it needs to be me.

I tug on the sleeves of Mami's jacket. I finally wore it today. I hope she's proud of me.

"Can I be honest with you all?"

"Even more than you already have been?" Kiko says. Anita laughs into her shoulder.

"I earned that one," I say with a smile, biding my time. I know what to say, but vulnerability still comes hard for me.

"When I was a kid, all I ever wanted was to captain my own team. I couldn't wait to give the inspirational speeches and instill confidence in everyone." I almost don't say the next part. "I thought I could make someone feel the way I never did. Like I was good enough, something to be proud of.

"And then I became captain of my high school team, but by then, it wasn't about motivation or spirit or heart for me. Soccer was all about winning. It was about where we ranked in the state, how many goals I shouldn't have missed, who I should tell my coach to bench. I was constantly picking at flaws and issues and trying to make everything perfect all the time. Trying to control whatever I could."

The girls start to sit up, their eyes on me with undivided attention. "I lost sight of what really mattered." I pause and look at Leticia, who holds my gaze.

"I thought, for the longest time, that the only reason I play soccer is because it's the only thing I'm good at, and if I was better at it than anyone else, that meant I was good enough. For people to care about me, for people to love me."

I swallow. "Or because I thought if I could control a team and a game, I could at least control *something* in this life, when there's so much I can't. And couldn't."

Claire meets my eye and nods in understanding.

"But none of that is the whole truth," I continue. "I play because it makes me *happy*. Because it connects me to other people and forces us to share our mistakes and successes as a team instead of experience them all by ourselves. Because when I make a tricky pass and my teammate receives it anyway or I'm in a tough spot and someone opens up for me, I feel like I can count on people. And they can count on me." I take a deep breath. "I count on all of you. I *believe* in all of you. Winning matters; of course it does. But the spirit of playing, of working alongside the other players on the field and making something magical happen with just our bodies and minds and heart, *that's* what really matters. I guess I just wanted to say thank you for showing me that again."

No one says anything at first. And then Marley springs up and wraps me in a hug, quickly followed by Claire and Gloria.

"Team group hug!" Marley shouts, encouraging everyone else to join. In the center of it all, I feel so much love, I might burst.

When they release me, I see fire reflected in every girl's eyes. They believe in me again. But more importantly, they believe in themselves.

I stick my hand out, palm down. "Purple Princesses on three?"

Marley's hand lands atop mine, followed by Kiko's, then

Anita's, then everyone else's: Claire's, Gloria's, Hayley's, Rani's, Natalia's, Bethany's. Our new teammates'. Leticia's.

"Count it off, captain," I say to her, risking it.

She fights a smile. "One, two, three—"

"Purple Princesses!" the team shouts, the words a rumble in my chest.

Everyone separates, moving to take their positions or get comfortable on the sideline. No one was too broken up over finally having subs.

I watch Leticia go toward her mark as a wing.

But I can't start this game, not yet.

"Leticia?"

She slowly turns, looking at me the same way she usually does. But that means something different now, I guess. Something I didn't understand before.

"I'm sorry for pushing you away," I say. "I'm not used to accepting that people can see anything good in me. Especially people who are so talented at seeing the bad in me."

Her lips twitch at the corners.

"You don't have to forgive me for what I said in that video or for running away after." I take a leap of faith and drop to my knees. She startles, eyebrows shooting up to disappear under her curls.

"You're not proposing to me, Princesa?"

A laugh breaks out of me. "No. But I am apologizing. Hands and knees, groveling and all." I stare up at her beautiful face, the sun glowing behind her like the halo she always deserved.

"I'm only seeing knees."

I drop to all fours. She's holding back a smile. "I'm sorry, Leticia."

She blows out a long breath, then checks her nails. "I *suppose* I could forgive you. Under one circumstance."

I stand up and brush the mud and grass off my knees. "Another deal?"

She shrugs. "One more for the road, seeing as this is probably the last time we'll ever be on the same side of the field." Her voice goes serious. "No matter what happens out there, if we win or lose or go into the world's longest penalty kicks, you don't let it take away what you did this summer."

"Which is what?"

Lola blows her whistle, a warning that there's only one minute before the game starts. I look back to Leticia, a smile already blooming on my face. For the excitement of the game, but also because I'm looking at her.

She returns the smile and it's better than victory. "You had fun playing soccer."

The heat is brutal today, exhausting everyone minutes into the game. At least both teams are victim to the sun, as evidenced by Rani easily stealing the ball away from a sluggish Scarlet.

I call for her as I dodge a defender, distantly remembering being on this same field playing this same team weeks ago. I scored our first goal that time, hope climbing its way up my throat afterward. But I have hope already, so I pass up to Kiko once she's open.

She and Anita are almost as well matched as Leticia and

I are, so it comes as no surprise when Kiko gets to the corner and crosses beautifully to an already jumping Anita, who slams the ball into the net with her forehead.

My fellow Princesses erupt into cheers. And it's sweeter than that first goal of mine weeks ago. Because that was my goal, proof of my skill as a player. This goal is ours, proof of our skill as a team.

It feels damn good, no matter what happens next. But what happens next is just as brilliant.

The Scarlets feel the pressure of being down a goal, and they make us feel it too. With a couple of clever passes, they get past Rani, closing in on Claire and Bethany.

Claire did less training than every other girl on our team, with good reason, but the look in her eyes is deadly, even from as far back as I am, running to help her. She doesn't look like she needs it.

The Scarlet tries to fake her out. Claire favors her right foot, like most players, but she recovers in the blink of an eye and swipes the ball away with her left as clean as a professional. Before the Scarlet even knows she's lost the ball, Claire's already passed it up to Kiko.

The ball goes out a few minutes later for a throw-in, and as we rush over to defend it, I shout to Claire, "How'd you do that back there?"

She smiles. "I practiced playing around with my left foot after sitting out during Leticia's nondominant-foot scrimmage. I realized I could multitask on the phone."

My attention needs to be elsewhere, back on the game,

but hearing her say that is almost better than watching her stop that goal in its tracks. Almost.

By halftime, we're tied 2–2. Though Claire's play was gorgeous, the Scarlets weren't giving up without a fight, and they managed to get two good crosses in on Marley. But she also stopped three other goals herself. I know that technically those don't cancel out in any way that officially counts, but I can't help the pride they make me feel regardless.

Leticia and I work on our lineup while the rest of the girls cool down and guzzle their drinks. Sharing the same bottle of yellow Gatorade, we weigh decisions we never had to make until now about who to bench and who to keep on the field.

Hayley and Bethany can be swapped out for Angels we inherited. Gloria will go back in as left wing, and the rest of the girls will stay put for the time being.

"You know, I never thought I'd live to see the day we make decisions this efficiently without any arguing," Leticia says as she passes me the bottle.

"I'm pretty tired, but I can find something for us to argue over if you'd like." I take a long sip and hand it to her again. "Our right wing is pretty decent, but I'm willing to propose benching her for the sake of a disagreement."

She clucks her tongue. "No, we can't do that. Otherwise who is going to help our passably talented center mid?" Another sip and she passes back the bottle.

"Damn, wish they could make things easier for us and

not work so well together." I down the rest of the drink. "Oh well, I'm sure we can find something to argue about later."

"We're talking after this game ends? I thought our relationship expired the second the summer season did."

I throw the bottle at her. She catches it, laughing.

"Hey, guys?" Natalia shouts. Leticia and I turn to face her and the rest of the team.

"Could we interrupt our favorite married couple to hear what the plan is?" Bethany asks. Selfishly, I feel less bad about having her sit out. It distracts me from the embarrassment of being caught flirting.

Leticia takes the teasing in stride though. "All right Princesses, listen up . . ."

The second half, as per usual, is more intense than the first. The stakes are higher than they've been all summer. This is the final game, the entire camp is watching, scouts are tracking our every move, and we're still tied with the clock ticking down fast.

The Scarlet goalie narrowly saves Kiko's shot and punts it to her team. Their center mid's fast, but so is ours, so we're neck and neck while I try to knock the ball out from under her. We're quickly approaching Marley, and the panic makes me sloppy, accidentally catching the Scarlet's foot instead of the ball.

The both of us go crashing down. It knocks the wind out of me, but not too badly. I sit up as I hear Lola blow her whistle.

"You okay?" I ask, offering the girl a hand up.

She's grimacing, but accepts it. Polite claps surround us as Lola calls a foul.

"Shit," I whisper to myself. We're nearly at the top of the box; this might as well be a penalty kick.

I jog over to Marley while they're still setting up the ball. She and Leticia trained for weeks on penalty kicks after we played the Clovers, but practice is always easier than a game and her fear is palpable even from a distance.

She starts rambling the second I'm in earshot. "We're tied and almost out of time, if—if they score on me, then we—"

"Marley," I interrupt. "It's okay if they score on you."

Her eyes widen. "You want me to miss the save?"

"Oh no no no," I quickly correct. "But if they make this shot, it isn't the end of the world. Just . . . do your best."

She blinks at me, almost like she doesn't recognize me. I understand the feeling. But then she nods, and I'm rushing to join the wall of Princesses between Marley and the Scarlet selected to take the shot. Leticia isn't a defender, but she's one of our tallest players, so she stands beside me.

"Are motivational speeches going to be a common occurrence for you now?" she asks. "Because I could use a cheerleader at my games next year."

"I hope the ball hits your face," I reply. But my mind does drift to what it would be like to cheer for Leticia at her games, to wear her team jacket outside the confines of that supply shed and my cabin.

"Once a fouler, always a fouler," she tsks. But her laughter and my daydreaming are cut short by Lola's whistle.

The Scarlet steps back and we start jumping, hoping to

block the shot. She runs for the ball and kicks, harder and higher than I feared she would.

The ball soars over our heads and I watch as it moves toward the upper right corner of the net. Marley was shifting left and in slow motion, she tries to correct her mistake. But it's too late: The ball is too far and she's not fast enough.

I start running anyway, inversely to everyone else. It's a risk, but I trust my team. After a moment that feels infinite, I spin around.

I see Marley throw herself in the opposite direction she'd been headed, leaping into the ball and wrapping her entire body around it.

She did it. She saved it.

Everything speeds back into full motion.

"Marley! I'm open!" I scream.

With a punt that would put Leticia Ortiz to shame, she sends the ball straight at me. I trap it with my chest and start moving. And then it's just me, the ball, the goalie, and one defender to go.

My heart is racing, my entire body surging with energy. It's a fast break not unlike the one I made during that playoffs game against Leticia all those months ago.

The time is ticking down. Lola will let this play run its course, but if I miss, we're going to penalties. Scarlets are gaining on me. Everyone is screaming. I swear I hear my dad's voice standing out in the crowd, even though I didn't spot him before the game and refused to look for him during it.

"Shoot it! Take the shot, Valentina!" he screams.

I'm closing in on the goalie and defender. They look ready. Something in me knows that if I shoot here, even if I get it past the defender, the goalie will catch it. I don't know this for sure, of course, but I can see it play out in my mind like a prophecy.

I can also see my glory if I make the shot. I can see the victory landing squarely on my shoulders.

It always all comes down to me and me alone, doesn't it?

Does it?

"Princesa!"

I see Leticia, outrunning the charging Scarlets. The relief I feel is so overwhelming, I almost drop to my knees as I remember the one thing you're never meant to forget when playing soccer: You have a team. You don't have to do it alone.

I cross the ball to Leticia and know it's going in before it even happens.

Still, it's a glorious thing to see, her magnificent kick in the same upper left corner I was eyeing for myself. The goalie was still facing me as it went in. She never even had a chance to see Leticia.

But I did. I always see her.

Lola blows the whistle and it's over, we won.

I start laughing and crying all at once. I shut my eyes against it at first, but when I open them, the tears stream down my face, happy and heavy and everything I forgot soccer can make me feel.

The rest of the team is miles away on the other half of the field celebrating, so I take this single moment for myself, before I run to her.

Leticia has the same idea, sprinting to me. And then we're throwing ourselves at each other, spinning around in a tornado of laughing and cheering. I think she's crying too. When we finally stop, we're just there, holding each other and this thing we've both won that isn't the game.

Then Kiko is leaping onto my back and pumping her fist in the air while Marley tackles Leticia in a hug, screaming about the goal she just saved. Bethany and Natalia are there seconds later, equally as ecstatic. They're followed by Claire and Rani and Hayley and Gloria and all the new girls.

We're a mess of limbs and hair and sweat. It's the happiest I've been in years. Not because we won—though that doesn't exactly hurt—but because we won together. Because it didn't come down to any one of us, it came down to all of us. *We* won this game. We won this tournament.

We actually fucking won.

The postgame high fives are a blur, but the Scarlet Fevers don't look sad. They got to play in a hectic, close game in front of all these college scouts. It's a victory in and of itself.

After I finish high-fiving the last Scarlet, a tall East Asian woman I recognize from months of cyberstalking Division I coaches stops in front of me.

"You're Valentina Green, right?"

"Castillo-Green," I correct. "But yes, yeah, that's me," I reply.

"I'm Lil Nakatsuka, the coach for Cal Poly Pomona's women's soccer team. We've been following you and your high school team for the past year, but I didn't expect to see you here this summer." I keep my mouth from falling open. Barely. "That final goal was an interesting play. You had what looked like a pretty clear shot, but you didn't take it."

My mind says she's disappointed, that this is another example of how I fail everyone, even myself. Since I don't have anything to lose, I say, "Respectfully, I didn't." She raises her eyebrows. "Something told me I wouldn't make that shot. I knew my teammate would."

She makes a noise of agreement. She almost looks . . . impressed? "You co-captained this team, correct? And captain your high school team?"

I try not to deflate. "For now, but I don't know what next year will bring."

"Well, if next year brings you any interest in Pomona, we'd love to invite you to practice with and meet some of our team." She digs around in her back pocket, pulling out a business card. I take it, numbly. This can't be real. "Give me a call come September and we can find a date that works for you." I keep staring at the card. "That is, if you're interested?"

"I am!" I shout, then catch myself. "Very interested, thank you."

She nods and smiles politely before excusing herself.

I start walking nowhere in particular. I'm wading through my thoughts and a sea of congratulations and pats on my back when a familiar hand grips my shoulder. I turn around and it's him, it's Dad. Even though it's only been a couple of weeks since I've seen him up close in person, it feels so different to be standing in front of him now.

"You could've made that goal yourself," he says, by way of greeting.

"No," I tell him, straightening my spine. "I would've missed."

"You've made trickier shots before."

"But I wouldn't have made this one."

I don't know if that's true, actually. But I don't regret trusting someone else when I wasn't sure. That doesn't make me a weak player, it makes me a strong teammate.

He stares at me, his face so similar to mine, yet so different. He made me this way, even if he didn't mean to. That doesn't mean I can't be someone else though. It's not too late for me. Maybe it's not too late for him either, but that's not on me to figure out.

I pocket the business card. I could show it to him, evidence that I didn't fuck up my life completely, that good schools still want me. But I don't owe him that.

"Thank you for coming," I say. "But I have something I have to go do."

I side step my father as he shouts after me. I'm sure I'll get a lecture later, but that's a battle for another day.

When I finally break from the crowd, I see her.

Leticia is sitting on the sidelines, peeling off her socks and shin guards. A few strands of hair flop onto her forehead as she frees her curls from her headband and waves at someone congratulating her from a distance. She looks sweaty and happy and flecked with mud and grass stains. She looks perfect.

She sees me coming. "Not a bad way to end the summer,

huh?" she asks. We share a knowing smile. "Saw that coach talking to you. Good news?"

"News for another time," I reply, waving off the future.

"Saw you talking to your dad too."

"You see a lot from down there, don't you?" I ask. "Nice goal, by the way."

She smiles as she stuffs her feet into slides. "It was all right. Some might even call it *lucky*."

I laugh, shaking my head. "I should've just taken the damn shot myself."

"Keep that in mind for playoffs next year," she says, leveling me with her gaze. "I expect to see you there. Captain or not."

"Playing against you on the actual *field*, outside of your little safety net?" I pretend to consider it. "I guess you've got yourself a deal." I reach out my hand.

Her warm palm meets mine, the rush of touching her still so new but so familiar at the same time.

I don't realize what she's doing until I'm already falling on top of her.

We burst into a fit of laughter, the sound so happy and breathless I almost don't recognize it as me. As us.

I prop myself up on my hands, still pressed chest to chest against her. "I suppose I earned that one."

"You have no idea how long I've been waiting for you to offer me your hand." Her words are distorted by laughter. "Seriously, I was ready to just trip over nothing on one of our runs I was getting so desperate."

"Does this mean we're even now?" I ask, suddenly realizing how close we are.

My hands cage her head. Ever so gently, I lean my weight on one of them and place the other against the soft skin of her neck. Right at her racing pulse.

"Not quite," she says breathlessly.

We move together at the same time, meeting in the middle. Our lips touch and it's everything I've ever wanted without knowing it.

She sits up while I slide into her lap, our mouths dancing lightly against each other. It's different than the kiss at the party was. Where that one was delicate, a question finally being asked, this one is confident. An answer that's finally been figured out.

One of her hands wraps around my waist, pulling us closer, while the other snakes its way up my face and cups my cheek. Both of my hands are buried in her curls, touching every soft, sweaty strand.

Holding her like this, being held like this, I can't imagine ever feeling like a disappointment.

Whistles erupt behind us. We separate just enough to turn our heads.

Kiko, Marley, Dina, and Ovie stand at the edge of the crowd, the rest of our team behind them, everyone whistling and clapping. Claire winks at me.

"Finally!" Marley shouts. "I thought they'd never make their moves."

Dina laughs, spinning her participation medal. "You have no idea."

We flip them off. Which, of course, just earns us more cheering.

I turn back to Leticia and lean into her, our foreheads pressed together. She kisses my nose, lightly.

"I hope you know this doesn't mean I'll go easy on you next year," she says, her mouth brushing mine.

I pull back. "Of course not. I mean, you *have* been in love with me since we were kids so—" She pushes me off her as I crack up. "No! Don't be embarrassed!" I get out between fits of laughter. "It's cute! Did you write about me in your diary? Please tell me you have hearts next to my name in your phone."

She throws grass at me. It makes me laugh harder.

"Big talk from someone who apparently called me a miracle to watch play."

I immediately cover my face with my hands. "Oh god."

She pries them away, back on teasing offense. "It's sweet that seeing me play is one of the defining reasons you play soccer. I feel so honored."

I kiss her again to shut her up. Then move my hand down her neck slightly, resting just above her skyrocketed pulse. "Nice heartbeat you've got there. Anyone ever teach you how to feel for that? Did it have lasting effects on your sexuality?"

She squints at me, smirking. "Just for that, I'm stealing your plays and teaching them to my team."

I kiss her again, because I can. I could kiss her a million times and it'll never be enough, it'll never get old. I do it once more. "Game on."

EPILOGUE

COACH IS GOING TO KILL US. Running late to playoffs two years in a row is not a great look. At least Dina and Ovie hold the record with me.

"There was traffic! I'm sorry!" I shout as we throw our bags down and trade our sneakers for cleats.

Coach lifts a disbelieving eyebrow. "I'm guessing their captain is running late too?"

I fiddle with the red jacket around my waist. "She may or may not have arrived in the same car as us."

Ovie and Dina are trying so hard not to laugh.

Coach's mouth is frowning, but her eyes show her amusement. "Hurry on then."

I meet her at the midfield line, the ref already waiting for us.

"Try to keep your hands off me this game," Leticia says, smirking.

"Won't be hard when you're wearing that ugly uniform," I reply.

She gasps. "Valentina, are you asking me to *strip*? In front of a *referee*?"

The ref looks back and forth between us. They're the same person as last year. "Am I going to have a problem with you two?"

"Ignore them! They're dating," Ovie says, jogging over to join me. "Sorry, we had an issue with my gloves. But I'm here. Co-captain reporting for duty."

Dina wasn't lying when she said she didn't want to be captain. Ovie, on the other hand, thrived at it over the summer. When Coach heard all about me and my Princesses, she told me she was reconsidering her decision about me. But if sharing a team with Leticia taught me anything—other than that she may not, in fact, be the worst person I've ever met—it was that I work well with someone in charge beside me.

Nepotism allegations of course came back around. But Ovie earned her spot at the helm of our team, same as I had to earn it back.

"Um, okay," the ref says. "Tigers, your call." They flip the coin in the air and catch it on the back of their hand.

"Heads," Leticia says.

It lands on tails. We choose to start and stick to our current side. "Now shake hands and take your positions."

Leticia shakes Ovie's hand, then turns to me.

"Good luck out there," she says.

I accept her shake. "I don't need it."

"Are you sure?" she asks, running her thumb lightly over

the back of my hand. "I had a *really* good trainer over the summer."

"And don't you forget it."

She winks at me, then moves to take her mark as right wing. Her wrist healed properly enough to play goalie again, but she's expanded her horizons. She'll probably take up the net in the second half, but for now she's on offense. Which means she's mine to stop.

I move to take my position too, at the center of the field.

We could win this game, we could lose it. But that's the point. *We* will do it.

Leticia and I aren't teammates anymore, but she showed me what it means to love soccer, and even myself, again.

I look at her, then at Dina and Ovie. Briefly, I look in the stands and see Dad's same scowl. Same readiness to judge.

But I also see Marley, who's fifth-wheeling with Kiko and Anita, and Claire and her boyfriend. They've all got their phones out, FaceTiming the game to the rest of our old team.

Matteo sits beside them, already cheering. Even Jorge looks up from his notebook to salute me.

I love soccer, but it's not all that I am. A lot of people love me beyond what I can do while playing it, and every day I remind myself to never forget that.

The whistle blows.

I take a deep breath and start moving forward.

ACKNOWLEDGMENTS

MUCH OF THIS BOOK WAS WORKED on while I was wading through the depths of freshly grieving my mom's unexpected death. I'm grateful for everyone who showed me patience and kindness in the face of such an unimaginable loss, many of whom I know through publishing.

Thank you to the whole team at Sandra Dijkstra Literary Agency, especially Jennifer Kim, Andrea Cavallaro, and my incredible agent and advocate, Thao Le. I'd already started two different potential sophomore books, but when I said I wanted to write sapphic soccer-rivals-to-lovers, you showed me nothing but support.

Thank you to editor extraordinaire, Rachel Diebel. We made another book and our sapphic soccer dreams come true, all in one go! Thanks for indulging all of the Ophelia references.

Thank you to everyone at Feiwel and Friends and Macmillan who helps bring my books to life, including Jean Feiwel, Avia Perez, Liz Szabla, Rich Deas, Holly West, Anna

Roberto, Kat Brzozowski, Dawn Ryan, Emily Settle, Foyinsi Adegbonmire, Brittany Groves, Kim Waymer, Leigh Ann Higgins, Teresa Ferraiolo, and Kelsey Marrujo. Thank you Jackie Dever, Marielle Issa, and Katy Miller for your diligent copyediting and proofreading. Aurora Parlagreco and Be Fernández, thank you for bringing Valentina and Leticia's beautiful sapphic tension to life with this stunning cover!

I'm grateful for every single reader whose early and ongoing excitement for *Ophelia After All* and "*Soccer Gays WIP*" has helped me continue writing and publishing these books of my heart.

Thank you to my wonderful therapist for being excellent at her job.

So much love for my publishing besties! Thank you to Jake Maia Arlow, Joelle Wellington, and Christina Li for always beating me at Catan and inciting chaos in the group chat.

My d.a.c.u. loves: Tashie Bhuiyan, Chloe Gong, Zoe Hana Mikuta, and Christina Li (again), thank you for every writing Zoom and speedy response to my panicked publishing questions. New York did more for my grieving heart than words could ever convey. Snicky Snack forever.

Special shoutout to Christina for being a 24/7 cheerleader for this book from (literally) day one. VaLeticia and Hamlet love you! That's why you're here three times!

Apologies to the babies, Luke and Leia, for forgetting you in my debut's acknowledgments. You took over my bed and bark at everything in a five-mile radius. You also got me out of said bed every day for your morning cookies when the grief wanted me to stay wrapped in blankets forever. Gracias, perritos.

Gratitude and apologies to everyone who ever played on a soccer team with me. Soccer is in my blood, so it'll always have a place in my heart alongside the years I spent playing/watching/practicing it.

Thank you to the friends who've continued supporting me as I venture further into this whole author thing, including but not limited to: Velma, Essance, Dania, Monika, Yitmarak, Ara, Cynthia, Joanna, Catherine, Emily, Claudia, Maggie, Oliver, Kylee, Adri, and Chris.

Stacey Manos, everyone deserves a friend like you in this lifetime. Kei Nakatsuka, thank you for forcing me to take Contemporary Queer Literature with you. I randomly told you about my first editor rejection before anyone else, and we've been paddling through publishing and life together ever since. Thank you to the Bub Community, Al and Jen, for indulging my every bookish rant and update. It's us forever, my loves.

Thank you to my big family for your endless encouragement and love. Grandma Mac, Grandpa Mac, Abuela Mireya, and Abuelo Pacho, thanks for enrolling all of your kids at the same soccer field once upon a time, leading to lifelong friendships and my parents' marriage. I know Grandpa and Abuelo are cheering together from the other side now.

Myung, thank you for embodying what it means to be a best friend, first to my mom and now to the rest of our family. You're the greatest cheerleader and future bodyguard

I could ever ask for. You get all my publishing secrets straight from the source now.

Dan, thanks for helping Mom with the terrible title suggestions for this book. Bree, sorry I played so badly on our team in high school. I'm another book closer to winning the Nobel Prize first. Love you, nerds.

Abuela, gracias for every day you took me to lunch, let me write on your sofa while you watched telenovelas, and then fed me ice cream con melocotones. You have no idea how much I needed it. Besitos.

Dad, I genuinely couldn't have written this book without you (sorry it happened to be the one with the shitty dad, lol). You helped structure my fictional teams, outlined drills and plays, and answered a million questions. More than that, you celebrated every success, listened to every concern, reminded me to be proud of myself, and kept me going during the hardest moments of both of our lives. Thank you for never being my soccer coach and for always being my best friend. Love you, mwuah mwuah.

Mom, I'm deeply sorry that I didn't name this book *Socc' It To Me*, *Rock 'Em Socc' 'Em*, or *Goals and Holes* like you suggested. You were a creative genius ahead of her time but I didn't want to get blacklisted from publishing. Maybe in another life, I used those titles, you got to read my books, and I never got a wrist tattoo of your handwriting on a rainy summer day in New York City. In this life, Vale and I both lost our moms too soon. Te quiero por siempre, Mami. Besitos, and thank you for this life. You're with me every day.

Thank you for reading this Feiwel & Friends book.
The friends who made *You Don't Have a Shot* possible are:

Jean Feiwel, Publisher
Liz Szabla, Associate Publisher
Rich Deas, Senior Creative Director
Holly West, Senior Editor
Anna Roberto, Senior Editor
Kat Brzozowski, Senior Editor
Dawn Ryan, Executive Managing Editor
Kim Waymer, Senior Production Manager
Emily Settle, Editor
Rachel Diebel, Editor
Foyinsi Adegbonmire, Associate Editor
Brittany Groves, Assistant Editor
Avia Perez, Senior Production Editor